The Chef

Banana Split

"In *Banana Split*, Josi Kilpack has turned a character that we've come to love as an overzealous snoop and given her the breath of someone real so we can love her even more. **This is a story with an ocean depth's worth of awesome!**"

> —Julie Wright, author of the Hazardous Universe series

"Josi Kilpack does an excellent job with the setting and creating a believable plot with *Banana Split*. The Sadie Hoffmiller series continues to be **one of my favorites.**"

> —Heather Moore, author of *Daughters of Jared*

Pumpkin Roll

"*Pumpkin Roll* is different from the other books in the series, and while the others have their tense moments, **this had me downright nervous and spooked.** During the climax, I kept shaking my head, saying, 'No way this is happening.' Five out of five stars for this one. I could not stop reading."

> —Mindy Holt, www.ldswomensbookreview.com

Blackberry Crumble

"**Josi Kilpack is an absolute master** at leading you to believe you have everything figured out, only to have the rug pulled out from under you with the turn of a page. *Blackberry Crumble* is a delightful mystery with wonderful characters and a white-knuckle ending that'll leave you begging for more."

> —Gregg Luke, author of *Blink of an Eye*

Key Lime Pie

"I had a great time following the ever-delightful Sadie as she ate and sleuthed her way through **nerve-racking twists and turns and nail-biting suspense.**"

> —Melanie Jacobsen, author of *The List* and *Not My Type*,
> http://www.readandwritestuff.blogspot.com/

Devil's Food Cake

"Josi Kilpack whips up **another tasty mystery where startling twists and delightful humor mix** in a confection as delicious as Sadie Hoffmiller's devil's food cake."

> —Stephanie Black, four-time winner of the Whitney Award for
> Mystery/Suspense

English Trifle

"***English Trifle* is an excellent read** and will be enjoyed by teens and adults of either gender. The characters are interesting, the plot is carefully crafted, and the setting has an authentic feel."

> —Jennie Hansen, *Meridian Magazine*

Lemon Tart

"**The novel has a bit of everything. It's a mystery, a cookbook, a low-key romance and a dead-on depiction of life.** . . . That may sound like a hodgepodge. It's not. It works. Kilpack blends it all together and cooks it up until it has the taste of, well . . . of a tangy lemon tart."

> —Jerry Johnston, *Deseret News*

TRES LECHES CUPCAKES

OTHER BOOKS BY JOSI S. KILPACK

Her Good Name
Sheep's Clothing
Unsung Lullaby
Daisy

CULINARY MYSTERIES

Lemon Tart	*Blackberry Crumble*
English Trifle	*Pumpkin Roll*
Devil's Food Cake	*Banana Split*
Key Lime Pie	*Baked Alaska* (coming Spring 2013)

Tres Leches Cupcakes recipes

Download a free PDF of all the recipes in this book at
josiskilpack.com or shadowmountain.com

TRES LECHES CUPCAKES

CUPCAKES

A CULINARY MYSTERY

Josi S. Kilpack

SHADOW
MOUNTAIN

To Nancy and Jenny

for their friendship, new and old.

How it has blessed me.

Library of Congress Cataloging-in-Publication Data
Kilpack, Josi S., author.
  Tres leches cupcakes / Josi S. Kilpack.
    pages cm
  Summary: Sadie Hoffmiller is working undercover for the BLM on an archeological site in New Mexico when she stumbles across a pair of recently deceased bodies and becomes involved in the black market world of Indian artifact theft.
  ISBN 978-1-60907-170-7 (paperbound)
1. Hoffmiller, Sadie (Fictitious character)—Fiction. 2. Cooks—Fiction.
3. Murder—Investigation—Fiction. 4. Archaeological thefts—Southwest, New—Fiction. I. Title.
  PS3561.I412T74 2012
  813'.54—dc23   2012023497

Printed in the United States of America
R. R. Donnelley, Crawfordsville, IN

10   9   8   7   6   5   4   3   2   1

PROLOGUE

It was the cold that woke her.

Sadie reached out to pull the plush, soft-as-kitten's-fur blanket to her chin and settle back in for a couple more hours of sleep; the fire she lit in the evenings always burned out in the early-morning hours, inviting the autumn chill back in. But instead of finding the comforting softness she expected, her hand brushed across rough stone and rubbed gritty sand beneath her fingers. A breeze passed over her, rippling the silky fabric of her blouse that afforded no protection from the cold night air.

She wasn't in her apartment. Why not?

Then she began to remember.

Her body tensed as equal amounts of confusion and memory swirled together, like two children trying to talk over each other as they both explained their version of events. From the bits and pieces of her recollections, she knew she was in the New Mexican desert. She'd been at the Balloon Fiesta, the annual hot air balloon festival in Albuquerque. She had been selling cupcakes there—Lois's tres leches cupcakes to be exact—but then . . . then something had happened. Someone had brought her here, far away from the tourists and balloonists and anyone else whom she could call to for help.

The Cowboy.

But he'd been sent by someone else. Langley? Standage? She wasn't sure. But she knew the Cowboy had brought her here to kill her. He said she'd crossed a line.

What line?

Why couldn't she remember?

She must have made a run for it. How had she gotten away? They'd come after her—the Cowboy and the man she didn't know. And then . . . then . . .

What had happened then?

Sadie attempted to sit up, but her head spun, convincing her to lie still again and catch her breath. Then she rolled to her side and used a large rock, gray against the blackness behind it, to pull herself up, though her joints and muscles screamed in protest. As her eyes traveled up the side of the hill above her, she could make out the scraggly silhouette of brush against washed-out desert dirt. Had she fallen? She looked toward the bottom and saw that the hill she was on continued for several more yards, ending in an arroyo. She'd come to a stop at a ledge of sorts near the middle of the incline. Perhaps the rock she'd used to help her sit up had stopped her descent. None too gently, it seemed.

Once sitting, she put a hand to her throbbing forehead and gasped in pain at her own touch. She pulled her hand back. Even in the minimal light of the crescent moon, she could see the contrast between her pale skin and the dark stain on her fingers. Knowing the stain was blood made Sadie's throat tighten and her hand shake from something other than the cold.

Where was she? What would happen next?

Fear began to take over. It was hard to breathe, and her body seemed to curl in upon itself involuntarily though her back and hip protested. Everything hurt. *What had happened?* How long had she been here?

"She went this way," a voice said from somewhere above her, the words carrying on the wind. Another voice answered the first, but Sadie couldn't make out what was said. She didn't need to. What she needed to do was hide. Quick. Though she couldn't remember everything, she knew that if they found her—whoever *they* were— she'd never make it back to Santa Fe.

Sadie knew firsthand how well the desert could hide a body.

Tres Leches Cupcakes

Cupcakes
1½ cup all-purpose flour
2 tablespoons cornstarch
1 teaspoon baking powder
¼ teaspoon salt
5 eggs
1 cup granulated sugar
½ cup butter, softened
1 teaspoon vanilla extract

Preheat oven to 350 degrees. Mix flour, cornstarch, baking powder, and salt in a small bowl. Set aside. In a separate bowl, beat butter for 1 minute until very smooth. Add sugar and mix well. Add eggs one at a time, beating until yellow and frothy. Add vanilla. Add flour mixture in three batches and beat an additional minute. Fill cupcake liners halfway. Bake for 15 to 20 minutes, or until tops are lightly browned and an inserted toothpick comes out clean. Do not overbake. Cool completely.

Makes approximately 24 cupcakes.

Glaze

1 (5-ounce) can evaporated milk (or half of a 12-ounce can)
1 (11-ounce) can of sweetened condensed milk
1 cup cream, coconut milk, half and half, OR whole milk

Mix milks together. When cupcakes are cool, carefully slice off the top crust to expose the sponge cake. Drizzle the milk mixture one spoonful at a time over the cupcakes, allowing the cake to soak up the milk in between additions. (Cupcakes typically hold between 1 and 2 tablespoons of glaze.) Once milk seems to be pooling at the top of the sponge cake, cover the cupcakes and refrigerate for at least six hours.

Note: An easy way to add glaze is to use a medicinal syringe. (You can find them in the pharmacy section of your local grocery store.) Instead of slicing off the tops of the cupcakes, simply inject the milk one syringeful at a time.

Cinnamon Buttercream Frosting

1 cup butter, softened
3½ cups powdered sugar
3 teaspoons vanilla
1 to 1½ teaspoons cinnamon
½ teaspoon nutmeg
Dash of salt
Milk, as needed

In a mixing bowl, whip butter until smooth. Add 2 cups of powdered sugar and mix well, scraping the sides of the bowl as needed. Add vanilla and mix well. Add remaining powdered sugar, cinnamon, nutmeg, and salt. Mix; add milk as needed to create a smooth, but thick frosting. Pipe frosting onto cupcakes using a 1A tip, or spread frosting over cupcakes with a butterknife or spatula.

See page 328 for additional recipes and ideas for tres leches cupcakes.

CHAPTER 1

Ten Days Earlier

I've got a visual through the sliding glass door of the apartment," said Caro's voice through the static of the walkie-talkie. "Copy, Churrochomper?"

"Copy, Dunebuster," Sadie said while depressing the button on her hand unit. "Can you identify the occupants?"

"Hold on." Caro was an exercise buff, an excellent cook, the wife of an engineer, and trying to adjust to her empty-nest lifestyle. She was also a cousin to Pete Cunningham, Sadie's boyfriend. Sadie had known all those things about Caro when she moved into Caro's mother-in-law apartment in Santa Fe six weeks ago. Sadie had also expected she and Caro would get along well. She *hadn't* expected Caro would also be a wannabe CIA operative. But if Sadie had learned anything over the last couple of years, it was that circumstances brought out parts of people's personalities even they didn't know existed.

"Two males," Caro continued, "mid-twenties, eating Cheetos and . . . wait . . . not Cheetos. Stand by, Churrochomper."

"Ten-four, Dunebuster." Sadie could see Caro from her vantage point on an obliging rock beside a cypress tree, but just barely—Caro's black hoodie and yoga pants blended well with the darkened landscape.

It hadn't taken long for Sadie to settle into New Mexico. She had needed to stay under the radar due to an unresolved threat that had been haunting her after a near-deadly trip to Boston almost a year ago, and Santa Fe was turning out to be the perfect place to hide. What made it even better was that Pete had lined up an opportunity for Sadie to act as an undercover informant for the Bureau of Land Management. Caro was helping her with the paperwork portion of the job tonight.

"Cheese doodles," Caro said over the walkie-talkie. "I repeat, the subjects are eating cheese doodles."

That wasn't really the type of information Sadie needed to collect, but she could remember her own naïve overexcitement on her first few cases so she didn't bother saying anything to Caro about observing insignificant details.

"Can you confirm subject sixteen?" Sadie asked while looking at the clipboard in her hand and finding number sixteen on the list. She tapped the point of her pen over the name Kyle Langley. His address was apartment number 28 at the Colonial Hills complex.

"Affirmative," Caro replied. "Definitely sixteen. Lizard tattoo on right forearm is in view."

Sadie smiled to herself and wrote a big, fat check mark next to Kyle's name. "And the other subject?"

"Might be subject nineteen. Can't confirm . . . wait . . . what's his hat preference?"

"Braves," Sadie said, scanning down to number nineteen on the list. "Atlanta Braves."

"Confirmed. Yes, I do believe it's subject nineteen. I've taken photos for further verification."

"Perfect," Sadie said into the speaker before checking Cesar Montoya off the list as well. Seventeen of the twenty-six names on the list were checked off now, meaning she was closer than ever to completing her assignment.

"I'm moving away from the lookout point," Caro said. "Repeat, I'm moving *away* from the lookout point and will rendezvous at predetermined location in oh-three minutes. Dunebuster over and out."

"Churrochomper over and out," Sadie said. She got up from where she'd been sitting, but remained in a crouch as she headed back down the embankment that acted as a natural barrier between the elementary school parking lot where they'd left Caro's car and the apartment complex they were staking out.

It really should have been Sadie who made the visual verifications—she was the official informant after all—but Caro liked the trench work so much that Sadie couldn't tell her no. It was fun to share the experience with someone else and, seeing as how this was Sadie's first foray back into the world of private investigating, having Caro at her side made all the difference in keeping Sadie's anxiety at bay. Sadie wasn't the woman she used to be before Boston, but she was making progress. Caro was helping more than she knew. She made Sadie feel safe, and needed—two things that were very important to Sadie right now.

Sadie reached Caro's royal blue Neon—a *terrible* car for investigative work; it was so conspicuous—several seconds before Caro appeared over the berm and used the button on the key fob to unlock the doors. Once Caro reached the driver's side door, they both entered the vehicle on their respective sides, pulled the doors closed in tandem, and buckled their seat belts as though following a well-rehearsed choreography.

Caro pushed back the hood of her sweatshirt, then started the engine and smoothly reversed out of the space before exiting the parking lot altogether. She sat up straight with both hands on the steering wheel, pulled her shoulders up to her ears, and squealed. "That was so fun! Where to next?"

"We're done for the night," Sadie said with a laugh at Caro's enthusiasm.

Caro's shoulders slumped, and she leaned back against the seat with a frown. "Really? Already?"

"I'll have more work tomorrow night," Sadie said. "Can I see the camera?"

Caro, pouting slightly, reached into the kangaroo pocket of her hoodie and handed over Sadie's compact design DSLR camera with 12x stabilized zoom, 1/2000 shutter speed, and face-recognition technology. Sadie compared the pictures on the camera to the pictures she'd taken with her cell phone on the sly at the dig site. The men were, in fact, subjects sixteen and nineteen.

"Why can't we just track down the whole list right now?" Caro asked. She used her fingers to smooth her chin-length bob. Caro's mother was a Mexican immigrant who came to the US in the 1950s with her family to work and fell in love with a gringo—Pete's uncle, Wynn. Caro had inherited her mother's features: light brown skin, dark eyes, envious curves. She took pride in both cultures, never having chosen one above the other in order to define who she was. "I'm not tired," Caro assured her. "And we're on a roll. This was the quickest verification we've done yet."

"That's because Mr. Langley owns his own apartment." A lot of the other crew members were somewhat nomadic, living with friends and family while they moved around to different job sites. That was likely why subject nineteen was there; he was probably sleeping on the couch. "Regardless of that, I don't have photos of the rest of the people on the list yet." Sadie lifted her phone as a visual reminder of her process. "I have to talk to the subjects first, *then* get their photo, *then* confirm their address, and *then* get additional photos, if possible."

Caro continued pouting, and Sadie couldn't help but laugh again. "What did you ever do for fun before I got here?"

"I can't even remember," Caro said, looking thoughtful. "Watched TV mostly, I guess, and nagged my husband to take me places. But playing private investigator is so much better."

"You're not playing at anything," Sadie said with a shake of her head. "You're doing it, for real."

"It's so exciting," Caro said with a contented sigh. "Have I convinced you yet to stay in Santa Fe forever so we can open up a PI business together?"

"You know I can't do that," Sadie said, ignoring the pang of envy she felt for Caro's normal life. "But you ought to look into it for yourself. You're a natural."

Sadie was a natural too, but living underground like she was meant she couldn't own a business. The car she'd been driving since coming to New Mexico was even in Caro's name, though Sadie paid the lease payment. Officially, Sadie lived . . . nowhere, and it would stay that way until Pete felt certain it was safe for Sadie to return to Garrison, Colorado. He was tracking the person who made the threat on Sadie's life, but he had yet to uncover an actual lead that led to an actual arrest. Until he did, he wanted Sadie far away from anywhere that could put her in danger of being attacked again— which meant anywhere she'd be expected to go.

After nearly a year of hiding, and a debilitating battle with anxiety and depression, however, Sadie was beginning to feel that it wasn't worth the toll it took on her and her family and friends. She missed her hometown and her friends and the purpose she'd once had. But Pete didn't feel she was safe and, although the situation was far from ideal, Sadie trusted his judgment more than her own. And Caro was wonderful. That helped immensely.

"Maybe I *will* start my own company," Caro said with a jaunty shake of her shoulders. "It's got to be more interesting than working in a dental office, I'm sure. Then I'll hire you under your other name, *Sarah.*" She gave Sadie a sidelong look, and Sadie rolled her eyes at Caro's reference to the name Pete had chosen for her: Sarah Worthlin. Sarah *was* Sadie's legal first name—Sadie was short for Sarah Diane—and Pete felt it would make it more natural for Sadie to answer to a name already familiar to her. Caro and her husband, Rex, called her Sadie though, which Sadie preferred.

Caro's phone rang, and she fumbled for her earpiece on the dashboard. "Hello," she said brightly. Her voice was flatter when she spoke again. "Hey, Rex, yeah, we're on our way home."

Sadie squirmed; she hadn't ever come right out and asked, but she suspected Rex didn't know what they were really doing on their evenings "out." Not that Sadie would accuse Caro of lying to her husband, but Sadie couldn't imagine that Rex would be okay with his wife sneaking around Santa Fe and Los Alamos, confirming addresses of the people Sadie worked with.

While Sadie had hit it off with Caro as though they were lifelong friends, Rex hadn't been nearly as personable. In fact, Sadie sometimes worried that he resented her being there at all. She hoped it wasn't true and that Rex's quiet demeanor and tendency to leave the room when Sadie entered was a type of chivalry. Pete thought a great deal of Rex, and so Sadie tried to keep her opinion of the man who owned the home where she was staying more in line with Pete's opinions. She found Caro and Rex to be a rather odd couple. Caro was vivacious, outgoing, and engaged in multiple pursuits. Rex did little other than watch sports on TV, fish on the weekends, and go to work every day.

Work.

Sadie stifled a groan and glanced at the dashboard clock as her thoughts shifted. It was 8:52 P.M. which meant that in just over seven hours she would be parking her car in the vacant lot on Airport Road, loading up into the D&E Salvage vans, and heading out to the desert again. She knew it was important to start early in the day, when the ground was still cold and moist, and it was sort of nice to end before the day got too hot and dry, but it would be day nine of this horrible job.

When Pete had presented her with the opportunity to do a little undercover work for the Bureau of Land Management in New Mexico, she could not have been more excited. She'd been in Santa Fe for about a month by then, and growing increasingly bored. She'd been flattered to be offered the job, and she'd stepped out of the van on day one brimming with enthusiasm.

Unfortunately, working as an amateur digger at an ancient burial site hadn't lived up to her Indiana Jones expectations. It was hot, it was dirty, it was tedious, her back was killing her, and no one working at the dig looked like Harrison Ford. Thank goodness there were only two workdays left in this week; at least she'd have the weekend to recover before going back out again.

The other part of the job—the undercover informant part—was fairly straightforward. She was supposed to get to know the crew members and develop profiles for each one of them. She hadn't been told why she was developing these profiles, which drove her a little crazy. Pete felt the secrecy was necessary so that she wouldn't have any biases. Even so, she had a theory that her job had something to do with artifacts being sold on the black market.

The BLM was the agency charged with enforcing the laws regarding antiquities, and there just didn't seem to be many other reasons for the BLM to want information about a crew working an archeological site. Regardless, she was determined to prove to the faceless BLM people that she was the right person for the job. Who knew what it could lead to in the future?

The actual archeological work, though, was awful. Day after day she chipped pieces of broken pottery out of the ground for hours on end, stopping only now and then to sneak a picture of her fellow crew members. The days seemed to last forever, and by the time she left the site each afternoon, she was coated with dust, her fingers were raw, and she was completely exhausted. The only relief was coming home to a hot shower.

"Okay," Caro said, sounding irritated as she spoke to the invisible voice in her ear. "We'll be home in less than ten minutes. Bye."

Caro took off the earpiece and tossed it back on the dashboard before glancing at Sadie. Her face brightened immediately. "Want to stop at Keva and get a smoothie or something?"

"I'd love to," Sadie said sincerely, "but I've got to get up in seven hours." She didn't point out that Caro had told Rex they'd be home in ten minutes.

Caro frowned. "I don't know how you stand that job."

"Me neither," Sadie said with a shake of her head. Caro had been the sounding board for all of Sadie's complaints, which were plentiful.

"How many more days?"

"I should be done by Monday," Sadie said, scanning her

paperwork, and making a note of the nine people she hadn't talked to yet. Three people a day for the next three workdays should finish it off.

She hoped that once she'd turned in the profiles, she could stop working at the site; unfortunately, no one had told her as much. She needed to believe it for her own emotional stability, but deep down she feared she'd have to stay on the crew throughout the duration of the job in order to maintain her cover. If it came to that, she might have to break her own leg to get herself out of the work.

She took a breath and tried not to fantasize about broken bones. *One day at a time,* she reminded herself. *One hot, dirty, dry, miserable day at a time.* Then, with a little luck, she'd wow the people who'd hired her and be extended better opportunities in the future. They couldn't get much worse . . . at least she hoped not.

CHAPTER 2

Y ou brought these cookie bar things?"

Sadie looked up from where she was digging Thursday afternoon to see who'd spoken to her. It was Margo Kauffman—one of the nine names left on Sadie's list.

"I did," Sadie said. Bringing baked goods every morning had helped her make friends at the site, especially with the young men who treated her like a favorite aunt, and therefore told her pretty much everything she wanted to know. Margo was in her late thirties or early forties, Sadie guessed, and she kept to herself enough that Sadie hadn't been able to connect with her yet.

"They're really good," Margo said. She popped the last bite of the dulce de leche bar into her mouth and wiped her hands on her pants, which would only make her hands dirtier since she'd been digging for hours.

"Thank you," Sadie said, not sure whether she should take a break to talk or finish the jar she was uncovering. It was the first intact piece she'd worked on so far, and she was being extra cautious in hopes of keeping it in one piece. A lot of the pottery the crew uncovered was as fragile as eggshells, often victims of hairline fractures.

14

If handled too roughly, the item often crumbled in the hand of the digger attempting to preserve it. She decided to talk and dig, unwilling to abandon her project when it was so close to being out of the ground. "I love to bake."

"And I love to eat," Margo said with a smile. "We're a match made in heaven."

Sadie looked up at her and smiled while hiding her surprise at the inclusive comment.

"Is this your first dig?" Margo continued as she sat down in the dirt next to where Sadie was working; a little puff of dust plumed when her bottom hit the ground. She pulled a crushed pack of Camel cigarettes from one of the pockets in her khaki cargo pants—basic uniform for diggers—removed a cigarette and lighter out of the crumpled cellophane, and lit up.

Sadie was glad the breeze took the smoke away from her; if she had to be around cigarette smoke, she preferred it to be outdoors.

"It's my second dig," Sadie said, sticking to the story Pete had helped her create. Her hands were getting sweaty inside the latex gloves she was required to wear. She considered taking them off until she was ready to pick up the pot but she didn't do it for fear she'd forget to put them back on and touch the pot with her fingers; she didn't want to get any oils from her skin on the artifact. "I went on a tourist dig near Phoenix last summer. I guess you could say I fell in love with it." *That* was an absolute lie.

"So now you're an official dirt geek like the rest of us, huh?" Margo took a long pull off her cigarette and let it out slowly. Margo's too-yellow-blonde hair hung behind her shoulders in two braids. A turquoise bandana was tied kerchief-style over her head, and she wore a men's white dress shirt unbuttoned over a green tank top. She was slender and strong, and her overly tanned skin testified to a lot of time spent in the sun. "Dirt geek," the nickname assigned to those who dug for a living, was a very good title for Margo.

"I guess so," Sadie said, feeling just a little bit proud to claim the title even if she despised the actual work. "Do I get a T-shirt or something?"

Margo laughed as she exhaled another lungful of smoke. "We'll have to talk to HR about that. Until then, the perpetual squint, uneven fingernails, and dust that never fully washes off will have to do."

Sadie smiled. Margo had seemed intimidating from afar, but talking to her now showed her to be more personable than Sadie had expected. "How long have *you* been digging?" she asked, chipping away at the solidified dirt clinging to the jar.

"Eighteen years," Margo said after exhaling again. "I graduated from ASU with a few years of fieldwork under my belt and never looked back."

"How long have you been with D&E?" D&E Salvage was a privately contracted salvage archeology company hired to clear archeological sites in the Southwest area of the United States—Arizona and New Mexico, mostly. Once hired, they were responsible for properly removing, cataloging, and warehousing the artifacts or repatriating them back to the tribes claiming contemporary heritage. This particular job was to clear out a burial site recently discovered by a construction company when they attempted to put in a road leading to a new Ranchette community northwest of Santa Fe.

"I've been with D&E about two years," Margo replied. "Since I moved to Santa Fe."

"And do you like working for them?"

"Sure," Margo said with a slight shrug. "They pay pretty well, and they let me do the bodies."

Sadie looked up quickly, surprised by the flippant comment. It had taken her by surprise to learn that so many members of the crew regarded this as just another job—like landscaping or washing cars. It was disappointing to think that Margo might be equally callous toward the work, especially since she'd just said how much she loved it.

"Those monkeys aren't careful enough for bones, and D&E knows I'll do the job right."

Sadie felt better about that explanation and moved forward with the conversation. "Is that why you don't work with the rest of the crew?"

Margo nodded but her gaze drifted to a mesa in the distance. "I get priority for the women and children. You can usually identify the gender by what funerary is buried with them. The crew gives me my space so that no one gets in the way of my work." She nodded toward Sadie's jar, one of the many items buried with the people interred there. Sometimes there were jewelry or weapons, but Sadie was new and so she was given the pottery, something most of these diggers regarded as a dime a dozen. "The other crew members might end up doing more bone work if I can't get it done on my own. But I'm fast. I like to be the one who brings people up."

"You take it pretty seriously, then," Sadie commented, stealing glances at Margo while she kept working. She picked up her spray bottle and gave the jar a few squirts of water to remove the dust layer hiding the black-and-red design someone had hand painted almost a thousand years ago. It was like bringing the item back to life.

"These were real people with real lives," Margo explained, a bitter edge to her voice. "And their loved ones never expected them to be dug up in order to make way for some rich person's swimming pool."

"So you make sure they're treated right," Sadie summarized. It seemed silly to compare her approach to the jar to what Margo did with the skeletons, but Sadie felt the same kind of reverence. She also had to admit to a little jealousy toward Margo's work. Would she ever get to do a body? Maybe she'd enjoy the work more if she could do something that important.

Margo took a final drag of her cigarette before snubbing it out in the dirt and rolling the butt into a tissue from her pocket. D&E had been very clear during orientation that no one was to leave anything at the site. Margo put the tissue back in her pocket and then looked hard at Sadie. "I could use an extra set of hands today."

It took a few moments to realize what Margo meant, but once Sadie understood, she sat up straighter—no small feat for her poor back that felt fused into a slouchy curve. "With the bodies?" she said quietly but with an eager tone she hoped wasn't inappropriate.

"I found a family plot," Margo said. "They probably all got sick at the same time and were buried together. The bones are mixed in and it's going to take me the rest of the day to separate them for proper cataloging. Bill said I could ask a crew member to assist me and, quite frankly, I don't want to work with any of those guys." She nodded toward a group of guys who'd taken a break to play hacky sack outside of the dig area. "I've been watching you. You do good work, even if you're slow."

Sadie tried not to let the comment sting and instead focused on the compliment. "I'd love to help," she said. "I'll be over as soon as I finish this."

Margo nodded, thanked her, and then stood, not bothering to brush off her pants—what was the point when they all left the site covered in dirt anyway?

When Sadie stood up fifteen minutes later, she *did* brush the dirt off her sleeves and pants, creating a miniature dust cloud in the process. Most of the dirt settled right back into her clothes, but she felt better for having at least tried to get clean. The shower she'd take once she got back to Caro's was sounding better by the minute.

She pulled a plastic bag out of one pocket of her cargo pants and a Sharpie out of another. Using her thigh as a solid surface, she wrote the grid number, time, and her name on the outside of the collection bag—all part of the cataloging process. She put the intact jar into the bag, removed the paper strip that exposed the sticky fold-over, and sealed the bag, satisfied with her work.

It was a lovely pot, about four inches in diameter and six inches tall, the neck barely narrower than the body. She couldn't help but think about what a fun conversation piece it would be if she could take it home and display it on her mantel—her very first intact pottery jar from the time she played archeologist. That would be illegal, of course, but it was still just a tiny bit tempting. She continued to admire the pot as she headed to the converted camp trailer where the artifacts were stored.

Roberto, a big fan of her baked items, was in charge of cataloging. He typed all the information she read off from the bag into his computer before reaching down for the item—his workspace was a few feet above her.

Sadie was handing it up, sad to see it go, when Cesar, one of the more boisterous members of the crew and number nineteen on her list, came around the corner of the trailer fast and bumped her shoulder. The slick plastic slid through her still-gloved hands. She fumbled to catch the pot. Roberto grabbed for it too, but to no avail. The pot crashed to the ground at her feet.

Dulce de Leche Bars

1½ cups flour
1½ cups quick oats
1 cup brown sugar
¼ teaspoon salt
1 cup butter, softened
1 (13.4-ounce) can dulce de leche
1 cup Heath toffee bits or chocolate chips
½ cup chopped nuts (optional)

Preheat oven to 350 degrees. Combine dry ingredients. Cut in butter with pastry blender or fork until crumbly. Reserve ¼ cup for the topping, then press remainder of the mix into an ungreased 9x13 pan. Bake for 10 minutes.

While crust is baking, soften dulce de leche in a small saucepan over low heat (about 5 minutes). Spread dulce de leche over hot crust. Sprinkle with toffee bits and the rest of the crumb mixture. Add nuts if desired. Return to oven and bake 25 to 30 minutes.

Let cool 15 minutes and then run a knife around the edges of the pan to loosen.

Let cool completely and cut into bars.

Makes 24 bars.

CHAPTER 3

Sadie gasped and quickly picked up the bag as though she could somehow undo the last three seconds. What had been a perfectly shaped jar with beautiful symmetry and design was now a bag of pieces. Sadie's throat tightened, surprising her with the sorrow she felt.

"Sorry," Cesar said, making a face while handing over a plastic bag of his own. As soon as Roberto took his bag, Cesar hesitated a moment as though trying to think of what else to say, then left without another word.

Sadie cradled her bag like it was a dead pet, telling herself not to cry. After several seconds, Roberto carefully took the bag from her hands. When she looked up at him, he smiled sympathetically.

"Most of what we find is already broken," he said, just a hint of an accent in his words.

"But this wasn't," Sadie said, replaying in her mind the way she should have handed it up, more carefully or with both hands. "It's stayed together for hundreds of years, and I'm the reason it's in pieces."

"Cesar is the reason it is in pieces," Roberto said, turning toward the shelves inside the trailer. She watched him put the bag on a specific shelf, then add some notes to his computer, probably changing the description from pottery to pot shards. When he finished typing, he met her eye again. "The Navajo believe that everything has a life: rocks, trees, pots. They think we should leave all of this in the ground and let it die too, rather than keep it alive somehow. Maybe this supports that belief more than the pot going to a warehouse, where it will sit until someone decides what to do with it or steals it in hopes of making money from the black market."

Sadie nodded, but his comments didn't make her feel any better. Pete had educated her on the current state of antiquities when he told her about this job. So many artifacts had been taken from the ground in recent years, or seized from pothunters who dug them up illegally, that there weren't enough museums to house them. Instead, there were warehouses and storage units all over the Southwestern United States filled with artifacts that were just waiting for a chance to be studied, or in some cases, displayed. There was also a multimillion-dollar black market that sold to private collectors or anyone else wanting to skirt the laws regarding ethical archeology. Sellers got rich, while buyers surrounded themselves with historical contraband. Were any of those options better than leaving an artifact to die, as Roberto had said?

"Thank you," she said to Roberto, trying to sort it out in her head. There were so many opinions on what was right and what was wrong in regards to archeology. Sadie hadn't decided what she thought about it, but she did know she'd wanted that jar to stay in one piece and she felt responsible for the fact that it no longer was.

She turned away from the trailer and headed toward the far corner of the four-acre dig site where the graves of a hundred or so people who'd lived almost six hundred years ago were located. The nearly invisible mounds, weathered from centuries of wind and rain, were all that remained on the surface. On her first day, the project supervisor, Bill Line, had called them "Anasazi"—ancestors of the current Hopi, Zuni, and Pueblo tribes.

The dig site was divided into three sections and cordoned off by orange surveyor's tape wrapped around sticks hammered into the ground. One section had already been emptied, catalogued, and smoothed over, little blue flags specifying where the graves had once been. The middle section had blue, orange, and red flags—orange identified where items had been removed, and red marked areas containing bones and artifacts that still needed to be brought up. As the graves were completely emptied, Mr. Line would inspect them, check them off, and allow them to be filled; a blue flag would then communicate the status of that grave. There were only half a dozen blue flags in section two.

Margo was at the far end of the third section, which only had a couple orange flags amid the red. Section three had only recently been opened to the diggers so the majority of the crew were still finishing up the second section.

When Sadie arrived at Margo's dig area in section three, she was shocked to see the jumble of partially uncovered bones. As she looked closer, she could see parts of five different skulls: two large—adults—and three smaller ones of varying sizes. Her throat tightened again. A whole family, gone. Or had there been other children left behind? Orphaned and missing their parents, brothers, and sisters?

"You said they were sick?" Sadie asked.

Margo looked up at her briefly. "A severe drought is thought to have caused the Anasazi to struggle for food. Without proper nourishment, disease ran rampant. This burial site was likely used over a few years' time. It's assumed the majority of the Anasazi simply abandoned their homes and moved farther south to escape the changing conditions."

"Abandoned their homes," Sadie said. "Like those cliff dwellings at Bandelier?" She pointed to the west; their dig was only a mile or two from the eastern boundary of Bandelier, a national monument preserved by the federal government. Sadie had gone there with Caro when she first arrived in Santa Fe. She'd walked where the cliff dwellers had walked centuries earlier and marveled at what they'd created from stone and mud.

"Probably," Margo said. "They left behind their day-to-day equipment that wasn't essential, and their dead. Now we dig it all back up."

Sadie moved around the dig area, a six-by-six-foot square Margo had segregated with a line drawn in the dirt. "It's so sad," she said, looking at the skeletons.

Margo just nodded and went back to where she was chipping dirt from between two rib bones. "Yeah," she said evenly. "Very sad." She paused for a moment. "But at least this family was together, and they'll come up together too. There are worse things."

In Sadie's mind, the family dying together was about as tragic as it could be.

Margo continued, "Last week I heard Bill talking about some sites by Mimbres being blown up."

"Blown up?"

Margo nodded but kept digging. "Pothunters find a site and use dynamite to blow it up, then comb through the rubble for items they can sell. Most of what's there gets destroyed, but they can be in and out in a matter of hours, long before anyone can find them and arrest them for theft. Maybe they get a dozen pieces that survive the blast; maybe they get twenty."

"That's horrible," Sadie said, imagining the senseless destruction of sites like this in the name of profit. "They must destroy more than they take away."

Margo nodded. "The bones are always left behind, though, broken and scattered across the desert." She paused, and Sadie noticed the catch in her voice. "At least these people get respect." She dug in the dirt for another moment. "Those pothunters don't care. It's all about money and power."

"Power?" Sadie repeated.

"It's a rush for them to have something they aren't supposed to have—something they feel would have belonged to them until the government made laws taking it away. Finders keepers is kind of a mantra for a lot of the pothunters. It's a high for them to beat the system they feel infringes on their rights."

"Oh," Sadie said, realizing how complex this issue was. She was such a novice in her understanding of things. "So, you've never . . . found anything?"

Margo paused, then leaned back on her heels and put her hands on her knees, still holding her chisel and small hammer. "A couple summers ago, I went hiking down by the Guadalupes in the southeast—there are all kinds of hidden crevices and small caves honeycombed through the rock there. Not everything was abandoned when the Anasazi left, some things they hid—valuable or sacred things. I'd never found more than an arrowhead or a broken pot here and there, but I'm always looking. To find things in situ is a remarkable experience." Her eyes sparkled a little bit. "So, while I'm hiking, there was this freak storm."

Margo went back to the chipping while she talked. "I ran for this overhang, which wasn't significant except that due to the angle of the rain it offered me some protection. There was a shrub growing to one side, and I pushed back behind it a little bit only to find that the shrub had grown over the entrance of a very small cave opening. I had to army crawl to get through the opening but inside . . ." She paused in both word and act, obviously reliving the moment. "Inside was some kind of shrine. There were carvings on the walls, and intricate pottery filled with beads and small bones. It was absolutely incredible to see so much stuff in its original place. I stayed for hours, just sitting and looking around this cavern someone had worked so hard to design; somewhere someone had chosen to secure these sacred things they probably expected to come back for one day." She paused another moment, then went back to work on the bones, leaving Sadie hungry for more information.

"What did you do with it?" Sadie asked, trying to envision the setting in her mind. Even with her limited understanding of the world of antiquity, she imagined such a cave would be quite the find for a university or archeological group.

Margo shrugged. "Nothing."

"Nothing?" Sadie asked, almost disappointed.

Margo shook her head. "I guess that's not true. I enjoyed it," she said wistfully. "I absorbed the spirit of it—the sacredness of the site—and the reverence I felt the people intended for it. Then I left, carefully covering my tracks and adding what was left in my water bottle to the roots of that divine shrub, which was likely the only thing that had protected the place that long." Margo sat back on her heels again and looked up at Sadie. "This stuff doesn't belong to us," she said, waving her hand over the dig site. "Just because we *can* take it, doesn't mean we *should*. It was a very personal victory to me to have been able to leave that cave without disturbing even a single bead. Not many people could do that. I'm proud to say that I did."

"I'm not sure I could," Sadie said, hoping she wasn't revealing too much. She could still imagine that pot on her mantel at home.

Margo smiled at her, assuring Sadie she understood, then leaned forward over the tangled bones once more. "I couldn't have when I started, but I can now."

Sadie very much admired Margo's devotion. From what she'd read, most people wouldn't have treated that shrine as Margo did. Pothunters would have taken every last item—perhaps even chipping the petroglyphs off the wall. Archeologists would have put the items in a museum, or maybe just in storage. That Margo took pride in her ability to walk away was no trivial accomplishment. Chances were good that another explorer would one day find the cave and deplete it entirely; maybe they'd even blow up the entrance like those pothunters Margo had talked about in order to make it easier to empty.

"Well, why don't you tell me what to do," Sadie said, breaking out of her thoughtfulness. "I'm at your disposal."

Sadie spent the rest of the afternoon following Margo's orders. Sometimes she chipped away dirt like Margo did, though not as fast; other times she catalogued the bones Margo removed and then took the items to Roberto, who put them on the "Bone" shelf.

It was tedious work, and yet Margo never faltered. She wanted the whole family bagged and catalogued by the time they had to leave the dig at five o'clock. She didn't like leaving partials out overnight, she said. While they dug, they talked. Sadie told her mostly-fictional story of coming to Santa Fe—well, Sarah Worthin's story—and Margo told Sadie about her two failed marriages and her gypsy-like travels. She liked Santa Fe, though, and was thinking about staying for a while. There were often long stretches of silence, but Sadie got used to those as well. They weren't awkward, just circumstantial.

A little after three o'clock, Sadie put the last of the foot bones from the final skeleton in a bag—Margo liked to move from head to toe—and took it to Roberto, confirming they were done with the grave and getting an orange flag to put in the now-empty ground so that Bill could inspect it. When Sadie returned, Margo was standing at the edge of the dig site, smoking another cigarette.

Sadie wasn't sure what to do next. She wondered if she should return to digging pots in section two, but she wanted to keep helping Margo. It was nice to have someone to work with, and the skeletons were more interesting than the artifacts. She decided to wait to ask for instructions until Margo finished her smoke break.

She began wandering in between the nearly invisible mounds in the third section, most of which were adorned with little red flags indicating they hadn't been cleared out yet. Time had worn the mounds almost even with the ground, which is why the burial site hadn't been discovered until a bulldozer ripped through the first four graves.

It was strange to think that each of these slight bumps on the ground had a body beneath it. She let her eyes scan mound after mound until her gaze stopped on one mound that seemed larger than the others. Sadie moved toward it, coming to a stop a few feet away. Was it another mass grave? Was that why it was bigger?

She heard someone coming toward her and looked up at Margo before turning back to the mound of dirt. "This grave is different," she said. "Bigger, and the shape of it is more succinct. Do you think it's another mass grave?"

"It doesn't look like the one we just uncovered. Mass graves are wider, not taller," Margo said, walking around the mound, looking at it closely. "Wanna dig it? So long as there's only one body down there, I bet the two of us could bring it up before it's time to leave if we work fast. Might be a leader of prominence with more funerary items than usual."

Sadie couldn't help but smile. It was a small adventure, but an adventure all the same.

Within five minutes, the two women had their shovels out, carefully digging through one half-inch of dirt at a time until Sadie's shovel hit something solid. She made eye contact with Margo, and they both lowered their shovels in tandem and picked up their trowels, carefully probing the dirt around the object. A minute later, Sadie sat back on her heels to make sure she was really seeing what she thought she was seeing.

Margo also stopped. Also stared, then she said quietly, "Is that . . . denim?"

CHAPTER 4

The two women shared a look before silently agreeing to dig a little further to make sure, but within another minute it was obvious that the buried body was wearing jeans.

"I'll go get Bill," Margo said, leaving Sadie to stare at the partially uncovered leg and try to make sense of it. She'd come to terms with the idea of digging up bones from centuries ago . . . but a recent burial? How long had it been there? It. Sadie shook her head and stood up to relieve the cramp in her legs just as Margo returned with Bill and two of the younger crew members. The men immediately began digging, though Margo harangued them with instructions on where to dig and how far down to go down with the tips of their shovels. She took her digging seriously.

Within five minutes, a full leg was exposed. Within a few more minutes, the trademark button fly of the Levi's company and several inches of what looked like the bottom hem of a sweatshirt was revealed.

Bill made a cutting motion with his hands, and the crew members stopped digging, waiting for him to give instructions. He stared at the partially uncovered body, then shook his head and swore.

"This is going to add another week to the dig—no question. So much for the early finish bonus."

Margo and Sadie exchanged an unimpressed look but remained silent.

A few more seconds passed before Bill took off his hat, wiping his sweaty forehead with the back of one hand. Several other members of the crew had realized something was going on and gravitated toward the newly dug grave. Bill seemed to notice them for the first time.

"Stop digging for the day," he barked while scanning the growing crowd. "We're done here. The vans leave in ten minutes. Stow the tools and load up." He turned to Margo and pointed. "You," he said, then turned to point at Sadie, "and you, stay for the police." He turned back toward the trailer and pulled his phone out of his pocket. He took a breath and dialed a number.

"I prefer bones," Margo said softly, drawing Sadie's attention. "Old, dry bones."

"Have you found bodies before?" Sadie asked. "I mean . . . like this."

Margo nodded. "Sort of," she said. "In Arizona, a junkie tried to break into a trailer left on the dig over the weekend. We found him Monday morning—overdose. It's a sight and a smell you never forget. This one's been in the ground long enough that the smell's worn off, I guess. I've never found anyone recently . . . *buried*."

"I wonder how long he's been in the ground," Sadie said.

"Months at least," Margo said, nodding at the only portion of uncovered skin that was visible: a hand that was sunken, dry and discolored.

Sadie had to look away. She'd seen a documentary on the rate at which bodies decompose based on climate and covering, but she couldn't remember what they'd said about deserts.

"Whoever brought him here had to know this was a burial site, right?" Sadie said, waving toward the other graves in section three. It couldn't be a coincidence.

"I guess so, huh?" Margo commented, walking around the grave and cocking her head to the side. "We should finish digging him up. Get a better look at him."

Sadie immediately shook her head. "It's a crime scene now. We'd contaminate it. Plus Bill said to stop digging."

"They're going to bring in a bunch of cops to dig him up. You and I can do a better job." She didn't wait for an answer, just dropped to her knees and grabbed her trowel, digging around the side of the body. It was easier digging than the other graves—the dirt hadn't solidified around the body. Sadie looked toward the trailer. Where was Bill?

"I really think we should leave it alone."

Margo didn't answer as she kept digging.

Sadie shifted her weight and realized that despite her objections, she was itching to drop down into the dirt beside Margo and dig too. Her own reaction surprised her. It had been just six months ago that a run-in with a dead body had lit the tinderbox of anxiety and depression Sadie had been trying to ignore. She'd returned home to Garrison soon after, and in the months since that time, had made great progress in coming to terms with what her therapist had deemed post-traumatic stress disorder. She still had her moments—still had nightmares now and again—but she'd learned that staying busy and not becoming too self-focused had helped her stay ahead of most of her problems with it. An occasional Xanax helped too.

That she wanted to help dig up a body, when accidentally

running into one had been so overwhelming last April, was odd but she hoped that it meant she'd made more progress than she'd realized. And yet, the "success" of her curiosity aside, this *was* a crime scene.

She was only mildly aware of the rest of the crew loading up in the vans that would take them back to Santa Fe until the first van pulled away, leaving a cloud of dust behind. She expected the next one to leave soon after, but the engine didn't start up. She looked from Margo—still digging—to the trailer—Bill was still inside—and then to the second van just as someone called out, "Looks like we've got another one!"

Margo looked up from her work, caught Sadie's eye, and together they hurried toward the area almost directly across from them in section three.

Shel, a crew member Sadie had profiled on her first day, stood on the perimeter of the dig site, almost at the head of a . . . well, a head. He was leaning on his shovel and looking appropriately shocked by what he'd uncovered. Another crew member was pacing back and forth in front of the grave, and Sadie suspected he was the one who'd shouted out the discovery.

Shel continued to stare at the body for a moment, and then quickly dropped his shovel and walked away from the dirt-covered hair and decomposed face showing above the ground. Sadie couldn't be sure, but she thought he pulled a phone out of his pocket before he disappeared around the parked van.

Bill showed up a moment later and swore again. Pushing his hand through his hair, he ordered everyone out of the van and told them to grab shovels and verify that every as-yet-untouched grave contained Anasazi bones. "If there are more fresh bodies out there, I want the police to deal with them all at once."

Sadie waited for someone to object, but no one did, which meant she had to. "This is a crime scene, Mr. Line," she said as crew members climbed out of the van and grabbed shovels. He turned to look at her and put his hands on his hips. Not a good sign. A few of the crew hung back, but others took off toward the remaining mounds of dirt. Sadie took a breath and pulled together her confidence. "We can't dig anymore."

"Until the cops get here, it's my dig."

Sadie shook her head with more force, losing some of her anxiety in the face of his . . . wrongness. "You can't do that," she said. "It's illegal and it can mess up the pending investigation. We need to leave everything as we found it. We may have already accidentally destroyed evidence. But there won't be anything accidental about us continuing to dig now that we know."

"My dig," he repeated with clipped words. "And my freaking bonus that just went down the toilet. Salvage archeology is already the redheaded stepchild of any development like this." He waved his hand at the raw desert surrounding them. "All the construction company sees is that they have to waste time and money on what, to them, is as important as dirt. This"—he pointed at the body Margo had gone back to digging up—"is their worst nightmare because what was already a pain in the neck just got ten times worse."

"I hardly think *this* is all that fond of being a part of it either," Sadie said, waving at the bodies they had unearthed. "These bodies are not supposed to be here and—"

Bill turned away and headed for his trailer, dialing another number on his phone.

Sadie hurried after him. "This is a big mistake, Mr. Line," she said as she marched in an attempt to keep up with his long strides. "A terrible, horrible mistake."

She stopped in her tracks as an awful crunch sounded to her left. She spun around and saw Kyle Langley, whom she'd researched just the night before, pull his shovel out of what was obviously a grave of antiquity, the dirt barely rounded above the flat desert.

"What do you think you're doing?" Margo yelled, jumping up from where she'd been excavating and storming toward Langley.

He put the point of the shovel in the dirt again and hurried to step on it before she reached him. The lizard tattoo on his forearm moved with his muscles as he pushed down on the shovel.

Margo wasn't fast enough to prevent the secondary crunch.

"Bill told us to dig," Langley said.

Margo grabbed his shovel, pulling it away from him with surprising force. She swung the shovel up and grabbed the other end of the handle, holding it in front of her with both hands like a bow stick. Sadie had trained with bow sticks during her self-defense class, but she'd never mastered the weapon; she'd hurt herself enough times with it that the teacher suggested she concentrate on her hand work.

When Langley grabbed for the shovel, Margo pushed it toward him, catching him in the chest, and causing him to stumble backwards. "What the—"

"You're not digging for rocks!" she yelled, taking a step toward him, which caused him to fall back another few steps. "You just crushed a skull, you idiot."

"Bill told us to dig," Langley said again, but some of his fervor was gone. His eyes darted back and forth as though looking for someone to back him up. Sadie was the only person close enough to do such a thing.

Margo was still advancing toward Langley, who was looking at her as though she were a crazy woman. Afraid she was going to hurt him, Sadie hurried forward and put a hand on the shovel's handle. "Margo," she said in a reassuring tone. "It's okay."

"It's not okay!" Margo said, rounding on her and causing Sadie to be the one to backpedal. "These are people. They deserve respect!"

"I know," Sadie said, putting her palms out in a placating gesture she hoped would calm Margo down. "He's caught up in the energy, that's all." She looked around for Langley, wanting him to confirm her defense, but he had scurried over to join a friend who was digging up another mound. Sadie clenched her teeth as she scanned section three and saw at least a dozen people digging. She hoped Bill got in big trouble for this.

"It's not okay," Margo said again, but with a catch in her throat that drew Sadie's attention back to her. Tears filled her eyes as she stared down at the sloppy dig marks Langley had left behind. She fell to her knees at the graveside and, with her hands, began pulling at the dirt, gently uncovering a delicate, small human skull, the top crushed.

The reverence and sorrow of Margo's movements seemed out of place following her anger with Langley. Sadie knelt down beside her, staring at the eye sockets that had once belonged to someone's child before looking up at Margo. Silent tears ran down her cheeks as she carefully removed the skull from the ground. There was something more than archeology and respecting this grave behind Margo's tears.

"Get me a bag," Margo said, wiping at her eyes with a dirty hand and leaving tracks across her cheek. She hadn't put gloves on before extracting the skull. It was against procedure to handle anything without gloves on, but everything happening on the site right now was against procedure.

Sadie pulled a plastic bag from her pocket and held it out toward Margo.

"Grid 33," Margo said, reciting the cataloging information without taking the bag.

Sadie pulled out her Sharpie and wrote down the grid information, the item description, the date and time, and noted Margo as the digger, then held the bag open so Margo could place the skull inside it. She then reached into her other pocket and handed Margo a pair of vinyl gloves—she always carried extra of everything.

Margo put the gloves on before carefully picking up every tiny piece of bone broken off by Langley's shovel and adding it to the bag.

"I'm not leaving until she's up," Margo said quietly, drained, as she went back to digging.

"Okay," Sadie whispered back. "I'll help you." She looked at the rest of the crew, still digging, and gave up the fight to preserve the crime scene, opting instead to be very clear in her report of what Bill did to create the chaos. That was information the BLM would certainly be interested in.

Margo continued to cry as she dug out the jaw, and then the clavicle. She moved with incredible efficiency, and Sadie kept up with the labeling and bagging, only stopping once to return to the original grave, now fully uncovered to show the man's plain blue sweatshirt, to gather Margo's tools. Then she took a moment to text Pete what had happened.

When Sadie returned, Margo was brushing away dirt from the exposed pelvis with her gloved fingers—tender and soft as though not wanting to hurt the ancient bones. She was still crying.

"Margo?" Sadie said, putting the tools down beside her new friend. "Are you okay?"

"I'm fine," she said, tears dripping off her face and into the dirt.

"I just want her out of the ground. I want to make sure no one hurts her again."

"Okay," Sadie said, removing another bag from her pocket and wondering what was behind the emotion. It was more than this body, Sadie felt sure of that, but Margo seemed too fragile to answer any questions right now.

They continued digging and cataloging for another thirty minutes. Sadie could not have been more relieved when an approaching cloud of dust in the distance announced the police. She finished filling in the information on the bag she had in hand, then stood and hurried it over to Roberto just as the squad car pulled to a stop.

She pulled out her phone to see if Pete had responded to her text. He had, and she read the words twice.

Don't say anything about the undercover work. Stick to your story. I've made a call to the BLM contact. I can't believe this.

Sadie let out a breath and deleted the text in case the police wanted to look at her phone. She slipped the phone back into her pocket. *You and me both.*

CHAPTER 5

Sadie gave her statement to the police late Thursday afternoon and was then driven back to the carpool location along with the remaining crew. It was a surprisingly quiet drive; no one wanted to be the one to broach the silence and by the time the D&E van pulled into the parking lot, the opportunity was lost.

The story was on the news that night and there were a few follow-up notes about it over the weekend. On Saturday, the police reported that initial forensics had confirmed both bodies were male, Hispanic, and possibly illegal immigrants. Both had been killed by a gunshot to the head at point-blank range. The men didn't match any missing persons reports filed in the last six years, and they hadn't been buried at the same time, however, both murders were estimated to have happened within the last year. Further testing would be needed. In the meantime, the public was asked to inform police if they had any information. By Monday, the story of two bodies dug up from an ancient burial site was old news.

The lack of new details was frustrating and Sadie reviewed the order of events over and over again. Details began to rise to the surface of her memory—things she wanted to make sense of. Why were the bodies there? Why had Margo been so upset? And then there was Shel. He'd kept digging and discovered the second body even after Bill told him to stop.

Pete didn't know anything more about the case than she did, and Agent Shannon, Sadie's contact from the Bureau of Land Management, had told her via one phone call—the first time Sadie had even heard the woman's voice—to be patient. Ho boy, being patient was not Sadie's strong suit. But she didn't dare go around the BLM to ask for information from the police. She didn't know how the jurisdictions worked.

To keep her mind and hands occupied, she'd been baking like a madwoman, freezing most of what she made for a later date, something that was a bit odd to her because she liked the process of cooking her favorite items as much as eating them, so freezing simply denied her the pleasure of creation later on. Still, she needed to stay busy, and baking was her old standby. She should really take up some hobbies other than cooking and investigating murders.

At least Pete was coming to visit this weekend, after he finished some training he was heading up in Denver. Sadie couldn't wait to see him. But the weekend felt so far away.

Sadie wondered if she'd go back to the dig at all—D&E had sent out a form e-mail explaining that they would be in touch when and if the dig reopened. As much as Sadie hated the actual work, she missed having purpose—and a dual purpose at that. The last nine names on her list remained unresearched, waiting, like everyone else, to see what would happen next.

"Well," Caro said after Sadie had voiced her concerns about whether or not she'd go back to the dig site, "I told Lois I'd help her with her booth at the Fiesta. I'm sure she wouldn't mind an extra set of hands if you don't go back."

"That would be fun," Sadie said, transferring the dulce de leche bars she'd made that morning to a clean plate.

Lois was Caro's good friend and the owner of her own cupcake catering business. For the second year in a row, Lois had a booth at the upcoming Balloon Fiesta in Albuquerque—an annual hot air balloon festival that Sadie had heard about, but never actually been to. Sadie loved the idea of helping Lois with her cupcakes, but she knew if she never resolved her questions about what had happened at the dig, she would remain frustrated. She wanted more than newspaper articles.

"I'm going to run some errands," she said, making sure the plastic wrap was good and tight around the plate. She'd decided to talk to Margo for a variety of reasons, but mostly because Margo was the one person from the dig that Sadie felt connected to. Finding that body together had made them into an unexpected partnership.

"I'll come with you," Caro said as she started gathering up the bills she was sorting.

Sadie hurried to talk her out of it as gently as she could. "Well, after the library I was going to stop at Margo's. She's the woman I worked with at the site that last day. She was really upset about everything. I want to make sure she's okay."

"Oh," Caro said, reading between the lines. "It would probably be awkward if I came, wouldn't it?"

Sadie made a regretful face. "Probably. Sorry." While waiting to be cleared to leave the site that night, Margo had smoked her way through half a pack of cigarettes while Sadie came up with a hundred things to talk about in hopes of keeping Margo at least a little bit distracted. It hadn't helped much. Seeing all the graves open had devastated Margo. It was as though the bodies were her own people—despite her Caucasian ancestry—and she took the fact that they weren't being properly removed as a personal failure. At the same time, once she got over the initial, intense shock, she seemed a bit embarrassed by her reaction. Sadie hoped that her impromptu visit wouldn't be too unwelcome.

"That's okay," Caro said, trying to be a good sport. She fanned the bills back out on the table. "You know where she lives?"

"Background check," Sadie said with a casual shrug. Didn't everyone do background checks on their acquaintances? Granted, Sadie hadn't done a full report on Margo yet, but it had taken less than five minutes for her to find the address. Like Kyle Langley, Margo had her own place—she was easy to find. "I won't be gone very long—maybe an hour. I could stop and pick up the tortillas for the Tostadas Compuestas. You still wanted to make that tonight, right?"

"That'd be great. I'm almost out of Monterey Jack cheese, too, if you don't mind." The chili con carne was already simmering in the slow cooker, filling the house with the most delectable smell.

Sadie assured her she didn't mind, but by the time she was on the road, her eagerness to talk to Margo had moved to the top of Sadie's list of errands. The library and the Mexican market weren't going anywhere.

Margo's duplex was on the other end of town, so it took a good ten minutes before Sadie pulled up in front of the very basic adobe structure. Caro had shown her some traditional adobe in the re-stricted section of the city where everything had remained authentic, but the majority of the "adobe" was made of a stucco-type material.

Parked in the driveway on Margo's side of the duplex was a 1970s model Land Cruiser with faded green paint and some stick-ers on the back window: "Bark Less Wag More," which Sadie didn't understand, and a familiar blue "Coexist" sticker.

Sadie took a breath, hoping to calm her nerves as she focused on her objectives: first, make sure Margo was all right, and then see if she could answer some of the questions Sadie couldn't ask anyone else. Just talking to someone else invested in the dig would be a relief.

Sadie reached the front door and knocked rather than ringing the doorbell. No one came to the door, but Sadie was sure Margo was home since her Land Cruiser *was* in the driveway. She knocked louder, and this time heard movement from inside. Several seconds later, the doorknob turned and the door began to open. It stuck slightly before being yanked all the way open. Margo looked as though she'd just woken up despite the fact that it was almost noon. Her hair was down, but tangled, and she wore mismatched sweats.

"Hi, Margo," Sadie said, giving a little wave with her free hand.

"Sarah?" Margo said, using Sadie's undercover name. She lifted a hand to her hair as though she could fix the damage. "What are you doing here?"

"I just thought I'd stop in and see how you were," Sadie said, feeling her instincts kick in. "And I brought you some dulce de leche bars," she said, holding out the plate.

"You didn't have to do that," Margo said, looking embarrassed. Sadie knew they were both thinking about Margo's reaction at the dig site. "I'm all right." Then she looked at the plate that Sadie had extended toward her. "I sure did like those, though."

Sadie smiled even wider. "I was also hoping you might have some info on the dig. I haven't heard anything other than what's been on the news."

Margo finally reached for the plate. "Do you want to come in? I mean, it's a mess, but if you don't mind."

"I don't mind," Sadie lied as Margo pulled the door open all the way and ushered her inside.

Besides the stale and thick stench of long days of chain smoking, there were piles of clutter everywhere. Clothes, books, magazines. Things weren't piled in a hoarding kind of way, just in an "I don't care" attitude that often plagued people who lived alone. Though to a far lesser degree, Sadie herself had fallen victim to that same attitude once her children had moved out. Luckily, she'd nipped that particular bad habit in the bud. Margo's house was a testament of what a good decision it had been for Sadie to cure herself years ago.

Margo closed the door, but had to really push to get it to snap back into the frame, making the whole apartment shake slightly. "I left the door open one night and it rained—the water warped the entryway." She waved toward the parquet flooring near the door, which was warped, dull, and lighter in color than the rest of the floor that was mostly covered with a large area rug in need of vacuuming. "The warped boards catch the door."

"Wood floors are tricky," Sadie said, trying to ignore the puffy pillows of dust and hair accumulated by the baseboards. "Can you sand it down?"

"Maybe," Margo said with a shrug. "I haven't tried. Don't know how long I'll be here, and I already broke a window lock so I won't be getting my deposit back, whether I fix it or not."

Margo turned toward the small kitchen with the plate of treats, placing it on top of the dish drain, which was the only space free of dishes, pop cans, and miscellaneous papers. "I guess I fell asleep on the couch," she said, reaching up to scratch her head. "When I'm not waking up at three A.M. my body tries to make up for all the sleep it's missed over the years."

"No problem," Sadie said, holding her purse with both hands in front of her.

Margo lifted a corner of the plastic wrap and snuck part of one of the bars, popping it into her mouth and then nodding in approval before wiping her sticky hand on her sweatpants. One pant leg was pulled up to her knee.

"So did you get called back, then?" Margo asked as she came back into the living room.

Sadie pivoted to follow her across the room. "Called back?"

"Yeah, to the site? Thursday?" Margo sat on the couch, waving Sadie into the recliner.

"I didn't get a call," Sadie said, sitting down on the very edge of the chair. It was gray velour, but it had several stains that Sadie wasn't going to take chances with. A 1980s style green-and-pink nylon jacket was thrown over the back. Had she missed the callback from D&E, or had they just not called her?

"Oh, well, Bill said it would be a light crew called in to finish it up. You probably didn't get called back 'cause you're so new."

"It probably didn't help that I told Bill to leave the graves alone." Sadie knew that hadn't been one of her best career moves.

Margo shrugged in agreement. "That whole thing was a disaster," she said, her voice somber. "He should have listened to you. We all should have. If the graves weren't all opened up, I think we could have convinced the police to bring the bodies up more delicately—maybe even keep some of us on to help." She leaned forward and picked up a package of cigarettes lying on the coffee table, tapping one out of the cellophane package before seeming to remember she wasn't alone.

"Do you mind?" she asked, lifting the cigarette slightly in one hand and fingering her lighter in the other.

Sadie did mind, sort of, but it was Margo's house and Sadie wanted to get to know her better so she shook her head. "But you're okay?" she asked, reflecting back on Margo's reaction at the dig. "You seemed pretty upset at the site."

Margo put the cigarette between her lips and waved away Sadie's question. "I'm a purist," she said, the cigarette bobbing up and down as she talked. "To me, the fact that these bodies are a thousand years old makes no difference. Anyone would be horrified if someone took a crowbar to their grandma's casket in hopes of finding a wedding ring on her corpse, but somehow *these* people are just bones." She shook her head and flicked her lighter, going almost cross-eyed as she lined up the flame and the cigarette. She inhaled deeply, then exhaled slowly, and Sadie watched her shoulders relax.

"I've never met anyone who takes it as seriously as you do," Sadie said, wondering why that was so. Though she didn't think Margo was hiding anything, her attitude still seemed extreme.

"Sometimes it feels like I'm the only one," Margo said after exhaling and leaning back against the couch. "Me against the world of 'archeology for profit.' At what point do the *people* not matter anymore? How long do they have to be in the ground before no one cares?"

All kinds of religious answers came to Sadie's mind, about what happens when people die and what the purpose of life was, but she'd no sooner considered taking the conversation in that direction when Margo sighed and looked up with a change-the-subject smile. "It sure is weird, though, isn't it? Fresh bodies buried in an ancient site."

Sadie nodded. "Really weird." She had to keep her hands together in her lap so as not to start straightening the cluttered coffee table. Margo leaned forward to tap off her ash in a coffee mug. Sadie had to repress a shudder; every time she saw someone do that, she imagined accidentally drinking cigarette ash.

"Did you ever see the other body?" Margo asked.

"Just what you and I saw together at the very start. The paper speculated that they were illegals," Sadie said. "If that's the case, the families couldn't report their deaths for fear of deportation, right?"

Margo frowned. "Yeah, maybe."

The smoke in the room was getting thick, and Sadie felt the urge to cough but cleared her throat instead.

"It's too bad you're not going back on Thursday."

Sadie was embarrassed all over again. "Yeah. Do you know anyone else who was called back to the crew?"

Margo shook her head. "I'm not tight with anyone on the crew," she said, then straightened. "Although I have Langley's number. I guess I could ask him." She riffled through a bunch of junk on the coffee table before excusing herself to her bedroom—which was also a mess from what Sadie could see through the doorway—and returning a minute later with her phone.

"Isn't Langley the guy who dug into that grave? The one you almost beat with a shovel?" She knew he was, but she didn't want to seem too familiar with the crew and risk blowing her cover. Mostly, she was surprised that Margo was friends with him. They certainly weren't on good terms at the dig last Thursday.

Margo nodded, scrolling through her phone. "My Cruiser broke down a couple of weeks ago. Langley towed it to a repair shop—he's got a sweet truck—and he drove me to work for the next couple of days while they were fixing the starter. Ah, there he is." She started typing on her phone, then pushed a button and set the phone aside.

"Are you still mad at him?" Sadie asked, wondering what Margo's text message had said.

Margo narrowed her eyes. "Furious," she said, quick and sharp. "But if he's on the crew too, I want to know." She glanced at her phone. "Assuming he'll even reply to my text."

"There's something else that's been bothering me," Sadie said, deciding this was as good an opportunity as any to ease into the other purpose for her visit.

"Yeah?" Margo asked, lifting her eyebrows expectantly.

"Shel—the guy who found the second body—he was digging after Bill told everyone to stop."

Margo looked to the side and pondered that for a few moments. "That's right, Bill *had* told everyone to stop, hadn't he? Even us. He didn't want us to keep digging up that first body."

Sadie nodded. "Shel's only been working with D&E for a month. He said they paid better than the last company he was with and—"

Margo's phone chirped and she picked it up, reading something before looking up at Sadie. "Langley got called back to the dig too."

"Oh," Sadie said, feeling like chopped liver.

"Anyway," Margo said, putting her phone down again, "even though he's new with D&E, Shel's been working digs for years, right? He knows better than to keep digging."

"Right, and everyone else had stopped. Plus the first van had left already so there could be no doubt he knew that the dig was closed for the day."

"Yeah," Margo said, "that's weird." She paused for a moment, then picked up her phone again. "Want me to find out what he has to say about it?"

"You have Shel's number too?"

"No, but Langley might. They hung out a fair amount on the site. I bet he could put us in touch with Shel."

Sadie leaned forward, all tingly with anticipation. "What would we say to him?"

"Ask him why he kept digging," Margo said matter-of-factly.

It was hard to argue with her logic, so Sadie didn't bother. Margo pushed a few buttons on her phone, then held it to her ear.

"He better answer," Margo said. "He owes me." A second later she straightened. "Langley? Yeah, I'm good. . . . Yeah, I'm on the crew starting on Thursday too. . . . Hey, I'm looking to get in touch with Shel, and you guys seem to be buddies, so . . . I just need to talk to him about something. . . . No big deal. . . . Seriously, no big deal." She rolled her eyes at Sadie and Sadie smiled at her encouragingly. "Yeah . . . I'd prefer in person."

Sadie startled slightly—a face-to-face meeting? Of course those were always more effective, but they could be intimidating all the same. Then again, maybe only Margo would go. Sadie wasn't sure if that thought was a relief or a disappointment.

Margo paused for a few more seconds. "Langley," she said in a flat, even tone. She was too calm—and a little scary. She leaned forward, completely focused on the call. "You owe me for what you did to that little girl. If you know where he's going to be, then tell me and we're square." Then she was quiet again, listening.

Sadie swallowed, really glad she wasn't in Langley's shoes right now.

"I know where that is. North end, right?" Margo said after several seconds passed. "What time should I run into you guys? . . . Perfect, I'll look for you."

She hung up and tossed her phone back on the coffee table. "Looks like we've got a double date tonight," she said, getting to her feet with a triumphant smile. "They'll be at The Conquistador. I wouldn't call it classy, but for a bar, it's not a total dive."

"Oh," Sadie said with more surprise than she'd have liked Margo to hear. Suddenly everything was moving really fast. "A bar. Right. I can go to a bar."

Margo cocked her head to the side. "Have you ever been to a bar?"

"Sure," Sadie said, thinking of the time she and Gayle ended up at a bar in Fort Collins; they were getting a flat tire repaired at the auto shop next door and needed some place to eat. It had been dark and smoky inside the flat square building, but it had played good music and the soup of the day, Chicken Tortilla, had been surprisingly good. It even had avocados in it. Maybe this bar would have some really good food too.

Margo picked up her phone again. "Give me your number and address, and I'll pick you up at nine tonight."

"That late?"

Margo smiled slightly. "You've never been to a bar in your life."

"I have," Sadie declared, nodding her head to further convince Margo that she was familiar with the bar scene. "Nine o'clock is great. But what if they stand us up? Langley didn't seem . . . happy about this."

"If they stand us up, then we'll know one of them is hiding something," Margo said with confidence.

"Oh. Good point."

"Trust me," Margo said. "This will be perfect." She lifted one arm and took a sniff of her armpit, making Sadie wince and look away. "I better take a shower though."

Sadie let herself out of Margo's after they exchanged phone numbers.

After stopping at the library and then at the Mexican market for the tortillas, Sadie told herself it was silly to be so worried about going to a bar. Margo wasn't worried. But Margo and Sadie were very different women. *But with the same goal,* she reminded herself. She'd been fine at that bar in Fort Collins, and she'd be fine here too. Besides, she'd seen *Cocktail* and *Coyote Ugly*—she knew what she was getting into.

Tostadas Compuestas

Chili con carne
2 pounds course ground pork or beef (pork tastes better)
4 tablespoons red chili powder
2 garlic cloves, minced
4 tablespoons flour
4 tablespoons oil
1 medium onion, chopped
1 teaspoon salt
1 tablespoon ground cumin
1 tablespoon oregano
4 cups hot water
Tomato juice, as needed

In a large mixing bowl, combine meat, chili powder, garlic, and flour. In a large, heavy skillet, heat oil over medium heat. Add onion and sauté until tender. Add meat and cook until brown. Add salt, cumin, and oregano. Add water and simmer, uncovered, for 1 hour. Add tomato juice as needed if chili becomes too dry. Add additional amounts of salt, cumin, and oregano as needed to get the flavor you prefer. Keep mixture warm on stove until the tortillas are done being fried.

Note: For a slow cooker version, brown meat according to recipe, then transfer to a slow cooker. Add seasonings, three cups of water, and one cup of tomato juice. Cook on low for up to 8 hours, or on high for 2 to 3 hours.

Tostadas

2 quarts oil, for frying
Corn tortillas (3 to 4 per person)
Cheese, grated
Lettuce, shredded
Sour cream
Pinto beans, warm
Tomatoes, diced
Guacamole (optional)

In a deep, heavy saucepan, heat oil over medium to medium-high heat. (You know the oil is at the right temperature when you can drop a small piece of tortilla into the oil and it floats to the top and starts to sizzle. If it sinks to the bottom, the oil is not hot enough. No bueno.)

Stack the tortillas three at a time and make 4 slits, about an inch out from the middle on each side, forming a rough square pattern in the center of the tortilla. Set a cooling rack over a sheet pan to drain and cool the shells. Drop the tortillas one at a time into the hot oil. When the tortilla floats back up to the surface, press a soup ladle into the middle of the tortilla so that the edges fold up and around the ladle. This will form the shape of the tortilla bowl.

Hold the ladle in place for 3 to 4 minutes. Remove the ladle and flip the tortilla over to check brownness. You want the tortilla to just barely have some color. If it looks too golden, then it will taste overcooked. Place the tortilla bowl upside down on the rack to drain and cool.

Once all the tortillas have been fried, layer the additional ingredients according to your preference. Enjoy!

Note: If using canned pinto beans, drain and rinse them. Add them to a small saucepan with a small amount of fresh water, and heat up before serving.

Note: Caro always puts the cheese into the tortilla shell first, so that the chili makes it all gooey and melty. Mmmm.

Note: Caro is offended that I put "Optional" after guacamole.

Chicken Tortilla Soup
www.ourbestbites.com/2011/02/chicken-tortilla-soup

Albuquerque International Balloon Fiesta
www.balloonfiesta.com

CHAPTER 6

The room Sadie stayed in at Rex and Caro's house was referred to as "the apartment," but was really just a large bedroom, complete with a small table and sitting area, its own fireplace, and full bathroom. They had designed it for Rex's mother who had lived with them up until four years ago when she'd passed away. Their daughters had shared it after that, certainly enjoying the independence it afforded them.

It did not, however, have its own outside entrance, which meant Sadie had to come and go through the front door of Rex and Caro's home. She didn't mind, of course, but couldn't help thinking that the resell value would have been much improved if they had added an exterior door.

It reminded Sadie of her friend, Fiona, an avid gardener who'd ripped out her only full bath in favor of a greenhouse area she felt sure would work well with the existing skylight. After the remodel, the house was left with one bathroom complete with a shower, which was fine with Fiona since she had issues with the unsanitary nature of bathwater.

The greenhouse never quite worked as well as she'd hoped it

would—there wasn't enough light, and it looked downright strange to have a greenhouse inside your home. Five years later, Fiona decided to move and had to put the full bath back in because the market had gone soft and she couldn't compete with all the other two-bath homes on the market. It cost her nearly $12,000. Point being: resell mattered, even if you weren't planning to move soon.

At five minutes to nine, Sadie was putting the final touches on her hair when she heard the sound of an engine in the driveway. She peeked out her window that overlooked the front lawn and saw Margo's faded green Land Cruiser come to a stop. Having had hours to think about what the night might become, Sadie was a bundle of nerves. A real-life bar! At night!

She grabbed her purse and turned off the light in the apartment before sneaking past the living room where Rex was watching a sport fishing show. Caro was organizing her photo box—twenty-five years' worth—and pouting a little at not having been invited to go to the bar too.

Sadie had anticipated her reaction and so had waited to tell her until after they'd made the Tostadas Compuestas—little taco salads in corn tortilla bowls—one of Caro's favorite family recipes. Caro might have been more inclined to argue about it if she hadn't already promised Rex she'd spend the evening with him. Watching a show about marlins while sorting photos didn't seem quite date-worthy, in Sadie's opinion, but then she hadn't been married for thirty years either. She and her late husband, Neil, had celebrated their eleventh anniversary a few months before he died of a massive heart attack, leaving her a widow and a single mother of their two adopted children. She'd always envied those people who had long, comfortable marriages, but she understood that there were trials to be had there too.

Sadie shut the front door quietly behind her and headed toward the Land Cruiser. Margo met her on the front walk, bringing Sadie up short as they appraised each other. Margo was wearing quite a bit of makeup, including some bright red lipstick that looked like wet paint. Sadie tsked in her mind over the tight pink tank top that left too little to the imagination. Margo was trim and athletic, but she was close to forty; and regardless of age and fitness level, modesty was a good rule of thumb for any woman.

After a few seconds, Margo shook her head and smiled sympathetically. "You can't go to a bar looking like that."

Sadie looked down at her khaki capris, cute brown sandals with just a hint of a heel, and flowing patterned blouse with a little ruffle at the neck. Caro had helped her reinvent her wardrobe with regular shopping trips to the fabulous boutiques in Old Town. Sadie was better dressed than she'd been in years.

"I thought I looked nice," she said, frowning. She eyed Margo's top again and hoped she wasn't supposed to dress like *that.*

"Exactly," Margo said, taking Sadie by the shoulders and turning her back to the house. "Too nice. It's not that kind of bar."

Fifteen minutes later, Sadie stood in front of the full-length mirror attached to the back of the bathroom door in her apartment and pulled at the black fitted T-shirt she usually wore underneath other shirts, not by itself. It hadn't fit this well a year ago, however. One of the positive side effects of Sadie's trip to Kaua'i last spring was that she'd lost her appetite and, in the process, dropped nearly twenty pounds. Of course, she'd gained half of it back once she came home thanks to a six-week trip to England with her two children. But within a week of returning from *that* trip, she was in New Mexico and Caro was dragging Sadie to her Zumba and spinning classes every day.

Sadie hated the bikes, but the Latin American dance class was kind of fun. She didn't have Caro's moves, but the other people in the class didn't seem to mind that she flopped around like a drunken monkey in the back of the room. She'd lost five pounds of the weight she'd gained back. Though she felt arrogant to say so, even to herself, she looked good in the top Margo had picked out for her. In addition, Margo had chosen a pair of Sadie's straight leg jeans and folded them up into too-wide cuffs. A pair of silver ballet flats out of Sadie's closet and a chunky turquoise necklace of Caro's that Sadie hadn't returned yet completed the outfit to Margo's standards.

While Sadie changed her clothes, Margo had gone out to her car to get her purse—for finishing touches she said. She was already back by the time Sadie stepped out of the bathroom to reveal her new, dirtied-up-barfly look.

"Still a little dressy," Margo said, slapping Sadie's hands away when she folded her arms over her stomach. "But better."

Dressy? Jeans and a T-shirt? "Can I wear some footsy socks with these shoes? Otherwise my feet will sweat."

Margo laughed, then started rummaging in her purse.

Sadie took that as permission and found a pair of black booties. Once her feet were back in the shoes, Margo handed her a tube of lipstick. Apparently her barely-there lip gloss wasn't bar-worthy either. The glossy red wasn't totally wrong for her complexion, but the darker color meant she had to take a minute to darken her eye makeup and blush so that it all coordinated.

Margo used some aerosol hairspray to make Sadie's chin-length, salt-and-pepper hair a little bigger before pronouncing her ready for the bar scene.

Sadie looked one last time at her semi-trashy reflection before grabbing her purse, again, and turning off the lights of the apartment, again. Thank goodness she wouldn't have to worry about seeing anyone she knew while she was out tonight. Well, other than the members of the dig crew.

It was harder to sneak past Caro this time. She'd looked up when Sadie and Margo had come back inside, and was therefore alert when the two of them headed for the front door. She lifted her eyebrows, but Sadie just smiled and waved without stopping. Caro would be waiting up when Sadie came in tonight. Guaranteed.

It was a quarter after nine when they got into Margo's Land Cruiser, but when Sadie shared her worry about being late, Margo just laughed.

"I can see I'll need to be the leader for this expedition," she said once they were on the road. The inside of Margo's Cruiser was as cluttered as her house, and suddenly Sadie was glad she hadn't worn her nicer clothes.

"I can live with being your wingman," Sadie said, relieved. She was relearning her investigative skills but was already intimidated by this situation. Plus, Margo knew Shel and Langley better than she did.

Margo drove through a part of town Sadie was familiar with, but then turned on a road Sadie hadn't been down before and drove for a few miles into an area that looked nothing like the Santa Fe Sadie had seen so far. Instead of the Pueblo Deco building designs and meticulous xeriscaped lots, the businesses here were square and squat, with bright paint jobs, and flashing neon signs in blackened windows. The *other* side of Santa Fe it seemed.

At a stop sign, Margo lit up a cigarette, rolling down her window as if that would keep the smoke from bothering Sadie. Her plan did not work, but Sadie appreciated the gesture.

After passing half a dozen bars, a tire store, and two auto

body shops, Margo pulled into the parking lot for a bar called The Conquistador. The building consisted of whitewashed cinderblock, too-orange trim, and a neon Bud Light sign in the window. Hitching rails were up against the front, making them completely useless if someone were actually to arrive by horse.

Once out of the Land Cruiser, Sadie stood up straight, eyeing the building and trying to convince herself that she was comfortable and confident. Such positive affirmations were helpful to her in coping with her anxiety, and her anxiety was knocking on the door . . . hard.

Margo finished off her cigarette, a perfect ring of red lipstick around the filter, then dropped it in a large ashtray by the door that looked like it was full of gray sand . . . and a few dozen cigarette butts. Sadie hurried to keep up with Margo's long-legged strides, determined not to let her out of her sight for the rest of the evening. Ninja skills aside, Sadie didn't want to fly solo on this mission.

The inside of the bar was as dark and smoky as Sadie had expected it would be, with faded felt sombreros hanging from the ceiling and peanut shells on the floor that Sadie tried to avoid. Walking on them felt like she was stepping on cockroaches. Mexican rugs were tacked to the walls, but their once-bright colors were muted and yellowed from age and smoke. There were a couple of pool tables in the back, a long shiny bar to the right, and clusters of tables to the left. Sadie didn't see a jukebox, but there was Mexican music playing from somewhere, barely loud enough to be heard over a few dozen voices talking and laughing. Were bars always this busy on Monday nights?

Margo scanned the room and then began moving toward a table on the far side. Sadie dutifully followed and recognized Shel, Langley, and another member of the dig crew named Garrett sitting around the table. Whereas Shel was broad-shouldered, but relatively short—five foot nine Sadie guessed—Langley was thinner, taller, with reddish hair. His pale blue eyes stood out against his fair complexion that was liberally sprinkled with faded freckles. He really shouldn't have a job that required so much sun. The bright colors of his lizard tattoo stood out against his pale forearm.

Shel was talking with a waitress who wore a large men's dress shirt that came to mid-thigh. The sleeves were rolled up to the elbows and the front was unbuttoned one button lower than it should have been. The only other thing she wore—that Sadie could see—were bright blue cowboy boots. The other waitresses wore the same attire, but with different colored boots. Sadie was embarrassed on behalf of all of them.

"Hey," Margo said as she reached the table. She grabbed the back of Langley's chair and gave it a shake. "Fancy meeting you guys here," she said.

The waitress laughed at something and walked away. Shel watched her leave long enough that Sadie was embarrassed for him too.

Shel looked up at Margo and smiled. "What else is there to do in this town?" He flicked another look at the waitress leaning over the bar. Sadie pretended not to notice.

"No kidding," Margo said, pulling out a chair and waving Sadie toward it before grabbing an empty chair from another table—without even asking the people seated around that table—and pulling it over for herself. Sadie sat down between Langley and Margo and worked hard to appear casual, which was hard to do since the effort it took to appear casual defeated the very purpose.

The table was disgusting, the stained varnish chipping off in places. Sadie kept her hands in her lap and considered passing around the travel-sized hand sanitizer she always carried in her purse in case anyone else at the table was as grossed out as she was. Then again, maybe she needed to save it for herself. Mingled with the smoke and the yeasty smell of beer was the scent of chicken and hot oil. She was not the least bit tempted by any of the food offered here.

"What are we drinking?" Margo asked, hooking one arm over the back of her chair and kicking out one leg; she looked right at home.

Shel lifted a hand, raising two fingers when the blue-booted waitress looked his way, then leaned back in his chair and took a swig from his bottle.

"So I got called back to the dig Thursday," Margo said. "How about all y'all?"

Sadie glanced at Langley, but he didn't give away that he and Margo had already had this discussion. Instead, Shel and Langley confirmed that they too had been called back. Garrett hung his head a little bit.

"How'd you make the cut?" Margo said, looking from Langley to Shel.

"Luck of the draw, I guess," Shel said with a wink that made Margo's jaw tighten, though Sadie hoped she was the only one who noticed it. The waitress returned with two beers, and Shel pointed at Sadie and Margo, indicating the drinks were for them.

"Could I just have a Coke?" Sadie asked. Everyone looked at her and she shrugged. "I'm the designated driver." Never mind that it was Margo's Land Cruiser.

Margo gave Sadie a tight look, but Sadie wasn't about to drink a beer with people she didn't know and didn't trust.

"Ah, right," Shel said, taking her beer for himself. His eyes were already glassy, and he had that too-relaxed look of a man already well saturated. He hadn't come across as quite so arrogant at the dig site, which reminded Sadie why she didn't enjoy keeping company with drunks. Why on earth had she come to a bar?

Someone cheered from the direction of the pool tables, and the waitress left. Margo asked Shel and Langley if they knew what was going on with the dig.

"We went up there this morning for a bit," Shel said.

"You did?" Margo said, tensing slightly. Sadie knew exactly how she felt—left out.

"To catalogue the bigger stuff the feds pulled up before they razed everything," Shel continued with a shrug. "They had two bull-dozers there today. All the fill is in dump trucks, and the crew will be sifting through it."

"You're kidding!" Margo said, sounding horrified. She seemed to catch herself quickly, though, and took a breath. When she spoke, she tried to keep her tone casual. "It's a lot harder to do it that way. Makes a mess of the cataloging process."

"But it's faster," Shel pointed out. "The developer wants Bill to stick to the original time line as much as possible."

Never mind there were two men found dead there, Sadie thought to herself. Why was it so easy for people to discount that? A second later, she thought about the other hundred or so bodies buried there originally and what Margo had said about there not being as much difference as people seemed to believe.

The waitress returned and put a glass bottle of Coke in front of Sadie. The cap had already been removed.

"Thanks," Sadie said to her, loving the nostalgic bottle. Her grandparents had had cases of pop in glass bottles at their house. Sadie and her brother and sister would take the empties back to the neighborhood grocer and earn five cents per bottle. They felt rich walking out with a dollar apiece.

"Is the sifting being done on site?" Margo asked.

Shel shrugged. "Yeah—a few hundred yards away from the original dig. They're getting screens and metal detectors to help it go faster."

Sadie thought about the pothunters who blew up burial sites— would this result be much different? "How much longer do they think the job will last?" she asked.

"Four or five more days is all," Shel said, grabbing a few peanuts out of the bowl in the middle of the table. He cracked off one end and sucked out the peanut. Sadie hated peanuts in the shell. So messy. He dropped the shells on the floor, which she liked even less. Wasn't it a safety hazard to have peanut shells on the floor where inebriated people were trying to keep their balance?

"Bill says there's another job starting out by Chapelle at the end of next week," Langley added. "It'll be full crew, and we ought to be done with the Ranchette job by then."

Would Sadie work the new dig? Did she want to?

"That's good," Margo said with a weighted tone. "So, Sarah and I were talking about when we found those fresh bodies."

The men looked at her expectantly. She got right to the point, staring hard at Shel. "Why did you keep digging?"

CHAPTER 7

All three men seemed startled by Margo's question. It was all Sadie could do to contain her own surprise. She had expected they would ease into things rather than get to the point so quickly.

When none of the men answered, Margo continued, "Bill had told everyone to stop digging for the day before you found that second body, Shel. So why were you still digging?"

"I didn't hear Bill tell us to stop," Shel said, but there was tension behind his forced casualness.

"No, you heard him," Margo said with a quick shake of her head. "I was there when he announced it—everyone stopped digging." She leaned forward to stare at Shel before turning the pointed look to Langley.

Sadie took a drink of her Coke, trying to hide her unease, and scratched at some of the flaking varnish on the table. When she realized it might not be varnish at all, but petrified crud instead, she put her hands in her lap.

"Didn't everyone else stop digging, Langley?" Margo pressed.

"Um, yeah," Langley said, looking at the bottle he was turning in his hands.

"Shut up, Langley," Shel said.

Margo turned to Shel again. "Bill had told everyone to load up in the vans, the first one had even left, but you kept digging. Why?"

Shel took a drink from his bottle and said nothing. He looked between the two women with narrowed eyes.

Margo turned to Langley again. "Why was he digging?"

Langley continued to stare into his bottle. "I don't—"

"Why, Langley?" she demanded. "Why was he digging in that *exact* place *after* being told to stop?" She dropped her voice, but held him with her gaze. "You owe me."

"Owe her?" Shel repeated, looking at Langley. "What's she talking about?"

Sadie knew Margo was referring to the skull Langley crushed in the digging fury that followed Bill's instructions to check all the graves, but Langley continued to stare at the bottle in his hands. Garrett looked confused, glancing between Margo and Langley as the interrogation continued. Sadie counted to three before Langley spoke. "He said the hill looked different."

"Shut up, Langley!" Shel snapped again.

Margo's eyes whipped to Shel, a triumphant look on her face. "So you *did* hear Bill say to stop."

"So what if I did?" Shel said, leaning back in his chair as though wanting to appear casual. He failed, though, due to the tension still radiating from him. "I'd noticed that hill earlier in the day, and then after the first body came up, I thought we ought to check. It wasn't a big deal."

"Actually it was a *really* big deal," Margo said. Her words were calm, but intense. "If you'd have left it alone, Bill wouldn't have told us to open up every grave like that."

"So what?" Shel said, shrugging. "We dug 'em up faster."

"Except we didn't dig them up," Margo snapped, losing her cool. "We *opened* them up, which is totally different. We completely compromised the cataloging, and now they're sifting the bones instead of letting us do it right. You really screwed it up, Shel."

"Those bones are worth less than the dirt they're covered in." Shel's words lacked the bravado Sadie expected though, and he shifted uncomfortably in his seat. If he didn't believe it, why did he say it?

Sadie looked away from Shel's duplicitous expression and took another sip of her Coke while trying to think of something—anything—to say. She wasn't much of a wingman so far.

"We are hired to preserve them," Margo said, her eyes as focused as a laser beam on Shel. "That means treating them with the same care and respect we'd give our own family."

Shel looked down at his beer bottle, his jaw tight with anger.

When Margo spoke again, Sadie could tell it was taking all she had to keep her voice calm. "And then you were hired back on the dig. That seems a little strange too, doesn't it?"

Sadie considered excusing herself to the restrooms. The tension was getting to her, and she had half a Xanax in her purse which would keep the rising anxiety from getting the best of her. Yet the confrontation was a tiny bit exciting too.

"It's all about who you know, isn't it, Shel?" Langley muttered.

"Shut up, Langley."

"What does that mean?" Margo demanded, looking between the two men.

Neither of them answered, though Sadie noticed that Shel tried to strike an even more casual pose. She wasn't buying it, and she doubted anyone else was either. Rather than hiding whatever it was he wanted to hide, he was making it even more obvious that he *had* something to hide in the first place.

"I've been with D&E for years," Langley said. "I don't think there's any question as to why I got called back." The implication that there was a reason other than seniority that got Shel back on the job sat in the center of the crud-encrusted table. "Maybe you ought to tell them why you kept digging. Maybe you ought to tell them *who* told you to dig in the first place."

"Langley," Shel said between his teeth. "Shut. Up."

Margo pounced on this new information, leaning further toward Shel. "So you went against a direct order from Bill because someone else told you to dig? Did you know there were fresh bodies at the site, Crossbones?"

Crossbones? What did that mean?

Sadie saw Shel clench his fist on the table. She felt her heart pounding from the growing tension, and her hand tensed around the Coke bottle in response. She watched him closely. Garrett shifted in his seat and glanced around the bar as though considering the other occupants and wishing he were at their table instead of this one.

"He sure did," Langley said, fast and crisp, suddenly confident. There was a challenge in his eyes. A pushing. A threat?

Sadie watched as his words registered on Shel's face, triggering a new level of anger and . . . fear?

Shel suddenly lunged across the table toward Langley, but Sadie had been watching the coil of anger behind his eyes. With a flick of her wrist, Sadie turned the Coke bottle in her hand sideways, jumped forward, and bashed it onto the bridge of Shel's nose.

Coke spilled all over the table, and Shel went careening backward so fast that it wasn't until his chair, and perhaps his head, cracked against the concrete floor that Sadie fully realized what she'd done. Everyone at the table screamed or cursed, jumping up and back as the quick change of mood and circumstance caught everyone off guard.

Sadie blinked at the Coke dripping off the table, then turned to see Margo looking at her in shock.

The entire bar was frozen, except for the music, which sounded tinny and sparse in the instant silence.

Shel struggled to his feet while everyone stared, cupping both his hands over his face. Once upright, he pulled his hands away to reveal his mouth, chin, and hands covered with blood.

Sadie had hit him harder than she'd meant to, and she wondered if she should apologize.

He looked down at his blood-covered fingers, then up at the three of them standing across the table while Garrett, who was closer to Shel, started moving away. Shel narrowed his eyes, and in one movement, he grabbed the edge of the table and threw it over.

Margo, Langley, and Sadie tried to jump out of the way but ended up running into each other and the people from the table behind them, their feet sliding on the peanut shell-covered floor. Coke and beer went everywhere; Sadie dropped her Coke bottle as she stumbled over someone's foot. She grabbed the back of a chair, hoping to save herself, only to realize someone was sitting in the chair. They tumbled to the ground together—the woman screaming and swearing while Sadie tried to apologize. She heard someone laugh, and from a few feet away someone else yelled "It's on!"

People were enjoying this?

The entire bar seemed to erupt an instant later, and Sadie scrambled up from the sticky floor only to duck a punch. Who wanted to punch *her*? A moment later, she didn't duck fast enough and a fist hit the side of her neck.

With her neck throbbing, she put her arms up in a protective block while trying to back out of the crowd. The next time an arm came toward her, she hit it as hard as she could in order to deflect the blow. There were easily a dozen people fighting as a mob now, everyone throwing random punches. For real? People just jumped into a fight and started punching whoever was in their way?

How did this night go from asking a few questions to a full-on barroom brawl?

Sadie caught sight of Langley holding some guy in a headlock. Margo was yelling at a man in a cowboy hat in the epicenter of the fight. Sadie wondered who he was—she'd never seen him before—and why Margo was so angry with him. The drinks had mixed with the scattered peanut shells and created a slippery mess all over the floor.

Sadie pushed toward Margo and grabbed her arm, trying to pull her out of the fray just as Shel appeared, getting in Margo's face and screaming at her. Before Sadie could get her away, Margo threw a punch, catching Shel under the right eye. He responded like a wild animal, swiping at her and anyone else in striking range.

Where were the bouncers? Shouldn't someone break this up? She didn't see Garrett in the mix. She hoped he wasn't involved, the poor boy seemed completely baffled by the direction of the discussion earlier, and she'd hate for him to be drawn into this as well.

Sadie heard glass break, and she pulled Margo again only to have someone step hard on her foot, causing her to stumble and lose her grip on Margo's arm. Sadie pushed the person away, which earned her a push back. What a nightmare! The shouts were getting louder. Something hit the back of her head and made the room spin. She had to get out of the pileup. She reached for Margo again, but she was gone. Sadie couldn't even see her now. She had to save herself!

Sadie started elbowing and pushing her way toward what she thought was the outskirts of the madness, getting pushed back almost as often as she made progress. She started yelling too, and she threw a few jabs of her own as adrenaline coursed through her veins. If the group could understand she didn't want to be in the middle of the fight, they would let her go, right? She was beginning to feel the panic rising in her chest when she heard a whistle and authoritative shout. Thank goodness someone was putting an end to it!

The fighting mellowed a little, though there were still several people proceeding unheeded. Sadie continued toward the edge of the crowd—her eyes fixed on an exit sign at the back of the bar—her only goal self-preservation.

A hand grabbed her arm and threw her to the side; she tripped over a chair, but someone else caught her from falling completely.

"Thank you," Sadie said, wondering if this same person hadn't punched her at some point in the last few minutes. Her head throbbed and her lip burned. She reached up to make sure she wasn't bleeding. Her hand came back red, but she quickly realized it was lipstick.

"Nobody leaves," a booming voice said over the din of the crowd.

Sadie looked toward the main doors where a uniformed officer blocked the door, his hand on the gun in his holster. Another officer, built like a Viking, had waded into the middle of the fight, and there was more shouting as he flung people out of the group one at a time. The last two people to be broken up were Shel and Langley, both of them bloody as they stared at each other, chests heaving. Sadie couldn't see Margo or Garrett anywhere.

"What happened here?" the Viking officer asked, looking from one to the other.

Shel turned away, scanning the crowd, and then he pointed at Sadie, who tried to shrink backward into the closest shadow.

He narrowed his eyes and his nostrils flared. "She started it!"

CHAPTER 8

"You're not really arresting me, are you?" Sadie asked the female officer who pushed her across the threshold of the police station an hour after Shel's accusation. Sadie's shaking hands were cuffed in front of her, and her anxiety was still building. She'd listened to her rights, dutifully put her wrists forward for the cuffs, and patiently endured everything based on the belief that the police would let her go once she was away from the bar. It was all part of an act, right? She was a BLM informant, for heaven's sake!

"You started a fight," the female officer said from behind her. "That's disorderly conduct down here in New Mexico."

"I didn't start a fight," Sadie contended, glancing over her shoulder at the officer who was staring straight ahead. "I blocked Sheldon Carlisle's attempt to start one. He's the one who should be arrested, not me."

"He was arrested too," the officer said. "Eyewitnesses confirmed the two of you as the primary aggressors."

"But I was trying to stop him!"

The officer walked up beside Sadie and grabbed her arm as if

Sadie might make a run for it now that they were in the police station. "Then you failed, didn't you?"

"Is that a crime too?"

The officer gave her a look that made Sadie aware of her own cheekiness, and she ducked her chin. The woman was nearly six feet tall and wore her hair pulled up into a severe bun; Sadie didn't want to call her out too much. "So what happens now?"

"Sit," the officer said, pointing to a bench along one side of a long white hallway. "We'll get you booked in a few minutes."

Booked? Really? Sadie sat down, swallowed, and tried not to let her thoughts run away from her, but she'd seen way too much TV to not be absolutely terrified of being taken back to a cell full of thugs and drug dealers. Pete and Agent Shannon had told her not to tell anyone about her informant status, but surely they hadn't meant in a situation like this, right?

Pete!

She'd told him she was going to the bar with Margo to ask a few questions, and he'd been hesitantly supportive. Pete would know exactly what she should say; in fact, he would probably tell the police about her informant status himself and then everything would be okay. She hadn't even thought to text him before they'd put the handcuffs on her.

"Can I make a phone call, please?" she called out to the officer who'd retreated to a desk on the other side of a half wall.

"Not yet."

"Doesn't everyone get a phone call?" Sadie said. It was practically cliché, right?

The woman looked her over and held her eyes. "Not yet," she said again, slower this time as though trying to make sure Sadie understood.

Sadie sat there, trying to think affirming thoughts until another officer told her to stand and follow her down a hallway.

"What's your name?" the officer asked once she had Sadie sitting in a chair next to a desk.

"Uh, my name is . . ." Should she give them her fake name, Sarah Worthlin, like she had told the cops at the dig site, or should she give her real name? Would that mean her real name would be published in the newspaper? If so, she could be tracked to Santa Fe.

"Name," the woman said again, watching Sadie closely. Annoyed.

"Can I please make a phone call first?" Sadie begged. She needed to talk to Pete in the worst way.

The woman swiveled in her seat and put her face within inches of Sadie's. She'd had tuna for dinner. "Give me your name," she said in slow, clipped tones.

Sadie's heart rate took off like a shot. "Sarah Diane Wright Hoffmiller," she said quickly, though she whispered it just in case. Heat washed over her at having told the truth. The truth was supposed to set you free, that's what everyone said, but she felt sure she was making a mistake. Oh, she needed to talk to Pete!

Sadie was almost in tears by the time the officer had finished taking her pictures, fingerprints, and shoes—thank goodness she'd worn those footsy socks and didn't have to walk around barefoot. Or maybe they had booties they'd have offered her, like at a hospital, if she hadn't had her own. They led her to a holding cell that was basically a big concrete room about twenty feet square with bars on the front, a cement bench running the length of the back wall, and a stainless steel toilet in one corner—no privacy whatsoever. Sadie was so glad she hadn't drunk that entire Coke.

Seeing the cell looming before her made it all so real. The police had really booked her. She was really in jail! And they hadn't let her make a phone call. Did Pete still monitor her from Colorado? What if he found out she was in jail before she had a chance to explain? He'd think she was trying to hide things from him again, but she wasn't. She was dying to call him.

"What happens now?" Sadie asked the officer who was walking in front of her. She tried not to let the emotion show in her voice as they approached the cell meant for murderers and Mafia kings.

"We'll finish your paperwork, figure out bail, and set a court date to appear before a judge. Then you can make some phone calls."

"How long will that take?" It was almost midnight. Caro must be worried sick! Sadie felt tears coming to her eyes and pushed them down. She could not cry in jail; she'd be beaten up for sure. But she felt so bad for the stress she was causing Caro. Would Caro call Pete when Sadie didn't come home?

"However long it takes," the officer said without emotion.

The sound of the big metal barred door opening was horrible, and she had to swallow the tears again.

The only thing in her favor was that the cell was empty. What she wouldn't give for a bottle of bleach and a scrub brush.

The officer walked away, and Sadie tried to think positive thoughts. If she were a mystery novelist or a journalist, she might be able to see this as a valuable learning experience! But she wasn't either of those things. She was a retired elementary schoolteacher with really great reflexes—surely that wasn't criminal.

She paced for the first hour, sat on the bench for the second hour, and gave in to tears for the third. She was just recovering when an officer came for her. She was certain she was being freed—pardoned from the terrors of having been actually arrested—but instead they took her down the hall and put her into another cell almost exactly the same as the first one except in this one there was a rough-looking bald woman who appeared to be passed out on one end of the cement bench.

Sadie asked about her phone call again, but was told "Not yet" for the fourth time. She prayed her new roommate would stay asleep and sat down as far away from her as possible.

Sadie watched the bald woman for nearly thirty minutes, trying to prepare herself for how to react when she came out of her stupor. Should she try to make friends? Every time she heard a noise outside the cell, she held her breath and straightened, waiting to get permission to make her phone call or be informed that there had been a mistake—it had to be close to three o'clock in the morning now, right? Cameras were mounted in every corner of the cell, but she was afraid to try to get anyone's attention for fear she'd get in more trouble, or wake up the bald woman. Luckily, her cellmate kept sleeping, and eventually Sadie propped herself up in the corner and let herself relax, just a little. She closed her eyes in hopes of finding some level of calm amid all the anxiety, and prayed she'd be let out soon. She wasn't sure how long she could hold everything together under these circumstances.

"Hey."

Sadie felt herself jolt before blinking her eyes open to see a big round head a couple feet from her own face. Moving away from the bald woman who was violating her personal space was reflexive, but the concrete bench didn't allow much room for retreat, and instead of putting distance between her and the scary woman, Sadie tumbled onto the concrete floor. She quickly scrambled to her feet and pressed her back against the wall, still trying to wake up completely. She didn't want to think about all the horrible things she'd touched when her hands hit the floor. What time was it? How long had she slept?

"What's wrong with you?" the bald woman said.

"Nothing," Sadie said quickly. She realized she was pressing herself flat against the cinderblock wall, fingers splayed and everything. She forced herself to relax somewhat, but smiling was beyond her abilities. "I—I was asleep," she said dumbly, then feigned a yawn and a stretch. "Tough waking up sometimes, ya know?"

The woman stared at her with big, dark eyes surrounded by saggy, pockmarked skin and no eyebrows at all.

"You want breakfast?"

"Breakfast?" Was it morning already? The police had taken her watch along with everything else removable, and without windows in the cell, she had no idea what time it was. Was it possible she'd slept for a few hours?

"It's coming in a few minutes. You want yours?" The bald woman cocked her head to the side in what Sadie took as a challenge.

"Nope!" Sadie said, shaking her head. "I'm not hungry."

The woman smiled, revealing surprisingly good teeth, then stood up and returned to her end of the bench. She didn't say anything else, and Sadie moved back to her corner. She was so tense her jaw hurt.

A few minutes passed before she heard clangs and footsteps from the other side of the bars. Sadie held her breath but didn't move. *Please be coming to let me out*, she pleaded in her mind.

Sadie's cellmate darted to the door before a guard appeared with two Styrofoam trays holding Styrofoam dishes filled with food. The bald woman motioned Sadie to come forward and get one of the trays, which Sadie hurried to do. She returned to the bench and sat with the tray on her lap until the guard left, at which time she put the tray on the bench and pushed it toward her cellmate.

"Thanks," the woman said, pulling the tray closer to her side while she ate her bowl of oatmeal.

"You're welcome," Sadie said, although she was pretty sure if she hadn't shared, she'd have been sorry. She thought of the breakfast burritos Caro made nearly every morning—simple, filling, delicious—and had to close her eyes as her longing to be back at Caro's nearly overcame her. Tears pricked her eyes, and she blinked them back quickly.

She walked up to the bars in hopes of finding a clock somewhere. She couldn't see one, however, just doors with windows in them at either end of the hallway. When she turned around, the bald woman was drinking down the juice from the bowl of peaches and watching Sadie over the rim of her bowl. She wore a man's T-shirt and had some letters tattooed onto the back of her fingers.

As hesitant as Sadie was to talk to this woman, there was no one else to talk to, and she was suffocating from the lack of information. "Do you know what time it is?"

"Breakfast is at 6:30," the woman said after finishing off her peaches and reaching for the fruit on Sadie's tray.

Six thirty? She'd been here for seven hours already? Sadie turned back to the bars and held on to them with both hands even though she knew they were filthy from thousands of other unwashed hands that had held these same bars. "They didn't let me make my phone call."

"Yeah, sometimes it takes a while." This woman spoke from experience. "You makin' bail?"

"I don't know," Sadie said, looking down both sides of the hallway again. "I'm not even sure how bail works."

"Someone puts up money or stuff to make sure you come to your court date."

"How do I even get a court date? Will I go in front of a judge?" Would she have to wear one of those horrible orange jumpsuits?

"Sometimes you go to a judge, but lots of times they go by the schedule."

Sadie looked over her shoulder. "Schedule?"

"Bail schedule—assigned amounts based on what you done."

"Is disorderly conduct on the bail schedule?"

"That what you done?" the woman asked. She'd worked through both breakfasts and now held a Styrofoam cup of coffee in each hand.

"That's what they *said* I did," Sadie clarified, looking back out of the bars before accepting no one was coming. She sat down on her end of the bench again, keeping her hands in her lap in hopes of touching as few surfaces as possible.

"I hear ya," the woman said with a nod.

"And then, if I get bail but don't show up for my court date, Dog the Bounty Hunter comes after me?"

The bald woman snorted and drank from one of the coffee cups. "Court opens at eight, things get moving after that. First arrest?"

"Sort of," Sadie said, thinking about how her interference with a police investigation a couple of years ago had resulted in a few hundred hours of community service and an official arrest record. "I turned myself in last time, and I knew most of the officers." Specifically, she knew Pete, who had been with her throughout the entire process, which had been calm and fluid and necessary. Did Pete know she was here yet? Did anyone know? She realized she should have asked the guard who brought the breakfast tray about her phone call. Caro would be worried sick.

"What you do to get disorderly conduct?" the woman asked after she'd finished off her own coffee and started on Sadie's.

"There was a bar fight, and someone said I started it."

"You came out pretty good," the woman said. "Both your eyes isn't black."

Sadie rubbed her left elbow. Her back ached, though she couldn't be sure it wasn't from sleeping against the wall. "Yeah, I guess I was lucky in that way. But it wasn't my fault—we were just asking some questions and then everything went really wrong."

"Maybe you asked the wrong questions."

"Yeah," Sadie said dryly, "of the right person it seems." Why else would Shel have reacted the way he had unless he had something to hide? He knew someone—someone who told him to dig and who helped him get rehired to the smaller crew assigned to finish up the dig. Sadie shook her head. She didn't want to think about that anymore. She should never have gone to the bar. And why had Margo been so aggressive? Where was she now?

"What bar didja fight at?" the woman asked.

"The Conquistador."

"On Valero?"

Sadie looked at her. "You know it?"

"Sure," the woman said. "Not the kind of place a lady like you goes to though. What'd you go there for?"

"I needed to ask some people some questions," Sadie said again, letting out a heavy breath while reviewing how few answers she'd received.

"What kind of questions?"

Sadie cast a sideways glance at the woman and realized she should be more evasive. She didn't know anything about this person other than the fact that she was in jail. And that didn't necessarily say glowing things about her character . . . though Sadie was there too, and she was innocent so perhaps she shouldn't be so judgmental.

"What are you in here for?" Sadie asked by way of changing the subject.

"The cops always bring me in when Mack and I start fightin'," she said, shrugging. "Just 'cause I'm bigger."

"Oh," Sadie said.

"Mack'll bail me out after work. What kind of questions were you asking at that bar?"

"Oh, nothing important." She managed a smile, wondering if it was standard etiquette to share stories between convicts. "I'm Sadie." She considered putting out her hand to shake over their budding friendship, but that seemed a little out of place. Only after giving her name did she consider whether she should have said Sarah. Too late now.

"Lily," the woman said before polishing off the other coffee and then turning to eye the toilet in the corner.

Sadie's breath caught in her throat; Lily had just drank two cups of coffee. Oh dear.

A door opened at one end of the hallway, and Sadie leaped to her feet, barely restraining herself from running to the bars again. Though she no longer felt in fear of her life from Lily, she was still eager to get out. She was holding her breath when she heard the door close and then footsteps come closer. If they let her out, even just long enough to make a phone call, Lily could have her privacy.

When none other than Pete Cunningham came into view, Sadie's mouth dropped open. After a moment of pure shock, Sadie ran across the cement floor, reached through the bars, and grabbed both his hands.

"Pete!" She let go of his hands and reached for his face, but the crossbar blocked her arms so she grabbed the sleeves of his jacket instead. There could be no more beautiful sight than this—Pete Cunningham!

"I can't believe you're here," she said through her tears, letting go of him with one hand so she could wipe her eyes. She pulled her hand away to see a thick black smudge of mascara; she'd forgotten how much makeup she'd worn last night. "Did you drive all night? How did you know? They wouldn't let me call you. Have you talked to Caro? I'm not really under arrest, am I? No one's even questioned me since I got to the station. Did I mention they wouldn't let me call? Is that even allowed?" She realized she was rambling and stopped, just staring into his face instead, taking in every detail and trying to read his expression through that bland detective-mask he wore. Was he angry? Worried?

"You okay?" he asked in a careful tone, looking past her.

"I'm fine," Sadie assured him. She waved over her shoulder. "This is Lily. She's been very nice."

Pete nodded in Lily's direction, not breaking the mask. "Then maybe I should leave you in here—it might be safer that way."

He started to smile at his joke, but the mere idea brought on a fresh round of tears and soon Sadie was unable to see his face through the black mascara curtain.

"I'm kidding," he said quickly, gently.

"Please get me out of here," she said through her tears. "Please, oh please, get me out."

Breakfast Burritos

½ pound chorizo sausage (other types of sausage can be used, or
   omitted altogether)
8 eggs, beaten
1 (4-ounce) can diced green chilies, drained
2 tablespoons mayonnaise
8 flour tortillas

Brown sausage in large skillet over medium-high heat, drain.
Remove from pan, drain oil, and set aside. In the same pan, add
beaten eggs and cook until scrambled, but not yet dry. Add chilies and
sausage and finish cooking. Remove from heat. Add mayonnaise and
mix. Place a large spoonful of sausage-and-egg mixture in the center
of a warmed tortilla and fold into a burrito.

Serves 8.

Note: Shawn prefers regular country sausage; Breanna prefers
no sausage at all.

CHAPTER 9

S adie practically flew through the holding cell door as soon as it opened and would have buried her face in Pete's shirt if not for the fear of ruining it with her smeared makeup. He let her hug him for only a few moments before pulling away. He straightened the lapels of his jacket and leaned forward to whisper in her ear, "I can be your boyfriend in an hour, right now I need to be a police officer."

Sadie nodded, and fell in love with him all over again. He put his hand at the small of her back and guided her out of the cell area into the office portion of the police station. Sadie kept her hands clenched into fists at her side to keep from holding his hand.

The police returned her shoes, and Pete got permission from an officer to let Sadie use a private restroom. She nearly cried all over again when she saw her reflection. It was a testament to Pete that he'd still let her out of that cell after seeing her in such a state.

A few minutes and several paper towels later, she felt present-able enough to join Pete and the officer in the hallway. Pete led her through a few doors as though he knew the place, which she found odd until she remembered that Santa Fe had been his hometown once. He'd even been an officer here years ago when he first began his career. Was that why he'd been able to get her out personally? Had he asked favors of his old friends?

Another officer escorted both of them to an interrogation room where Sadie wrote out her statement of what had happened at the bar. There was no drama, no questioning, and Pete sat next to her the whole time. After giving her official statement, she and Pete followed the officer down a long, narrow waiting room with an exit sign above the door on the far end. Sadie could barely take her eyes off that sign. Was freedom really so close?

A glass wall separated them from an officer sitting behind a desk. A slit in the glass allowed papers to be passed back and forth. Pete gave the officer Sadie's name—her *real* name—and the officer shuffled through some papers before passing some through the slot.

Sadie scanned the top paper and then looked up at Pete. "You posted bail?"

He nodded like it was no big deal, but Sadie was mortified. "I was really arrested then?"

"Yes, Sadie. You were really arrested. Didn't they tell you that?"

"Well, I thought maybe they would realize it was a mistake and change their mind." She'd even hoped for an apology.

"That's for the judge to decide." He pointed at a specific line on the paper. "Your court date is set for the thirteenth. That's when you get to explain your side."

"Is it like *Law and Order* where I'm one of the hundreds of people cycled through?" She thought about those orange jumpsuits again. They wouldn't make her wear one if she wasn't in jail, would they?

"Not quite," Pete said with an amused smile. He pointed at the line where she was supposed to sign her name. After she signed her name, he turned the page and pointed to another line while explaining what it was she was signing: basically that she agreed to come back for her court appearance and if she didn't, Pete would lose an awful lot of money.

Sadie didn't ask many questions; she'd have signed just about anything to get out of there. She finished and slid the papers back through the slot in the glass.

"I'll pay you back," she said to Pete.

"Don't worry about that. You can have a seat." Pete waved toward the bench lining the wall across from the glass-enclosed officer. "I'll be right back."

The officer who'd escorted them to the waiting area opened the interior door for Pete, but then stayed near Sadie, who sat down at the far end of the bench, as close to the exit as possible.

Now that the ordeal was almost over, she was surprised she hadn't had a full-blown panic attack. Six months ago she'd have been rocking back and forth in a corner, and although it was nice to reflect on the progress she'd made, a breakdown still felt entirely possible. Maybe it would happen when she came back to court and tried to explain her innocence. What if they didn't believe her? What if she went back to jail?

She took a deep breath and focused on being so close to freedom. Positive thinking—that was key. That Pete was here was an additional balm to her soul. Everything was better with Pete.

She heard a door open and looked up, expecting to see Pete, but startled slightly to see Shel following an officer into the waiting area instead. She swallowed and shrank back against the wall, but not before Shel saw her. He narrowed his discolored eyes at her, at least as much as he could considering the substantial swelling. Surely there was some kind of rule about arrestees being together, right?

She listened to the officer tell Shel the same kind of things Pete had explained to her a few minutes earlier. Sadie frowned. Who was bailing Shel out?

A buzzer sounded from the other side of the narrow room. The officer guarding the door crossed the room and opened the outside door that was just a few feet away from Sadie. She held herself back from running through that door.

"Mornin', Benny," the officer said as a man came inside.

"*Buenos días*, Paul. How are you?"

The man was dressed like any other cowboy—jeans, cowboy boots, a gray felt cowboy hat, and denim shirt—but he had an accent she hadn't expected. She took a second look at his face, noting dark eyes, dark skin, and a thick black mustache that not only covered his top lip, but hung nearly to his chin on either side of his mouth.

"I hope you get paid overtime for comin' so early," Officer Paul said.

Benny grunted and slid his hands into the front pockets of his Wranglers, rocking back on the heels of his well-used cowboy boots. Sadie wondered if he was a bail bondsman, but he didn't cross the room to sign anything. Instead he looked toward Shel and lifted his eyebrows. "Are you ready? I need to load fifty head of cattle before eight."

Sadie looked at Shel who nodded, finished signing a paper, and crossed in front of Sadie without looking at her. The officer who'd escorted him returned to the inner part of the station, and brought back a plastic bag, which Sadie assumed held Shel's personal effects.

Sadie kept her focus on the man bailing him out, or picking him up, or both. She didn't think a bail bondsman would be transporting cattle, but picking up Shel did seem to be part of Benny's job. Did he bail people out for work all the time? Was that why he knew Paul so well? There was a logo embroidered on the left pocket of his faded denim shirt. Sadie couldn't read it from where she was, but she kept her focus intently trained on the emblem.

"Let's go, then," the cattleman—Benny—said, stepping out of Shel's way to let him go through the door first. In the process, he moved close enough to Sadie for her to see that the logo consisted of a circle with some kind of design inside and words around the outside. Gold River Ranch? Cold River Ranch?

The man turned away from her before she could confirm what it actually said. Shel disappeared outside, having ignored Sadie completely.

Benny said good-bye to the officers, tipped his hat slightly in Sadie's direction, and left, treating the whole thing as though it were perfectly normal to bail people out of jail first thing on a Tuesday morning.

"You ready to go?"

Sadie hadn't heard Pete return, but jumped to her feet, nodding quickly. "I'm so ready."

CHAPTER 10

Pete finished checking her out of the police station and listened to her version of events on the way back to Rex and Caro's house. When she finished, he updated her about what had happened on his end. When she'd first come to Santa Fe, Pete had informed some of his former fellow officers about Sadie's situation. Sadie had suspected as much since he always seemed to drop a bug in someone's ear when she came to a new town.

When she'd been arrested last night, one of those old friends had called Pete, and everyone in the department had given Sadie her space while they waited for him to arrive. Sadie would have appreciated knowing all of that last night; she was still annoyed not to have gotten her phone call.

"It was a unique situation," Pete pointed out.

It was hard for Sadie to argue with that. She was a pro at creating "unique situations."

"How did you get out of your Tuesday classes?" Sadie asked, thinking about the training he was supposed to be heading up right now in Denver.

"Don't worry about it."

Sadie's heart sank. "It's so bad that you don't want to tell me?"

"It's okay. It worked out."

"Pete," she said, her voice soft and repentant. "I'm so sorry. I made a real mess, didn't I? Are you in trouble?"

Pete glanced at her, then looked back out the windshield. "I couldn't *not* leave, Sadie."

"But what about your classes?" she asked again.

"I told them I had a family emergency. I don't know what they did to cover for me."

"I'm so sorry," Sadie said again. She was touched that she'd been included in his idea of "family," and yet she couldn't help but wonder what would happen when they found out the real reason he'd left. And they would find out. They were cops, and Sadie had made things hard for Pete and, in the process, the entire Garrison Police Department, more than once. For all her talk about blame and fault for last night's bar fight, she knew who carried the burden of any fallout Pete might experience in the wake of all of this.

"I thought I was going to the bar to get some very basic information—which I *fully* planned to share with you and the police. I had no idea this would happen," she said.

Pete reached over and gave her hand a squeeze. "I know you didn't do this on purpose. But when you put yourself into these things, you can't always control the outcome."

Sadie felt tears come to her eyes at the reprimand, gentle as it might be. "I don't know what's wrong with me. Why can't I just leave things alone?"

He gave her hand another squeeze. "Because you are who you are," he said, giving her a soft smile so she'd know he wasn't angry. Maybe he *should* be angry. "I gotta say it's kind of nice to see your moxie back." He winked at her before returning his attention to the road. The sentiment warmed her more than she could say.

"But I *am* worried about this," Pete continued. "Your name's now on public record where anyone can find it. Other than an official witness protection program, I'm running out of ways to keep you safe."

Sadie let those words ring in her head. Since Boston, Pete had utilized every option he could think of to protect her from the threat that loomed over her. The threat had sent her to Hawai'i for several months and into an emotional firestorm unlike anything she'd ever been through before. The fallout from *that* situation had sent her home for a week, then into hiding in Europe for six weeks, and then finally to Santa Fe. Now where would she go? Where *could* she go? Beyond those questions, *should* she go anywhere? Pete was still nervous about her being found, but did she want to keep living this way?

"I hate knowing that I put you in this situation this time. I'm the one who got you this job and then—"

"This is not your fault," Sadie said. "There's no way you could have known what was in that dig."

"But I arranged it and—"

"Are you seriously saying this to me?" Sadie cut in. She turned to face him and stared at his profile as he watched the road. "After all these years of telling me this type of thing isn't my fault, *you're* going to take the blame? Does that mean these other things *are* my fault? That I *have* been responsible every other time?"

"That's not what I said," Pete said quietly. He paused as though gathering his thoughts. "I'm just . . . you were . . . It was supposed to be safe here."

"Maybe we need to stop trying so hard to keep me safe," Sadie said, facing forward again. She felt Pete's hand tense in hers. "It's been almost a year now and nothing's happened. Maybe we're over-reacting and—"

"Your life was threatened," Pete said. "And I don't think what happened in Boston has been forgotten by anyone involved."

"Then maybe it's time to call it out," Sadie said, though the idea gave her butterflies. "I miss my home, Pete. I miss my life. And the future I want with you has been put on hold in the name of protecting me. Can't I return to Garrison and get an alarm system? Is hiding really the best option?"

Pete shifted in his seat, his mouth pulled into a thoughtful frown. After a few seconds, he shook his head. "I don't know," he said, his words showing how tired he was, emotionally and physically. "If something were to happen to you, Sadie . . ."

"But I'm in trouble of one kind or another everywhere I go any-way," Sadie reminded him. "I can't seem to avoid it, and I'm making things so hard for so many people. I don't know how much longer I can do this—how much longer *we* can do this, really."

Pete clenched his jaw but said nothing.

"Will you at least think about it?" They both needed time to absorb the option. "I don't have to go back now. But, like you said, my name is now public record in Santa Fe, which makes me no safer here than I would be back home."

"You can't leave until your court date," Pete said. "Unless we were convinced you weren't safe here . . ." He shook his head. "I'll think about Garrison after your court date is over."

He let go of Sadie's hand in order to make the turn onto Rex and Caro's street, but as soon as the car stopped, she took off her seat belt and leaned across the middle console of his car to give him a kiss. She wasn't convinced she was right, but she would rather face the threat than waste more time with this partiality of existence that, while not horrible, certainly wasn't ideal. The last year had been full of difficulty and learning experiences. Sadie felt stronger now, more sure of herself, and ready to take whatever might come next. Or at least she thought she was ready.

She looked into his beautiful hazel eyes and reflected on how lucky she was to have a man like him in her life. "Thank you for coming," she said. "I love you, Pete Cunningham."

He smiled while shaking his head slightly. He placed his hand against her cheek. "So help me, Sarah Diane, I love you too."

CHAPTER 11

Caro gave Sadie a big hug when she walked through the front door before peppering her with questions Sadie tried her best to answer. After a couple of minutes, Caro seemed to realize that Sadie was exhausted. Pete had driven all night and was dead on his feet too, so Caro encouraged them both to get some rest. Pete took the extra bedroom, and Sadie went to her apartment, took a hot shower, and then crawled into bed, pulling the super soft blanket to her chin, almost crying with relief of being here—safe and secure— with Pete only a few rooms away. She made sure to offer a prayer of gratitude before she drifted off to sleep.

It was almost three o'clock in the afternoon when Sadie woke up, horrified to have slept so much longer than she'd planned. Even so, she made sure to make herself presentable before she dared leave her apartment. She chose a mid-calf-length sundress she'd bought in Old Town and some red flip-flops to match. She wore her hair in a smooth bob, rather than her usual slightly messy "do," and managed to hide the bruise on the side of her neck with some foundation. The knot she had on her head wasn't visible, but she winced when she smoothed her hair one last time. Bright colors, subdued makeup, and conservative hair seemed a good start toward helping Pete forget everything about her appearance at the jail that morning.

Pete was at the kitchen table eating potato chips from the bag and reading something on his cell phone, but he stood up when he saw her, crossing the room to give her a hug before pulling back and looking her over. "Did you sleep well?"

"Better and longer than I'd expected to," Sadie said with a gracious smile. As bad as she felt about the circumstances that had brought him here, it was so nice to be with him. "How about you?"

"I got up about an hour ago." His cell phone vibrated on the table, and he looked at it with an expression of surrender and uncertainty. As he replied to the text message, Sadie noted how quiet the house was.

"Is Caro here?" Sadie asked as she headed toward the fridge to make Pete and herself some lunch. Potato chips were not a sufficient meal, and she was pretty sure Caro had everything for her delicious Cinco de Mayo chicken salad; she usually kept the chicken part mixed up and in the fridge so that the other ingredients could be easily thrown together.

"She had to go to work," Pete said, still texting. "She tried to call in, but no one could cover for her. She said to tell you she'd be home around six thirty and not to worry about dinner, she'd pick something up."

"That's right, it's Tuesday." Caro only worked three days a week—eleven to six on Tuesdays, Thursdays, and Fridays—so Sadie made dinner on those three nights. While Sadie thought it was sweet for Caro to offer to pick something up for dinner, after Sadie's time in lockup, she looked forward to embracing the freedom of making a meal. Sadie would simply text Caro to let her know—

She reached for her cell phone before remembering it was in

the bag of personal effects the police had returned to her at the jail. Sadie was in no mood to go look for it right now; she had a man to feed!

"Could you text Caro for me and tell her thanks for the offer, but that I can do dinner?"

Pete looked up at her. "Are you sure?"

She gave him a don't-you-know-who-I-am? look, and he chuckled before tapping away on his phone. She glanced at the clock and was gratified to know she had plenty of time to eat with Pete and still put together dinner in time for Rex and Caro to enjoy after they got home from work.

Since coming to Santa Fe, Sadie had learned how to make several wonderful recipes from Caro; it was fun to add new favorites to her Little Black Recipe Book, a journal she'd filled up with the very best recipes she'd found over the last thirty years. She'd choose one of those recipes to make tonight as a way to thank both Caro and Rex for their patience with her.

"How are things in Denver?" Sadie asked while putting the salad fixings on the counter. She broke up lettuce into a bowl she'd retrieved from a cupboard.

Pete blew out a breath and leaned back in his chair. "Rough. I have to be back in Denver tomorrow morning. I had hoped I could stay, I really don't want to go, but . . ."

"That's okay," Sadie said, feeling horribly guilty again. "I'm sorry you had to leave in the first place. I'll be fine."

"I'll come back Sunday for the Balloon Fiesta," Pete said. "Maybe by then we'll both have an idea of what to do from here on out. Will you be extra careful in the meantime, though? If anything seems out of place, let me know or go directly to the police station. I don't want to take any chances, but I don't see any options other than keeping you here for now. I've got a guy in Garrison monitoring things very closely—if for any reason we think you're in danger, he'll let you know."

"Thank you," she said, hating how much work she was for people. "I'll be extremely careful for as long as I'm here."

Pete returned a text message while Sadie added the chicken salad mixture to the lettuce and tossed it together. Once the lettuce was coated, she divided it between two plates and topped it with some of the crumbled bacon Caro stored in a Tupperware in the fridge. She wished she had time to fry the bacon a little bit, so that it was warm and crispy, but Pete would need to leave soon if he hoped to get back to Denver before midnight.

"Thank you," Pete said when she slid the plate in front of him a few minutes later. "Is this Caro's famous Mexican chicken salad?"

"The very same," Sadie said. "But I added bacon to it. Everything's better with bacon."

"Of course," he said, giving her a smile before savoring that first bite. Sadie loved watching people take the first bite of things she prepared. It was one of her most favorite experiences in the whole world.

After a few bites of his meal, his phone rang. He read the caller ID and excused himself for privacy, and Sadie was rinsing her dishes by the time he finished his call and returned to the kitchen. Pete came up behind her and snaked his arms around Sadie's waist and rested his chin on her shoulder. Sadie closed her eyes and drank in the smell and feel of him, wondering when their lives would return to normal. Then again, what was normal for them? She'd met Pete during her first murder investigation—had their lives ever really been normal?

"Ah," she said, turning to face him and wrapping her arms around his neck. "This must be my boyfriend you were telling me about."

He kissed her ear and hugged her tighter.

"I've got to go," he finally said quietly, sadly.

Sadie looked into his eyes, knowing she'd keep this image of his face in her mind until they saw each other next. "My returning to Garrison might put an end to this hiding once and for all," she said, further supporting her campaign. "We can move on with our lives together."

"Don't tempt me," Pete replied, smiling softly at her. "I don't want to make a decision in my own best interest if it means putting you at risk."

"I'm at risk everywhere I go, remember? You've said yourself that I can't seem to keep myself out of trouble, and every time I end up in the middle of one of these situations, I'm at risk all over again."

"I know," Pete said. "I just keep hoping that whatever draws you to these things—"

"Or draws these things to me," Sadie cut in. "I have not gone seeking them for a very long time."

"Either way, I keep expecting that this disaster-streak is done. That last time was really the *last* time."

"And yet, even if that were true, I'm still hiding." She tightened her arms around him.

"I know," he said, bending down to kiss her softly on the mouth. "But are you sure you're ready? Living in Garrison felt overwhelming to you not too long ago."

"I've made some good progress since then. I haven't had a panic attack for months, and I feel like I'm ready to go back to my old life. I'm ready to go home and see what happens. I'm ready to see where this thing between you and me might go."

He let out a deep breath but was unable to hide a smile. "I'll think about it."

She smiled and went up on her toes to kiss him again and seal the deal. "Good," she said, pulling back slightly. "Now, you need to finish your salad. Can I also make you a sandwich for the road?"

Ten minutes later, Sadie walked Pete to his car and handed over two sandwiches, a bag of cookies from the freezer, and some string cheese in a paper bag. They lingered over the good-bye kiss, wanting the moment to last as long as possible.

Pete finally opened the car door, but before he got inside, he reached down and picked something up from the floor on the passenger side. He handed it toward Sadie. "You don't want me taking this to Denver, do you?"

She immediately recognized the bag of her personal effects from the police station. "Thanks," she said, taking the bag and imagining what a mess it would have been if he hadn't found it until he got back to Denver.

He kissed her one more time—longer and harder than he usually allowed himself to—then, without saying anything else, he let her go and got into his car.

She recovered from that final kiss enough to tuck the bag under her arm and wave until his car disappeared, trying to swallow the lump in her throat. A year ago they had gone to Boston. It was supposed to have been a very different turning point for their relationship than it ended up being.

But she wasn't giving up on them. Not now. Not ever.

Caro's Cinco de Mayo Chicken Salad

2 large boneless, skinless chicken breasts
½ cup picante sauce
½ teaspoon ground cumin
¼ teaspoon salt
¼ cup sour cream
2 tablespoons mayonnaise
1 ripe avocado, chopped
1 cup diced celery
Bibb or leaf lettuce
4 crisply cooked bacon slices, crumbled

Cut chicken breasts into ½-inch cubes. Set aside. In a 10-inch skillet, combine picante sauce, cumin, and salt. Add chicken and cook about 4 minutes, stirring frequently until done. Transfer contents of skillet to large mixing bowl; cover and chill.

To serve, combine chicken mixture, sour cream, and mayonnaise; mix well. Add avocado and celery; mix lightly. Spoon chicken salad onto lettuce-lined salad plates or mix together with torn lettuce in large mixing bowl. Sprinkle with bacon.

Serves 4.

Notes: In a pinch, you can use 8 ounces of canned chicken, skip the cooking, and mix up the salad immediately. Also, a handful of chopped green peppers add great flavor and texture. This salad is also great with tortilla chips or wrapped in a flour tortilla. Mmm!

CHAPTER 12

Sadie plugged her now-dead cell phone into the charger in her apartment and then headed back to the kitchen to start dinner. Within twenty minutes, she had everything she needed combined in a pan on the stove. She knew posole was one of Rex's favorite meals; it was even his mother's recipe and, although written as a slow-cooker recipe, it was easy to convert to a stove-top version. The flavors might not blend quite as well, but it wouldn't be too different, so long as she used canned chicken, which she did. She was pouring corn bread batter into a baking dish when she heard the door from the garage open.

"Hi, Rex," she said in an upbeat tone she hoped covered the discomfort that still lingered after what happened last night. She wanted to wait to explain until she could talk to him and Caro at the same time. As always, things felt a little strange with just Rex and Sadie together. "Dinner will be ready by the time Caro comes home." She glanced at the clock, it wasn't quite six. There was just enough time for her to bake the corn bread, finish the dishes, and set the table before Caro got there.

Rex busied himself with emptying out his lunch cooler. When

he finished, Sadie expected him to head to the living room and turn on the TV, but he didn't. When she looked up, he was watching her. Rex was tall and broad shouldered, with a square face and coarse dark hair cut into a crew cut left over from his years in the Army. Sadie tried not to be intimidated by him, but his usual posture was imposing, and right now it was even more so.

"Is everything okay?" Sadie asked.

"You made things difficult around here last night."

"I know," Sadie said, wishing she'd apologized before he brought it up. "And I'm really sorry about everything that happened. The police wouldn't let me call anyone or I'd have called you guys first thing." Well, first thing after she talked to Pete.

He continued as soon as she stopped speaking, giving the impression that he had not listened to any of her explanation. "Caro was about out of her head with worry until Pete called us, which wasn't until after midnight. You didn't even tell her where you were going."

Sadie shifted her weight from one foot to the other, unsure of how to respond to his hostility other than with humility and truth. "I told her I was going to a bar with Margo," she said calmly. "I had no idea that—"

Rex smacked the counter, and Sadie jumped back a step.

"She didn't know where you were or where to look," he nearly yelled, his face darkening as he released the rage she suspected he'd been holding back since entering the house. "But she was about ready to check every bar in town lookin' for you. It caused a real ugly argument between the two of us."

"I'm very sorry," Sadie said again, careful this time. Rex had never been as warm as his wife, but Sadie had also never seen him angry. She felt he was overreacting, but didn't want to be dismissive of her fault in this situation. "You have both been nothing but accommodating of me, and the last thing I wanted to do was cause this kind of . . . concern." Was that the right word? Was he *concerned?* It felt different than that, bigger. Judging from the pinch around his eyes and the hard line of his jaw, her apology wasn't making much headway. "It won't happen again, Rex. I promise."

He stared at her for a couple of seconds, but his expression did not soften. "It might be a good time for you to come up with somewhere else to stay."

Sadie's heart started pounding. "You want me to leave?" she asked quietly. Really? Just like that?

"I think it's for the best," he said, sounding a little calmer now that he'd given her the ultimatum. "I've been a good sport about you stayin' all this time, but I've hit my limit. It isn't good for my wife to be so involved in this kinda thing. It's causin' trouble between us."

Dueling perspectives wrestled in Sadie's mind. Up until last night, she'd worked hard to be a very good guest. She cooked dinner as often as she could, paid rent for the apartment, and did her share, if not more, of the housework; all in the name of pulling her own weight and easing the burden. It didn't seem fair that he would discount all of that. But then again she didn't know how bad the argument had been between them last night or how worried Caro had been. In the end, dueling perspectives aside, she wasn't going to stay where she wasn't wanted.

"I'm certainly not about to overstay my welcome," Sadie said tightly. She was tempted to try to explain again what had happened and insist he not treat her like a child. Yet, no matter how hard she tried to justify going on the defensive, she couldn't skirt around the fact that she'd caused a great deal of trouble for two good people who had only ever wanted to help her.

"I'm glad to hear we're on the same page, then," he said. "It'd be better for Caro and me if she thought it was your idea to go sooner rather than later."

Sadie pinched her lips together and inhaled through her nose. She was not okay with lying to Caro, but did she want to cause more trouble between the people who'd opened their home to her? She was suddenly itching to call Pete and get his opinion. However, Rex was waiting for her to agree; what should she say?

"I can get a hotel," Sadie said, neatly sidestepping the issue without committing one way or another. She turned away from him to stir the posole. She lowered the heat, already packing in her mind.

"Caro wouldn't understand if you left too soon. You can stay through the weekend, but I 'spect you to have something set up before Monday. 'Til then, we all go on like you and I didn't have this talk."

Sadie took another breath in order to keep from saying how uncomfortable she was with him wanting Caro to believe a lie, but she nodded and returned to the corn bread without another word.

Once Rex left the room, Sadie used the kitchen phone to call Pete, since her phone was charging in the other room, but ended up leaving a message. Then she had nothing to do but try to sort out her thoughts. She did not agree with how Rex was going about things, but even if he was being a jerk about this, he'd let her come into his home and she'd made things hard for him. She hated feeling responsible for that, yet it also reaffirmed her resolve to return to Garrison. She was running out of places to go faster than she thought.

Crock-Pot Posole

2 (14.5-ounce) cans golden hominy, drained
1 (4-ounce) can chopped green chili peppers, not drained
1 medium onion, chopped (about ½ cup)
2 cloves garlic, minced
1 pound boneless, skinless chicken breasts and/or thighs, cut into
    1-inch pieces
1 (14.5 ounce) can tomatoes, cut up and not drained
2 (14.5 ounce) cans reduced-sodium chicken broth
1 teaspoon dried oregano, crushed
½ teaspoon ground cumin
1 teaspoon chili powder
¼ teaspoon cayenne pepper (optional)
½ teaspoon salt (or more to taste)
2 tablespoons snipped fresh cilantro
Sour cream (optional)

Place hominy, green chili peppers, onion, garlic, chicken, tomatoes, chicken broth, and spices in a 3½-, 4-, or 5-quart crockery cooker. Cover and cook on low setting for 5 to 6 hours, or on high setting for 2½ to 3 hours. Stir in cilantro. Garnish each serving with a dollop of sour cream, if desired.

Makes 8 to 10 servings.

Note: You can use canned corn in place of hominy. Canned chicken works great, too!

CHAPTER 13

Rex kept to himself until the front door opened and Caro called out "Hello."

Sadie took a breath. She'd hoped Pete would return her call before Caro got home, but he hadn't. She'd have to handle this on her own.

"Hi," Sadie called from the kitchen, glad that her voice didn't sound as tight as her stomach felt. She'd considered eating her dinner in her room so as to steer clear of Rex, but knew that it would worry Caro. Sadie heard Rex enter the kitchen to greet his wife, and she turned around in time to see Caro walk right past her husband and come directly to Sadie. Her eyes were wide as she looked Sadie over and put her hands on Sadie's upper arms.

"How are you? Okay? Did you sleep? Oh my gosh, what happened to your neck?"

Sadie caught Rex's expression over Caro's shoulder as he watched them for a few seconds before turning back toward the living room. Sadie felt a wave of sympathy for his position. He was trying to protect his wife, and Sadie had become a threat.

"I'm okay," Sadie said, deciding to downplay everything. She didn't want to trigger too much more of Caro's curiosity. It was a shame because Caro would be the perfect person to appreciate Sadie's Coke-bottle-to-the-nose maneuver and her encounter with bald Lily. But Sadie needed to pull away, which made her sad. "We just went to the bar to talk to a guy and things got out of hand. My arrest was a mix-up. I'll have a court date where I'll get to explain the mistake." She wished she was as calm about it as she'd made it sound.

"But you went to jail," Caro said in an almost reverent tone, her eyes still wide and brimming with curiosity. "What was it like? Was it awful?"

"It *smelled* awful," Sadie said, smiling in an attempt to lighten the mood. "But it didn't turn out too bad. There was only one other woman in the cell with me, and she was nice enough. I was sure excited to see Pete, though. I'm sorry I had you so worried. They wouldn't let me make any calls."

"Oh, I wasn't that worried," Caro said, letting go of Sadie's arms. "I just wish I could have gone with you last night." She smiled big and wide, reminding Sadie of her own naïve beginnings in the world of investigation. Everything was so simple and obvious then—follow the threads to see where they'd take you. Now, she knew too much about where those threads could lead. She was still curious—all her questions still swirled in her mind—but these days she went in with a bit more caution and realistic expectations than what she saw in Caro's eyes right now.

"Well, dinner's ready," Sadie said, turning to get some bowls out of the cupboard. "If you want to get Rex."

Dinner was awkward, but Caro didn't seem to notice the tension between Sadie and Rex. She kept asking Sadie about what had happened the night before, but after enough of Sadie's flat answers which were meant not to encourage her, Caro went on to talk about the three-year-old twin girls who'd come into the dental office for their first appointment. They'd reminded her of her daughters, so she'd helped keep them distracted while the dentist "counted their teeth" and "painted" them with fluoride.

After dinner was over, Rex returned to the living room where he turned on a basketball game, and Sadie and Caro cleaned up the meal. Sadie tried to steer the topics of conversation away from her arrest, but she didn't know how to skirt the topic entirely without being downright rude, which she was loathe to do to her friend.

Caro suggested kicking Rex off the TV so they could watch a Netflix movie. "He can watch it in the bedroom," she said. No way was Sadie going to do that. She used the excuse of a headache—not entirely a lie—to escape to her apartment.

Once there, she lit a fire in the fireplace grotto in the corner of the room, then spied her laptop computer set up on the desk. Having her best investigative tool right there waiting for her had her thinking over some of her remaining questions. First and foremost, what was Shel's tie to this Gold River Ranch or Cold River Ranch? From the background check she'd done on him, Shel was new to the area and had been working for D&E, not a ranch. Information that didn't fit was unsettling, and yet the answer could be simple to uncover. She started with a basic Google search, which confirmed that *Cold* River Ranch was an organic cattle ranch located just outside of Santa Fe.

The ranch's website had a complete history of the Standage family, immigrants who'd started the ranch back in 1914. The ranch had survived the Great Depression due to the family's wise financial planning and because the ranch had access to water supplied by an underground spring that ran along the south end of the property.

They were currently one of the only cattle ranches supported almost entirely by green energy, as solar panels and two windmills on the west end now provided all the power necessary.

Impressive, but she couldn't see how it was connected to Shel.

She went back to the initial report she'd worked up on Shel, but could still find nothing on the surface to connect him to the ranch, though he had attended the University of New Mexico several years earlier.

She went back to the Internet and searched for any community commentary about the ranch. She found several instances of donations and support of various nonprofit organizations; it seemed the ranch was very generous. Finally, she found an article about Ethan Standage, heir to the Cold River Ranch but also a champion of current laws maintaining proper preservation of historical emblems.

Sadie felt a red flag go up in her mind. Shel was working on an archeological dig site, and Ethan espoused preservation of artifacts. Was *that* the connection? It was frail at best. A knock at the door interrupted her from learning more about Ethan Standage, and she minimized the browser window quickly.

"Come in," she called as she stood up and turned toward the door.

Caro opened the door. "I made some hot chocolate," she said. "I could add a shot of brandy if you think that would help your head. Would you like some?"

It had been a surprise to Sadie that hot chocolate was so popular in New Mexico, but it was offered everywhere coffee was served, and it was always *so* good. What excuse could she possibly make to pass on Caro's fabulous homemade hot chocolate?

"The hot chocolate would be perfect," Sadie said, giving into the temptation. Besides, saying no would seem so out of character that Caro would know something was wrong. And her stomach may never forgive her if she denied it the opportunity.

On her way out of the room, she took her cell phone off the charger. Hopefully Pete would call her soon; she really needed to talk to him about what had happened with Rex.

Sadie could hear the whistles and squeaks of the basketball game from the living room TV. She sat at the kitchen table, and Caro passed her a mug.

"I just got off the phone with Lois," Caro said after blowing across the top of her own mug.

"Oh yeah?" Lois was a friend of Caro's who owned a bakery a few blocks from Old Town and had a booth at the upcoming Fiesta. Sadie and Caro had gone to the bakery at least once a week since Sadie's arrival, and they had even helped out with a catered order a few weeks ago when Lois was shorthanded. It was fun to work in a commercial bakery, and Lois was a high-energy sweetheart who made Sadie feel right at home.

"She asked if we were still able to help with the booth at the Fiesta this weekend," Caro continued.

"She doesn't mind having a . . . wrongly-imprisoned potential felon working for her?"

"I told her it was all a big mistake, and she said she could use the help."

"I'd love to," Sadie said, relieved to have something to do and thinking, sadly, about how this may help her transition out of living in Caro and Rex's house. The Fiesta could serve as an excuse for her to get a hotel in Albuquerque for the rest of her time in New Mexico. She glanced at her phone and willed Pete to call her. She really needed his perspective on this.

She took a sip of her drink and felt her whole body relax as the warmth enveloped her chest and drifted throughout her arms and legs. Sensational. "Does she need any help in the bakery beforehand? I don't have anything to do with my time."

"She didn't mention that," Caro said, shaking her head. "But I'll ask her and see."

The home phone rang and Caro excused herself to answer it while Sadie sat up straight. She'd called Pete from Caro's home phone, maybe he was calling her back on that number.

"Nikki," Caro gushed, identifying her daughter as the caller. "How are you, sweetie?"

Sadie leaned back in her chair, turned her attention to her own phone, and realized why Pete hadn't called her—she hadn't turned it on. Duh. The screen came to life moments later and immediately informed her that she'd missed several calls and three text messages. The text messages and the first four voice mails were from Caro last night, each message sounding a bit more frantic than the last. Sadie felt horrible knowing she'd caused her friend so much worry, but it supported what Rex had said about how concerned Caro had been, despite her attempts to make it sound like she hadn't been too upset.

The final voice mail was from Margo. Sadie had looked for Margo in the crowd last night as the police cruiser had pulled away from The Conquistador, but she'd been unable to find her.

"Hey. It's me. I need to talk to you. Call me back as soon as you can. This is bigger than you thought, and I'm going to need your help with something. I apologize in advance for . . . well, just call me ASAP."

Sadie could feel her eyebrows pull together as she played the message a second time, listening to every word. What was Margo pre-apologizing for? After listening a third time, she toggled through her phone and confirmed that Margo had left the message around one o'clock in the morning—the same time Sadie was in jail. Where was Margo calling from? What had she figured out? *Bigger than you thought?* Had Sadie even gotten to the point of "thinking" anything in particular?

"Is everything okay?" Caro asked as she returned to the table. Sadie hadn't noticed her end her phone call. Sadie's thumb hovered over the CONNECT button to call Margo back, but Rex's words came back to her: *"It isn't good for my wife to be involved in this kinda thing."*

"Everything's good," Sadie said, putting her phone back on the table and pasting on a smile. "How's Nikki?"

"She's fine," Caro said in that longing, I-miss-my-kids tone Sadie knew from experience.

Sadie gave her a sad, sympathetic smile. "It's quite an adjustment, isn't it?" If not for having her dad to take care of when Shawn had left for school, she wasn't sure how she would have handled her own empty nest. Of course, Dad passed away not long afterward, but that adjustment had been different.

"In so many ways that I never considered," Caro said, then glanced over her shoulder and leaned forward. "The hardest part has been Rex."

"Does he miss them that much?" Sadie asked, genuinely surprised. Most men adjusted much easier than women did when the kids left home. Rex, specifically, didn't seem like the type of man who would waste much energy pining for his daughters.

"No," Caro said, then softened her quick reply. "I mean, he does miss them, but since they left, he wants all my free time—every minute I used to devote to the girls."

"Oh," Sadie said, shifting uncomfortably in her seat.

"He's talking about taking partial retirement next year. He's fully vested next April, so he could cut back to twenty-four hours a week and take some of his pension and still keep his health insurance." She paused and shook her head. "Honestly, Sadie, I think I might kill him."

Sadie startled. She'd helped unravel too many murders to not react to threats, even idle ones. Caro continued, unheeded.

"I spent all those years raising the girls, and they were great years. I loved them. But a few years ago, I started this mental list of all the things I wanted to do when they were gone. I wanted to cut back at work, volunteer, make handmade quilts, and learn to cook with tofu—which actually turned out to be a poor goal to set, but anyway—I wanted to travel and buy a cute car and do all those things you can't do when the kids come first, you know? Since they left, I've really been able to explore my own interests. It hasn't completely filled the void, but it's certainly helped. And it's been so much fun." She smiled, looking past Sadie thoughtfully. "I go to lunch with my friends, I took a calligraphy class, I get to cook with mushrooms—both my girls hated mushrooms—I'm in the best shape of my life and really enjoy my 'me time.'" Her face fell and her eyes snapped back to Sadie. "But Rex hates it. He doesn't like that I have all these new things I'm interested in that don't include him. Never mind that I took care of everything for all those years so he could take hunting trips, and go to school and work, and not have to worry about home and family. I even cared for his mother for over a decade when she came to live with us. These days, when he's around, he wants all my time, all my attention. As much as I enjoy spending time with him, I have so many other things I want to do that have nothing to do with him. He wants us to do things like redo the tile in the kitchen together or watch TV—so not my idea of a good time." She paused to take a sip of her hot cocoa.

"Maybe you can find some things you both enjoy," Sadie started, but Caro was shaking her head before Sadie finished.

"He doesn't want to do any of the things I want to do. I've even suggested things like scuba diving lessons or getting season tickets to the Lobos games—you know, things I think he'd enjoy—but he gets irritated by them, won't even try. He's turned them all down. He was a linebacker in college, Sadie—sexy and full of energy. What's happened to him?"

"Transitions are difficult," Sadie said, willing her phone to ring and interrupt the increasingly uncomfortable conversation.

Caro smiled, softening the lines in her face. "You coming when you did was such a blessing. It seemed to change the dynamics just enough for things to feel more like they used to be, before it was just Rex and me." Her smile widened even as Sadie found it harder to keep her own smile in place. "It's like you being here made it easier for Rex to give me a little more space. And there's someone else for me to talk to and be with—someone adventurous and fun. It's been so great to have you, and"—she looked away guiltily for a moment before meeting Sadie's eyes again and looking a little embarrassed, but a lot sincere—"I don't miss my girls as much since you came." She took another drink before returning the mug to the table, holding it with both hands. "Anyway, that's the long answer to 'it's been hard,' but it's not so bad anymore."

Call me right now, Pete! "You and Rex have been great," Sadie said, carefully. She hated that she couldn't return Caro's enthusiasm. "I can't thank you enough for letting me stay all this time."

Caro's eyebrows came together as she seemed to properly interpret the tone of Sadie's voice. She sat up a little straighter. "You're not going anywhere, are you?"

Sadie took a breath and said a little prayer for help on how to say this the right way. "Pete thinks I need to move on, what with the arrest and everything. My name's on public record now." Sadie hated lying, and she felt even worse when Caro reached across the table and put her hand on Sadie's arm.

"Please don't go," she said, tears actually coming to her eyes. "Can't the police block your name or something? Can't the judge do that so you can stay?"

Sadie covered Caro's hand with her own. "I don't know what's going to happen, exactly," she said, hoping to let her down easily. "But you have been amazing to me, and I can't thank you enough for everything you've done. I've loved being here."

Sadie's chest ached with regret. *This is not the way things should have gone.*

"I knew it wouldn't last forever," Caro said, removing her hand from Sadie's arm and taking another long sip of her cocoa. She looked away, a kind of forced nonchalance in her tone and posture. She couldn't hold it long, though, and after a moment, her shoulders sagged. She let out a long breath, and when she looked up at Sadie, her eyes were sad. "Are boredom and annoyance grounds for divorce, do you think?"

"Oh stop," Sadie said, trying to laugh off the comment. "You don't want a divorce." She kept her tone soft. "You guys just need to find a way to better adjust to a new life. Maybe you can talk to him, really open up about how you feel."

Caro shrugged and seemed to blow off the idea. She took another sip of her drink, then stood and took her mug to the sink. "Don't go unless and until you have to, okay?"

"I'll do my best," Sadie said, wondering how she would talk to Pete about this without betraying Caro's confidence. "Until then, let Lois know I'm happy to help at the bakery any way that I can."

Mexican Hot Chocolate

2 (12-ounce) cans evaporated milk (or regular milk if you like; it
  won't be as rich)
1½ teaspoons ground cinnamon
1 teaspoon vanilla extract
¼ teaspoon ground nutmeg
Pinch of cayenne pepper
1 cup semisweet chocolate chips

In a medium saucepan, whisk together milk, cinnamon, vanilla
extract, nutmeg, and cayenne pepper on medium heat. When mixture
is hot, but not boiling, add chocolate chips. Stir until chocolate is
melted. Reduce heat to low and simmer 5 minutes. Whisk and serve.
If desired, dust finished mugs of hot chocolate with cocoa powder.
  Serves 4.

Note: To cook in a slow cooker, combine all ingredients, cover, and
cook on low for 2 to 3 hours, stirring every 15 to 20 minutes.

CHAPTER 14

Wednesday morning, Sadie hid in her room with the lights off until she heard Rex leave for work and Caro leave for her spin class. One bowl of leftover posole—surprisingly good for breakfast—and a clean kitchen later, Sadie texted Margo again. Before going to bed the night before, she'd sent two text messages and then called—it went straight to voice mail and there was no response to her texts. Sadie was eager to find out what Margo had discovered Monday night. Having a goal also helped distract her from the situation with Rex and Caro.

Pete had finally called Sadie back around ten o'clock, and Sadie told him about Rex's ultimatum. Pete had wanted to talk to Rex, but she made him promise not to. She wasn't going to stay where she wasn't wanted, and she didn't want to cause more discord between Rex and his wife. Sadie didn't tell Pete about her conversation with Caro regarding her marital issues—it didn't seem appropriate.

Once she was showered, dressed, fixed up, and ready to go, Sadie checked her phone for a reply from Margo. Nothing. However, there was a text from Caro inviting Sadie to lunch and then to Lois's bakery to help with the cupcakes.

Sadie frowned. She hated the necessity of creating some distance in their relationship so as to make her leaving easier on both of them. She bowed out of the lunch, but agreed to help with the cupcakes; she loved working at the bakery and needed something to do. If not for having her retirement plans derailed by her odd penchant for murder investigations, Sadie may very well have opened up her own corner bakery.

Margo's Land Cruiser wasn't in the driveway when Sadie pulled up to the duplex, but Sadie went to the door anyway—just in case. She knocked, waited twenty seconds, knocked again, waited some more, and then leaned to the side and tried to peek into the living room. There was the narrowest of gaps between the edge of the window and the mini-blind, but not enough to see much of anything.

She pulled out her phone and called Margo again, but like the other attempts, it went straight to voice mail. Sadie didn't bother leaving a message. She put the phone back into her purse, which she hiked up further on her shoulder. Margo had been called back to the dig starting on Thursday. Could she have been asked to start a day early? Was that why she wasn't home?

But the unanswered calls and text messages didn't sit right with Sadie as she headed down the sidewalk toward her car. Halfway there, she paused and turned back to look at the front of the duplex, her eyes moving from Margo's door to that of her neighbor's only a few feet to the right. Maybe Sadie wasn't ready to give up just yet.

"Hello," Sadie said to the young woman who answered the door a minute later. She had a darling towheaded little boy on her hip and the quick, ponytail hairstyle of young motherhood. "I'm a friend of Margo's next door and wondered if you'd seen her around today. I need to get in touch with her, but she's not answering her phone."

The girl shook her head. "I haven't seen her today," she said, bouncing her toddler higher on her hip. "Sorry."

"Could you tell me when you last saw her?"

"Our paths don't really cross much. The last time I saw her was Monday. I was going grocery shopping without my sidekick." She jostled the little boy, and he smiled shyly while putting two fingers in his mouth. "She was leaving too, and we waved at each other."

"Do you know what time on Monday?" Sadie asked, wondering if it was before or after they'd gone to the bar.

"Um, let's see, Max was already in bed, so it was after 8:00— maybe 8:30?"

"Was her Land Cruiser here when you got back?" Sadie asked, already knowing the answer. They were in the middle of a bar fight at 9:30.

"I really don't remember," the girl said with a shrug, but a concerned expression crossed her features. "Is it important?"

Sadie smiled so as not to worry this girl too much. "Oh, I don't know," she said, trying to sound flippant. "I was with her on Monday and haven't been able to get a hold of her since then. I'm just wondering if she's been around. I'm sure her phone just died or something. I'm Sadie, by the way." She put a hand to her chest since the screen door between them prevented a handshake, not to mention the fact that the girl's hands were full. As soon as she said her name, though, she remembered that Margo knew her as Sarah. Oops.

"I'm Alison, and this is Max."

"Hi, Max," Sadie said, lowering her head to smile at him. He promptly hid his face in his mom's shoulder. Sadie commented on how cute he was and asked his age—fourteen months. By the time they finished the small talk about the baby, Alison was the one to go back to Sadie's original topic.

"Ya know, I hear Margo come and go a lot," Alison said. "Her front door sticks and the whole duplex kind of rattles when she has to pull it shut."

Sadie nodded. "I remember that from when I was here on Monday; those warped floorboards catch the door."

"Right," Alison confirmed. She leaned against the doorway after moving Max to her other hip. "She used to work these crazy hours and left at, like, four in the morning. Woke me every single time, but then I don't sleep all that deeply these days." She smiled at Max, and he pulled into her shoulder again. "But come to think of it, I haven't heard her come or go the last couple of days, and I haven't seen her car in the driveway."

"Nothing yesterday?"

"No, and I was home all day. Well, I'm always home all day." She gave Sadie a tired smile that Sadie well understood. Sadie had been a stay-at-home mom until Shawn started all-day school. Those had been wonderfully exhausting years. "And I don't think she came home Monday night, unless she went in through the back, but she doesn't seem to use the back door much—even though the front door sticks so bad." From the way she said it, Sadie could tell Alison found it a little rude that Margo would insist on using the disruptive door when there was a perfectly acceptable alternative. She had a point.

"Huh," Sadie said, looking at Margo's door again and wondering if it was locked. She thought back to the message Margo had left on her cell phone: *This is bigger than you thought.* Where had Margo been when she made that call?

"Are you sure everything is okay?" Alison asked.

Sadie turned back to the neighbor. "I'm sure it is," she said, forcing a soft smile. "I was just trying to get in touch with her. Um, would you mind if I left you my number and then when she comes home, could you call me?"

"Sure, or I can have her call you herself."

"Either way would be great." Sadie dug in her purse for the little notebook she always carried and a pen. A few seconds later, Alison pushed open the screen door with her hip and Sadie handed the paper through. They said their good-byes, but as soon as Alison's front door was shut, Sadie headed back toward Margo's side of the duplex. There was a six-foot-tall cedar fence enclosing the small backyard; Sadie had seen the patio through a window Monday.

It took Sadie about three seconds to reach over the gate and open it from the inside. The hinges creaked horribly—proving the gate wasn't used very often—but no one in the neighborhood seemed out and about enough to notice. She closed it carefully and headed up the back steps, justifying that she'd done the best thing first—she'd talked to the neighbor—before she resorted to breaking and entering.

She tried the door. It was locked, but she always carried her pick set with her these days, and within thirty seconds, she was working on the basic cylinder lock with a five-pin deadbolt. Tricky, but not too tricky. Though Sadie preferred the pick gun, an electric version that was fast and easy, the whirring noise always sounded so much louder than it really was when she was already doing something she wasn't sure she should do. But, then again, she was pretty sure she *should* do *this.* Sadie didn't think Margo would be upset with Sadie checking up on her due to the circumstances, and trying to clear this kind of activity through Pete would only connect him to it, so she didn't bother asking herself if he'd approve. The goal was to find Margo, and Sadie just needed to confirm that she'd come home after the bar Monday night. If she hadn't . . .

It took less than a minute to unlock the door and slip inside.

"Margo," Sadie called out softly as she carefully shut the door behind her. The back door entered into the kitchen that smelled like old cigarettes and garbage. "It's just me, Sadie—er, Sarah."

The apartment was eerily silent. Sadie moved further into the kitchen, taking in details and wondering if she would know if something were out of place. The apartment was such a mess that nothing stood out to her. The only thing that would likely draw Sadie's attention was if the apartment were cleaner than it had been on Monday—which it certainly wasn't. Not for the first time, Sadie mentally thanked her parents for making her do chores as a child so that living like this had never been a consideration.

The stale smell of cigarette smoke hung heavier in the air as she got closer to the living room, but the smell of fresh tobacco wasn't mixed in with it. There *were* a couple dulce de leche bars missing from the plate still balanced on the dish drainer, but Margo could very well have eaten them before picking Sadie up Monday night. The plastic wrap hadn't been secured after the last sampling, and when Sadie checked, the bars were rock hard.

Sadie headed toward Margo's bedroom, her heart rate increasing. She'd been in places where she didn't belong before, and she'd stumbled onto things she would rather not have seen. In an instant, all those situations flashed through her mind, completely freezing her in place as she thought of how often she'd walked into a nightmare. Reality mixed with a heavy dose of pure fear descended on her like a curtain.

What was she doing here? Why on earth would she want to invite another horrible situation into her life? Her chest felt tight as she turned around and moved toward the back door, noting how clammy her skin felt and how shallow her breathing had become.

All she needed was to have an anxiety attack in a home she'd entered illegally. And what if she *had* found something? Would she have called Pete and confessed what she'd done while asking him to call an ambulance?

Her hand was on the knob of the back door, but she stopped before fleeing from the apartment. Running hadn't worked so well in the past, and she'd learned many things about the power of fear in the last several months. Giving in made it worse in the long run.

She pressed her forehead to the cool wood of the door. Closing her eyes, she took several deep breaths of the pungent air and began counting her inhalations and exhalations, calming her body down as she allowed her thoughts to catch up with her actions. It took a few minutes for Sadie to talk through what she was doing here and consciously process the facts as she knew them. So far, everything Sadie had seen in the apartment validated the hypothesis that Margo hadn't come home, but Sadie could still make sure before she left. If there was something ugly to discover, not discovering it wouldn't make it go away.

Once in full control of herself—well, maybe not full, but *mostly* in control—she turned back to the living room and walked slowly to the bedroom, scanning everything on her way there to make sure nothing was different than she remembered it on Monday. Nothing stood out. The mug Margo had been tapping her cigarette ash into was still on the coffee table. The same jacket was thrown over the back of the stained chair.

The bedroom door was open, and Sadie held her breath as she entered, scanning the floor and letting out a sigh when there was no body to be discovered. "Good job," Sadie said, complimenting herself on having pushed through the fear. Not finding a body seemed like an adequate reward for her decision. The clothes Margo had worn to the bar were not among the piles of clothing on the floor, but the sweats she'd been wearing Monday afternoon were on the unmade bed, where Margo would have slept if she'd come home that night.

Nothing stood out in the bedroom or bathroom, so Sadie continued her slow walk to the back door wondering what had happened between Monday night and now. The fact that Margo wasn't here—and didn't seem to have *been* here—thirty-six hours after leaving that cryptic message worried Sadie a great deal. Where could she be? Perhaps the better question was, where should Sadie start looking? Alison would call her if Margo came back here, which freed Sadie to look somewhere else.

It made sense that the last place Sadie had seen Margo should be the first place she'd start her search—The Conquistador. Going back to the scene of such upsetting events was not an exciting prospect, but the only other option was to do nothing. That seemed a very poor choice to make.

She thought about asking Caro to come to the bar with her—there was no doubt in her mind that Caro would jump at the opportunity—but she shook the idea away almost as quickly as it had come. She needed to leave Caro out of this, no matter how much she wanted a partner. She was on her own.

CHAPTER 15

Sadie found it a little sad that being open at 11:30 in the morning was a worthwhile business decision for the owner of The Conquistador. Sadie parked next to a dusty gray sedan—one of four cars parked out front—and pushed through the door and into the interior that looked exactly like it had two nights before except not as crowded. Was there a reason people didn't want to drink with sunshine pouring through the windows and fresh flowers on wrought-iron tables? Maybe a little Josh Groban playing in the background?

She stood in the entryway for a few seconds, allowing her eyes to adjust to the dimness. The same Mexican music was playing as before, and as Sadie scanned the room, she noticed that the table she'd been sitting at Monday night was gone—had it been broken in the fight? She couldn't remember. No one had bothered to rearrange the other tables and chairs to fill the empty space. Sadie quickly looked away, feeling guilty for all that had happened—even though it wasn't her fault. There were still peanut shells all over the floor, and her shoes made sticky sounds as she made her way to the bar where she waited for the bartender to see her. He did eventually, and came her way.

"What'll you have, sweetheart?" He had gray hair and a full beard, and his eyes crinkled when he smiled at her.

It had been a long time since someone had called Sadie "sweetheart," and it made her smile less forced than it had been. "I'm just looking for some information, if you've got a minute."

"Well, as long as the crowds stay contained, I can probably give you a little time." He waved at the six or seven people scattered around the room, and then gave Sadie a wink. "I guess things got a little wild here the other night, so I've been asked to keep a sharp eye."

"Oh, right," Sadie said, adjusting her purse strap and glancing at the place of the missing table again before looking back at him. "That's actually kind of why I'm here. I guess you weren't working Monday night?"

"No, ma'am," he said, shaking his head. "I'm the day tender for the very reason of avoiding scenes such as that." He leaned closer. "The day-drunks are much better behaved." He winked again.

"I'm glad to hear it," Sadie said while trying to come up with what she could ask him if he hadn't been there that night. "Do you know how many people ended up being arrested that night?" She only knew about Shel and herself. No other women had been put in the cell with her, but it still seemed like a good idea to make sure Margo hadn't been taken in after Sadie left, maybe taken to another jail, though that would be strange.

"I believe it was just the two—the guy and gal who started it."

"I'm pretty sure only he started it," Sadie said, unable to miss an opportunity to defend herself. "I mean, all she'd had to drink was a little Coke . . . I think."

"Not what I heard," he said, shaking his head. "Customers were saying she was already hammered before she even walked through the door. Wasn't here even ten minutes before she started yelling and screaming and carrying on. Tried to break a bottle over some guy's head—that don't work so good in real life. In the movies them bottles is made of sugar, or so's I heard."

"Who told you that?" Sadie responded sharply, then cleared her throat. "I think the story must have gotten exaggerated."

"No, they really do use sugar glass in the movies," he replied. "I seen a video of it on the computer. My granddaughter showed me."

"I meant that the *man* must be the person who started the fight. The woman was probably just defending herself or her friends."

He cocked his head to the side and eyed her with a little more consideration. "How would you know that? Were you here?"

"I were . . . I mean, I was," Sadie said, then hurried to explain. She didn't want to get him thinking she might be the woman accused of starting the fight. "A friend of mine was here as well but we got separated and I'm trying to track her down. I was hoping maybe someone here would know what happened after the police took . . . uh, after the police left. I'm hoping someone remembers my friend."

"We got closed down for the night," the bartender said. Someone waved at him from the other end of the counter. "Be right there," he said before pointing over Sadie's shoulder. "Mike was here, though."

She looked over her shoulder as the bartender explained that Mike was the guy in the Red Sox baseball cap and Tapout T-shirt. She turned to thank the bartender, but he was already moving down the bar.

Sadie stood up and turned toward Mike, but he must have overheard because he'd already stood up from his table and was coming toward her with an amiable smile on his boyish face. He had light brown skin, dark hair that poked out from beneath his hat, and blue eyes. She guessed he was part Native American.

"So they let you out already, huh?" he asked when he reached her.

"Pardon me?" Sadie said, but she could feel the heat rising in her neck. He recognized her from Monday night? Oh dear.

"You're the lady who started the fight, right?" He leaned against the bar, bracing himself with his elbows as he looked her over in a way that made her want to fix her hair.

"I really didn't start it," she explained, standing up straight. "Shel—the man who *actually* started it—was lunging toward my friend. I just reacted like anyone else would have done."

"Hey," he said, raising both hands as though in surrender. One hand held a longneck bottle of beer. "It was the most exciting night I've had in months, I'm not complaining." He smiled and took a long drink of his beer.

He was young, mid-twenties, Sadie guessed. What was he doing in a bar Monday night and again today? Didn't he know there was a whole world out there? And yet, maybe his pending alcoholism could work in her favor. She sat back down on her barstool and struck a more casual pose.

"I'm glad someone enjoyed it," Sadie said. "It was quite horrible for me."

He shrugged and slid onto the stool next to her, both of them with their backs to the bar, facing the tables and patrons. "But they let you out?"

"I made bail," Sadie said as though she always made bail easily when arrested following the barroom brawls she was wrongly accused of starting. She put out her hand. "I'm Sadie."

He held out the hand not holding his beer and grabbed hers in a single shake. "Mike."

"Nice to meet you, Mike," Sadie said before leaning her elbows back against the bar behind her. "I was with a friend on Monday and I'm trying to track her down. Any chance you remember her? She was blonde, about five foot seven, with bright red lipstick."

"White chick?"

"Yes," Sadie said, embarrassed by her faux pas. "She's white." In a lot of other places there'd be the assumption that whoever she talked about was Caucasian if she didn't point out otherwise, but not here. Caro had told her about a friend who was blonde-haired and blue-eyed but considered herself a Pueblo because of her great-grandmother's ethnicity. She took great offense to being called white, even though that's what she appeared to be. Apparently Sadie hadn't taken Caro's education on the social diversity as seriously as she should have.

"You've just described half the female clientele of this fine establishment," Mike said with a laugh. "The other half are brown-skinned with dark hair and dark eyes. They still wear the lipstick, though."

"She had braids," Sadie said, picturing Margo as she'd looked Monday night. "And a . . . very tight pink top." A thought came to mind—could the too-tight shirt have attracted the wrong sort of attention?

She saw recognition dawn in Mike's eyes. "She was at the table with you, right?"

Sadie nodded, a bit disappointed that it was Margo's immodesty that sparked his recollection, but grateful that he remembered her all the same. "Yes. When things got . . . going, we were separated and then I . . . I was, you know . . . taken in."

"Right," he said with a nod, leaning one elbow on the bar and staring at the far wall as though pondering. "She left after you did, I think. Well, I mean we all left after you did."

"I heard it got shut down."

"Yeah, two hours early. Cops." He sounded rather disgusted that the police would do such a thing, but as long as he wasn't blaming her, Sadie could handle his perception of things.

"Did you happen to notice my friend after the bar closed down for the night?"

"She left with a guy."

"Willingly?" Sadie blurted, earning her a curious look from her new friend. "I mean, she and I came together, so I'm just surprised she left with someone else."

"She looked willing to me," he said.

"Did you see if they took her car? It's an old green Land Cruiser."

"Bunch of stickers on the back?"

Sadie nodded.

"Yeah, they talked for awhile and then she drove off in it, headed toward Tesuque, following the guy's car."

"He knew she was following him? They planned it?"

Mike gave her an odd look. "Yeah, I guess."

"What's Tesuque?" Sadie asked, repeating his pronunciation in her mind: *tuh-soo-key.* Was it a landmark of some kind?

"Tesuque Pueblo," Mike clarified.

"Oh, a reservation?"

"No, a pueblo, the land the tribe lived on historically rather than new land *reserved* for them to live on now."

"Sorry," Sadie said, hoping she hadn't offended him. "I'm not from here."

"I figured that," he said with a slight smile. "Otherwise you'd know what Tesuque was and why a pueblo isn't a reservation."

"And my friend was going there?" Why would Margo go to a reservation . . . a *pueblo* late at night?

"She was going that direction," Mike clarified. "There are some houses and ranches out that way too."

"Do you know the man she left with?"

"I've seen him a time or two. He's not a regular, though."

"Can you describe him, or his car?" Sadie asked even though she only knew three men from the bar last night.

"Reddish hair," Mike said, "About my size, I guess."

Langley, Sadie thought to herself. "Any chance you noticed a tattoo on his arm?"

Mike paused for a moment, then nodded. "Yeah, I think so, something green."

So, Margo had followed Langley somewhere. "What time did the bar close down?"

"About ten thirty," Mike said. "By the time I got to Southern Exposure, *Letterman* was just starting."

His comment distracted her from Margo for a minute. "You went to another bar after this one closed down?"

"Sure," he said, finishing off his beer. "The night was still young."

Sadie felt her smile turn sad. "Do you mind if I ask why a man as young and bright as yourself spends his days and nights in a bar?"

His smile faded too, and he looked at his beer. "Lost my job a few months ago. There's just not much left to do with my time."

"Are you a married man?"

"My girlfriend up and left about the same time I was canned."

"I'm sorry," Sadie said sincerely. It was sad to see someone so young without direction. "And I know you don't know me, but do you mind if I offer you a little advice?"

"Get a job?" he said dryly. "I might have heard that one before."

"No, find something to be passionate about."

"I told you, she left me."

"Not a woman," Sadie said. "Something worth investing in for the rest of your life. Maybe you like to paint, or lift weights, or make the perfect brisket."

His eyebrows pulled together.

Sadie was just getting started. "Jobs come and go, but passion can last a lifetime. It makes the hard times bearable and the good times easier to find. Isn't there something you love to do? A hobby or a talent you enjoy?"

"I like drinking."

"Unfortunately that won't bring you the same satisfaction as putting yourself into something you love." She looked at him expectantly until she saw his expression change.

"I like horses," he said quietly. "I was working on a ranch, but they had to downsize. I got let go and had to move back in with my mom." He made a face and the disappointment rolled off him in waves. "I can't imagine doing anything else, but jobs are scarce. My ranch wasn't the only one to downsize."

"Then volunteer somewhere," Sadie said. "I bet there's a stable around here somewhere that would love an extra set of hands. Or you could go to school and become a veterinarian or a tech or an equestrian masseur. You seem like a nice man; it would be a shame if you wasted away in a place like this. God gave you gifts with the hope that you would use them, especially at a time like this when things seem so dark."

He regarded her closely, carefully, and she smiled and put a hand on his arm, giving him a little squeeze. "This isn't the life you were meant to live, Mike. But thank you for being here today when I needed your help." She stood up. "I've got to go look for my friend, but I wish you the best."

CHAPTER 16

Sadie left her number with Mike and asked him to call her if he remembered anything else or if he saw Langley at the bar later. Giving out her number and using her real name made her a little uncomfortable after being so cautious all these months. But it seemed like a good risk, and she didn't want to cut herself off from additional information. Mike had put the napkin with her number on it in his pocket and wished her luck before ordering another beer.

Once in her car again, she made some notes to track down Langley's phone number, and maybe Garrett's too. They could likely fill her in on what happened after she'd left. Since she was right here, though, she decided to drive in the direction Mike had indicated and see where Margo had headed.

There wasn't much on the road to Tesuque—another bar, a storage facility, and what looked like a manufacturing plant of some kind. The road narrowed, and though she passed a crumbling cinderblock building with a "For Lease" sign in the window, there wasn't much else.

Sadie took it slow, scanning the sides of the road and pulling over to allow other cars to pass her. She wondered if she wasn't looking for a needle in a haystack. She didn't know the area or where Margo could have been going. Why would she follow Langley anywhere? He must have invited her somewhere, and she must have been interested enough to trust him. The message Margo left Sadie indicated some kind of discovery or realization—but about what? How was Langley connected? What was Margo apologizing for?

Sadie looked in her rearview mirror. Santa Fe was slowly blending into the desert skyline the farther away she got. The buildings were soon behind her, and she entered into what seemed like miles and miles of rolling desert hills dotted with cedar, pinion, and juniper trees. Gates barred access to several dirt roads, some of which seemed to lead to buildings in the distance, and Sadie became even more discouraged. If Margo had gone through one of those gates, Sadie would never spot her vehicle from here—assuming it was still there. Then Sadie saw a sign that caused her to stop her car in the middle of the road.

COLD RIVER RANCH

An arrow beneath the words pointed down a blacktopped road. A tingle rushed through her. She put on her blinker. Half a mile in, the way was blocked by a wrought-iron gate complete with an archway that rose up from either side of the road. In the middle of the metal arch was a rendition of the same logo Sadie had seen on Benny's shirt at the police station and on the website.

Sadie rolled down her window to get a better view of the thick iron gate. The desert breeze was cool enough to feel refreshing without being cold. The gate wasn't fancy, just metal posts four feet tall, welded onto crossbeams at the top, center, and bottom of the gate.

Upon further inspection, she could see a post set alongside the road six feet in front of the gate, topped with a number pad.

She pulled up until her window was even with the device that she assumed allowed entry if someone entered the correct code. She put the car in park and got out to get a closer look at the ranch. The gate wasn't like those she'd seen on TV in front of celebrity homes. If someone really wanted to enter they could simply climb over the gate, or through the three-rail fencing that wrapped around the property. But the gate was closed all the same, and it held tight when she shook it—not that she necessarily wanted to go in.

Beyond the gate—a mile at least—was a large adobe homestead with a U-shaped driveway looped in front of it. Behind it, there were numerous outbuildings, including a metal grain silo that rose up behind a weathered barn almost as big as the house. There was plenty of what looked like open range, liberally sprinkled with cattle. The cedars and pinions thickened as the property stretched back, then rose into the Sangre de Cristo mountains.

Was Langley affiliated with the ranch too? Sadie scanned the horizon as though Margo's Land Cruiser might appear in the distance. How would Langley have convinced Margo to follow him to the ranch? Sadie turned back to look at her car parked by the pin pad. She could easily imagine Margo's Land Cruiser idling behind Langley's truck as he punched in the code, then easing on through to whatever lay inside the compound.

How did these pieces connect together? Where did Shel fit in? And Langley? And *where* was Margo?

As Sadie approached her car again, she noticed several cigarette butts on the ground.

Sadie lifted her head slightly, looking again at the area of road where Margo's Land Cruiser would have idled if Langley had punched in the code to allow them inside. She also thought of the cigarette Margo had thrown into the ashtray just before they entered the bar Monday night and specifically the bright red lipstick ring on the filter. It had taken Sadie some serious scrubbing to get the dark red lipstick off her lips the next morning. What if . . .

Sadie scanned the dirt, rock, and dry desert grasses on the edge of the road. She kicked at a couple tufts of brush, trying to peer beneath them. She squealed when a thin, dusty green lizard darted out from beneath the sagebrush, quickly disappearing beneath a rock. It took her a moment to catch her breath. She could handle lizards, it was surprises that got the best of her.

Would Margo have just dropped her cigarette? Or thrown it? There were dozens of butts mingling with the red-brown dirt, but Margo's lipstick was bright red and the cigarette would be new. Sadie moved further from the asphalt, still scanning the ground carefully. And then she saw it.

Goosebumps broke out across her shoulder blades, and even though it was exactly what she'd been looking for, she almost couldn't believe she'd really found it. She hurried a few steps forward and bent down, reaching beneath the skeletal remains of a tumbleweed caught up on sagebrush when she heard the sound of an engine.

Her head snapped up, and she looked first in the direction of the ranch. No one was coming from the ranch side of the gate, so she turned around to see a white truck come to a stop behind where her car blocked the road, right where Sadie imagined Margo's Land Cruiser would have been waiting for entrance. She glanced back to the ground where she'd seen the red-ringed cigarette butt.

"Can I help you, *Señora?*"

Sadie focused on the man leaning one elbow out of the truck

and looking at her curiously. It took a beat for her to realize it was Benny from the police station yesterday. She stood even straighter, wondering if he recognized her as well.

"What you doing over there?" Benny asked when she didn't answer.

"Uh, I . . ." She looked at the ground: powdery red dirt, washed-out sagebrush, tumbleweeds, and the occasional piece of litter, bleached by the sun. And Margo's cigarette butt. She couldn't admit she was looking for that, though. "I saw a lizard," she said quickly, then pointed to the place where she'd seen the lizard disappear. "I . . . I was hoping to catch it for my nephew. He was too fast for me, though—the lizard, not my nephew."

Benny narrowed his eyes at her as she stood in the brush and tried to look casual.

"What are you doing at the ranch?"

Oh, yeah, the ranch. Sadie glanced toward the hacienda, then back to Benny. "I made a wrong turn," she said as she began walking back to her car. She'd come back for the butt later. "I was about to turn around when I saw the lizard. Sorry I'm in your way."

"Hey," he said again, peering at her as she got closer to him out of necessity. "I know you, *sí*?"

"Uh, I don't think so," she said, counting on the fact that he hadn't paid her as much attention as she'd paid him at the police station. She avoided his eyes all the same though, and angled more sharply toward her car. "I'll move my car so I'm not in your way."

She heard the click before she saw his door opening. It blocked her path, and she stopped as he stepped out of the truck. He wasn't tall, but he was imposing, with an air of confidence and suspicion that made Sadie uncomfortable. He wore what looked like the same denim shirt he'd had on the day before and the gray felt cowboy hat with sweat stains on the brim; whatever he did on the ranch required him to work hard. He had the deep lines on his face of a man who spent a lot of time in the sun and a sense of ownership she found a little confusing. Benny just worked at the ranch; he didn't own it. From what she'd read online, Edward Standage was the owner of the ranch—and he was sixty-something and Caucasian.

Benny looked at her with distrustful brown eyes and then glanced toward the brush she'd been pawing through before he pulled up. He wouldn't see the cigarette, would he?

Only if he knew what she was looking for.

He took a couple of steps toward where Sadie had been standing, allowing Sadie to step past him and the door of his truck. She immediately headed toward her car again. Her hand was on the door handle when Benny spoke up.

"Come to the *casa* with me," he said.

She looked over her shoulder to see that he'd crossed his arms over his chest and was attempting to smile, but the kindness he seemed to be trying to communicate didn't reach his eyes.

"We have many lizards you can take home to your nephew. I'll have one of the ranch hands catch one for you and put it in a box."

"Uh, that's okay. I've already taken too much of your time." She quickly pulled open her door as he began walking toward her, causing her heart to speed up. There was a time when Sadie would have accepted his invitation and taken advantage of getting to the heart of the investigation. But her curiosity had taken a back seat to fear. Putting herself in danger no longer seemed exciting.

"Don't go," he said, still smiling that distrustful smile. She slid into the driver's seat, but he kept talking from behind her. "Come with me. I give you a tour of the ranch, *sí*?"

"Um, no thanks," Sadie said. She didn't look at him as she pulled the car door closed. The window was open, so she looked at him in the side mirror and added, "I've got somewhere to be. My nephew is waiting for me."

"Where were you going when you made the wrong turn?"

She didn't answer but instead shifted into reverse. With his truck behind her, there was barely enough room for her to execute a tight three-point turn, but he got back into his truck and pulled back and to the side, making it easier for her to use the worn dirt on the sides of the blacktop to complete the turn. She smiled and waved at him as she passed his truck.

He inclined his head, not bothering to smile any more.

She watched him in her rearview mirror for as long as she could. He didn't go through the gate, and as she reached the end of the road, she thought he got out of his truck again. She wanted to think he didn't know what she was really looking for, but what if he did recognize her from the police station? If Margo had come to the ranch Monday night—and Sadie was all but certain she had—and if Benny knew she and Margo were friends, would he guess Sadie was looking for evidence?

She turned onto the main road and drove back toward Santa Fe. Her anxiety level slowly evened out and her breathing returned to normal. She thought through everything she'd learned that morning and it didn't take long to reach the conclusion that she had to go to the police with what she knew. Maybe *they* could go back for the cigarette butt. She didn't know how she'd explain a second appearance at the ranch, or how she'd talk herself into taking the risk of going back.

She pulled her phone out of her purse and sent a text to Caro so she wouldn't worry.

I'll meet you at the bakery as soon as I can. I need to do something first.

She then took a breath and texted Pete.

Margo hasn't been home since Monday night. I'm going to report it. Who should I talk to at the station?

CHAPTER 17

Detective Marcus Gonzalas had been friends with Pete for over twenty years and, despite his ethnic name, looked as Caucasian as anyone with the last name of Hansen or Smith. Whenever Pete came to Santa Fe, they went fly-fishing on the Pecos River and, in Pete's words, "solved all the world's problems." As soon as he shook Sadie's hand, he invited her to call him Marcus, which made her feel like they were old friends too.

Marcus was in his late fifties, same as Pete, but with less hair and more belly, which reminded Sadie how lucky she was to have met a man of Pete's age with such refined good looks. Marcus led her back to an interrogation room without making a big deal about her arrival. It was nice to already feel trusted by this man; he trusted Pete and Pete had assured him Sadie was just as trustworthy.

They didn't waste much time with small talk, and Sadie agreed to have their conversation recorded. She told him everything she suspected and everything she'd figured out, leaving out only the part about her picking the lock in order to get inside Margo's apartment. Luckily, he didn't ask if the door had been locked or not.

He took notes while she talked and asked a question here and there, but mostly he just listened.

"Benito Ojeda, or Benny, is the ranch foreman," he said when Sadie finished explaining about the road that ended at Cold River Ranch and Benny giving her a hard time. "He takes his job very seriously. I wouldn't take it personally."

"He tried to get me to go to the ranch with him," Sadie reminded him. That seemed outside Benny's job description, and there was something unsettling about the way he'd watched her and, in her opinion, tried to lure her to the ranch. "Plus he bailed Sheldon Carlisle out of jail yesterday."

"I'll look into the bail situation, but the ranch has had a couple run-ins with some environmentalists the last few years, and so they beefed up security—no pun intended. I'm sure that's why he came across the way he did this afternoon." He gave her a half smile, and she returned it out of politeness, even though she felt as though she were being placated. "Benny's been running the ranch hand-in-hand with Edward for nearly thirty years, and he's taken the lion share of the workload these last five years after Lacey got sick. He's just doing his job."

"Lacey?"

"Lacey Standage, Edward's wife. She developed some respiratory issues that required her to move to a lower elevation. She's living in Oregon now, and Edward divides his time between the coast and the ranch. Ethan will eventually take over the ranch but in the meantime, Benny's doing a lot of the management. Honestly, I'm not sure how he keeps up. It's not a small ranch by any means."

"You seem to know a lot about the family."

Marcus shrugged a shoulder. "They're pillars of the community, you could say, and I've lived here all my life. Anyhow, we'll go back and look for that cigarette butt by the gate and talk to Benny. Anything else?"

"No, that's everything."

He nodded, then looked at the notebook and tapped his pen on the desk in a way that almost looked as though he were rereading his notes, except that his eyes were fixed instead of moving over the words.

Sadie waited him out, wondering what he was thinking about so hard and wishing he'd think it out loud. It was hard for her to give information and yet not know everything the police knew.

After a few seconds, he made eye contact with her again. "Will you excuse me for a moment?"

"Sure," Sadie said, even though it made her nervous for the first time since she'd sat down. She didn't like being left in interrogation rooms, though she would never feel truly alone with the mirrored wall on her left. It made her feel like she'd done something wrong.

He thanked her and left the room. She tried not to think about people watching her from the other side, evaluating her movements, talking about the things she'd said—judging whether or not she could be trusted. Wasn't coming to Marcus with the information proof enough that she could be trusted?

It felt like several minutes before Marcus returned, but was probably less than two. "Do you have time to come down to the impound lot with me?"

"Impound lot?" Sadie repeated. "Like, for cars?"

"You said you drove in Ms. Kauffman's Land Cruiser on Monday, right?"

Sadie nodded.

"We impounded a vehicle last night that meets the description of her Land Cruiser you just gave me. It's waiting to be processed, so a conclusive owner hasn't been determined or notified, but I'd like you to take a look, just in case."

Sadie's throat immediately thickened as she stood up. "I've got time," she said, but she couldn't help wondering how many green late-70s model Land Cruisers there were in Santa Fe.

Sadie drove with Marcus to the impound lot a few blocks away, and in the process, he updated her on the vehicle. A teacher at an elementary school had reported it that afternoon. It had been parked in the faculty-only lot since Tuesday morning.

They pulled up to a chain-link fence with razor wire at the top and wheels at the base of the gate portion. Marcus pushed a button on a key pad not that different than the one she'd seen at the entrance to Cold River Ranch. A voice said hello, Marcus explained who he was, and the chain-link fence buzzed, then moved to the right. When the fence had pulled back completely, Marcus entered the lot and wound through several lines of vehicles until he pulled up beside Margo's Land Cruiser.

"It's hers," Sadie said tightly.

"You're certain?" he asked. "Would you like to take a closer look?"

Sadie didn't need a closer look, but she got out anyway and walked around the vehicle. The "Bark Less Wag More" sticker in the center of the back window and the "Coexist" bumper sticker were just as Sadie remembered them. "It's her Land Cruiser," she said. "I'm absolutely certain of it."

She stepped to the passenger window and looked around the interior, glad that there was no trunk, nowhere a body could be hidden. Why would Margo abandon her Land Cruiser? There was no escaping the ominous probability that she hadn't done it by choice. The teacher who reported the car had seen it parked at the school

Tuesday morning. If they kept hours similar to Sadie's when Sadie had been teaching school, that would have been somewhere between seven and eight o'clock in the morning—ten hours since Margo would have followed Langley to the ranch.

"We haven't cracked it open yet," Marcus said, interrupting her thoughts. "We'll do a thorough search when we do, since you're worried about her."

Sadie stared at the Land Cruiser a few seconds longer. "We've got to find Kyle Langley. He's the last known person to have seen her." She'd already told him that, but it bore repeating.

"*We* will," Marcus said, emphasizing that *she* was not part of the *we*, though his tone was kind. He opened the passenger door of the police car for her, signaling an end to the field trip.

Sadie took the cue and got into the car, but she felt sick to her stomach as she tried to imagine a reasonable explanation for Margo to abandon her Land Cruiser.

However, based on the last two years of Sadie's life, it was very, very hard for her to be optimistic. Sadie already suspected the BLM was aware of something criminal related to the dig crew—why else would she have been put there as an informant? To then find recent bodies and have Margo go missing after they started making inquiries cast a dark shadow on the disappearance. An uneasy feeling sat like iron in Sadie's stomach.

"You said the Land Cruiser was found at an elementary school?" she asked as they left the lot. "Was that school near the ranch?"

"Nope, the school's on the west end of town."

Her momentary disappointment was quickly overshadowed by a new realization. "Which school?" Sadie was familiar with just one elementary school in this town. It sat behind and to the west of the apartment complex Langley lived in on that end of town. What were the chances?

"Ponderosa, I think. I'll have to double-check at the office though."

Sadie caught her breath. "Ponderosa Elementary on Santaquin?" She and Caro had parked in that lot and climbed the ten-foot high embankment to get a view of Langley's apartment complex less than a week ago.

"I think so," Marcus confirmed, not hiding his surprise as he glanced at her. "What do you know about it?"

She didn't answer right away because she was visualizing how the school and complex related to one another. They were reached from different streets, one block apart, but they shared a property line along the back side.

"What?" Marcus prodded when she didn't explain right away.

"Kyle Langley lives in the apartment complex behind that school," she said. "The complex is called Colonial Hills. Langley lives in number twenty-eight."

"And how on earth would you know that?"

Oh yeah, she hadn't told him about the BLM stuff. And it didn't sound as though Pete had said anything either. Shoot. "Um, can I call Pete first?"

CHAPTER 18

It was almost an hour later—after three o'clock—before Sadie was given permission to leave the police station. She hadn't been able to get ahold of Pete. And so, without his blessing, she'd told Marcus about her BLM status on the dig site and the report she'd developed about the members of the crew. She could feel his walls go up as she explained herself, even though she finished with, "I'm sorry. I was told to keep it to myself."

Another detective called Agent Shannon on the phone in one room while Marcus talked to Sadie in another. It would have been nice to feel like she was doing the right thing, but she felt like a naughty child in trouble with everyone. The police now knew she hadn't been completely forthcoming the first two times she'd given her statement, and Agent Shannon knew Sadie had disregarded her insistence that Sadie keep her undercover role a secret until the BLM was ready to make it known to local law enforcement. She felt like she'd let everyone down. Finally, Marcus left her alone with that mirrored wall, then came back a few minutes later, thanked her for the information, and told her she could leave. He'd call her, he said, as soon as he had news. She'd dared to feel as though they were friends earlier in the day, but that feeling was long gone now.

Sadie left with a rock still in her stomach, and asked herself in a hundred different ways what else she could have done. There were no answers, not firm ones anyway. Yet she really was trying to be upfront with as many people as possible. She dreaded having to talk to Pete tonight and relay everything that had happened. How much more of this could he take before he threw his hands up and said the complication she brought into his life just wasn't worth it? It was Sadie's greatest fear that he would say that to her one day. It nearly brought tears to her eyes just thinking about it.

It was close to 3:30 when Sadie pulled into the parking area behind the building Modern Cupcakes by Lois shared with half a dozen other businesses in the strip mall east of Old Town. The bakery was nestled between a tanning salon and a real estate office. Caro's blue Neon was parked by the back door, and Sadie wondered if she should just go home, pack her things, and head to Albuquerque. Would it be easier for everyone if she just left?

But Margo was still missing, and Lois needed help baking cupcakes, and taking off without a word to Caro would be devastating. Sadie couldn't do that to her. Not after everything Caro had done for her and Caro's confession last night.

Sadie let herself in the back door like Caro had told her to, causing Caro to look up from where she was putting cupcake liners into muffin tins. She paused for a moment, then put down the stack of liners and hurried across the room.

"Where have you been?" Caro asked when she reached Sadie and gave her a quick hug. "I've been calling and texting for over an hour."

"Sorry I'm so late," Sadie said, though she could tell that Caro wasn't angry, just genuinely concerned.

The desire to unload everything that had happened tugged and pulled at Sadie's determination not to involve Caro. How was she supposed to pretend she was unaffected by Margo's disappearance and the discovery of her Land Cruiser? Didn't Sadie deserve someone to confide in, someone to assure her everything would be fine? If she confided in Caro, however, she'd be making things more awkward with Rex, and interfering in an already strained marriage was not the solution.

"I'm sorry," Sadie said again, hanging up her purse on a hook near the back door and steeling herself against giving into the desire to explain. She did not have that luxury. She instead casually explained that she'd been talking to the police and hadn't gotten Caro's messages because she'd turned off her phone at the station per their request—which was true. She retrieved her phone from her purse and turned the ringer back on, showing it to Caro to prove she wasn't making things up. "Things took longer than I expected them to."

Caro's eyebrows pulled together, and she looked hard into Sadie's face. "What's going on?"

Sadie clamped her teeth together, determined not to say anything else.

Caro put a hand on Sadie's arm, her expression softening with even more compassion. "What's wrong, Sadie?" she asked, her tone warm with sincere sympathy. "You know you can talk to me, right? You know I'm your sounding board, don't you?"

"I can't," Sadie said in a pleading voice after pushing away another wave of temptation. "I'm sorry."

"Why can't you?" Caro asked, then her sculpted eyebrows rose as though she'd just discovered something. "Did the police tell you not to talk about it?"

It was an out, and likely the only one Sadie was going to get. She nodded, but felt horrible about the lie.

Caro took a step closer. "Not here," she said quietly as someone came through the swinging doors that connected the bakery to the sales counter. "But you know I won't say a word to anyone else. We'll talk later."

"Caro, could you—oh, hi, Sadie." Lois smiled brightly, picking up the cupcake liners Caro had put down and deftly putting them into the tin cups as though it had been her job from the start. Lois was a petite woman, with dark hair and dark eyes behind her glasses. She was always smiling, always full of energy.

Caro let go of Sadie's arm and turned back to her friend. "You needed me to do something?"

"Yes. Could you go to the bank for me? It must be twenty-dollar-bill Wednesday or something and I'm almost out of change. Molly doesn't come in for another hour so I can't leave the front. Do you mind?"

"Not at all," Caro said, reaching behind her back to untie her apron.

Lois finished putting liners in one pan and pulled another pan forward. A bell sounded from the front of the shop, and Lois abandoned the pans and headed through the swinging doors, throwing a "Thank you!" over her shoulder as she did so.

"We'll talk later," Caro said to Sadie again with a smile as she handed over the apron she'd been wearing. Sadie took it without comment. Caro followed Lois to the front, and Sadie moved to the table with the muffin tins, picking up the stack of liners. Too many more requests from Caro to confide in her, and Sadie would fold completely.

Caro left the shop a few minutes later, Lois stayed busy up front, and Sadie finished lining the tins and tidying up the kitchen, which was the best she could do without having any clear instructions. Though things still weighed heavily on her, there could not have been a better distraction than the bakery. Lois was meticulously organized, with every shelf and piece of equipment labeled and stored in a logical location. The smell of caramelizing sugar and sponge cake hung like gossamer in the air, relaxing Sadie a little more with every minute that passed.

A timer dinged, and she pulled open the huge convection oven, and got a whoosh of warm air in her face. She closed her eyes and inhaled the delicious aroma of the 200 cupcakes—well, 192 really—baking. There was just the slightest hint of golden brown on the edges of the back cakes, so she touched a few tops and, satisfied when they bounced back appropriately, she grabbed some oven mitts from a hook on the wall and went about moving the pans to the rolling baking rack where they could cool. She was just finishing up when another timer dinged; the lower oven was finished baking too. She removed those cupcakes as well, then went out to update Lois who was finishing up with a customer who looked about ten months pregnant.

"You took them all out yourself?" Lois said as she followed Sadie back into the bakery area—the front was empty for the moment. Lois inspected the racks of cooling cupcakes, then turned to Sadie with a smile. "You're a quick study. Thank you."

Sadie gave a humble smile, but appreciated the compliment very much. "You're welcome," she said, grateful to have done something right. "What else do you need help with?"

Lois looked at the clock and frowned. "You don't, by chance, know how to make stabilized whipping cream, do you?"

"Of course," Sadie said, standing a little straighter. "Do you put vanilla in yours?"

Lois smiled and brought her hands together as if in prayer. "You are my new best friend! Let me show you where everything is."

The stabilized whipping cream wasn't for the cupcakes Sadie had just taken out of the oven; it was for the two hundred tres leche cupcakes that had spent the morning soaking up the three-milk glaze in the cooler at the back of the shop.

Lois helped Sadie bring the trays out, then showed her how to fill the hollowed portion in each cake—made with an apple corer before the three-milk glaze was added—with the stabilized whipping cream. By the time Lois had finished showing Sadie how it was done, Sadie was excited to attack the project.

"Once they're filled, I finish them up with a swirl of cinnamon buttercream frosting and a white chocolate dot on top. The buttercream is already bagged and in the cooler. You'll want to let it sit out for fifteen minutes before you pipe it. Are you sure you're okay to do this on your own?"

"This is heaven," Sadie said, grinning widely and aching to get to work. She looked back at the cupcakes she'd be filling. "Are these for the Fiesta?" It was only Wednesday, early to complete the cupcakes not needed until Saturday morning.

"No," Lois said, "I have a special order tonight—two hundred each of my tres leches and dulce de leche cupcakes. The dulces are done already, boxed and ready in the cooler. But the tres leches have a few additional steps I haven't been able to get to. I've got to get them to the Palace Street Gallery by five thirty." She could not have smiled any bigger, showing how very proud she was of the job.

"Oh, wow, a gallery?" Sadie said, fanning Lois's excitement. "How exciting to be a part of that."

"I know," Lois said, bringing her shoulders up to her ears as she grinned widely. "It's this beautiful historic building in Old Town, which is exciting in and of itself, but the cupcakes are for Ethan Standage's annual art exhibit. Someone told him about my signature tres leches cupcakes, and Ethan himself came in to sample them a few weeks ago. He said they were just what he was looking for."

"Ethan Standage," Sadie said, too familiar with the name but trying not to react. "As in the Cold River Ranch Standages?"

"Yeah," Lois said, nodding. She started measuring out the gelatin for the stabilized whipping cream into a glass bowl. It was almost four in the afternoon, a slow time for any food establishment, but Lois wasn't about to waste a second of it. Sadie grabbed a measuring cup and headed for the sink to fill it in hopes of keeping up with Lois's practiced movements.

"He's an artist?"

"A photographer. He exhibits his annual heritage line at the Palace Gallery a few days before the Fiesta every year. He's very talented, and apparently has excellent taste in cupcakes as well, since he chose mine." She grinned again just as a ding from the front made her hurry toward the dividing door, leaving Sadie to ponder this new discovery while working on the biggest batch of stabilized whipped cream she'd ever made in her life.

She mixed the gelatin and set it aside while whipping the cream, all the time wondering why so many roads led to the Standage family. The second question was perhaps even more important: Was she willing to follow those roads and see where they led?

Dulce de Leche Frosting

2 sticks unsalted butter, softened
4 cups sifted powdered sugar, divided
2 teaspoons vanilla extract
¼ cup heavy cream or milk, divided
1 (13.4-ounce) can of dulce de leche, divided (found in the Mexican
   food section of your grocery store, or at a Mexican market)
Dash of salt

In a large mixing bowl, cream butter. Slowly add 2 cups powdered sugar. Add vanilla and half of the cream and half of the dulce de leche; mix until well blended. Add the remaining cream and dulce de leche and blend well. Add salt. Continue adding up to the remaining 2 cups of powdered sugar until you reach desired consistency. Mix on medium for about 2 minutes to achieve a smooth and creamy result.

CHAPTER 19

Sadie tried to talk herself out of the idea that began forming in her mind while she worked on the cupcakes, but she was difficult to convince. When Caro returned and set right back into asking about what had happened at the police station, Sadie used the gallery exhibit as an excuse to change the subject.

"Have you ever been to one of Ethan Standage's exhibits?" Sadie asked.

Caro hadn't, but talked in awe of Standage's talent. He'd done a community presentation about still-life portraiture last year that Caro deemed "brilliant." Sadie asked if Caro knew Benny, the foreman at the ranch.

"Mexican guy, right?"

Sadie nodded.

"Just by name," Caro said. "He's been working there since he was a kid, I think. How do you know Benny?"

"He bailed out the guy who was arrested with me Monday night," Sadie said. She realized her mistake when Caro got that excited look on her face and started asking more questions about the bar fight, the arrest, and Sadie's return trip to the police station. So much for trying to change the subject.

When Lois came back to check on things, Caro verified with her that the cupcakes were for the Palace Street Gallery. "Do you want Sadie and me to take them over for you?"

Sadie had filled half the cupcakes and was refilling the pastry bag with stabilized whipping cream in order to fill some more. Caro's question was the exact one Sadie had been forming in her own mind. She'd love to see this part of Ethan Standage's life up close, and she couldn't help but think it was some kind of gift to have this opportunity, like a little package with a tag that read "Open me!"

"Could you really drop them off for me?" Lois asked, her eyebrows going up as her hands came together in that pleading gesture again. "I was going to take them over myself, but if I could spend another hour here instead, it would give me a head start for tomorrow."

"We can totally drop them off on our way home," Caro said. She looked over at Sadie, lifting her eyebrows expectantly.

"Sounds great," Sadie said.

Molly showed up to run the front counter, which allowed Lois to come help them in the back. She mixed up enough cupcake batter to fill the lined pans and put them into the oven to bake before helping Sadie and Caro finish the cupcakes for the gallery. With Lois's help—which felt like two people—they got the cupcakes filled and frosted in no time. Caro topped each peak of frosting with a white chocolate disk placed at a jaunty angle, while Lois added a sprinkle of powdered sugar mixed with cinnamon. Sadie put the finished cupcakes in the teal bakery boxes; Lois's signature color that set her apart from the traditional pink-and-white boxes most bakeries defaulted to.

The visit to the police station and impound lot had distracted

Sadie from lunch—something that rarely happened to her—and handling all these cupcakes had reminded her that she hadn't had anything to eat since her bowl of reheated posole that morning. When Lois offered them both a cupcake, Sadie didn't even bother being polite about making sure Lois was sincere.

She'd never had a "wet" cupcake before and worried it would be messy as she peeled back the liner. The cupcake, however, had absorbed the glaze pretty well and though it was a little sticky, what were some sticky fingers in comparison with heavenly deliciousness?

"This is amazing," Sadie said between bites. "You developed this recipe yourself?"

Lois gave a humble shrug, but her smile revealed her pleasure at the praise. "I love playing around in the kitchen. What can I say?"

The cupcakes were due to the gallery by 5:30; Caro and Sadie were fifteen minutes early as they drove along the front of the whitewashed building. The gallery was two stories high with tall windows set along the front and columns that supported a balcony that looked more decorative than functional. The roof had the traditional terra-cotta tiles layered across its slight pitch. Black shutters flanked the long narrow windows, while two huge clay pots displayed bright geraniums, adding just the right touch of warmth and color. They parked behind the gallery and each carried a box through the service door.

A middle-aged white woman with platinum hair pulled back in a twist introduced herself as JoAnna, the event coordinator for the gallery. She wore a pink and white housedress but Sadie could see the hem of a fancier blue dress beneath it. She had marbled gray Crocs on her feet. Some women might judge such an ugly shoe harshly, but Sadie owned a pair of Crocs herself and knew that sometimes comfort had to trump visual appeal. She did hope JoAnna had a different pair of shoes she'd be wearing to the showing though. Santa Fe was known as the "City Different" due to an abundance of unique cultures and lifestyles, but wearing Crocs to an art exhibit seemed too eclectic even for this city.

JoAnna directed them through a doorway and instructed them to go up the stairs against the left side of the gallery, where they'd find a table set up in the loft. "The serving room is the furthest door on the left, behind the table. Go ahead and stack the boxes in the fridge. I understand they need to be served cold, right?"

Caro nodded just as JoAnna's phone rang. She waved them toward the stairs as she hurried to answer it. "Palace Street Gallery," she said in a chipper tone.

Sadie followed Caro, but they both slowed as they entered the exhibit area so as to take it in while heading toward the stairs.

High ceilings with intricate crown molding gave the illusion of a room bigger than it really was, and a partition in the middle provided both a focal point the crowd could rotate around as well as extra wall space to display the uniform 18 x 18 framed photographs. The gallery had knotty hardwood floors, shiny at the edges and worn in places where thousands of feet had trod. A staircase was built into the south end of the building, leading up to the loft. Each of the walls was painted in one of the traditional Southwestern colors: aqua, coral, lavender, or gold. The bold colors emphasized the white mattes surrounding each black-and-white photograph. It was a striking showcase.

As they passed through the gallery, Sadie noted that each photo featured an artifact as the focal point. "Where does he find these artifacts?" she asked. "On Standage land?"

Though laws had been enacted in the 1970s to prevent people from taking artifacts from public lands, if someone owned the land where items were found, they retained ownership and could then display or sell the items so long as they included the correct provenance—paperwork about where and when the item was found. Burial sites were precluded from this rule, however, and anything associated with graves was legally owned by the contemporary tribe. Based on Sadie's understanding of how things worked, and the recent enforcements of these laws, it felt strange to see artifacts displayed so openly. Was the BLM aware of these photos? Had they investigated the pieces displayed here?

Sadie had read about people who had slowly dismantled entire settlements of ruins located on their privately owned land, selling off the history bit by bit.

"These aren't from Standage land," Caro said from a few steps ahead. "Ethan takes these intense exploration trips twice a year, repelling into slot canyons and seeking out hiding places no one else has found before."

"But it's illegal to take artifacts from public land," Sadie said, looking at the photographs differently as she and Caro rounded the staircase and moved up to the loft. If Ethan Standage was involved in artifact theft, it opened up a whole new possibility in regards to Shel and Langley's connection to the ranch. "How does he get away with displaying his proof so publicly? I thought he was a vocal preservationist."

"He only photographs the items," Caro said. "He leaves them where he found them, and he keeps the location secret. That's kind of his motto: 'Take pictures and leave footprints.'"

"Oh," Sadie said, almost disappointed to have her budding theory shot down so quickly. She looked at a picture of an elaborate woven basket as she rounded the corner of the staircase and tried to come up with another explanation about the

Standage-Shel-Langley-archeology connection. Maybe Shel and Langley were preservationists too?

Upstairs, at the far side of the open loft area, a long table was set up and covered with white tablecloths, puckered and pleated to create a textured surface. Tiered serving trays and cake pedestals were waiting to be filled. Ribbons the same colors as the walls were woven among the folds of white fabric, adding a breath of color to the display. A doorway behind the table led to a room complete with a refrigerator, countertops, and a large table—basically a kitchen without a stove, though there was a microwave.

Sadie glanced at the cheap plastic clock above the fridge. It was 5:25. "Is someone managing the refreshment table?" she asked as Caro balanced her box in one arm and pulled the door of the refrigerator open.

"I don't know," Caro said. The shelves had been removed from the fridge, leaving a big open space for them to stack the cupcake boxes. Caro put hers on the bottom, then turned to get Sadie's.

"The exhibit opens at six, and there's no one here to serve," Sadie said once her arms were empty.

"I'm sure someone will be here soon," Caro said, letting the refrigerator door close and following Sadie back to the loft. On their way to get the next set of boxes, they passed two young men on their way up the stairs, each of them holding a commercial dishwasher tray full of glassware.

By the third trip upstairs, Sadie could hear JoAnna barking orders at the half dozen people dressed in black who had gathered near a display table at the front of the main floor. One of the men they'd passed on the stairs had cleared away the serving trays on part of the table and was setting out narrow, fluted glasses. His name tag read THOMAS. Another man was on his way up the stairs, carrying a wooden case of champagne bottles. A sample bottle of the champagne was displayed in a silver wine bucket for the benefit of the guests. Loathe as Sadie was to admit it, the cupcakes seemed a little informal compared to the rest of the gathering. She wondered why Ethan Standage had chosen cupcakes over gourmet cheeses or fancy chocolates.

"Are you two keeping up the serving table?" Thomas asked when they came out of the serving area empty-handed. He did a poor job of hiding the fact that he was looking them over head to toe. Every other "worker" Sadie had seen, him included, was dressed in all black. Caro wore khaki pants and a teal buttoned-up shirt while Sadie was dressed in jeans and a blue-and-white striped T-shirt.

"We're just delivery," Caro explained. Sadie glanced at the clock. The gallery would open soon. Where were the servers?

"I see," he said, looking a little less confused as to why they weren't in the right uniform. He glanced at his watch and straightened a line of glasses. "I hope they hurry, then."

Sadie and Caro agreed, wished both men a good evening, and headed downstairs. Sadie wanted to take more time and look over the photos, but it felt presumptuous to do so. Several workers were still hurrying back and forth taking care of last-minute details, and Sadie didn't want to get in the way. Maybe she'd come back tonight as a guest. She'd get another cupcake if she did. That alone was worth getting dressed up for. The exhibit was open to the public, right?

"Thanks, ladies," JoAnna said as she blew past them on her way to another part of the gallery. She'd taken off the housedress, revealing a lovely light blue dress, and had swapped her Crocs for silver pumps Sadie feared would have her limping by the end of the night. The showing went until ten.

"You're welcome," Caro said to JoAnna's retreating figure. They were almost to the back entrance when Sadie put a hand on Caro's arm.

"Hang on a minute," she said impulsively before turning to follow JoAnna.

She found JoAnna in a small office, thumbing through a stack of papers, pulling out one now and then and putting it aside. Invoices, maybe?

"Do you need help with the serving table tonight?" Sadie asked from the doorway.

"I don't think so," JoAnna said, distracted as she considered one of the papers, then kept it in the main stack. "We hired a couple of guys from La Fonda. Didn't you see them up there?"

"Yes, they're up there," Sadie said. "But I had the impression they weren't expecting to serve the cupcakes."

JoAnna looked up, a concerned expression on her face that passed a few moments later. "It's just cupcakes and champagne, I'm sure they can keep up."

"You know, I could help with the cupcakes," she said. "It would be no trouble."

JoAnna looked at her thoughtfully, and Sadie hurried to make the deal even sweeter. "The boys could then pass drinks rather than stay upstairs. No charge, of course. Consider it a thank-you gift from Modern Cupcakes by Lois. This is wonderful exposure for us."

"Really?" JoAnna said, looking unsure.

"Really," Sadie said with a smile. She waved toward the front of the gallery. "I know how intense events like this can get, and I'm happy to take over that one small part in order to free everyone up from having to worry about it."

JoAnna's eyes moved toward Sadie's clothes.

"I live a few minutes away and can be in uniform before the gallery opens."

JoAnna paused another moment, then broke into a wide grin. "Deal. Thank you."

Sadie found Caro texting by the back door and explained what she'd done as they headed toward their cars.

"What a great idea," Caro said, her bright eyes wide with excitement. "This will be fun!"

Sadie hadn't offered Caro's help, but obviously she expected to be a part of it. Normally, Sadie would love the company.

"What about Rex?" Sadie asked. Caro hadn't mentioned what her plan was for dinner; Wednesday was always her day to cook.

"He's a big boy," Caro said dismissively. "He can forage for himself. It'll be good for him. I'll meet you at home, and we can drive back to the gallery together."

"Maybe Rex would like to come to the showing," Sadie offered. "You two could come to the exhibit together, and maybe get dinner once things quiet down enough that I can handle things on my own."

Caro waved away the suggestion and pulled open the driver's door of her car. "He'd be a curmudgeon," she said. "I'll see you at home."

Feeling as though she had no choice, Sadie got into her own car and followed Caro home. She was starving, but she didn't have time for a full meal. Maybe she could grab something if Rex wasn't in the kitchen.

Sadie had bought a pair of black stretchy dress pants during one of her and Caro's shopping trips a few weeks ago. It had built-in minimizing panels in the front and at the sides, slenderizing Sadie's figure in a way that was worth the $85 she paid. She paired the slacks with a black three-quarter sleeve, scoop-neck top. She really, really wanted to wear the turquoise necklace she'd worn the other night, but none of the other workers at the gallery had worn jewelry, and so she erred on the side of conformity.

Luckily, Sadie didn't see Rex during the quick stop, and within ten minutes, she and Caro were back in Caro's car and headed for the gallery. Sadie ate a handful of crackers and a string cheese during the drive, feeling sufficiently held over, though far from satisfied. Snack food wasn't a real meal, but it turned off the hungries, and for that she was grateful.

At least she had another cupcake to look forward to. It wasn't a meal either, but the satisfaction level would be much higher.

Newspaper article about Indian antiquities
www.deseretnews.com/article/700182124
/Warehouse-protects-thousands-and-thousands-of
-looted-Indian-antiquities.html

CHAPTER 20

They arrived with only minutes to spare before the front doors opened. A dozen people were already visiting with one another on the sidewalk out front. The champagne boys were very happy to see Sadie and Caro, and the shorter of the two, Darron, stayed at the table while Thomas headed downstairs with a tray full of glasses in anticipation of serving the first visitors.

Caro and Sadie set out three dozen cupcakes and then familiarized themselves with more of the loft area—three separate visiting rooms opened into a common area where the serving would take place. They decided to take turns going through those rooms every fifteen minutes or so and picking up stray glasses, napkins, or liners even though each room had its own garbage can.

Sadie wasn't sure what she expected when the doors opened, but there was an almost anticlimactic hush to the conversations that whispered up to the loft area, and it was almost ten full minutes before the first of the guests made their way upstairs. Within half an hour, however, she and Caro were staying busy keeping the table stocked and the visiting rooms clean, while Darron poured champagne and retrieved empty glasses from pretty much every horizontal surface. They developed a good rhythm, Sadie staying mostly in the kitchen area while Caro stayed out front where she knew a surprising number of people.

Before they knew it, it was nearly eight o'clock. Caro had finished her first glass of champagne and started on a second, and they were running low on cupcakes. By 8:30, they'd put out the last of the cupcakes—people must have taken seconds. It seemed impossible that four hundred people had come through the gallery in two and a half hours.

Sadie broke down the empty bakery boxes and washed down the counters, leaving the serving area as clean as it had been before they arrived. Darron had joined Thomas on the main floor, so Sadie took a few minutes to place their dirty glasses into the plastic dishwasher trays. She suspected the glasses were on loan from La Fonda, and later tonight, they would be run through the commercial dishwashers and returned to their usual residence on a shelf somewhere in the historic hotel.

By the time she joined Caro, who was talking to yet another friend, in Spanish, there were only two dozen cupcakes left. Sadie felt guilty eating one of the last cakes, and wished she'd eaten one in the beginning when she wouldn't feel so bad.

When Caro finished her conversation, she suggested they leave the dessert table to its own devices and go look at the prints on display.

"That's a great idea," Sadie said. She'd no sooner said those words when several people on the main floor turned toward the back of the gallery. Moments later, champagne glasses were put down and applause broke out. Sadie leaned over the half wall as far as she could to see what had caused such excitement, but she couldn't see far enough.

"Ethan must be here," Caro said, pointing at the large wrought-iron clock on the front wall of the gallery. "I heard someone say he was coming around nine. He's going to give a little speech, I think." It was 8:40.

Sadie was curious to see the man of the hour, the man whose family ranch seemed to have swallowed Margo whole, but reminded herself to be patient. It had never been her intent to introduce herself to him. She just wanted to be in his space and see him up close.

They made their way downstairs, and Sadie picked up a brochure from the small table set by the front door. Caro was stopped by yet another acquaintance, giving Sadie time to browse the beautifully designed brochure, complete with thumbnail-sized copies of some of Ethan's prints. On the back was a message from Ethan:

The sense of immortality one can take from history is priceless, and I consider it a privilege to do my part in preserving those things that have survived generations, bringing a piece of that immortality with them. With Light and Lens it is my goal to keep the cherishing of these sacred items alive while allowing those same articles to complete their own existence; everything has a right to die, but that does not mean that its life cannot be treasured by those who have followed in the footsteps of the Ancients.

Sadie thought it sounded a little pedantic. The tone was all about reverence and respect, and yet wasn't he exploiting those very items as well? She read the rest of the brochure while Caro finished her conversation. Learning that Ethan had graduated with his master's degree in anthropology from the University of New Mexico a few years ago diffused some of her cynicism. Currently, he taught one class each semester at his alma mater. Was he going to give up his career in order to take over the ranch? It seemed that his passions went wide of his family's industry, yet his mother was in poor health and his father was traveling extensively in order to be both a husband and ranch owner. At the bar, Mike had said several ranches had downsized lately. How had Cold River Ranch been affected by the economic conditions that had seemed to impact other people in the cattle industry?

The brochure explained that each of Ethan's prints was a one-of-a-kind original and that following the production of each piece, Ethan destroyed all electronic copies. Sadie didn't know a lot about the photography art market, but she supposed that destroying digital negatives, which were eternal in theory, was a pretty unique thing to do.

Sadie easily picked out Ethan Standage from the crowd, though she could only see him when people moved out of the way. She guessed he was in his early thirties, but he had the young Bohemian look: overgrown hair, a casual "I'm too busy to shave" growth of beard, and silver-rimmed glasses. He wore a charcoal dress shirt with no tie and a black corduroy jacket. He also wore jeans and designer cowboy boots—the perfect blend of cowboy, artist, and yuppie all rolled together. His teeth were perfectly straight and blindingly white when he smiled, making him look more Hollywood than tree-hugger. He didn't seem particularly comfortable in the crowd, which Sadie found interesting.

Half a dozen people surrounded Ethan near the table where he was selling his books at the front of the gallery. The serpentine flow of the crowd would take Caro and Sadie to him eventually, so Sadie turned her attention to the pictures, just as Caro said *adiós* to her friend.

"So, he really photographs these pieces but leaves them there?"

Sadie asked Caro. It seemed suspect to her. She thought about the discovery of the cave Margo had told her about in the desert, and how careful she'd been to not touch anything for risk of destroying it. Ethan claimed to believe the same thing, but he had to pose the pieces for the photos, taking them out of situ in the process. There was hypocrisy there.

"Yep," Caro said, accepting another glass of champagne from Darron's tray when he passed by. Her third, Sadie noted, while deciding she'd be sure to drive home. She shook her head when Darron offered her a glass of her own.

"I wonder how much they cost?" Sadie looked at the picture of the basket she'd glanced at earlier that evening. The black-and-white photograph was so well contrasted that she could see the intricate design details within the weaving. The basket had been propped against a rock, putting it at an angle, and it showed fraying along the side, either from use or erosion. It was a beautiful picture.

"Oh, gosh," Caro said, laughing uncomfortably as she waved her champagne glass through the air. "Tens of thousands of dollars, hundreds maybe."

"That much?" Sadie asked, turning toward her friend in surprise. People talking near them looked over, and she lowered her voice. "That's unreal."

"These are the *only* prints," Caro said, gesturing toward the gallery wall in front of them. "He destroys even his digital copies so that these are one-of-a-kinds."

The brochure had said as much. "But a hundred thousand dollars?" Sadie repeated. "For a photograph?"

"This is all there is," Caro said, giving Sadie her full attention. "These items are hidden; not available. Ethan spends months out of the year on his expeditions. No one else will be finding these items, which makes the photographs equally valuable. It's the chance to own something without destroying it. Some would say the photos are priceless."

"Okay," Sadie said, understanding what Caro was saying, but still finding the logic flawed. "Why not make five hundred prints and sell them for forty bucks each?"

"Don't you see?" Caro said, her eyebrows raised. "This *is* history." She pointed at another photograph. It was of a double neck jar with one handle intact, and the other one broken. Black lines were painted across it, so meticulous that it seemed impossible that the design was done by hand. The jar sat on top of a flat stone, a prickly pear cactus in the left side of the frame. Another striking piece. "This is the *only* pot like this out there, but it's not available. The photo, however, is. He only makes one print in order to maintain the excitement of ownership for people who understand the mentality of what he does. One pot, one photo. He's not interested in gracing the walls of tourists' homes; he's appealing to collectors and people joined to the heritage he captures."

"How do people know this is the only print?" Sadie asked, wondering if everyone just blindly believed like Caro did. Did no one question Ethan Standage and his conflicting motivations? "What if he doesn't really destroy the print and makes and sells other copies too?"

"He'd be caught," Caro said, shaking her head. Sadie noticed that she was talking louder than usual, likely from the champagne. "He publishes an anthology of the pieces each year. It's the only other format through which he displays his photos. In the books, he talks about the item and its history and region. Not enough info for anyone to find the items' locations, but enough to give credibility to his work. Then he sells the original picture in a sealed and signed frame, as well as a few other shots of the piece from every angle—not posed, just for reference and insurance reasons. Anyway, if he sold duplicates, someone would find out. No one wants a numbered print of these pieces, they want the *only* print. It's Ethan's hook, so to speak."

Sadie looked at another print on the wall. "How long has he been doing this?"

"This is the exhibit's tenth anniversary. The pieces will be on display for a couple of months, then whatever isn't sold will go into catalogue sales."

Sadie did quick math in her head. If Ethan took just fifteen photos a year—he'd done twenty-three this year—and sold them for an average of fifty thousand dollars, he'd have brought in three quarters of a million dollars every year for ten years—or seven and a half million dollars over the last decade. Holy cow!

One photograph was of a wolf effigy. Another featured a carved antler showing incredible detail, though part of the carving was worn smooth—perhaps from water dripping into its hiding place? In other frames, there were baskets and pots, and one was of a partially uncovered skull, only the eye sockets above the ground, as though the skeleton were watching the crowds as they looked upon it.

"They are amazing," Sadie said as the spirit of the pieces settled upon her despite her determination not to fall under the spell. She tried not to visualize having one of these prints in her own home, but the temptation of ownership got stronger by the minute . . . until she reminded herself of the price tag, then the feeling quickly dissipated. Between Sadie's husband's life insurance, her brother's careful investing, and her own self-discipline, Sadie was well cared for financially, but something like this was galaxies away from her reality.

It was hard to imagine anyone could afford to hang fifty thousand dollars on a wall.

Caro nodded while admiring a print of a partially broken pot. The broken shards were laid out on the ground, but if you looked closely, you could see the hairline cracks running through the intact portion of the pot. The background was dark, and Sadie wondered if Standage had photographed the pot just as he found it, hidden somewhere, not daring to move it for fear of it crumbling further. Sadie had encountered many pots like this on the dig, and she thought about the one intact pot she'd brought up; only for it to lay in pieces at her feet. It was painful to think about.

She stopped to look at a photograph of an intricately carved pipe, the remnants of feathers still tied to the end, grains of sand trailing from the bowl.

Caro raised her hand to touch it, it looked that real. "They're beautiful," she whispered reverently. "I've never seen his prints, just the anthologies."

"Do you own any of his anthologies?"

Caro shook her head. "Maybe I'll buy one tonight. They're lovely books."

They were nearly to the end of the display, within a dozen feet of Ethan Standage, when a sudden hush fell over the crowd, and everyone turned toward the front of the gallery. A large man with a cowboy hat stood in front of Sadie, causing her to go up on her tiptoes and step from one side to the other until she found a gap between other people's heads that she could look through. Ethan stepped up onto some kind of platform; Sadie couldn't see it, she only saw him rise a few feet.

"Welcome, welcome, *bienvenidos*," he said as a final ripple of whispered conversation faded from the room. "I thank each one of you for coming to the exhibit tonight. I returned to Santa Fe just this morning and, as always, was overwhelmed with feelings of being home again." The room applauded, and he gave the crowd a nervous smile before clearing his throat and speaking again. "It is always such a humbling experience to put my year's work on display and to see so many people coming to join me in celebrating it. Today marks ten years of artifacts captured for the sake of timeless reverence." A smattering of applause broke out, and he hushed it by pressing his palm down in the air, an odd tension to his face.

Again, Sadie had the impression that he didn't want to be there, didn't want to make a speech at all. She wondered if anyone else noticed.

He cleared his throat and continued, "When I was a boy, my *abuelita* would make the most delicious tres leches cake, and I chose that as the theme of this year's exhibit."

Caro elbowed Sadie softly, and they shared a smile at the connection he'd just given to the desserts Lois had provided. That's why he was willing to suffer all those sticky fingers. Sadie looked around the gallery, noticing for the first time all the different white flowers and white swaths of fabric draped over the windows and tables. Did all his showings have a theme?

"For *Abuelita*," Ethan continued, "tres leches cake was a connection to her Mexican heritage, but she once told me that it also represented three elements of her life—religion, nourishment, and the need for something sweet now and again." A polite chuckle rippled through the crowd. Ethan smiled and spoke as though every word he said was memorized. "Over the years, I have found my own three milks—*tres leches*—that have nourished me and given me purpose in my life. My personal representations of the three milks—the three essential elements of balance—are temporal reverence, spiritual acuity, and creative expression. Temporal reverence is about the care with which we reverence the earth and its resources, understanding that without its succor, all else is lost. Spiritual acuity is about remembering from whence we came and the purpose of existing as we do." He paused and stared at the floor, seemingly out of place for a moment. Someone started to applaud and that snapped him out of his wandering thoughts. Was he drunk? He hurried to speak louder, before the clapping caught on. "The, uh, creative expression is all about how we give a piece of ourselves"—he put a hand on his chest—"to the world around us. *That* is the nourishment and sweetness I hope to share with the world. My own tres leches."

He took his hand from his chest and waved it, palm up, in a slow arch, encompassing the gallery and causing many patrons to follow the trajectory of his fingers and look at the prints on the walls a second time. A woman behind Sadie sniffled. Another woman standing a few feet ahead of them was wiping at her eyes.

For Sadie's part, she couldn't help but think about the fact that the twenty-three prints on the wall could sell for upwards of a million dollars. Sadie wasn't opposed to people making money, but for her, the pseudo-spirituality of Ethan Standage's "tres leches" was lost in the extreme profitability of his work. Did he know that the original tres leches cake was actually developed as part of a marketing gimmick to increase sales of canned milk? She'd no sooner thought that, however, when Caro turned toward her, her eyes glassy from unshed tears.

"I love that," she whispered. "Tres leches—what nourishes him, nourishes all."

Sadie nearly pointed out the dichotomy, but held her tongue. She was on Ethan's turf, and Caro was working on her third glass of champagne. Arguing the contradictions of this man was out of place. Sadie wondered what the Standage family thought of Ethan's art. Were they supportive? Since he made millions of dollars, they probably were.

"So I thank you," Ethan said, bowing slightly toward the crowd. "For being a part of this journey I am on, and for validating my life's ambition, which is to preserve those things that will be lost forever so that we might not forget who we are and who has blazed the trail before us."

The room erupted with applause. He thanked everyone again and stepped down from his platform, looking relieved. Maybe he just wasn't comfortable speaking in public. Within a few minutes, the crowd was moving and mingling again. Ethan made his way to the back of the room, and the crowd tightened around him.

Sadie and Caro made their way to the table filled with anthologies. Last year's book was *Eagle's Point*, and the year before it was *At Morning's Light*. She and Caro both picked up a book and began thumbing through the pages, commenting on the artistic appeal of the layout. In addition to the photographs, there were large portions of text. Sadie skimmed a few pages, enough to appreciate the depth of information Ethan included. His knowledge of anthropology was apparent in the detailed descriptions he gave of the time periods and the people who would have used the items.

"So Ethan isn't a collector himself?" Sadie asked.

"The Standage family has an extensive collection of their own," Caro said, putting down the book she'd been holding and picking up another one. Her words were sounding a little fuzzy. "It's all from their own land, or purchased over the years. When he was at NMU, Ethan photographed several of the more unique pieces and compiled them into a book as part of a project for one of his classes. I've heard that's when he fell in love with photography," she explained, scanning the table. "Here is a copy of the Standage collection," she said triumphantly, pulling the thinnest of the books from the table. There were only a few copies left. "I've heard these are hard to find." She opened the book and started flipping through the pages, admiring the colored photographs; the rest of the anthologies were all black and white.

"I think I'll get this one," Caro said, closing the book. "Though I'd really like the *Tres Leches* one too." The cover for *Tres Leches* featured the pipe photograph they'd admired earlier. Caro put her empty glass on a tray of empty glasses, and Sadie hoped that meant Caro was done with the night's beverage refreshment.

Sadie wasn't sure whether to buy a book of her own, and she scanned the room again, looking at the faces of the attendees—Ethan's supporters. Were Caro's opinions of Ethan's integrity reflected in the general consensus of these people? It was after nine thirty, and the room was still full. They could have brought another hundred cupcakes for a crowd this size.

Sadie looked up at the loft and noted that the crowds had thinned considerably. She and Caro needed to remove the trays that were surely empty by now. Maybe she'd get started on that so they could go home and she could work on learning more about Ethan Standage. She was turning back to Caro when a familiar face in the loft crowd caught her attention. More importantly, it was a familiar set of eyes that startled her—black and blue eyes to be exact.

Shel.

The swelling had gone down some since yesterday morning, but the purple rings under his eyes were darker now that gravity had pulled the pooling blood to the thin-skinned area. He stood on the edge of the loft with a glass of champagne in one hand and stared down at her.

Sadie refused to look away and stared right back while wondering why he was here. She'd already connected him to the Standage ranch through Benny bailing him out, and to the archeology through his work. Was he also connected to the artistic part of Ethan's life? How?

After a few seconds, Shel pointed to one of the doors at the top of the stairs that led to one of the sitting areas, and jerked his head toward it. Then he turned and headed for the door, disappearing a moment later, and leaving Sadie with a difficult decision to make that turned out not to be that difficult after all.

CHAPTER 21

"Caro," Sadie said, tapping her friend on the shoulder. "I'll be right back."

"Where are you going?" Caro asked. There were two people ahead of her in line for the cash register.

"Upstairs," Sadie said, her eyes on the door Shel had disappeared through. "I'll just be a minute."

Caro turned back to the cashier, and Sadie climbed the stairs slowly, hoping to center herself and not appear as anxious as she felt. Before entering the room, she looked back at Caro long enough to see that she wasn't watching.

Sadie slipped through the doorway and shut the door behind her, but stood with her back against it and her hand on the knob in case she needed to make a run for it—or needed something to brace herself with while she kicked Shel in the face. The taupe-painted room was furnished with a set of nice leather couches and a wicker coffee table with a glass top. A variety of watercolors hung on the wall depicting the New Mexican desert.

Shel was standing in front of one of three long, thin windows that were framed by elegantly carved, bright white trim. He turned to face her when she closed the door. His expression wasn't angry, which served to make her even more suspicious.

His face looked worse up close, all the individual colors easier to see. When she was black and blue—which had happened more often than she liked to admit during her recent various adventures—she tried to stay home as much as possible. And *she* could get away with foundation in a pinch.

"I didn't expect to see you here," Shel said, setting down his half-full glass of champagne.

"I didn't expect to see you here either."

He paused as though waiting for her to say more. When she didn't, he continued, "I guess it's a good thing. I wanted to apologize for Monday night."

Of all the things he could have said, an apology wasn't what she'd expected.

He put his hands in the pockets of his Dockers. "I was pretty drunk," he explained with an apologetic shrug as he rocked back on the heels of his scuffed dress shoes. "And things got out of control. Are you okay?"

"Am I okay?" Sadie repeated incredulously, finally finding her voice. She tried to balance his current humility with his arrogance of Monday night, but the equation didn't make sense. "I got arrested because of you."

Shel let out a breath. "I know," he said dropping his chin. "And I'm really sorry about it. Like I said, I had too much to drink. It doesn't look like you were hurt too bad; you're not limping or anything. That's good."

Sadie still didn't know what to make of the apology, but she was willing to see it as an opportunity to get some information, provided she proceeded carefully. "I've got some bumps and bruises, but nothing serious. Sorry about your nose."

He waved away her apology. "I've had worse. Though I'll be telling everyone I know that the other guy was twice my size, if you don't mind."

Sadie smiled at his joke, then they lapsed into silence. He was almost charming, but it was at such odds with the man from the bar on Monday night that she didn't dare let her guard down entirely.

"Anyway, I'm sorry."

"It's okay," Sadie said. She gathered her courage so as to take full advantage of the opportunity. "Do you remember what we were talking about that caused everything to explode like it did?"

He hesitated, but then nodded.

She kept her voice low and sincere when she spoke again, hoping to invite his trust. "Why did you keep digging, Shel?"

His expression sobered quickly, and he turned to the window again, his back to her. She watched his shoulders rise with a deep breath and then fall as he exhaled. "It's a complicated answer, which leads to more complicated questions that I don't know the answers to."

"Someone told you to, right?" Sadie said for him. Langley had said as much at the bar. "You knew the bodies were there."

"I didn't *know* anything. I still don't."

"We'd already found a body," she said when he didn't elaborate. "But you knew there was another one. Did you have something to do with the bodies being there in the first place?" She gripped the doorknob behind her back tighter than ever, ready to run if fire leaped into his eyes. She'd just accused him of being an accessory to murder at the very least. Him freaking out would not be an unexpected response.

"No," he said strongly, shaking his head but showing far less reaction than she'd expected. He continued to look out the window as he spoke. "I'd noticed a burial mound that looked out of place. When you guys found that first body, I took a chance and dug into the one I'd seen. I was right, but it was stupid. It would have been dug up eventually. I just . . ." He let out a breath. "I acted rashly."

"You made a phone call right afterward," she said. He turned to look at her. "Who did you call? Was it the person who told you about the bodies?"

He said nothing, and Sadie pushed even further. "Surely you know that whoever told you there were bodies buried at the site may very well be the person who put them there in the first place."

A flicker of doubt crossed his face, and he looked toward the door but then quickly shook it off. "It wasn't him."

"Him?" Sadie repeated, going through all the other men she knew of who could be associated with this. Only one came to mind. "Langley?"

Shel looked genuinely confused. "Langley? What does Langley have to do with this?"

"You tell me," Sadie countered. "What part did he play in the operation?"

"Langley wasn't involved in this at all. I told him too much over some beers one night, and then on Monday, he totally turned on me when you guys showed up at the bar."

Shel seemed to believe what he was saying.

"Have you talked to Langley since Monday?" Sadie asked.

"No, and I don't plan to. I'm leaving tomorrow, going back to my old crew in Arizona. I'll be glad to leave New Mexico behind again—my luck has never been very good in this state, but I think I've learned my lesson this time."

"What brought you here in the first place?"

His eyes looked wary again. "The job with D&E."

And yet he could go right back to his old job in Arizona? That meant he hadn't been fired from his former position and would be welcomed back. So why come to work in New Mexico at all? "What's your connection to Cold River Ranch?"

His jaw flexed, which meant the ranch was a sensitive subject, and that Sadie was getting closer to whatever secrets he was hiding. "The ranch foreman bailed you out of jail. Is he a . . . friend?"

"A friend of a friend," Shel said, looking at the ground for a few seconds before looking up with a more resolute expression. A buzz sounded from his pocket and he pulled out his cell phone, reading and replying to a text message. It was the same phone he'd used at the dig after digging up that second body. Maybe she could pass that information on to the police and they could trace the number somehow. He finished with his phone and put it back in his pocket. "I need to go."

"What about Margo?" Sadie asked, still needing answers.

Shel let out a breath and his eyes narrowed. "Don't tell me she's here too. I'm not sure I can sincerely apologize to her. The woman's insane. Did you hear her call me Crossbones? Like I'm in some kind of motorcycle gang or something. Honestly, the woman is nuts."

Would he dare say such things about Margo if he had something to do with her disappearance? "The police are looking for her," Sadie said, taking note of his surprised reaction. "She followed Langley from the bar Monday night. It's the last anyone has seen of her. I think they went to Cold River Ranch. And then the foreman—Benny—bailed you out of jail a few hours later. Did he take you to the ranch too?"

"No, he took me to the apartment I share with a couple other guys." He didn't seem to understand why this was important to her.

"Did he bail you out as a favor to someone else? This friend the two of you share?" Shel *had* to be connected to Ethan—he was at Ethan's exhibit tonight and he'd been bailed out by Ethan's foreman. But Shel had been working so hard to keep that information to himself that she was loathe to confront him with it directly. In the process she might miss out on information he would willingly give up.

"She left with Langley? No one's seen her?"

"The police found her Land Cruiser this morning, parked since Tuesday morning near Langley's apartment."

"Langley?" Shel repeated, looking off to the side as though thinking very hard about something.

Sadie tried to wait him out, but she couldn't help but push again. "Margo called me after you and I were arrested," she said, hoping her instincts about telling him more of the story were accurate.

His expression grew even more troubled. Whatever he was putting together in his mind was causing him a great deal of concern.

"She left me a message saying that she needed my help." But she wasn't in fear of her life, Sadie remembered. At least, she wasn't when she left the message. "She never came home. She isn't answering her phone."

"I—I need to go," Shel said suddenly, moving toward the door.

Sadie stood her ground, her hand still on the doorknob and her body blocking his way.

"Margo's my friend," Sadie said. "Please tell me what you know. Maybe it will allow me to help her." However, Sadie's sympathies toward Shel were triggered now too. Was he caught up in something he didn't understand?

"I don't know anything about her," he said. "But . . . let me see what I can find out." The tightness of his jaw and resolute look in his eye showed growing urgency.

Sadie needed more answers, but she knew that tenacity might not be the best way to get them at the moment. "Let me give you my number," she said, pulling her phone out of her pocket. "And let me get yours as well so we can keep in touch."

He hesitated, but then went ahead and gave her his number before typing hers into his own phone and labeling it "Sarah from Dig." Sadie didn't bother to correct him; there was no point in confusing him further. She finally moved aside and let him leave before following him out to the loft. He didn't say good-bye or apologize again, instead he took the stairs two at a time and disappeared through the front door. She stared after him, hoping he would really call her when he learned something. Had she handled that correctly? What if she never saw him again and this was her only chance to get information? Had she blown it?

"Where have you been?"

Sadie startled. She'd been so wrapped up in her thoughts that she had forgotten all about Caro, who was now standing in front of her at the top of the stairs with her arms folded across her chest. Worry had pulled her brow together in a deep furrow. "Who was that guy?"

Sadie looked back into Caro's confused and angry face. "Sorry," she said, trying to catch up and smile as though everything was normal. "Did you already get a cupcake, or are they gone?"

"A cupcake?" Caro repeated, throwing her arms out in a gesture too dramatic for the situation. "I'm not talking about a cupcake, Sadie!" she almost yelled. Several heads turned to look at them. "Who was that guy? What were you doing in that room?"

"Caro," Sadie said, quietly, remembering how many drinks Caro had had and hoping she would follow Sadie's example of calmness even as her face got hot. She put her hand on Caro's arm, but Caro shook it off. "Calm down, it's okay."

"It's not okay!" Caro said, tears suddenly overflowing and rolling down her cheeks. "I thought we were friends, Sadie. Why are you shutting me out?"

CHAPTER 22

Nothing short of divine intervention could have calmed Caro down. Luckily, that's exactly what happened. Father David, the pastor from Caro's church, was at the exhibit, and when he heard Caro carrying on, he ascended the stairs and was able to pull her into a corner to talk with her quietly, while Sadie tried to pretend people weren't staring.

Finally, Sadie went to clean up the serving table. Several minutes later, Father David brought a contrite but still weepy Caro back to Sadie. Assured that Sadie would see her home safely, he walked them to the back door—past an oblivious JoAnna—and watched until Sadie waved at him before getting into the driver's seat. Caro was somber, sniffling all the way home while she looked out the passenger window. Sadie wanted to blame the champagne, but she knew it had only numbed the filters that had kept Caro from pushing the issue of Sadie pulling away.

In the garage, Sadie shifted into park but let the car idle. "Caro," she said, quietly, "I'm sorry that I can't talk to you about all this stuff anymore. It's—"

Caro looked at her with red eyes. "Why can't you? I'm not going to tell anyone else. I thought we were a team."

"We were when I was working on the reports, but now with the police involved and everything, it's complicated."

"But to not tell me *anything*? Nothing at all? Why don't you trust me anymore?"

Sadie didn't know what to say. Her goal of not hurting Caro wasn't working, but she didn't know how to fix it either. The truth would hurt her just as much. "Of course I trust you, Caro. It's just gotten complicated and legal and stuff, and I just can't talk about it," Sadie said, trying to choose her words carefully. "I've been . . . told not to involve you."

"You have?" Her voice shook, and she wiped her eyes. "What did I do wrong? I know I said too much about my relationship with Rex last night; I could tell you were uncomfortable with it. Is that why you won't talk to me?"

Sadie touched Caro's arm. "It has nothing to do with that," she said, though she feared the discord between Rex and Caro was a big part of Rex asking Sadie to leave. "I wish I could explain." Caro was assuming it was Pete or the police who had instructed her to stay silent. If it was one of them, Sadie could at least promise to fill her in later, but she couldn't even do that. What would Caro say if she knew it was Rex?

Because it *was* Rex, the temptation to just tell Caro was strong; it would let Sadie off the hook, and perhaps save their friendship from being damaged, perhaps beyond repair. But the potential fall-out of Caro's marriage was too high a price. "I'm so sorry," Sadie repeated quietly.

Caro looked away, staring at the door that led into the house but making no move to go inside.

Sadie turned off the car and pushed the button that closed the garage door behind them. "I'm going to Albuquerque tomorrow. There are some things I need to do down there," Sadie said, hating to drop the bombshell when Caro was already upset, but thinking maybe it was better than upsetting her all over again tomorrow. "I'll still be able to help Lois with her booth at the Fiesta, but I think it's best for me to leave."

Caro nodded, still looking away.

"Thank you for everything you've done to help me, Caro. Staying in your home is the most comfortable I've felt in a really long time. You're one of the kindest women I know, and I'll always treasure your friendship."

"You know, I could find out what's going on myself," Caro said, almost too quietly to be heard, though what she said was more shocking than the tone of her voice.

"Excuse me?" Sadie said, stalling as she processed her surprise at what sounded like a threat.

Caro finally turned toward her and lifted her chin, though it was still trembling. "You're not the only one with skills, you know. I can help you with this. I know I can."

"It's not about that, Caro. And I'm not investigating. The police are. I'm out of it, and you need to stay out of it, too."

Caro turned away and let herself out of the car without another word.

Sadie watched her go through the door to the house and hung her head. *Please let it be the champagne that fueled her threats of digging into this.* Maybe she should just go to Albuquerque tonight, rip off the Band-Aid all at once. But she had two months' worth of living to pack up, so she may as well get to it. Luckily, Caro worked tomorrow, so Sadie would be able to avoid another difficult exchange.

She got out of the car and entered the house. Rex's big black truck had been in the garage, but Sadie couldn't hear the TV. The house was uncomfortably quiet, and Sadie imagined that Caro had already gone to her room, where she was probably crying.

Sadie was a few steps into the kitchen when her phone signaled a text message. She continued toward her apartment while pulling her phone out of her purse, but stumbled when the name of the sender registered as Margo.

I'm fine. Back off. Don't talk to anyone.

Sadie stared at the text, catching her breath before hitting reply. She'd already typed out part of a response asking if Margo was okay before pausing mid-word. Was it really Margo on the other end of this conversation?

A door shutting somewhere deeper in the house reminded her she was still in the kitchen. She hurried to her apartment and shut the door so she could concentrate and try to put the stress associated with Rex and Caro aside for a moment. She threw her purse on the bed and sat down on the edge of the mattress.

Sadie: Where are you?

Margo: With a friend.

Sadie: Where?

Margo: None of your business. Back off.

Sadie snorted. Not likely. How could she determine if this were Margo or not?

Sadie: I got your message on Monday. What did you want to talk to me about?

Margo: Nothing. Never mind. Just give me my space.

Sadie: I came over like you asked me to. You weren't home.

Margo hadn't asked Sadie to come over—the *real* Margo would know that.

Margo: Something came up. I'm fine.

This wasn't Margo, which meant Sadie needed to stay focused while drawing out as much information from the person as possible. She couldn't think about *why* it wasn't Margo.

Sadie: What happened Monday night?

Her shoulders tensed over the next several seconds as she waited for a reply. She braced herself for the response.

Margo: Back off!!!!!!

Sadie: I'm trying to help.

Margo: Youv been warned.

A rush of heat washed over her. Warned?

Sadie: Who is this?

She waited nearly thirty seconds, enough time to receive a response, then sent another text message.

Sadie: The police are onto you. They found Margo's Land Cruiser.

Margo: You have no idea what you're dealing with.

> *Sadie:* Unless I do, and then it's the other way around. Where's Margo?
>
> *Margo:* Keep this up and she's dead.

A jolt shot down Sadie's spine. The possibility of having something to do with Margo being hurt or killed was staggering. Sadie dropped her phone on the bed and pulled her knees to her chest. She stared at the phone, wondering what she'd just done. After nearly a full minute had passed, Sadie reached for her phone again and took a completely different approach.

> *Sadie:* What do I need to do to keep her alive?

She waited for a response, and waited and waited and waited. After a full three minutes, Sadie put her hands over her mouth and tried not to panic, but her heart was beating double-time. She had to go through her calming exercises in order to get control of herself before she called Pete.

"Detective Cunningham," he said, but Sadie heard the sleepy tone of his voice. A quick glance at the alarm clock made her realize it was after ten o'clock. He was likely still trying to catch up from the drive to Santa Fe and back yesterday.

"I'm sorry to wake you, Pete," Sadie said, wondering if she shouldn't have called at all.

"It's okay. What's wrong?"

Sadie relayed the information to him about the text conversation. "What do I do?"

"Call Marcus."

"This late?"

"Yes," Pete said, sounding resolute. "A threat has been made. He needs to know."

"Okay," Sadie said, her stomach in knots. Marcus had not seemed happy with her earlier. "Have you talked to him since this afternoon?"

"Just for a minute," Pete said. "He understands why we didn't tell him everything about the BLM right off the bat, and Agent Shannon filled him in as well. It's okay."

"Really?"

"Really. Call him right now, okay?"

"Okay."

She hung up, took a breath, and called Marcus. He sounded just like Pete had, meaning Sadie had woken up two police detectives in the last ten minutes. Awesome. She quickly told him about the text conversation she'd had with Margo's phone. When she finished, he was silent, Sadie's anxiety building with every moment.

"Come into the station tomorrow morning at eight."

"Tomorrow? Um, Pete said that since a threat had been made it was urgent."

"Pete isn't the detective assigned to this case," Marcus said in a controlled voice. "And there's nothing we can do about it tonight."

"Can't you track where the texts came from? Isn't it important to act quickly?"

Marcus was quiet for a few seconds, and it wasn't hard for Sadie to imagine him cursing her in his mind. "Tomorrow morning at eight," he said before hanging up.

Sadie closed her eyes, embarrassment and frustration arm wrestling each other for priority. She stared at her phone. Should she call Pete back and tell him what Marcus said? What would Pete do if she did? Would he call Marcus and try to convince him to deal with this right now? Sadie moaned at the very idea. That would be almost as bad as Pete trying to convince Rex to let her stay. Sadie dropped her head into her hands and closed her eyes, aching for some direction on this.

What should she do?

What *could* she do?

No inspiration came, and though she tried to have faith in Marcus's directive that it could wait until tomorrow, she knew she wasn't going to sleep with this burden weighing so heavy on her shoulders. Eventually she found herself at her computer. She pulled up Shel's BLM report and searched through information she felt she'd already memorized. What had she missed? His recent hire at D&E was still suspect, but that in and of itself didn't tell her much. That he was at Ethan's showing tonight was forefront in her mind, however. What was their connection?

Her eyes scanned the page until they rested on Shel's unfinished college experience: University of New Mexico. She pulled Ethan Standage's brochure from her purse; he'd attended UNM from 2000 through 2006. It took nearly twenty minutes for her to confirm that Shel had declared his major as anthropology while attending UNM—the same major as Ethan Standage—and that the years he'd attended the university overlapped Ethan's. It took twenty more minutes to find a single picture online that featured a young Ethan and a long-haired Shel taping beer bottles together at a frat party.

This was the connection she'd been looking for. And yet Benny, not Ethan, had bailed Shel out of jail. Maybe Ethan had sent Benny in his place. Hadn't Ethan said he'd just gotten back to Santa Fe this morning? Someone had given Shel a tip that led him to dig even after the first body was found, but Shel claimed to have never met

Benny before he'd posted bail. Had Ethan given Shel that tip, or had it been someone else entirely?

And then, within an hour of Sadie talking to Shel about trying to find Margo, someone had tried to pose as Margo with those text messages. Perhaps hoping Sadie would fall for it and back off? Who had Shel talked to after leaving the gallery? He'd said Langley's name before he left. Had he found him? Was Langley the person behind the text messages?

After affording herself a few minutes to write up her theory that Ethan, Shel, Benny, and Langley were all somehow connected, she reread her words and noted one more missing piece from this complicated relationship pedigree she was creating—Margo.

She closed the window she'd used to research Shel and opened up a fresh browser. She'd never worked up a report on Margo for the BLM—she'd been one of the last nine people on Sadie's list. If nothing else, maybe Sadie could spare the police trying to fill in the blanks themselves.

CHAPTER 23

"Her daughter was abducted and murdered," Sadie said the next morning as she handed Marcus the stack of papers she'd printed off as part of Margo's background check. "The killer was caught, but he never gave up the location of her daughter's body. He was killed in prison before he told anyone."

Sadie didn't know whether or not to be impressed with her stoic tone. She certainly hadn't been so calm when she discovered the information that put Margo's emotional behavior on the dig site into so much clarity. That was why Margo took archeology so seriously. She was finding her daughter over and over again, perhaps even trying to build the Karma that would eventually demand the same respect be given to her daughter's remains as she gave to the countless people she dug from the ground. Sadie's eyes were still puffy from the tears she'd shed over Margo's loss.

She'd fallen asleep at her desk once the tears were spent, but woke up a few hours later with a massive headache and a kink in her neck. Upon awakening, she found that her desire to find more answers had diminished in direct correlation to the difficulty of what she'd learned. Today, she had awakened ready to leave Santa Fe, ready to let the police put the pieces together without her, ready to prepare for whatever the next chapter of her life would be. This chapter was closed. Oh, please let it be closed!

Marcus took the papers and thumbed through them. "Huh," was all he said, which Sadie took to mean she should expound.

"This must be why she was so . . . confrontational with Shel that night at the bar, and then Langley must have shown her something relating to artifacts or bones for her to have followed him." She thought again about how Margo had apologized in advance for something. She wished she knew what that apology meant.

Marcus scanned the papers while she spoke, then finally put them down and leaned back in his chair, watching her. "This was the kind of report the BLM had you develop for the crew members?"

Sadie shook her head. "They just wanted address verification, name confirmation, and job history via my conversations with the employees. Basically I was double-checking the information from the employment applications to make sure everything matched up. This one is far more in depth because I wanted to understand Margo and see if she had any connections to any of the other people in this situation."

"And you don't know why the BLM wanted these reports?"

"No," Sadie said. "But I've developed a theory."

Marcus raised his eyebrows expectantly.

Sadie cleared her throat and sat up straight. "I was gathering broad-range information without prejudice, which means that they must not have had solid leads or else they would have sent in someone more experienced who would have a more detailed focus. I suspect they had figured out that a D&E digger was selling artifacts, but that was all they knew. I'm sure you already know that a salvage company is the perfect 'in' for a would-be black-market reseller of archeological items. Salvage companies are not as highly monitored as actual archeological digs since they are for-profit companies whose items generally go straight to warehousing or back to the tribes for reburial. A pot here and there, or a shell necklace smuggled off the site at the end of the day could be a pretty good second income to someone with a connection to the underground markets. Kyle Langley drives a late-model truck and has a pretty nice apartment too, with nice furniture and a big TV and things. I looked into him in more detail too after finishing this report on Margo." She paused for a breath. "After talking to Sheldon Carlisle last night, and reanalyzing everything I've learned, I also think the BLM might not be the only group with interest in that dig. Shel knew there were bodies at the site and he kept digging after being told to stop. Oh, and he went to school with Ethan Standage, who owns the ranch Margo went to after leaving the bar Monday night."

Marcus just nodded, which she found infuriating seeing as how she had just laid out everything she knew. She was certain the police had additional information, but his walls were up. She was simply a civilian, an informant, and someone he didn't necessarily trust.

"Did you guys go back for that cigarette butt at the ranch?" she asked.

Marcus nodded. "We did. We found it, and we're having it analyzed."

"Have you talked to the Standages?"

"It's not that simple."

"Margo's life is on the line here," Sadie said, feeling the fire build in her chest. "She's been gone for three days now, and I found a direct link between Ethan and Shel."

Marcus held her eyes. "I checked back on the dig site, you know. Shel has been fired. And neither Langley nor Margo has checked in for work." He didn't look defiant or defensive, just thoughtful as he regarded her closely. "If I tell you to leave this alone, would you take that advice?"

Sadie was so surprised by the question she wasn't able to form an automatic answer so she just spoke her thoughts. "After last night's research," she said, waving toward the papers she'd handed to him, "the idea of leaving this alone is more tempting than ever. I don't want to make things more complicated for the police, but . . . "

"But?"

"But I feel responsible for what's happened to Margo, and I'm very worried about her. I've been up front with you—you know everything I know now—but I can't help wanting more attention on this case, more people trying to find her. That you haven't even talked to the Standages, when we're almost certain she went to the ranch, makes me question whether entrusting it all to you is the best idea."

"Ouch," he said, still not looking defensive. "You don't have much faith in us, do you?"

"It's not that. I'm just worried about Margo," Sadie said, shifting uncomfortably in her chair. Sometimes honesty was awkward. "That's all. Not doing what I *can* do is hard for me, especially since I'm the one who started all this."

"You feel responsible for what happened to Margo?"

"Of course I do," Sadie said, suppressing the rising guilt. "I'm the reason we went to the bar that night." She waited for him to throw out platitudes about how Margo was the one who actually set up the meeting and chose to follow Langley afterward. Sadie could acknowledge those things were true, but it didn't change the fact that if Sadie hadn't gone to Margo's on Monday, Margo wouldn't be involved in this at all.

"And what if you weren't the reason she went to the bar?"

"I was the reason, though."

"What if you *weren't*?"

"But I *was*." Did he know how painful it was for her to say this out loud? Let alone to say it twice?

Marcus leaned forward slightly and tapped the stack of papers on the desk between them while holding her eyes. "What if I told you I already knew all of this?"

Sadie looked at the papers and felt instantly sheepish for assuming the police weren't investigating Margo too. It *was* hard to have faith in law enforcement sometimes, but had her distrust set her up to have wasted her time and make a fool of herself too? "Why would you knowing about Margo's daughter mean it wasn't my fault she went to the bar?"

He held her eyes for a moment, and then let out a breath. "I can't tell you everything, and I didn't know about Ethan being connected to Mr. Carlisle," Marcus said, his voice low and surprisingly trusting. "And the text messages worry me a great deal. You've already gotten dangerous attention, and now that you know this"—he tapped the papers again—"you've become even more vulnerable. I need you to stay out of this for your own safety."

Sadie stared at him. Her automatic response was to assume he was saying this simply to get her to back off, but there was an intensity in his eyes that spoke of something more.

"If you learn anything else after leaving here," Marcus continued, "I need you to bring it to me as soon as possible. And I need your word not to discuss this with anyone at all from here on out."

Sadie opened her mouth, but then closed it. She didn't know what to say—challenge what he'd just told her? Ask questions he'd already said he couldn't answer? But her mind was spinning, connecting dots she didn't know were connected until now.

Marcus must have seen the difficulty she was having. He took a breath. "You said that you think there may have been other people with interests in the site, and that Sheldon Carlisle had kept digging after being told not to—that's *one* other group besides the BLM, right?"

"And Langley, if he's involved somehow," Sadie said.

"There may be at least one other group involved, and we think Margo was part of it."

Sadie straightened and leaned forward. "What?"

"Because of your involvement with the BLM, we've collaborated with them on some matters involved in this case, and through them, we discovered some details about her history that weren't readily available to us before."

"The BLM has a history on Margo?"

Marcus nodded. "Margo used to be connected to an anti-antiquities trade group, a kind of straight-edge gang of heritage advocates who feel the federal government doesn't act fast enough to really curtail the black market trade. This group, Tribal Preserve, goes after pothunters and dealers themselves—burning down trailers, even destroying artifacts to keep them from the market if they have to. They send threats, scout out newly discovered sites, and gather evidence they then anonymously share with the government. They also draw a lot of attention from the dealers they work hard to stop. Margo testified against a relatively large dealer in the Northeast about ten years ago, which might be what led to her daughter's death."

Sadie gasped. She hadn't read anything about that. "They would kill a child over antiquities?"

"It was never proven one way or another, and the media kept it quiet because they've learned to be cautious about what they report—they get threats too. In fact, a few years ago, I talked to a journalist in Utah who said that the only time he'd personally received death threats was while he was working on a story about a black market ring he broke up."

Sadie had to repress a shudder.

"After her daughter's death, Margo left the States for awhile and worked some international projects. It seemed as though she'd broken ties with Tribal Preserve—they are primarily concerned with Native American artifacts. Then she suddenly reappeared here in Santa Fe a couple of years ago. The BLM came across her name when she hired up for D&E, and they watched her closely for a while, but she appears to be unattached to the group. Suddenly she's smack-dab in the middle of our crosshairs on this, and we're scrambling to put all this information together as quickly as we can in order to come up with the right plan on how to proceed from here on out. We fear there are some big guns involved in this situation."

"And yet you didn't care about the text messages she sent me last night."

"They had already been forwarded to our database. We got a court order to monitor her phone yesterday afternoon. We were tracing them as they happened, and I didn't have time to deal with you at the same time."

"I was scared to death," Sadie said, her chest hot with anger.

"I'm sorry," Marcus said, inclining his head slightly. "But we have a procedure to follow, and from everything we've been able to find, no one knows who you are. They all think your name is Sarah and the address on your application leads to an empty rental house. If you hadn't called me, I'd have followed up with you today."

Sadie's heart hammered in her chest. "Do you know who sent the text messages?"

"Not yet, but we know where the calls came from."

"Where?"

"I'm afraid I can't tell you that."

Sadie almost swore, but then took a breath, knowing that he'd already told her more than he'd expected to, and she didn't want to appear ungrateful. Instead, she focused on what she'd learned. "Oh my gosh," she said, sitting back in her chair as she realigned every exchange she'd had with Margo. "Was Margo on the dig to find the same thieves the BLM was looking for, do you think? Same as me?" Was that what she was apologizing for? Had she been planning to take Sadie into her confidence with that call Monday night?

"Possibly," Marcus said. "We are filtering and following the leads as quickly as we can, but doing so quietly is essential. Pete has told me I can trust you, regardless of some of your history that does not reflect that very well, and I am choosing to do so. But I need your word that you will step back and let us do our job—for Margo's safety as well as your own. Going to Albuquerque is a good idea. Going sooner rather than later is even better." He took a breath and then added in nearly a pleading tone, "Please don't ask me any more questions."

Sadie nodded, then paused, suddenly remembering something. "Margo called Shel 'Crossbones' at the bar on Monday," she said. "Shel didn't seem to know what it meant, but what if *Langley* did? What if that was Langley's code name or something for his artifact dealings? He'd have known then that Margo knew something she shouldn't know. It could be his motive for having her follow him out of the bar."

Marcus scribbled a note on top of the papers Sadie had given him. "I'll look into that."

"Does Pete know what you just told me?"

Marcus sat back, allowing distance back into their discussion. "No, but let me be the one to bring him up to speed. In the meantime, make sure you don't discuss this with anyone. You're already more involved than we would like you to be."

"Okay," Sadie said, sufficiently convinced to do things his way. "I can't believe Margo's daughter may have been killed for this."

"The antiquities market can be as bloodthirsty as drug cartels. There are very deep feelings involved from many different sectors, and when they cross one another, it's like lighting a stick of dynamite. We are quickly trying to cut this fuse, but we need as much cooperation as possible in order for that to work."

"I understand."

Marcus let out a breath and his shoulders relaxed slightly. "We'll also need your phone."

Sadie automatically tightened her grip on the handle of her purse, but not in surprise. Pete had checked in with her this morning and told her something like this might happen, so she'd already downloaded her contact list, text messages, and copies of her photos to her computer. "I thought you had all the text messages forwarded to your computer."

"I need to verify it, as well as check for photographs and other communications. It's how I prove that you aren't a part of this. It's how you get cleared of any suspicion."

Being cleared of any suspicion sounded good to Sadie. "Will I get it back?"

"Eventually, yes," he said. His demeanor seemed to harden back into that of police detective. "Because it was the method used to make the threat, we need to clear it through our technical forensics department before we can return it to you."

She took her phone from her purse and handed it to Marcus. "Do you know *when* I'll get it back?"

"I'll try to put a rush on it, but I can't make any guarantees," Marcus said. "Where will you be staying?"

"Here's the number I can be reached at until late this afternoon," she said, writing down Rex and Caro's phone number on the back of a business card he had on his desk. She'd already planned to pack up and be gone before either of them got home from work; now she simply had more reason to do so. She added her e-mail address too, just in case. "Then I'll go to Albuquerque."

"It won't be done today," he said. "But we could possibly have it sent to the Albuquerque station when we finish."

"Or I can come get it. I won't have much in my schedule, and I don't mind making the drive." Maybe not having her phone would also make it easier for her to stay away from everything. "I'll call you with the number to my hotel as soon as I get checked in. Or you can e-mail me anytime; I check my e-mail a few times a day."

"That would be good. Thank you for all your help," Marcus said sincerely. "Be assured that we are giving this priority attention."

The house was empty when Sadie returned, and it felt isolating to be in a home where she was no longer welcome without her phone connecting her to the world where she didn't feel all that welcome either.

She'd picked up some U-Haul boxes on her way home but put them aside as soon as she entered the house. Using Rex and Caro's phone, she called Pete and left him a message that she no longer had her phone but could be reached here until about three o'clock, at which time she planned to go to Albuquerque. She took a few minutes to put together some green chile stew, another favorite meal of Rex's, as a bit of a peace offering. She diced the potatoes that would need to be added later into a bowl of salted water and left it next to the Crock-Pot. Caro would know what to do with it.

Then there was nothing left to do but pack.

It was an affront to her organized ways not to make lists and charts that explained the contents of these boxes from bottom to top, but she didn't have time for the planning process. She hoped Rex and Caro wouldn't mind storing most of her stuff until she knew where she would be going after the Balloon Fiesta and her court date were over.

Bathroom supplies went in one box, nonessential clothing in another. The plush blanket she had fallen in love with went in with her jackets and shoes. Caro had helped her pick out that blanket on their very first shopping trip. She'd assured Sadie she'd love it, and she'd been right.

Sadie didn't think she'd collected too many things, other than clothes, during her stay, but she ended up with two whole boxes full of souvenir-type things she'd bought since arriving in Santa Fe. Each item reminded her of the good times with Caro, and she allowed herself to feel downright sorry for herself as she wrapped the more fragile pieces in newspaper. She reached for a sheet of newsprint to wrap up a beautiful ceramic bell they'd bought in Taos, when Ethan Standage's picture caught her eye.

She smoothed the paper out on the bed and read a recap of the previous night's exhibit—she hadn't realized she'd grabbed today's paper out of the recycle bin; Rex must have already read it. The article spoke of the ten-year anniversary and the basic process Ethan went through for his prints and anthologies, but toward the end there was a quote from Ethan that Sadie found surprising.

"I'll be cutting back on my photography for the next little while, but I still plan to have an exhibit next fall." Ethan Standage is widely known as the heir to the Cold River Ranch, which has been owned by his family for generations. When asked the reason for the change, Standage said, "I spoke tonight of the three facets of life I try to pattern my choices around: temporal reverence, spiritual acuity, and creative expression. I've worked hard to accomplish all of those things within my preservation and my art, but I've only been able to pursue those things because of the support and the legacy of my family, and my place, ultimately, is with them. I've been raised since my childhood to take over the ranch and I am eager to approach a new challenge. I am not leaving my art behind, but rather making room for more things in my future."

She couldn't help but wonder if this change could be connected to Shel having been told there were bodies at the site, or to Margo having gone to the ranch. Ethan's sudden devotion to the ranch felt a little bit like circling the wagons, pulling into the ranch in order to protect it or himself or something. But, Sadie reminded herself, she wasn't investigating. All those questions were for the police, and she would do well to leave them alone.

She placed the ceramic bell in the center of Ethan Standage's picture in the paper and proceeded to wrap it up tightly before putting it into the box and moving on to her next keepsake, and then the next, and the next. Each of them had a story connected to their purchase, most of them directly tied to Caro. Sadie looked forward to the day when she could think about her friend and the good times they'd had without feeling such heavy regret.

One of her favorite purchases was a woven table runner she'd bought from a Navajo woman who sold her pieces at a roadside shop.

She ran her fingers over the tight stitches. Sadie had bought it with the expectation of putting it across the sofa table behind her couch at home. She hoped that all this drama was at least getting her closer to that goal.

She realized while putting the table runner in the box that she'd almost forgotten about the rope hammock chair she'd also purchased in Taos. It had a long piece of wood from which the hammock chair portion hung, making it awkward to store. She'd put it under the bed. She got on her hands and knees in order to retrieve it, glad to have remembered it at all. When she was pulling it out, she noticed a box she didn't recognize. It wasn't very big—a large shoe box for hiking boots, probably, but it was pushed up against the wall at the head of the bed.

Sadie had helped Caro move out the girls' leftover items when she'd moved in, putting them into the smaller guest room further down the hall. They must have missed this box; it *was* hard to see. She pulled the box out and raised her eyebrows at the layers of packing tape wrapped around it.

The box wasn't heavy enough to contain the hiking boots it was made to hold, and nothing shifted inside when she shook it slightly, which meant whatever was in there was likely packed pretty tight. Since it wasn't hers, she knew she couldn't cut the box open without feeling guilty about it, so she simply put it on top of the stack of boxes she'd just packed up, then retrieved a Post-it note from the kitchen and wrote "This isn't mine. I found it under the bed." She stuck the note to the green shoe box, then set it next to the hammock chair on the top of the stacked boxes.

She did a final check of the room. She'd gotten everything it seemed—nearly two months of living all packed up and ready to move to wherever she went next. *Please help me get home,* she said in a silent prayer as she retrieved the cleaning supplies from beneath the bathroom sink and set about leaving the rooms cleaner than she'd found them when she'd moved in.

At two o'clock, the bedding and towels were in the dryer, and the walls, baseboards, windows, and bathroom were spotless. No one would even guess she'd been there, which made her sad, but she didn't dwell on it. She turned off the lights and closed the door on this chapter of her life.

She hadn't heard from Pete or Marcus, but she was surprisingly okay with that. Her desire to be in the middle of things was sufficiently tempered by what she'd learned that morning. Margo had been part of a vigilante group. Did that mean she'd used Sadie in pursuit of her own agenda? Not that Sadie could be offended by it, since she'd done the same thing in a sense, but it was an interesting shift nonetheless.

She wrote a note to Caro and Rex, thanking them again for having allowed her to stay and explaining the situation with her phone in case Marcus called. Then she cleaned the kitchen. She thought about backing out of helping Lois at the Fiesta, but she would be in Albuquerque anyway, and she really liked Lois. Besides, maybe working together would be the tender clay on which she and Caro could build a new foundation.

With nothing else to do, Sadie took a final walk through the house that had felt like home until just a few days ago. She would miss it here. She would miss Caro, and yet even with this lackluster ending, she was so grateful to have been here. She'd grown and become stronger, learned to trust herself again and regrow her faith in her individual purpose. Santa Fe had been a good place for her to be, and she would never regret having come.

Green Chile Stew

1 tablespoon oil
2 pounds cubed beef or pork stew meat
1 medium onion, chopped
1½ cups beef broth
1 (4-ounce) can chopped green chilies
1 teaspoon ground cumin
1 teaspoon garlic powder
Salt, to taste
Ground black pepper, to taste
2 large potatoes, peeled and cubed

Heat oil in a large pot over medium heat. Brown meat and onion until the onion is translucent. Add broth and green chilies. Stir in cumin, garlic powder, salt and pepper. Bring to a boil. Reduce heat and simmer for 1 hour. (Add more broth or water if needed while simmering.) Stir in cubed potatoes and simmer an additional 30 minutes, or until tender.

Note: Caro's girls like this stew boiled down until it's thick enough to use in a tortilla.

Note: It's worth buying pork stew meat when you can find it and freezing it for later. Pork is so good with green chilies.

Note: This is easy to convert to a slow-cooker recipe. Add browned meat and everything but the potatoes to a slow cooker. Cook on low 4 to 6 hours. Add potatoes for the final hour.

CHAPTER 24

Sadie woke up in Albuquerque and listened to the silence of her hotel for ten minutes before getting out of bed. It was strange to have an empty day all to herself. Sadie hadn't had one in months, and except for the continual thoughts on how much more fun Albuquerque would be with Caro, it might have been a nearly perfect Friday.

Sadie took one of the walking tours that began at the Albuquerque Museum of Art, History, and Science, and then went shopping at the cute boutiques in Old Town. But without Caro to tell her she looked *maravillosa*, she lacked confidence in her choices. She ate lunch in an open-air café—Frito pie with green sauce, as opposed to the red sauce—people-watching all the extra tourists the Fiesta had brought to town, and enjoyed the warmth of the sun as the light dappled through the trees overhanging the patio.

If only she didn't miss Caro so much. And Pete too, not to mention her children, to whom she hadn't talked for nearly a week. She feared she'd been pushing them away again, but she wasn't sure how to reassure them that she was okay. Why were her relationships so complicated?

She picked up a historical novel set in New Mexico from a little bookstore in Old Town and read it beside the hotel pool while getting a little color on her legs. After a conversation with Pete via the hotel phone, where he explained his attempts to help Caro understand things from a police perspective—the jury was out on whether it had been effective—Sadie went to bed early, depressed but so grateful to have purpose tomorrow in the form of helping Lois at the Fiesta.

Saturday morning dawned bright, beautiful, and lonely. The man at the front desk recommended the breakfast burritos at a small café, and Sadie thought breakfast in the park sounded wonderful. She was determined to enjoy every moment of the morning, and she loved the parks in New Mexico, little oases in the desert.

The café was set several feet lower than the road that ran in front of it, and required that the patrons drive past it, down a side road, and then into the entrance which looped around the building before ending at the parking area. Though the access was anything but convenient, she could only assume the food must be worth it, due to how many people were there at eight thirty in the morning.

Moments before entering the diner, she saw a man standing on the corner, set above her thanks to the strange placement of the café. He was looking her way—or at least he seemed to be looking in her direction. It was hard to tell because he wore sunglasses. She tried not to let it bother her as she entered the café and scanned the menu set high above the counter. She ordered a breakfast burrito that she hoped would be as good as Caro's and a side order of sopapillas. She was quite possibly addicted to the deep-fried bread and usually slathered hers with honey butter. She really should be as big as a house, she'd enjoyed so many of them these last weeks.

After waiting a couple of minutes, she thought about the strange man on the corner so she moved to the west side of the café in order to look out the windows. He was still there, though now he was talking on his cell phone in between glances he shot toward the café. She couldn't avoid the trepidation that took hold of her. Was he waiting for her to come out? Had someone sent him to spy on her? She tried to talk herself out of it—she'd accepted a long time ago that she was definitely paranoid. But that paranoia had saved her life more than once.

Once her order was ready, she left the café and pretended not to see the man still standing on the corner. She pulled out of the lot and took the driveway around and up to the main road, stopping at a stop sign a few yards from him. He didn't look at her. Maybe he was watching for someone else?

She must have idled too long, though, because he finally turned to look at her. She quickly looked both ways and pulled onto the street, glancing at him in her rearview mirror until the road curved and he was no longer in view. She stopped at a red light and noticed there were two women standing at the corner, staring at her just like the other man had been. Her heart started beating a little faster.

There is no conspiracy. You're being silly. But she watched the women in her rearview mirror as well until the light changed. Could there be a conspiracy? Multiple people planted along her path in order to keep tabs on her. What if there was?

She shifted her gaze away from the rearview mirror as the road came to a rise, giving her a clear view of the big sky ahead of her, filled with color like she'd never seen before. She automatically pressed down on the brake, earning her a honk from the car behind her. She sped up, only to have to stop after a hundred yards as a light turned red. It gave her some much needed time to take in the view.

The dots of color were hot air balloons, hundreds of them. They filled the expansive sky that stretched above the Rio Grande Valley. Some of the balloons were high, some looked only a few dozen yards off the ground, but they all looked *held,* as though the valley were a huge basket, cradling so many brightly colored Easter eggs. Sadie had never seen anything like it.

"Amazing," she whispered.

The car honked at her again, making her realize that the light had turned green. She pulled forward, and she noticed more people standing on the curb watching the balloons. And here she had thought they were watching her. Could she be any more ridiculous?

Her cheeks burned hot with embarrassment, but her self-recriminating thoughts were overshadowed by the incredible view of the balloon-filled sky and soon she'd forgotten all about her conspiracy theories. Her hotel was on the east side near the airport and the foothills of the Sandia Mountains; it was slightly elevated from the valley floor, giving her an excellent view. She passed her hotel and reevaluated her breakfast plans. She still wanted a park, but she wanted one that would allow her to bask in this sight. It took about ten minutes to find one, and she found herself a shade tree that didn't block her view, then enjoyed her breakfast while watching the balloons drift across the sky like colored clouds. They seemed to have nowhere they needed to be, separated from the hustle and bustle below them, content to trust the breeze to set their path. How Sadie envied them.

By eleven, the balloons had drifted away for the most part. They left behind a blue-linen sky and a feeling of peace Sadie had so desperately needed. Somehow, it made her think that maybe everything was happening exactly as it should after all.

Sopapillas

2 cups flour
½ teaspoon baking powder
½ teaspoon salt
½ teaspoon sugar
1½ teaspoons vegetable oil
Warm water (¼ to ¾ cup, depending on your climate: more
    humid = less water)
Oil
Honey

In a large mixing bowl, combine flour, baking powder, salt, and sugar. Add oil. Add water a little at a time, mixing as you go in order to form a smooth dough.

On a lightly floured surface, knead into a soft, slightly sticky dough. Let rest, covered, 20 to 30 minutes.

Meanwhile, in a deep pot or skillet, heat oil over medium to medium-high heat until it reaches 400 degrees. Divide dough into 12 equal portions and roll into balls. On a floured surface, roll each ball into a thin circle, about ⅛-inch thick. (The thickness is the key to success here. If the dough is too thick, the sopapillas will not puff up when fried.) Cut each circle into quarters.

Drop dough, one piece at a time, into the hot oil. The dough will sink slightly. When the dough resurfaces, push it back under the oil. This will make it puff up. After about 20 seconds, flip the dough over and cook the other side. After another 30 seconds, remove the sopapilla with a slotted spoon and allow to drain on a cooling rack set over a sheet pan. Keep the cooked sopapillas warm in the oven on the lowest setting while you cook remaining dough. To eat, tradition requires you to bite off one corner and pour honey inside.

Note: Sopapillas are also delicious when sprinkled with powdered sugar. And for a savory sopapilla, stuff the cooked sopapilla with pinto beans, lettuce, tomato, and onions.

CHAPTER 25

Fiesta Park was set in a low spot off of I-25, requiring cars and shuttles to drive down an incline to reach the parking area. Sadie parked in the general parking lot, then entered the park itself, looking from one end to the other as she took it all in. The park basically looked like a huge football field without goalposts, lines painted on the grass, or football players. A few stands of bleachers were set here and there along the perimeter, but they couldn't seat more than a thousand people, and from what Sadie had read about the event, far more would be expected, especially on opening day. Right now, the sheer expansiveness of the venue didn't make it seem very crowded, but she understood that morning and evening were the two most popular times.

A row of vendor booths ran the length of the east side, separated from the large grassy area by an asphalt road; large white tents stood at the north and south ends of the park. The booths offered every kind of hot-air-balloon-related souvenir imaginable, as well as hand-made jewelry, clothing, and pottery. Food booths, like Lois's, offered everything from Mexican dishes Sadie couldn't pronounce to typical fair food like chocolate-covered bacon, funnel cakes, and deep-fried Twinkies.

Sadie had arrived two hours earlier than Lois had said she'd need her help, but when she stopped to say hello, Lois asked if she could start right away. Lois's assistant—a Navajo woman by the name of Inez—needed to go back to Santa Fe to pick up another load of cupcakes; the chest refrigerator in the trailer could only hold so much, and the crowds had been good enough that they'd already sold through half the day's inventory.

Sadie had bought a five-session ticket to the Fiesta online weeks ago and had no qualms about putting off her tour of the grounds a little longer. She stashed her purse in the trailer, and Lois gave her a big hug before quickly explaining where everything was.

In addition to eight varieties of cupcakes—including her signature tres leches cupcakes—Lois was also serving bagels, an assortment of cookies, and Mexican hot chocolate. Half of the food booths were also serving hot chocolate, and Sadie considered tasting all of them to see which one she preferred. It still seemed strange that a hot drink was so popular in a desert, but she had no complaints.

Between the peaceful morning she'd enjoyed, the chance to keep her hands busy, and being back among friends, Sadie's heart felt twenty pounds lighter. She kept a close eye on the field where she'd been told all the balloons had taken off from this morning, but was disappointed that there were only half a dozen balloons in sight now. Some people were going up and down on short balloon rides that seemed to last about half an hour. At two o'clock, Sadie took a bathroom break. When she returned to the booth, she was brought up short when Caro looked up at her from across the counter. The pause was an awkward one.

"Hi, Sadie." The tone was even and centered, but their parting words hung heavy between them.

"Hi," Sadie said. "How are you?"

The look on Caro's face conveyed the doubt she felt about Sadie's concern. "Fine," she said, then nodded toward the shelf below the counter. "The police called to tell me your phone had been cleared. I picked it up on the way here, but I think it's dead."

"Oh, that's wonderful," Sadie said, hurrying around the counter and picking up her phone. "I mean, it's not wonderful it's dead, but it's wonderful to have it back. Thank you, Caro."

Caro didn't acknowledge Sadie's gratitude and turned to help a customer who'd approached the booth.

Sadie waited for a second, feeling awkward, then headed to the trailer Lois had parked behind the booth where Sadie had left her purse. She always carried a travel phone charger for situations just like this, not that she'd actually faced this situation before, and quickly plugged in her phone to charge up the battery. It wasn't any less awkward when she returned out front; Caro was helping a family make their selections from the glass-covered platters set on the counter.

Caro didn't go out of her way to talk to Sadie, and before long, Sadie retreated to the trailer, organizing things to make it as efficient as possible and helping Lois prepare a few batches of hot chocolate so she would have enough on hand when the crowds increased.

"Is everything okay between you and Caro?" Lois asked after they'd mixed up two batches of the cold ingredients they could store in the coolers until they were needed.

"Um, not really," Sadie said, not wanting to be dishonest but smiling in hopes it would soften the truth. "But I'm sure we'll work it out."

Lois certainly wanted to know more, but she seemed to understand that Sadie didn't want to say much more. She frowned and put a hand on Sadie's arm. "If there's anything I can do to help, let me know. Caro is one of my dearest friends, and though I haven't known you long, I've seen how much she's enjoyed your company. It would be a shame for that to come to an end."

Sadie thanked her and returned to the front where she helped a young family waiting at the counter. She handed over half a dozen cupcakes, then startled a little bit at the familiar face that was next in line.

"Uh, good afternoon," Sadie said, trying to hide her surprise.

Ethan Standage smiled politely but looked uncomfortable. "Are you Sarah?"

He knew who she was? "Uh . . . yes, my name is Sarah. Can I help you?"

"Yeah, uh, my name is Ethan Standage. I understand we have a mutual friend."

Shel. She'd walked away from this and left it behind her, right?

"I, uh . . ." He kicked at the ground and put his hands in his pockets, showing a similar nervousness he'd had when addressing the audience at his exhibit a few nights ago. He'd acted as if he didn't want to be at the exhibit that night, and he didn't seem to want to be here right now either, so why was he? A few moments later he looked up, but his eyes went to the menu board above her head. "I promised my chase crew some tres leches cupcakes."

Sadie knew that wasn't what he'd come here to say, but she didn't feel up to confronting whatever had really brought him here in the first place so she played along.

"They are quite remarkable, aren't they?" Sadie said. "How many would you like?"

"Let's go with a dozen."

"Certainly. Anything else?" Sadie retrieved a box from below the counter and removed the cover from the platter. Why was he here?

"No, just the cupcakes."

She carefully put the cakes into the precut holder set inside the box. "I heard you have a balloon here at the festival," Sadie said, telling herself she was just being polite.

"Yes," he said, pushing his glasses farther up his nose in such a way that would have been endearing if Sadie were open to attaching such kindness to his actions. However, the image of him as a criminal hiding behind his wealth and philanthropy was getting fuzzy in her mind. There was a tenderness about him, a vulnerability that didn't put him in the same category as Langley or Benny, or even Shel. "My family's ranch has entered a balloon for the last three years. It's been a great experience being involved in the events."

"That's wonderful," Sadie said, ringing up his order. "That will be $36." When Sadie had first heard that Lois sold her tres leches cupcakes for three dollars each, she'd been shocked, but after being a part of making them, glazing them, filling them, and frosting them, the price felt like a bargain. The other cupcakes were two dollars each, which felt more reasonable.

Ethan didn't bat an eye at the price and reached into his back pocket for his wallet. Sadie supposed that when you made a million dollars a year, you didn't complain much about the price of cupcakes.

"Have you ever been on a balloon ride?" he asked when she handed him his change. There was an eagerness in his face that, coupled with his opening comment about a mutual friend, had her carefully evaluating the question.

"I haven't," Sadie said.

"Would you like to?"

Sadie could feel Caro glancing at the two of them while ringing up a customer on her side of the booth. Ethan wanted to take her up in his hot air balloon? Should she be totally freaked out about the offer?

"It's one of the most amazing experiences you'll ever have," Ethan said, some of his confidence returning. "And it won't take long at all. It, uh, it would give us a chance to . . . talk in private."

Sadie looked past him to the balloons out on the field. "Which one is yours?"

"My crew's getting ready to inflate it right now. It will be up in fifteen minutes, but you can't miss it. It's bright yellow, with three eagle feathers wrapping around the circumference. Will you come?"

"Let me see if I can get away," she said before she'd properly evaluated the question or her answer to it. Was she seriously going up in a balloon with a man she believed was connected both to bodies found in the desert and to Margo's disappearance?

"I'll wait," Ethan said, his eagerness curious but not necessarily disturbing. He stepped out of line, and Sadie rang up the next person in line before finding Lois at the back of the booth talking to one of the Fiesta officials. She waited for them to finish their conversation, which ended with Lois giving the man a complimentary cupcake. Sadie explained the invitation and asked if she could leave for about forty-five minutes, fully prepared to take "No" as a sign that this was a bad choice.

Lois smiled instead. "You're going on a balloon ride with Ethan Standage! How exciting!"

When she relayed Lois's blessing to Ethan a minute later, his face lit up with relief and he nodded quickly. "Great, I'll see you soon, then."

"Thank you, Mr. Standage."

"Please, call me Ethan." He put his hand out, and Sadie shook it.

What questions did he have for her? What questions would she ask him in return? Nerves made her stomach flutter at the possibilities. She'd turned everything over to the police, but sometimes people told her things they would never say to an officer of the law. She had to do this, for Margo's sake, if nothing else.

She focused her thoughts and turned to the next set of customers—a young couple debating on whether to share one cupcake or each get one of their own. Sadie was against the sharing of baked goods; it wasn't good for any relationship, especially a new one. She was about to offer such advice when she caught Caro looking at her, a question on her face.

"What?" Sadie asked automatically.

"Ethan Standage is taking you up in his balloon?"

"I guess so."

"Huh." She turned to her next customer, leaving Sadie no choice but to do the same, though she kept glancing at Caro, wondering what was behind her question. She wanted to think that one of these days, she and Caro would be friends again and that they would overcome this difficulty, but Caro's mood today didn't seem to forecast that very well.

CHAPTER 26

"Have you heard of the Albuquerque box?" Ethan said half an hour later when he pulled the door of the balloon's basket closed and nodded to his crew to let go of the ropes holding the balloon on the ground.

"No," Sadie said as he reached past her and secured the door. There were benches built into either end of the rectangular basket, which was about eight feet long and five feet wide—bigger than she'd have expected. The burner hovered overhead, and she stared up into the envelope of the balloon, catching her breath at all the space inside the silken panels. She was seriously trusting her life to a wicker basket connected to a glorified parachute? She closed her eyes and prayed until the burner roared, and she opened her eyes to see that they were rising. Just like that.

Her stomach dropped, and she hung onto one of the leather loops positioned at intervals along the inside of the basket. Ethan pulled the burner cord again, and Sadie looked up to see the fire and heat waves distort her view for a few seconds. She felt the increased speed as the balloon lifted even higher. "What's the Albuquerque box?" she asked, though her voice squeaked. She cleared her throat and wished she had anticipated this experience better.

"It's the name coined for the wind patterns in the Albuquerque valley. Northern winds flow at the lower levels, and southern winds are higher. It allows balloonists to use the wind patterns to take off and land from the same location. It's why ballooning is so popular here."

"I'd heard the valley was ideal for ballooning, but I didn't know why. That's very interesting."

"It isn't always available, and it's most common in the mornings, but today is a perfect box. You're lucky to have your first balloon ride under such ideal conditions."

"Lucky me," Sadie said, but she was feeling a little green.

He smiled, then pulled the burner cord again, taking them higher. She could see nothing but sky and a few other scattered balloons. They went higher and higher, but Sadie managed to contain her panic and instead let her eyes focus on the valley with the goal of appreciating the amazing view. It *was* lovely, but she was still queasy.

When Ethan let several seconds lapse between pulls of the burner cord, Sadie realized they were level with another balloon several hundred yards to their left, but moving in the same direction—south. She'd left her jacket at the booth and hugged herself for warmth. The temperature had dropped quickly.

Now that they weren't going higher, she focused on Ethan and why he'd invited her here. He took a deep breath, held it a moment, then let it out. Sadie often did the same thing when she needed to calm down or to do or say something difficult. She waited him out, and a few seconds later he looked toward her. "Shel told you."

"Told me what?"

Ethan crossed his arms and looked at the bottom of the basket, covered with a piece of plywood. He took another breath and then said quietly, "About the bodies."

He'd inadvertently answered her unasked question. "I saw the bodies myself. You told Shel they were there, didn't you?"

He blew out a breath and ran his fingers through his long hair while nodding his head.

"How did you know?" she asked when he didn't automatically explain himself.

He sidestepped her question by asking a new one of his own. "Did you tell the police?"

"I told them everything I knew," Sadie said. She almost apologized before catching herself. There was something about Ethan that made her feel protective of him, but it bothered her to respond to him that way. "Have they contacted you?"

"I had a message from a detective this morning saying they needed to talk to me. I'm really freaked out. They think I had something to do with those guys being at the dig site, don't they?"

"You tipped off Shel. You knew they were there."

"But I didn't put them there," Ethan said with a pleading tone.

"Then how did you know about them?"

"I *didn't* know for sure."

"Okay, so you had a strong suspicion, and you were right—there *were* two bodies buried right where you told Shel they might be. It's going to be hard to split hairs on that."

Ethan looked at her for a few seconds, then busied himself with pulling the burner cord. They lifted again, but this time Sadie's stomach didn't roll. After a few seconds, he asked, "Who are you? Why are you even interested in all this?"

"My friend is missing, and I'm trying to figure out what's happened to her," Sadie said. She nearly told him about Margo's disappearance and her suspicions that it was connected to the ranch, but decided to hold onto that for the time being. Her goal was to determine what Ethan Standage knew, not show her hand. "She asked Shel a bunch of questions Monday night, and she hasn't been seen since."

"This is that Margo lady?"

"You know her?"

"No, Shel told me about her when I called him after listening to the message from the detective. I don't know anything about why your friend is missing, though. I don't even know who she is."

"But you knew the bodies were at the site."

"I *hoped* the bodies *weren't* there," Ethan said with more force than anything else he'd said.

"But you feared they were. Why?"

Silence. Was he already regretting saying too much? Yet, they were in a basket hundreds of feet above Albuquerque—surely he wasn't going to stop now.

"Look, my friend's life is on the line here," Sadie reminded him. "And the two men from the site are already dead. Holding back now isn't going to do anyone any good. You brought me here for a reason—why?"

"I just . . . I need someone to believe me. Shel says you're working with the cops but that you listen."

Sadie was touched by the compliment, and she hoped she could live up to it. "I'm listening, and I'm willing to advocate for you, but you're not telling me anything they don't already know. If I'm going to help you, I need to know what happened."

Ethan took a breath and a pained expression crossed his face before he relaxed just a little bit. "About six months ago, I received an anonymous tip, a letter mailed from Albuquerque that said my assistants were buried at a burial site in the desert northwest of Santa Fe."

"Your assistants?" Sadie said. *What assistants?*

"On my expeditions, I take a single assistant with me to help pack my gear and catalogue information. Teodor had worked with me for years, but he disappeared a few weeks before last year's fall expedition. I figured he'd gone back to his family in Mexico—I'd recently paid him well for his help. I hired Raphael, the nephew of one of the ranch hands to take his place. He had climbing experience, and he went on the fall and the spring expeditions with me. But then he disappeared a month after our return."

"You reported these disappearances, right?" The papers had said the bodies didn't match any missing person reports.

"No," Ethan said. "I hire . . . illegal aliens as my assistants." A look of justification leaped into his face as he continued. "They are good, hardworking men who have families they want to bring to the States the right way. They need money, and they need a good immigration attorney. I give them both in exchange for their secrecy and loyalty, both of which are essential to my work. Since I began these expeditions, I've helped two men bring their families here and begin the citizenship process. I've had a few others who ended up going back home once I paid them.

"When Teodor and Raphael disappeared, I assumed I was just having a string of bad luck with the men I chose. I had no reason to expect foul play, and because they're illegal, I couldn't go to the police even if I *was* worried about the circumstances. When I got the tip that they were . . . buried, I hoped it was some kind of sick joke."

"The tip told you they were at a burial site in the northwest desert. You could have looked for them."

Ethan looked south, but Sadie suspected he didn't see the

amazing view laid out before them. "I could have," he said quietly. "But I didn't want it to be true. I tried to forget all about it."

"How did Shel get work on *that* site?"

"When I heard about the newly discovered burial site in that area, I asked Shel to transfer to D&E and be my eyes and ears. I couldn't tell anyone official, you understand, and I couldn't connect myself to the site, at least not directly."

"You got him the job that quickly?"

"Frank Delam—the D in D&E—is a friend of the family. They're usually the company used for digs found by Parley Excavation; they'd discovered the site when they were excavating for a road. I called in a favor, and Frank was happy to employ a friend of mine in need of work."

"And all that effort was worth getting a phone call as soon as the bodies were discovered instead of when it hit the evening news?"

"Teodor and Raphael were my friends," Ethan said, a pleading tone in his voice. The balloon had started to sink again, and he pulled the burner for several seconds so they would rise back into the southern air currents.

"But you didn't report them gone. Even if they were here illegally, you didn't take the tip to the police even though you had reason to think it was true."

He looked past her toward the West Mesa. "Yes, I left them there because I hoped they weren't there at all. Part of me still hopes it isn't them, but everything in the papers seems to be supporting the fact that it is them. I hired someone to look for them in Mexico about the same time I asked Shel to work with D&E. I was in Mexico City following up on the investigation when Shel called me about the bodies being found. A few days later, I spoke to Raphael's mother—it was my last hope to prove that the tip really was a sick joke." He crossed his arms over his chest and stared at the floor of the basket again. "She hasn't heard from him in six months, since a few days before he went missing. I couldn't bring myself to talk to Teodor's wife after that. They have three children, and I don't know what she's going to do without him. He's been gone for over a year. I sent her some money through the investigator that I hope will help, but I'm just sick over this. I can't sleep, I try to make sense of it and I can't. They were good men—family men with goals and ambition. I don't understand what happened." He cleared his throat and turned away, attempting to hide his emotion.

"I'm sorry," Sadie said sympathetically. "I can see you truly cared about them and their families."

His back was still toward her, but he nodded, took a breath, and then turned around to face her.

"Why would someone kill your assistants, bury them in an old burial site, and then tell you where they were?" Sadie asked.

"I don't know," Ethan said. "The only thing I can come up with is that someone's trying to frame me."

"Why would they tip you off if they were trying to frame you?"

He shrugged again. "I don't know."

Sadie glanced down toward Fiesta Park, just a patch of grass from this far up, and processed through everything she'd learned these last several days. Then she turned back to him. "Were your assistants a threat to someone? Could they have both been involved with something criminal?" She meant criminal other than their status as illegal aliens.

"They were good men," Ethan said, running his hand through his hair again. "I don't understand how any of this happened. And then there's your friend who's missing, and Shel said that the guy he was with at the bar that night was dealing in artifacts, and it's all just such a mess."

"Langley?" Sadie said, perking up. "Shel said Langley was dealing in artifacts?"

"Yes."

"How did Shel find that out?"

"He said he talked to the guy Wednesday night after my exhibit and, even though the guy denied it, you'd told Shel some things that made him think this guy was dirty. That's also when he told me he was going to Arizona, that things were too much for him here. I couldn't blame him; I'd leave if I could get out of this that easily. But I don't see how a guy on the crew being involved with the black market has anything to do with Teodor and Raphael, yet this is going to come back to me. I feel . . . ambushed, and I don't know why, or what to do."

"You need to get an attorney and then tell the police the whole truth," Sadie said, trying to calm him. He shook his head but she continued. "I know that after keeping your secret this long it feels impossible to just put it all out there, but like you said, this is bigger than just you. Teodor and Raphael deserve justice. It can only be found if you help the police find it." Margo had said in her message that whatever she wanted to tell Sadie was bigger than she thought—did she mean this? What Sadie wouldn't give to talk to Margo about what she knew.

"Right." He sounded completely miserable and muttered, "How do I tell my parents?"

"Just tell them," Sadie said. "Tell everyone the truth. It's your only protection."

Sadie peered over the edge of the basket. They'd caught the northern air currents and were now moving closer to the festival grounds rather than away from it. They'd been gone for more than half an hour, but as they got closer to the landing area, Sadie realized she was running out of time to talk with him. "Ethan," she said, "after my friend left the bar that night, I think she went to your ranch with Kyle Langley."

"That's impossible. The ranch isn't open to the public, and I'd never heard of Kyle Langley until Shel mentioned him the other day."

"Do you live at the ranch? Were you there that night?"

"I keep an apartment near the plaza, and I was in Mexico the night Shel called me to tell me he'd been arrested. I didn't get back until Wednesday morning."

"Did you ask Benny to bail Shel out?"

Ethan nodded.

"I also ran into Benny on Wednesday," she said, then proceeded to tell him about their encounter. "I won't deny that he made me very uncomfortable."

"I'll talk to him," Ethan said, but Sadie could see that talking about Benny had raised his defenses. "We've had a hard few years at the ranch. We've had to cut back on our workers, and with my mother's health, it's been a strain on everyone. Benny's been the glue that holds everything together; I'm sorry he was rude to you."

"I didn't realize the ranch was struggling," Sadie said. The website hadn't mentioned that detail, but then again, a website wouldn't get into those types of things. "Is that why you're cutting back on your photography and turning your attention to the ranch?"

"That's part of it," Ethan said. "My mother's in poor health, and my father wants to spend more time with her and, then, all this business with my assistants and feeling like someone is setting me up— it's all kind of compounding to show me the only path I can really take right now. I need to get the ranch back on track and ease things up for my dad. I should have done it years ago, really. I'd appreciate it if you kept the status of the ranch quiet. We've worked hard not to make a big deal about it, and I've been able to help support it with some of the profits from my photography, but money isn't all that's needed—the ranch needs someone there, all the time, being attentive and aware. I'm only telling you this because I want you to understand where Benny was coming from. The ranch is his life, and like the rest of my family, he's dependent on its success—he's like an uncle to me."

He leaned over the side of the balloon and did something that made them descend faster than they had before.

"I won't tell anyone," she assured him, sensing the heaviness upon Ethan's shoulders. "Detective Gonzales is the man heading up this investigation. He's kind and will be fair with you."

Ethan nodded, but as they approached the landing zone at Fiesta Park, his mood became more and more somber, more and more scared.

"The sooner you call the police back, the better."

"I know," he said miserably. "I'll call them after I talk to my attorney. I promise."

They landed ten minutes later and parted with a handshake that Sadie turned into a hug. Everyone needed a hug now and then, and Ethan looked truly tormented. What she'd learned felt heavy to Sadie, who didn't know Ethan's assistants, but knowing that he cared for them increased her sympathy for the burden he carried.

Before stepping back into her work at the booth, Sadie ducked into the trailer and called Marcus, but ended up leaving him a message recapping her conversation with Ethan. She was following her own advice by being completely up front with everything she learned. After she hung up, she tried to push away the difficult discoveries of the day before returning to the booth, nearly running into Caro at the bottom of the trailer steps as she did so.

"Sorry," Sadie said, stepping to the side so that Caro could pass her by.

"I'm getting more cookies," Caro said by way of explanation, not that Sadie needed one. "It's going to get busy soon."

"Okay," Sadie said. How long had Caro been standing there? Could she have heard Sadie leaving the message for Marcus? She thought back to the comment Caro had made Wednesday night about investigating things herself, and she felt another burden of responsibility descend upon her weary shoulders.

"Caro?" she said.

Caro turned at the top of the stairs, her expression unreadable. "What?" Her tone was defensive and cold enough to convince Sadie not to make any accusation that would make things even worse between them.

"Uh, you look nice today."

Caro seemed startled by the comment. "Thank you," she said politely before entering the trailer.

"You're welcome," Sadie said to no one but herself before returning to the front and praying that the increasing crowds would distract her from her thoughts. She told herself she couldn't change what had happened to Ethan Standage or his assistants. She'd given him the best advice she had, but it was a poor balm for her heart that ached for the families of Teodor and Raphael.

Cupcakes, she told herself as she greeted a customer. *Focus on the cupcakes.* If only it were that easy.

CHAPTER 27

Inez returned from Santa Fe with an air-conditioned carload of cupcakes around three thirty—just in time. Sadie helped her unload the cupcakes to the freezers, then got swept into the early-dinner rush. At five o'clock, Molly, another of Lois's employees, showed up to help for the rest of the evening, and Lois told Sadie that she was free to go and enjoy the Fiesta.

"You're sure you don't need me?"

"I'm sure," Lois said, waving her away with a smile. "This is your first Fiesta. Go be a part of it."

Sadie couldn't deny how much she wanted to see the entirety of the festival. "What time do you need me tomorrow?"

"Is eleven too early?"

"Seven isn't too early," Sadie countered. "I have nothing else to do."

"Well, in that case, if you could come at nine, that would be wonderful. I just don't want to take your entire morning."

"I'm *giving* you my morning," Sadie said. She cast a look at Caro and wondered if she would be working tomorrow as well and if the awkwardness between the two of them was the real reason Lois was encouraging Sadie to leave. Caro seemed to know Sadie was watching her and pointedly turned away, rearranging the cookie platter.

Sadie retrieved her purse and phone from the trailer moments before Lois practically pushed her out of the booth with two Biscochitos cookies—the official cookie of New Mexico—and a cup of hot cocoa. There was no arguing with Lois, and so with a promise to be back tomorrow morning, Sadie left and enjoyed the dinner that was sure to give her a sugar-induced headache. It was delicious, though.

Once her hands were empty, she called Pete. He'd be leaving for Albuquerque first thing in the morning, and his excitement to see the balloons made Sadie smile; he'd been coming to the Fiesta since it had been a few taco stands and two dozen balloons lifting off from a park in Albuquerque.

Sadie sat on one of the bleachers and told him about her conversation with Ethan, inviting back all the mournful feelings she had successfully pushed away while she'd been working at the booth.

"Marcus hasn't called me back yet," Sadie said when she finished her explanation.

"He might not ever call you back. You're not a member of the investigative team. But you did the right thing passing on what you know."

"I know that," Sadie said, looking up at the sky and wondering when the balloons would come back. There was an evening event in less than two hours, but even the balloons that had been giving rides had disappeared. "It's just that every time I learn something new, I feel that pull to dig into the story again, and I have to start all over with the separation." She let out a breath. "It's a difficult balance."

Pete commiserated with her, reminded her that she'd done the right thing and that he'd be there soon to distract her. *That* sounded wonderful. They spoke for a few more minutes about Caro's coldness and Pete's training, which had gone very well despite him going AWOL for the Tuesday classes. Finally, Pete admitted to having some things to do before he left in the morning, and they said good night.

A beautiful sunset was turning the underbelly of the clouds dusty shades of pink and orange, and attendees were beginning to move out onto the big, grassy arena at the center of the park.

There were a few vans and trucks scattered along the field, and as the sun set, more vehicles drove out. Sadie thought it would be hard for the balloons to land with all these vehicles out there, but soon the van doors opened and the tailgates came down, revealing balloon baskets and large rolls of bright fabric. Apparently some balloons would be inflated right now. Cool. Sadie followed the crowds somewhat blindly, not sure where everyone was going but not wanting to miss it. She searched the sky again and frowned—not a balloon in sight.

The sun was almost gone when she looked across the field to see a bright splash of purple and blue begin to billow up from the ground. She turned the other direction where a green-and-black bubble was growing larger on the other end of the field, and she realized she'd been completely off base. The balloons must have come back from their mass ascension earlier in the day rather than float around the valley all day as she'd assumed. The balloonists were now reinflating them, but would they take off again for an after-dark show? Could balloons fly at night?

To her immediate left, a red, white, and blue mound rose up from the ground, the silky fabric shifting and rippling in the breeze that had picked up as the sun went down. She continued moving closer to the center of the field and then stopped and slowly turned in order to take it all in. Hot air balloons blossomed in every direction. Yellow, pink, white, orange. The sight nearly took her breath away.

"Step left! Step left!" a man shouted.

Sadie startled, but followed his instructions and stepped left moments before a long snake of nylon rolled right where she'd been standing. She traced the fabric back to a basket nearly thirty yards away from her. A woman was attaching the limp balloon to fixtures on the edge of the basket.

Sadie continued walking backward in order to get out of the way, only to have someone grab her arm to stop her. She looked up just as another long bundle rolled out a few feet behind her. The man who'd kept her from stepping into the balloon's path nodded to her as he let go of her arm. He tipped his cowboy hat in her direction before continuing across the field, which was becoming more and more colorful by the moment.

Sadie didn't even think to say thank you until he was too far away to have heard her, so she thought it instead and hoped it would still count. *Did he look familiar?* she asked herself, then shook it off. Was it so hard for her to be uninvolved that she was making up things to worry about? She thought back to her paranoia at the café that morning, when she'd thought the man on the corner was watching her. Ridiculous.

She spared only another moment on the cowboy before her attention was taken over by the balloons now on either side of her. Teams hooked fans to the basket end of their balloons. The fabric seemed dainty as the air stretched it toward the pale pink moon, which was just rising from the eastern end of the valley. Within two minutes, both billowing mounds stood taller than she was.

Other balloons across the field were fully inflated now, dozens of colorful droplets standing stark against the graying sky. A roaring whoosh sounded from behind her, and she turned to see a patchwork-designed balloon twenty yards away light up like a lightbulb; Sadie marveled that the silken fabric didn't catch on fire. The baskets were held to the ground by teams of men and women in orange vests pulling on ropes as the balloons attempted to rise. Burners would roar intermittently, lighting the balloons and making the seams stand out against the glowing interior. The sky got darker, but with more and more balloons lighting up, the view across the field was staggering. *Oh, Pete, I wish I were watching this with you!*

It wasn't until the two balloons nearest to her were fully inflated that she spotted Ethan's balloon on the west end of the field. Sadie hesitated, but then started walking toward it. Pete had told her not to expect an update from Marcus, but she could at least ask Ethan if he'd talked to the police yet—assuming he was here and not in Santa Fe this very minute. Each time a burner lit up, however, she stopped and felt the awe all over again.

The announcers began bantering over the loudspeakers, talking about the history of the Fiesta and how many balloons were on the field tonight—almost two hundred. Sadie walked faster, trying to keep the Standage balloon in sight. There was a white balloon with pink and purple flowers on it. Another balloon was shaped like a beer bottle, and yet another like a teapot. The Spider-pig balloon—a pig in a Spider-Man costume—had been one of the first ones fully inflated tonight; it was a real crowd-pleaser.

Burners still roared here and there across the park, producing enough hot air to keep the balloon shapes intact. She missed what the announcers said before they began counting down from ten. The crowd began to chant with them, and Sadie stopped walking, not wanting to miss whatever the countdown was leading up to. At the count of "One," balloons across the field roared together as burners engaged and two hundred hot air balloons glowed from their self-contained firelight.

A cheer erupted from the crowd as people clapped and whistled at the first "All Burn" of the Fiesta. Sadie couldn't help but clap as well. It was truly a magnificent sight, and Sadie's chest tingled with delightful excitement at beholding something so unique. How had she never attended this event before now?

Families had brought lawn chairs, and huge groups of people clustered in the open spaces, leaving only ten to fifteen feet between the spectators and balloonists. The men and women in or near the baskets, or holding the cords that kept the balloons from swaying too much in the breeze, looked serious and intent. Ballooning might be a hobby for these people, but it wasn't one they took lightly.

The wind was picking up, and the chase crews responsible for holding the ropes were struggling to keep some of the balloons upright. One chaser, a boy of about fifteen, was lifted completely off his feet when a gust of wind caught the wall of his balloon, pulling it hard. There was shouting and calling back and forth between the balloon teams. One man called out that he was taking his down, then another voice several yards away said the same thing about another balloon. Was it ending already? Would Standage take down his balloon before she got there? Sadie turned around and bumped into a man's chest.

"Ooph," she said, hurrying to step back. "I'm sorry, I wasn't looking where I was going." She caught sight of Standage's balloon over the man's shoulder before making eye contact, only to realize that of the thousands of people in the park, she'd run into the same man who'd prevented her from walking into the uninflated balloon fifteen minutes earlier. Could it be a coincidence that she'd run into him—literally—again?

Sadie didn't believe in coincidences.

The man in the cowboy hat smiled at Sadie in what she assumed was supposed to be a kind way before stepping out of her way without saying a word . . . again.

Sadie moved past him without saying thank you and refused to look over her shoulder to get a last glance at him. Instead, she picked up her pace in pursuit of her reason for being here—Ethan Standage. The Cowboy's presence rattled her however, and she thought more about the first time she'd encountered him. She thought she'd seen him before tonight. But where? When? Was he following her?

The big, yellow Standage balloon seemed to be straight ahead. It was on the edge of the field, close to many other balloons, but not as surrounded by the crowds that seemed to have amassed in the center of the field. She rounded a large family that was sitting, like everyone else, in the middle of the field, then moved around a mostly-inflated blue balloon with the name of a realty company emblazoned on it.

She heard the announcers begin another countdown. There must have been fewer speakers on this end of the field, because the voices weren't as loud, and though she was tempted to stop and enjoy the spectacular display of another All Burn, she was close enough to Standage's balloon that she didn't dare risk losing her momentum. As strange as it seemed, with her disconcerting thoughts about the Cowboy, Standage's balloon felt like a safe zone.

"Five!"

"Four!"

"Three!"

"Two!"

Moments before the crowd shouted the last number, she felt

something press into her back. A hand snaked around her stomach and grabbed her wrist, causing her to freeze.

"One!"

The roar of two hundred burners filled the air; Standage's balloon, only a dozen yards away, lit up as well.

A man's voice spoke in her ear. "Keep walking. If you stop before I tell you to, this knife will go clean through your ribs, puncture a lung, and you'll bleed to death before anyone knows what's happened."

Biscochitos

1 cup shortening—butter flavor works well
1 cup sugar, divided ¾ cup and ¼ cup
1 egg
3 cups flour
¼ teaspoon salt
1½ teaspoons baking powder
2 teaspoons anise seed, crushed or ground (or 1 teaspoon anise extract)
3 tablespoons brandy or apple juice
1 teaspoon cinnamon

Preheat oven to 350 degrees. Cream shortening and ¾ cup sugar together. Add egg. Mix well, then add flour, salt, baking powder, and anise seed. Mix well. Add brandy or apple juice and mix well. Dough will be a little crumbly, so add more liquid if needed and press together with hands. Combine ¼ cup sugar and cinnamon.

Roll dough out to ½-inch thickness and cut with cookie cutters. (Fleur-de-lis is the traditional shape.) Dust with sugar and cinnamon mixture. Place cookies 2 inches apart on cookie sheet.

Bake for 10 minutes or until golden brown. Cool on pan 2 minutes before removing to cooling rack.

Makes about 2 dozen 2-inch cookies.

Chapter 28

Though a momentary fear washed over her, a split-second later Sadie imagined herself twisting to the side and grabbing the man's hand that was holding the knife against her back. She'd done that move a hundred times in her self-defense classes.

"Try anything at all and Margo dies," the man said in a gruff whisper before she executed the move.

Sadie froze. "Margo?" she said under her breath. "Where is she?"

"I can take you to her."

After learning about Margo's involvement in the preservationist group, Sadie had experienced a resurgence of hope that she was in fact alive, perhaps hiding underground somewhere. Before then, keeping her quiet was the only plausible motive Sadie had been able to come up with for Langley leading her away.

Sadie's mind spun as he pushed her forward into a walk. She would be a fool to believe her captor, but if he had Margo . . . She hadn't been seen for five days. "Where is she? Why are you taking me to her?"

"Because you have somethin' we need."

"What?" They were quickly approaching a big white van parked on the edge of the field. Anxiety kicked in along with her observation skills. Some sections of paint on the door were brighter than others—a decal recently removed, maybe? She couldn't see the license plate or the make of the van. The Cowboy smelled like cigarettes.

"We're gonna have us a discussion about all of this, so just hold your pretty little horses." She could tell by his voice that he was smiling.

"I need proof," Sadie said, frantically trying to decide what to do. What if this was her only chance to find Margo? "I need to talk to her before I'll go with you."

"Oh, you're comin'," the Cowboy said. "I'm not really leaving that decision up to you."

When they were a few feet from the van, the side door pushed open, and a younger man jumped out. Seeing the gaping interior of the van—there were no seats, just space—gave Sadie a burst of fear, and she began struggling.

"I—" The Cowboy clamped a hand over her mouth, and she realized she'd waited too long to put up a fight. Between the second man and the Cowboy, they lifted her and threw her inside the van, stripping her purse from her arm in the process.

She tried to scramble to her feet as soon as she hit the floor, but the second man pulled the door shut before she could get up, and then he pinned her to the floor of the van by pressing his knee against her head. His hand was over her mouth as soon as she'd thought to scream, while the fingers of his other hand dug into the space just below her clavicle. Like her, he knew pressure points, and the pain and nerve cessation his actions produced rendered her nearly incapacitated.

She couldn't help but scream against his hand, though, as he pressed harder and harder. Fabric was pushed into her mouth, causing her to gag while forcing her to breathe through her nose. He moved his knee to her back, and then he pulled her arms back, quickly tying her wrists together—a process not much different from the calves she'd seen roped at a rodeo Caro had taken her to the first week she was in Santa Fe.

She tried to pull her wrists apart as much as possible to allow some space, but her captor tightened the knots until Sadie worried the bones would break if she resisted anymore. Her ankles were quickly tied together as well, sending her panic levels to the moon. Pieces of sand from the floor stuck to her cheek. She tried to catch her breath and maintain rational thought.

The van engine roared to life, and the second man hastily patted her down. Her pockets were empty except for her car key. She always kept her key on her person per Pete's advice; it had saved her life before. The man removed it and threw it onto the passenger seat of the van. Was her purse there too? She continued fighting.

"You'll only make this worse," he said while pushing her head down again, causing more sand to press into her skin.

She stopped fighting, and a few seconds later, he moved away from her completely. She could hear him shifting around as though trying to make himself comfortable. The van turned, then turned again, and then began picking up speed.

It was hard to breathe with the gag in her mouth, and she could feel the tightness building in her chest as she thought about Pete, Caro, Shawn, and Breanna—they wouldn't know what happened to her. They wouldn't know where to start looking. Was this what had happened to Margo?

As her breathing increased, it became more difficult to get air. The gag was choking her, and though she tried to calm herself, it wasn't working. She tried to lift her head, only to have it shoved against the floor. She tried to roll onto her back, but her arms were tied, and each time she lifted a shoulder, she was shoved down again. She needed to tell them she wasn't going to fight them, she just needed air. Panic set in, and soon she was kicking again and screaming behind her gag. She was dying, right here, right now. Her shoulders and wrists burned, but she almost couldn't feel it as the panic rose higher and higher.

"Stop," the man said, hitting her in the back of the head.

That only increased her panic. Logic had no play now; pure survival instinct took over. The man said something, but she couldn't register the words. Did he realize she couldn't breathe? Did he know he was killing her? She heard the other man's voice—the Cowboy—but his words didn't make sense either. She threw her right shoulder up and managed to get on her side. She kicked her bound legs like a dolphin until she flipped onto her back.

Things seemed better when she was staring at the ceiling of the van. She felt like she could expand her lungs at least, but she was still choking on the gag. The man who'd tied her up was sitting against the side of the van, staring at her while she thrashed around, kicking from side to side. The Cowboy was yelling. Sadie felt bile rising in her throat and looked at her captor pleadingly. She was going to die either by suffocation or by drowning in her own vomit if he didn't do something. Her attempts at screaming were little more than guttural sounds coming from her heaving chest. Light began to pop in her peripheral vision, and she continued to stare at him. Is this really what he wanted to have happen? Her dying in the back of this van?

Suddenly he leaned forward. She feared he was going to hit her, but an instant later the gag was removed from her mouth. It was like pulling out a drain in the bathtub. She stopped kicking. She coughed and sputtered and dry heaved as she turned her head to the side in case she threw up anyway.

The panic still swirled around her, its long, gnarled fingers squeezing her lungs and its dry voice whispering in her ear that she was as good as dead anyway. She should never have cooperated with them at the Fiesta. Amid the scratchy voice of the demon of her own worst fears, however, was the faint voice of logic: she could breathe now. She would not die. Not yet anyway. But it was hard to believe they had any other motive in mind than to kill her. She wanted to tell them she didn't know anything, that she'd told everything she'd learned to the police, but she had to get herself together first.

She turned away from the man and forced a little more air into her lungs with each breath she took. A little more. And a little more. She held each breath a little longer, not letting herself hyperventilate. Her thoughts began to slow. Her muscles started to relax, but then came the intense pain in her shoulders. Lying on her trussed-up arms like she was made her shoulders feel as though they were going to pop out of their sockets.

"Please," she said in a strangled voice. "Can I sit up? My . . . my shoulders."

"What's going on?" the Cowboy said from the front.

"I've got it," her captor said, and although she didn't dare expect much, he grabbed her arm and pulled her to a sitting position. The interior of the van spun for a few seconds, and her shoulders continued to throb. But at least they no longer felt like twigs ready to snap. She continued to take deep, gulping breaths. She tried to roll her shoulders, though it was nearly impossible to do so with her wrists tied together.

"Thank you," she managed to say once she'd overcome the vertigo.

He didn't say anything, but when she looked toward him, there was a look of uncertainty on his face. Maybe her thanks had thrown off his game plan. She could only hope.

The man had a long face, thin, no facial hair, and a gold chain around his neck mostly hidden by the top of his black T-shirt. He was younger than she'd expected, mid-twenties she guessed, Hispanic, with dark hair and eyes, brown skin and . . . was she imagining that he looked familiar too? An instant later she remembered the man she'd seen standing on the corner that morning when she'd come out of the café. She'd determined that it was the sky full of balloons that had his attention. But she felt sure this was the same man. She *was* being watched. But why?

"I saw you this morning," she said, realizing she had nothing to lose. He didn't deny it, just stared at her. "How long have you been following me?" She glanced at the Cowboy sitting in the front seat. They wouldn't have been following her all day if they simply wanted to kill her, right? "Why are you following me? Why am I here?"

At the Fiesta, the Cowboy had said she had something he wanted—what could it possibly be? Information? She thought of the ugly world of antiquities she'd learned about from Marcus. Black market thugs may have been responsible for the death of Margo's daughter. Were these two men part of that same dangerous group? Had Sadie drawn their attention? Her mouth went dry and her heart, so recently recovered from her anxiety attack, began to speed up again. It was all she could do to force herself to calm down, though her whole body was hot and her arms were shaking.

"Why were you talking to Ethan Standage?" the Cowboy asked from the front seat.

The sound of sirens caused all of them to pause as the second man moved to the back of the van and looked out one of the windows.

"They're not coming for us," he said when the sirens didn't get any closer. "Another car was weaving between lanes."

Sadie's fragile hope was quickly extinguished as her captor moved back to his position at the left side of the van. No one knew she'd left the Fiesta. No one was coming for her. That her captors weren't protecting their identities implied their expectation that she wouldn't have the chance to identify them later. She had to force herself to breathe again after that realization. In, out, in, out, until she didn't feel on the verge of another panic attack.

"I asked why you were talking to Ethan Standage," the Cowboy said again.

Oh, right, she'd forgotten his question. Her thoughts were still scrambled, and she needed time to think about the best answer. Why would her talking to Ethan be a concern for these men?

"Can I move to the side of the van to brace my back, please?" she asked the Hispanic man sitting a few feet away from her.

He stared at her for a moment, then nodded but made no move to help her.

"Thank you," Sadie said again, scooting backwards to the side of the van. It took several seconds to adjust her body so she was more comfortable, but she used the time to survey the inside of the van; unfortunately, it was pretty stark. There was a box against the opposite wall, and some rope behind the driver's seat, but the rest was just empty space. She did note that one of the two square windows on the back doors of the van was cracked in the lower corner. The details were paltry. Once she'd used as much time as she felt she could justify, she looked across the van at the younger of her two attackers.

"I was talking to Ethan Standage because he was buying some

cupcakes. Then he invited me to take a ride in his balloon." It was the truth.

"Right," the Cowboy said. "'Cause he invites middle-aged women to check out his balloon all the time. What did you talk about?"

"The Albuquerque box and his photography. Why am I here? Where are you taking me? Where's Margo?"

"Tell us what you talked to Standage about, and then we'll move on to talking about Miss Margo."

"Can we get on with this?" the Hispanic man shouted in the Cowboy's direction. "Who cares what she talked to Ethan about?" He turned to look at her. "How long have you known Margo?"

"A week," Sadie said calmly, deciding this was a question she could answer honestly. She noted that he'd said "Ethan" not "Ethan Standage" or just "Standage," like the Cowboy had.

"Did you ever go to her apartment?"

"Once," Sadie said before remembering that she'd also broken in on Wednesday, but she didn't feel inclined to amend her answer. Besides, the only thing she'd determined from that walk-through was that Margo hadn't come home. "Monday afternoon. Where is she?"

"Did she show you anything . . . valuable when you were there?"

"No," Sadie said, doing an instant mental tour of Margo's apartment. There was nothing there that couldn't be purchased at a secondhand store for cheap. "She didn't show me anything at all. We talked."

"About Crossbones?" the Cowboy said from the front seat.

"No." It was the truth; they hadn't talked about Crossbones. Sadie had only put together the possibility of Langley being Crossbones since talking to Marcus.

"Then what did you talk about?"

"We'd worked a dig site where fresh bodies were uncovered. We talked about that."

"And then you went to the bar looking for Crossbones."

"Margo might have been looking for Crossbones, but I'd never heard the name until that night. Right before . . ." Suddenly his profile sparked a flash of memory.

After the fight had broken out at the bar, and before the police had put an end to it, Sadie had seen Margo arguing with a man she didn't know. She'd thought it strange that in the middle of the frenzy, Margo was arguing with someone, but so much was going on that she hadn't dwelled on it for more than the moment she saw it. Looking at the Cowboy's profile now—the same perspective she'd had at the bar—confirmed that he was *that* man. Then Margo disappeared. Was this man Crossbones? He was involved before Margo disappeared—but why? How?

How many players were there in this game?

CHAPTER 29

I've answered your questions, now tell me where Margo is. You said you would take me to her."

He glanced at her in the rearview mirror, confirming that he'd heard the question, but he didn't answer and turned his eyes back to the road. The absence of stoplights and the rate at which they were driving made it clear to Sadie that they were on the freeway, going away from Albuquerque; they'd have been in the city by now if they'd gone south. Headlights illuminated the Cowboy's face every few seconds as traffic came toward them, and the sound of cars passing them on the left told her they were in the slow lane.

"I said she'd die if you kept fightin' me," the Cowboy clarified from the driver's seat. "Two different things."

"*Are* you taking me to her?" Sadie asked.

The Cowboy shrugged. "Maybe."

That meant no. Sadie swallowed and took a deep breath, trying to gather her courage. She had to throw them off their game somehow. "You were at the bar on Monday."

He glanced at her in the rearview mirror again. Blue eyes. Over-tanned skin. Mid-fifties.

She pushed further. "You were arguing with Margo that night. Why?"

"Because she had something I needed."

Had? "What?" Sadie thought back to Margo's apartment again. Clutter. Old furniture. Discarded newspapers. What could Margo possibly have had that this man needed?

"I'm hoping that you—as the closest thing she had to a friend— would be able to tell me that. We searched her apartment and her car real careful-like so as not to tip anyone off, and we ain't found it. Until we do, anyone who had anything to do with that woman ain't gonna be safe. You, though, have been a hard woman to find. You gave the wrong address on your employment application, and you use a couple different names." He tightened his grip on the steering wheel. "What for?"

"That has nothing to do with Margo," Sadie said—another truth, though only part of it.

"You can't expect me to believe that," the Cowboy said with a chuckle. "Any more than you expect me to believe you don't know where the property is."

"Property?"

"The item Margo stole, the item she's been hidin' from us. I'm thinking maybe all your coverin' up is 'cause you're one of her little friends who are out to save the world from people trying to make a livin' off a little history."

So these men weren't part of Margo's preservation group. "I don't know what you're talking about. I met Margo at the dig site. We worked together for one day, then met up on Monday, compared some notes, and went to the bar. If she had an agenda other than talking to some of the members of our crew, I don't know what it was."

"You did more than talk to members of yer crew. You were asking why Mr. Carlisle kept diggin'. Like you said, I was there. I heard the whole thing."

Was he connected to Shel somehow? Sadie wished she had more answers. "Then you know that's all we talked about before people started throwing punches."

"You have a fake name and a fake address, and you bested a man half yer age when he came at you. I want to know who you is, and what yer doin' here. I 'spect you know more than yer saying. Margo said she'd moved the item, and yer the only person she spent time with that we can figure out. So I think she handed it off to you. I think yer one of her freaky do-gooder 'ssociates."

"You're wrong," Sadie said bluntly. She could not give him what he wanted, but her fear was rising quickly as to what might happen to her if she couldn't produce whatever it was he was looking for. "The police are investigating Margo's disappearance. They're on to you."

He laughed. "Nice try, sweetheart. You *just* recognized me, and with all the festival hubbub, no one saw you leave."

"But you're connected to Langley," Sadie said, feeling her own need for this to be true. "And he'll lead them to you. Or Shel will."

He laughed again. "Langley ain't leading no one nowhere. Guy like that knows better than most that he's only valuable so long as he's useful. He stops being useful . . . and well, the body count rises."

Sadie felt her stomach drop. "Langley's dead?"

"Puts a whole new spin on the nickname Crossbones, don't it?" He laughed, deep and hearty enough that it dissolved into a cough.

Sadie turned away and stared across the van. These men were killers. She caught the second man looking at her with an expression she couldn't read, and she looked away, unable to meet his eyes and see the victory in them like she heard in the Cowboy's voice. Did she dare ask where Margo was again? The possible answer scared her.

"So Langley *was* Crossbones," Sadie said. She'd wondered as much, but then she'd also wondered if the Cowboy was Crossbones. "Was he a black market dealer?"

"Not a very good one," the Cowboy said. "Seein' as how Margo was on to him, and him drivin' that big, flashy truck around."

"You worked with him," Sadie said. "You're a dealer too."

The Cowboy grunted. "I'm whatever I need to be whenever I need to be it, ain't that right, son?"

Sadie glanced at the younger man, but he wasn't watching her. He was staring at the floor, his jaw tight and his hands clenched into fists on his knees. The Cowboy laughed and glanced at her in the mirror again.

"How do you know Sheldon Carslisle?" she asked.

"Can't say that I do—other than knowing who he is. Why? Was he friendly with Miss Margo? I didn't get that impression."

So he wasn't connected with Shel—assuming she could believe what he told her. She was tempted to test their knowledge of Shel's connection to Ethan, but the familiarity the Hispanic man had used when he said Ethan's name held her back. She couldn't be too free with handing over information; she might need to bargain with it later.

"And that brings us back to you. See, if you ain't the receiver of the property, then we have to really think about what your value is. If you're no use to us, then yer just a liability, 'specially seein' as how you're all sweet with Standage. Liabilities get buried here in New Mexico."

"Buried like Ethan's assistants?"

Both sets of eyes snapped to her in surprise, and her breath caught in her throat. Apparently they hadn't expected her to know this.

"Who told you that?" the Hispanic man asked, watching her intently.

She looked between him and the Cowboy, searching for direction on how to answer this. "The police did," Sadie said. "I told you, they're on to you. They know everything."

"Oh, no, they don't," the Cowboy whispered, but he was obviously bothered by this new information. The other man was still watching Sadie, but when she looked at him, he quickly looked away. Guilty? Scared? Who was he? At moments, she felt as though he were a hundred percent into this, and other times she had the feeling that he was being victimized somehow too. Yet he was the one who'd helped throw her into the van, tied her up, and knelt on her head.

"We're done talkin'. We got one more *amigo* who'd like to talk with you, but dependin' on what he decides, you might run out of road pretty quick, sweetheart. I suggest that if you're hiding something, you uncover it real quick. You done crossed a line when you was talkin' to Standage. Things'll only get worse for you if you're not the one to help us recover our property."

Sadie took a breath and quickly rushed through her options. There was only one possible course of action that she felt gave her any chance at all. The truth was, she had no value to these men. She didn't know what property they were talking about, and even if she did, she didn't have it. But they thought she did, or at the very least, they thought she might know something. If she could give them something, maybe she'd live to tell the truth to someone else.

The van slowed, and when he came to a stop after a slight decline and a left turn, Sadie suspected they were getting off the freeway. It was now or never. She took a breath. "I've known Margo since just before her daughter was killed."

The Cowboy's eyes lit up in the rearview mirror, and his whole body straightened. She'd told him something he wanted to hear. Good. The other man stared at her, but she kept her attention on the Cowboy. "I worked with another preservation group, and our paths crossed a time or two."

"Which group?" the Cowboy asked.

"I guarantee you've never heard of us. We're very discreet."

He narrowed his eyes. "You're lyin'. The whole point of those groups is to not be discreet."

"Tribal Preserve, yes, but not mine," Sadie said, brimming with confidence about something she knew far too little about. "We're the . . . I guess you'd call us the intellectual side of the preservationists. We deal with politicians and powerhouses, and we funnel some of the hands-on work to groups like Margo's. I haven't seen her for years though. Didn't know she was still involved until we met up at the dig site. She suspected Langley of stealing from the sites and brokering artifacts on the side, which is how he's connected to you guys, I assume."

"If she knew it was Langley, why'd she call Mr. Carlisle Crossbones?"

"She thought he was involved too," Sadie said. It felt good to tell some truth amid the story she was fabricating one word at a time. "*He's* the one who dug into that grave, after all. She thought she could get Langley to turn on Shel, and that seemed to be exactly what was happening until Shel attacked us."

He shook his head and muttered, "I knew you wasn't some grandmother when you blocked that punch."

Sadie shrugged as best she could, but her heart was racing. How long could she keep this up?

"Tell me about the property," the Cowboy demanded.

"No," Sadie said bluntly.

He narrowed his eyes again in the mirror. "Then how's I know you even have it?"

"You said someone else wanted to talk to me about it. I'll wait for him." Anything to buy more time, more opportunity. She was as limited as she could be in the back of this van. They were taking her somewhere, and once she was out of the van, she'd have more options than she had now. She'd also have someone else to deal with, but there would at least be somewhere to run.

The Cowboy didn't respond, and silence filled the van. She caught the other man looking at her again, but this time she met his eye and lifted her chin the way she imagined an artifact-preserving mob boss would do. He looked confused, but . . . interested, then finally pulled a cell phone from his pocket. "He's thirty minutes out," he said to the Cowboy a few seconds later, then typed out a response.

The Cowboy said nothing.

The van turned again, and the new road was not as kind as the last one—dirt, maybe. Without a seat to keep her in place, Sadie bounced on the floor of the van, killing her tailbone and shoulders. She winced when her head cracked against the side of the van, and she tried to press her back against the metal side in hopes that would help her keep her place. The panicky feeling she'd been trying to suppress was rising quickly. Every second they kept driving took her farther away from rescue, but she was scrambling to put together the rest of her plan and needed time for that too.

"If you're playin' us," the Cowboy said, finally breaking the silence as they bounced down the road, "I'll kill you slow and painful."

"I'd expect nothing less," Sadie said brazenly. Inside, however, she cringed and cried and prayed for help some more.

CHAPTER 30

The van finally came to a stop. Nothing but desert and scrub surrounded them. When the two men pulled her out, she didn't bother fighting. What was the point now that she'd told them she wanted to talk to the third man? They removed the rope from her ankles so that she could walk. Her legs tingled as the blood hurried back to circulate through the tissues.

The half-moon allowed just a blush of color on the red hills around them while reflecting silver off the pale sagebrush and black for the darker cedars and ponderosa pine. They weren't in the flat, barren desert, but in an area with rock formations, trees, and brush; perhaps they had come up against one of the national forests, but it was desolate all the same.

The headlights of the van were still on, lighting what might have been a path. The Hispanic man walked behind her, while the Cowboy led the way. It was cold, and Sadie remembered she'd left her jacket in Lois's trailer. Would someone discover it there and come looking for her? The chances seemed very slim; it was just a jacket left behind, nothing more.

After walking a few yards, Sadie glanced back to get a final look at the van, still filing away details in hopes they would come in handy later on. One headlight was dimmer than the other, and more yellow. She squinted and thought she could make out the Ford logo on the front grille when the Hispanic man pushed her forward, causing her to stumble and nearly lose her balance. Almost as soon as she faced forward again, the headlights shut off automatically, and she had to blink as her eyes adjusted to the new level of darkness around her. What year did automatic shut-off first start being used in Ford Cargo vans?

The Cowboy led the way around an outcropping of sandstone, blocking them from the area where the van was parked and relying only on the moon to light the way. He seemed to be following a dried-out creek bed that was smooth enough to appear reflective in the moonlight.

Sadie stumbled over a rock, and the other man yanked her upper arm to keep her from falling. He jarred her shoulder in the process, which made her stumble again. Determined to come across as cool, calm, and in control, she bit back the retort . . . several retorts actually. Thank goodness she'd chosen to wear her TOMS instead of flip-flops today. She wished she'd also chosen long pants after she scraped her shin on a rock and was pulled through a clump of sagebrush. She tried to watch the ground in front of her to avoid spraining her ankle until she realized that the farther from the road she was, the farther she'd have to go for help if she managed to get away.

She stumbled forward and pretended to be hurt, gasping and limping as though unable to put weight on her right foot. The Hispanic man pulled her up again. "Ow," she said through clenched teeth. He forced her to walk for another fifteen feet or so, but she moaned and limped as though she were in excruciating pain until the Cowboy turned back to see why they were so far behind.

"She's hurt," the other man explained.

Sadie put on a good show as she struggled to limp toward the Cowboy, as though not wanting to be left behind. "I think it's a sprain," she said, hobbling forward. "I've always had weak ankles."

"We'll stop here then," the Cowboy said after watching her take a few steps. "He can take her farther in if he wants to."

The Hispanic man loosened the grip on Sadie's arm, and she hobbled to sit on a rock. He checked his phone again. "He says he's about fifteen minutes out."

Sadie was surprised he still had service. He stood on her right side, blocking the way they had come, and her heart started racing as she tried to come up with the next part of her plan. How would she get away if he was in her path? She tried to breathe deeply to keep from freaking out—no sense using up her adrenaline before she made a run for it. Though where she'd run to was anyone's guess.

To her surprise, the Hispanic man leaned over and started untying the ropes on her hands.

"What are you doing, Horace?" the Cowboy said, marching toward them.

Horace! He had a name.

"Making sure nothing leads back to us," he said, glaring at the older man.

Sadie looked between them. To prevent someone tracing the ropes back to them meant he expected her to die out here, and yet she thought she'd done a good job of convincing them she was valuable. Did he not believe the story she'd told? She glanced at Horace as he untied the ropes and repeated his name in her mind over and over again to make sure she didn't forget it.

He finished with the ropes and shoved them in the pocket of

his baggy denim shorts. The Cowboy muttered under his breath, but Sadie couldn't make out what he said.

"So, where's Margo?" she asked once Horace had settled himself against a rock a few feet away from her, though still blocking the path she needed to use for her escape. She rubbed her wrists, still raw from the ropes.

They didn't answer her. She turned her attention to the Cowboy. He was the one in charge.

"Where is she?"

"Margo's dead," the Cowboy said, a half smile on his face.

The shock hit her like a sonic wave, and her whole body jumped. *Dead?* Sadie stared at the sand at her feet as tears rose in her eyes and a lump formed in her throat. He was lying. He was making it up to upset her . . . but . . . "Why?" she asked. She shouldn't have an emotional reaction if her relationship with Margo was professional, should she? "Why would you kill her if you thought she had what you want so badly?"

"First off, she said she didn't have it no more, and *then* she pretty much forced our hand."

Sadie knew what that really meant: Margo had put up a fight, maybe she got away from them, and they had to kill her to stop her. Her stomach rolled, and tears pricked her eyes, but she pushed the fear and sadness down. She would not meet the same fate. She wouldn't! She'd survive this and then get justice for Margo.

She glared at him, unable to keep her contempt to herself. "You're a sick, twisted, lying murderer."

He cut her off with a laugh, which stopped abruptly as he walked toward her, a swagger to his step. Sadie pulled back, completely forgetting the escape plan she'd been building as what he'd said kept her frozen in place. Margo was dead. Sadie couldn't save her.

"Everybody's gotta make a living," he said, then cocked his head to the side and regarded her. "But you can learn from her mistakes, ya know. Play nice and live to see another day." He reached out to run his thumb down her cheek. She pulled back as though he'd cut her, but she kept her eyes locked with his as she tried to reorganize her thoughts, which had scattered like so many pigeons. There was no way he'd let her live through this. She'd seen them; she knew they'd killed Margo and Langley.

"Who are you working for? Who's coming out here?"

"Whooee," he said, shaking his head and crossing the clearing to lean against a large rock directly across from her. "You do have a lot of questions in that pretty little head of yers, don't ya? Dangerous." He was twelve feet or so away and pulled a pack of cigarettes from his front pocket. The lighter flame lit up the Cowboy's face for a few seconds, then withdrew, leaving the silvery reflection from the moon on his hat and the red ember of his cigarette floating in the semidarkness.

A gust of wind blew around the rocks, raising goose bumps on Sadie's arms and making her shiver. She rubbed her upper arms in an attempt to warm herself up, but the coldness came from more than the night. She waited for him to speak again, but he didn't, content to slowly smoke his cigarette instead.

"It's a shame, really," the Cowboy said after nearly a minute had drawn out between them. "Getting rid of such fiery women as you and Miss Margo. The world could use a little more temper, if you ask me, especially in the lady folk."

"Then don't kill me," Sadie said dryly. His words about it being dangerous for her to know so much had hit home. Maybe she should have played dumb. But there was no reason for her to think they would keep her *alive*.

He laughed then coughed, raising his cigarette-free hand to his mouth as he hacked. Horace was texting on his phone again, and suddenly Sadie had found her moment far sooner than she'd expected.

She bent down and rubbed her supposedly injured ankle, then picked up a rock, then two. Neither man noticed. She set her eyes on the creek bed that had led them here, then took a breath and made a run for it, throwing one rock at Horace as he looked up in surprise and the second one a moment later, aiming for his head.

He ducked and lost his balance on the rock he had been leaning against, but she wasn't there to see the tumble. She thought she heard him swear as she ran past.

She was far more worried about the young, trim, Horace catching her than the smoking, potbellied Cowboy. As soon as she wasn't in their view, she darted left through a narrow gap between the rock and a ponderosa pine, assuming they would expect her to run to the van. She focused all her attention directly ahead, running from one tree to one rock then setting her sights on a new goal. She could hear the two men yelling and hoped it would cover the sounds of her footsteps.

Soon, all she could hear was the drawing of her own ragged breath. Thank goodness for Caro's fitness obsession and the weight loss she'd enjoyed because of it. Though she knew she wasn't fast compared to some, by her own standards, she felt exceptionally quick.

She passed another tree and darted right, setting her sights on a new rock, then another tree. Point A to point B. Point B to point C. One at a time. Move as fast as possible. This wasn't the first time she'd run through the mountains in an attempt to save her life, but this time her hands were free, and she had that past success to give her confidence. Confidence, however, was only one part of the equation. It was dark, there were *two* men behind her, and they *would* kill her if they caught up—of that she had no doubt.

She didn't dare look back for fear that one misstep would bring on the sprained ankle she'd faked earlier. How far had she run? A hundred yards? Two hundred?

Not far enough.

One more tree, she said, focusing her sights ahead as she felt her speed decreasing. The initial rush of adrenaline was wearing off, and she could feel the burning in her thighs and the bite of every rock beneath her feet—TOMS were not meant for running over rocks and sagebrush.

One more tree. She was almost there. She could hear nothing from behind her. She passed the tree and searched for her next goal, and saw . . . nothing. She looked down at the same moment she pitched over the edge and couldn't help but scream as the ground came at her.

Her flailing arms proved insufficient to catch her as she fell.

CHAPTER 31

Sadie was first aware of the rough stone beneath her fingers, followed quickly by the cold air and a growing sense of awareness, though her thoughts were splintered and frail.

Her head hurt. She was bleeding. She needed to hide until the panic of her body, and the memories of what had gotten her there, could combine and bring some sense. She felt as though she had been chased by a mountain lion—which she feared wasn't far from the truth. Someone wanted her dead. Her whole body knew it.

She had to hide, even if she didn't know why or who she was hiding from or even where she was. Wait, she did know where she was. She was in the desert. She'd been at the Balloon Fiesta in Albuquerque.

And she was hiding from the Cowboy. And the other man— what was his name?

"She went this way," a voice said from somewhere above her.

Another voice answered—the Cowboy—but Sadie couldn't hear what he said. Or were there three of them? Her head spun faster when she tried to stand. She rolled to her knees, then bit her tongue to keep from whimpering as shards of rock cut through her pants. She was so dizzy.

Within a few seconds, she realized she hadn't rolled to the actual base of the hill; in fact, she was only about halfway down. A portion of rock jutted out of the slope, complete with a struggling cedar tree. The rock had broken her fall and possibly caused her loss of consciousness. One side of the rock allowed the continuation of the incline, which ended about twenty yards down in a dried-out riverbed. The other side of the hill leveled off slightly and disappeared into shadows that offered the most promising chance of shelter. She moved in that direction, careful not to fall the rest of the way down the hill.

A particularly sharp rock jabbed into her knee, sending pain through her leg and bringing tears to her eyes. She took a breath, held it, and forced herself forward. At any other time, the heavy shadows would have seemed ominous. Who knew what could be in the darkness? But whatever it was—snakes, scorpions, horrendously freaky spiders intent on scaring her to death before the venom could do the job—it couldn't be worse than the Cowboy and his henchman.

For a moment she thought she saw a cave ahead, but quickly realized it was just rocks set against one another with a space in between. But it was enough to create an area of almost complete darkness amid the shadows of nightfall. She squeezed herself between two rocks. The air was colder by the stones, but they made her feel protected and hidden. She didn't know how much more ground she could cover. Her head was killing her.

She told herself she was safe, and focused on her breathing until she didn't feel like she was sucking air through a straw any longer.

Now and then she'd hear a word carried to her on the wind. She'd hold her breath all over again, willing them not to come closer.

At one point she heard movement just beyond her rocks; she sat very still and breathed as quietly as she could. The person, or animal for all she knew, moved away. She pulled her arms inside her shirt and hugged her knees to her chest as best she could, holding her body tightly as she began to shiver. How cold would it get tonight? If they were still looking for her come morning, they'd surely discover her hiding place. What were her options? Was there no hope?

There was always hope.

She tried very hard to believe it. She *had* to believe it.

"I don't see any sign of her."

Sadie froze, and the name Horace came to mind. Was that his name? He wasn't far away. She pulled her legs even closer to her body.

A voice answered him, but she couldn't make out the words.

"Even with flashlights we'd have a hard time tracking her. Have you looked at this place?" He was close, less than ten yards away, she guessed. Would the moonlight reflect off her clothing? Off the silver-gray streaks in her hair?

Another answer she couldn't hear.

"Wait," Horace said. "There's . . . there's a cliff at the bottom of this hill and . . ." She heard his footsteps; was he coming closer? "There's at least a thirty-foot drop. No way she survived that fall."

"You sure she came this way?" She could barely hear the Cowboy's words. He must be at the top of the hill. Did it really end in a cliff instead of the arroyo she thought she'd seen? Had she so narrowly escaped death twice in one night?

"I heard the scream and the fall, then nothing," Horace said. "We'll come back for her in the morning—assuming the coyotes haven't finished her off by then." She heard him turn away but didn't dare believe it.

"We ain't leavin' till we know she's dead."

"She's dead," Horace said, sounding angry. "They're all dead, just the way you like 'em."

"You watch your mouth!"

"Or what? You'll kill me too? We've put up with an awful lot we never counted on, but there's no way you could talk yourself out of that one.

"No one's going to find her body before morning," Horace continued. "And *Padre* says he needs us at the Fiesta. He wants us to . . ."

The voices drifted away. Sadie was so tense, she felt sure her muscles were turning to the same stone currently embracing her. She strained to hear an indication of . . . anything.

Finally she began to relax. But each ache and pain her anxiety had masked while on high-alert came back, and she groaned under her breath and tried to shift her position. Those men had brought her all the way out here, she'd seen their faces, they'd admitted to killing Margo and Langley. Why would they so quickly believe she was dead without any proof? It might be a trick.

She pulled her arms and legs in even tighter, though they protested, and she whimpered. She needed to conserve as much body heat as possible. She didn't dare come out and risk being discovered. She wasn't sure she could muster up the adrenaline she'd need for another run should they be waiting for her. She dropped her head onto her knees and focused on remaining calm and warm. It was going to be a long night, but if her discomfort meant she would live to see another day, it would be a small price to pay.

CHAPTER 32

Sadie had to stay focused and awake even though her body wanted to sink into oblivion. She was more than tired. She was mentally and emotionally exhausted and overwhelmed. Teetering on the brink of panic for so long had worn through her reserves, and she found herself crying into her knees. For Margo. For Langley even. A fair amount of self-pity mingled with the tears as well. The self-pity, however, was a reminder of the escape she'd made—both escapes. One from the men who had kidnapped her, and the other from plummeting to her death. There had to be a reason for that, right? There must be purpose to her still being alive.

To keep from drifting off, she started whispering to herself, outlining everything she knew about anything that seemed the least bit related to Margo's disappearance and Sadie's eventual capture. There were so many details to track, and she wished she had a notebook she could write them down in to make sure she wasn't missing anything.

Once she felt she'd verbalized everything she knew, she started putting the details together. Langley was Crossbones, and obviously he had some kind of a connection to the Standages, but Shel didn't know that, despite his own connection to Ethan. Langley didn't seem to have known about the bodies before Shel talked about them over too many beers. She didn't think the Cowboy and Horace were working for Ethan—otherwise why would they be so threatened by her speaking to him at the Fiesta? Why would they be so curious as to what they'd talked about?

Margo had something Horace and the Cowboy wanted—or at least whoever hired them wanted it—but they hadn't found it at Margo's house. They were desperate enough to find it that they'd hunted down Sadie, thinking she had it. But she didn't. She and Margo had only spent time together outside of work on Monday. One day. One hour, really. Why would anyone think that would create a relationship strong enough in Margo's mind to trust Sadie with whatever it was Margo was supposedly hiding?

Unless Margo had hidden it from Sadie too. Considering Margo's past associations, maybe she knew the item wouldn't be safe in her possession. The Cowboy had said Margo admitted to handing it off. But how would she have transferred this mystery item to Sadie without Sadie knowing? And what could the thing be? A computer disk full of incriminating information? Surveillance video? The item had to be of considerable value to draw so much attention.

They hadn't driven in Sadie's car, and Margo had only been to Sadie's apartment once, and she'd been right there with Sadie the whole time. Margo hadn't had an opportunity to hide anything. And Sadie had cleaned the room top to bottom just a couple of days ago and found nothing. Maybe Margo slipped the item into Sadie's purse, but Sadie had reorganized her purse just last night and hadn't found anything out of the ordinary. There simply was no opportunity for Margo to have handed anything off. Except . . .

Sadie gasped and straightened a tiny amount, enough for her

back to twinge in protest at the sudden movement. When Sadie had gone into the bathroom to change before they'd left for the bar, Margo had said she needed to get her purse from the Land Cruiser—for lipstick, she'd claimed. She was back before Sadie had come out of the bathroom, but she had been alone in Sadie's room for a short time. Enough time to have brought something in from the Land Cruiser and hidden it? Something hidden in a green shoe box, perhaps?

She thought back to the moment when she'd pulled the green box out from under the bed. It was too light to have held shoes, and taped up to prevent being tampered with. It had been under the bed, shoved into a dark corner, barely discernible. If not for the fact that Sadie had been clearing everything from her room, if she hadn't been leaving Caro's for good, she'd have never given that corner under the bed any attention at all. The box could have safely stayed there until Margo devised a way to get it back.

If Margo hadn't paid the ultimate price for whatever role she was playing, Sadie would have been hurt at having been used. As it was, she felt nothing but sorrow and a growing sense of urgency about the discovery. That box was sitting on top of half a dozen other boxes, in plain sight, waiting to be found. Margo had died for whatever was in that box; Sadie nearly had as well. The idea of leaving her hiding place made her tremble, but she'd heard no sign of movement for at least forty-five minutes; and they'd *said* they were leaving.

She waited until she'd accepted this next move as inevitable before carefully and slowly unfolding herself from the rocks. Her legs shook when she stood, and she had to hold onto the rocks and trees for those first few steps, while her muscles seemed to fall back into place. Every joint ached, every step was painful, and yet she had no choice but to move forward.

Every few steps, she would stop and listen for anything other than the rustle of wind through the desert grasses. She peered toward the bottom of the hill she'd fallen down, looking for the edge of the cliff Horace had said she'd fallen off of, but just as she'd remembered, it ended in an arroyo. Even had she fallen to the bottom, she would very likely have survived. Had Horace said it was a cliff in order to deceive her into coming out of hiding? If they were set to ambush her, she'd be pathetically easy prey right now.

She walked up the incline she'd fallen down—not nearly as steep as she'd thought—and crouched beneath a tree in order to listen and watch the area around her for any sign that the men were still there. She saw nothing, heard nothing, so she took a breath and continued forward. The half-moon didn't cast as much light as she'd have liked, but her eyes had adjusted, and she was grateful for any light at all right now.

She found the place where she'd made the sharp turn from the creek bed and looked both ways: the direction where the van had been, and the direction where she'd been taken. She spent a few minutes looking for the cigarette butt the Cowboy would have thrown into the brush before going after her. She found it and rolled it up in the cuff of her pants in hopes of preserving it for the police.

Then she cautiously moved back toward the van's parking spot and could finally breathe again when she saw that the van was no longer there. She continued to be hyper-vigilant of her surroundings, however. If Horace wasn't trying to lure her out, why had he said there was a cliff? She thought over a few other things Horace had done that seemed out of character: he'd removed the ropes from her hands, and perhaps the fact that he hadn't caught up with her even though he'd been less than a dozen feet behind her when she had fled indicated that he was an unwilling participant in the events of the night. It was paltry evidence to lead her to a positive evaluation of him—she remembered his aggressive treatment of her once she was in the van—but there was enough for her to question his dedication to the cause that the Cowboy seemed fully committed to. When she'd been hiding, he'd commented that things hadn't gone as he had wanted them to go, that too many people had been killed. He'd blamed the Cowboy for that. Could Horace have *let* Sadie get away? The possibility didn't give her many warm fuzzies since he'd still left her alone in the desert.

Sadie followed the dirt road in the direction they'd come from, her heart thumping in her chest as she relived what had happened. She scanned the desert around her while rubbing her arms to stay warm. It was so cold.

Would they come back to find her sooner than first light? How would Horace explain the lack of the cliff and therefore the lack of her body at the bottom of it? The dirt road joined a paved road, and the scraggly trees she'd used as a kind of cover became scarce, which would make her even more vulnerable, but what choice did she have? She had to get to that green box before anyone else did. The Cowboy had said she was hard to find, which meant they might not know where she'd lived in Santa Fe—after all, they hadn't found her until the Fiesta.

Everything hurt, but her head was especially painful, throbbing with every step. The blood had dried, but she was certainly not a pretty sight. She approached the two-lane road ahead, which she assumed led to the interstate. The sound of a diesel engine caused her to spin around and stare down the road several seconds before a single headlight came into view, lumbering in her direction.

As she watched it approach, her heart rate increased, and she looked around before hurrying to an empty ditch and ducking behind the berm to hide herself completely. It might be the men coming back for her. But the van hadn't been diesel, and she had seen two operating headlights on the van, one a little brighter than the other one.

Instead of the engine passing her by and fading into the distance, it seemed to be slowing down. She pulled herself further into the ditch, controlling her breathing and willing whoever it was to pass her by. They couldn't have seen her, could they?

She heard a door squeak open then shut. She clenched her eyes closed. Why would they stop here? Oh gosh, was she about to be shot in the head?

The sound of heavy footsteps approaching caused her to put a hand over her mouth to keep from whimpering. Then they stopped, directly above her. She stayed perfectly still, trying to convince herself that it was a coincidence.

"Hey."

She stayed where she was. Maybe there was someone else he was talking to, right?

"Hey," he said louder.

She swallowed and opened her eyes, tilting her head back as her eyes traveled up the large body of a man peering down at her. The single headlight lit him up from the back, making him appear that much more ominous. "You drunk, lady?"

Sadie shook her head, but couldn't find her voice.

"You sick?"

"No," she managed to say, though her voice shook.

"What you doing out here?"

"I, uh, need to get to Santa Fe," she said, slowly coming to her feet. She still had to look up at him, but at least he was right side up this time. He was Native American, with a large face and long, dark hair pulled back into a ponytail.

"That's why you're in the ditch? 'Cause you need to get to Sandifay?"

She looked past him to the truck. "Can you give me a ride to Santa Fe?"

"You are trouble," he said, narrowing his eyes at her. She scrambled out of the ditch, though she feared her stiff movements made her look like a zombie. He took a step back when she joined him at the side of the road.

"I'm *in* trouble," Sadie clarified. "And I have to get to Santa Fe. I can pay you when we get there—anything you want." Even though Caro was angry and hurt, she would loan Sadie the money after Sadie explained how her purse was still in the kidnapper's van. "Please, sir." She stopped fighting her emotion and let it shade her voice, though the burden of feeling her own fear made her knees weak. "My life, and the lives of others, depends on this. Please."

She hadn't realized she'd clasped her hands together, though the pleading was completely sincere. She stared at him, and held her breath.

"What happen to your head?"

Sadie raised her hand to the dried blood. "I fell," she said. "I can get it taken care of when I get to Santa Fe. I'll pay you whatever you want. Please."

He narrowed his eyes at her, then nodded. "Fifty dollars to take you to Sandifay."

"Yes, yes," Sadie said, nodding quickly enough that it made her a little dizzy. "I'll pay you a hundred dollars. Absolutely."

"And you ride with the boxes."

Sadie eyed the back of the truck that was filled with cardboard boxes of various sizes and containing who-knew-what cargo. "A hundred and fifty if I can ride in the cab."

He frowned, but she held his gaze. She understood why he didn't want her in the cab with him—he'd found her in a ditch in the middle of the night after all—but she didn't want to ride in the back of a pickup truck.

"Two hundred."

"Deal."

CHAPTER 33

Her driver took back roads to Santa Fe, which she didn't think was even possible. What would have been about twenty minutes—she'd realized that she was about halfway between Albuquerque and Santa Fe—ended up being over an hour. Neither of them seemed to be in the mood to talk, so Sadie looked out the window, and he hummed along to the country music playing on the radio, though he rarely got the tune right. She clenched her jaw to keep her teeth from hitting together when they hit a bump or pothole in the road—the truck definitely needed new shocks.

It was nearly midnight when they pulled up at the curb in front of Rex and Caro's house. The garage doors were closed, and the lights were out. She hated waking them but she'd promised to pay this stern man who had saved her with his truck. She headed up the walk and tried to straighten her clothes.

She automatically reached for the door handle to let herself in, then remembered she didn't live here anymore and had put her key on the counter when she'd left Thursday afternoon. Instead, she rang the bell and waited while finger-combing her hair that she felt sure looked like it belonged on a Troll doll. After a few seconds, she heard someone approaching and exhaled slowly. Moments before the porch light flipped on and the door opened, she realized the footsteps belonged to Rex. Great.

He was wearing a white T-shirt and flannel pajama bottoms. He spoke before she had a chance to say a single word.

"What happened to you?" He was staring at her head.

She touched the dried blood. "It looks worse than it is," she said, which was a lie. It hurt like crazy. "I know you'd rather I wasn't here, but I've got a situation and I really need to talk to Caro." She looked past him toward the hallway that led to her former apartment where the box was waiting. Surely Caro would have followed him out of the room.

His expression changed from confusion to . . . apprehension. "She said she was with you."

Sadie startled as her eyes snapped back to meet his. "What?"

"She said she was staying with you at your hotel in Albuquerque so she didn't have to drive back to the Fiesta in the morning. She's not with you? What's going on?"

The truck behind her honked, reminding her of her chauffeur. She held up one finger toward him, then turned back to Rex. "I need two hundred dollars," she blurted out. She pointed a thumb over her shoulder. "He gave me a ride, and I told him I'd pay him. I was going to ask Caro, but—"

"Where is my wife?" Rex asked, sounding angry.

"I don't know," she shouted at him. "But I will do everything I can to find out once I pay this guy for the ride. Do you have two hundred dollars?" She knew he did. They had a safe in their room where they kept some emergency cash.

"I don't care about your ride," Rex growled. "Where's my wife?"

"Oh, for heaven's sake," Sadie said, throwing up her hands.

"Can you set aside your pigheadedness for two seconds and listen to me? I need to pay this man—he saved my life. I need two hundred dollars, and I don't have time for your hardheaded, boorish ways right now!"

Rex narrowed his eyes, but turned and headed for his room. Sadie gave a thumbs-up to the man still scowling from the truck. She stayed on the porch, shifting her weight and holding herself back from going for the box. If she didn't think her driver would charge after her, she'd have chanced it.

Two minutes later, Rex walked past her without a word. He handed the cash to the man in the truck, then came back to the door while the truck growled and rumbled down the road.

"Now help me find my wife," Rex said, leading the way into the house.

Sadie followed him, hearing Caro's voice ringing in her head: *"You're not the only one with skills, you know."* Caro had overheard Sadie talking to Ethan Standage, and she'd been outside the trailer when Sadie left the message for Marcus about what she and Ethan had talked about during the balloon ride. What if those things hadn't been circumstantial? What if they'd played into Caro trying to figure out what it was Sadie wouldn't tell her? Sadie also thought about Horace saying they'd been called back to the Fiesta. Oh, heavens.

"When did Caro say she'd decided to stay with me?" Sadie asked as she walked to the phone in the kitchen to call Caro's cell phone.

"When she left this afternoon," Rex told her.

Caro's phone rang four times before going to voice mail. Sadie hung up without leaving a message. She rested her hand on the handset. "I'll call Lois and see if she knows anything. I think she said she'd forwarded the bakery calls to her cell."

She thumbed through the phone book while Rex paced back and forth across the kitchen floor.

The phone rang twice before Lois answered. Sadie immediately apologized for calling so late.

"It's fine," Lois said with a laugh. "Inez and I were just getting a head start on tomorrow. Is everything okay?"

"Actually, I'm looking for Caro. She isn't answering her phone, and I wondered if she was with you." Rex stopped pacing and moved closer to listen in. She pushed the button that transferred the call to speakerphone so he didn't have to breathe down her neck.

"Nope, it's just Inez and me. I haven't seen Caro since she went after you."

"After me? When was that?" Sadie asked.

Rex turned and headed for the other side of the room where he grabbed his car keys from the rack by the garage door. Without asking, she knew he was getting ready to go to Albuquerque.

"Um, I don't know, a little after six, I guess. She said she needed to talk to you. Is everything okay?"

"I'm not sure," Sadie said, though she felt sick to her stomach. "Can you please tell me exactly what happened?"

"A few minutes after you left, she asked if I needed her to stay— she said that she wanted to catch up with you. I'd hoped you two were going to work things out so I said we'd be fine and that I'd see her in the morning. She did catch up to you, right?"

"No," Sadie said, closing her eyes. "I didn't see her after I left the booth. I tried calling her just now, but she didn't answer her phone."

"Oh my gosh," Lois said after a few moments of silence. "What should I do? How can I help?"

"I don't know," Sadie said. "I need to talk to Rex and make a game plan. I'll let you know, okay? But until you hear from me, don't talk to anyone about this, okay? Just in case."

"In case what?"

"Just don't talk to anyone," Sadie said, turning and scanning the kitchen. Could Caro have left anything behind that would tip Sadie off? "And call her house if you hear from her. . . . Wait, actually call Rex's phone." She lifted her eyebrows toward Rex, who moved closer to the phone.

He gave Lois his number; she read it back and agreed to call.

Sadie hung up the phone and crossed the kitchen while processing through what had happened after she'd left the booth. Sadie began a search of the kitchen, looking for notes Caro might have made, phone numbers she might have written down somewhere.

"What are you doing?"

"Looking to see if Caro left behind any clues. I think she was investigating all this stuff—all the things I wouldn't tell her. I need to know what she knew." If Sadie was right, Caro could be in real danger. But Caro would also have been careful about leaving any notes behind. It was the first rule of investigating—one Sadie had learned the hard way—protect your information. She was sure Caro understood how important that rule was. "I need to call Pete." Pete would help her line things up, and he'd know what she should do next. Call Marcus? Go back to the Fiesta?

"We can call him on the way to Albuquerque. We're going to retrace her steps," Rex said, turning toward his room. He stopped and asked, "Do we need to take you to the emergency room to get your head checked?"

Sadie raised her hand to the scabbed-over cut, but shook her head. "There's no time, but thanks for the offer." Sadie looked at her dirty hands and clothes. She was a mess, and Rex was in his pajamas. It was a necessary evil that they take a few minutes to prepare themselves. "I should get cleaned up though."

He nodded and looked relieved. "We leave in two minutes."

"Okay," Sadie said, turning toward her old apartment.

"Sadie," Rex said.

She stopped and turned to face him. "What?"

"Is Caro having an affair?"

"What? No," Sadie said, shaking her head.

Rex pulled his eyebrows together, and his eyes went back to the dried blood on the side of Sadie's head. "Then what's going on here?"

Sadie took a breath. "I'll have to tell you on the way. We need to hurry."

CHAPTER 34

Sadie tried not to look at herself as she cleaned up a little bit, but the streaks of mud and blood were difficult to clean up without looking at her reflection. Her hair was atrocious; she had to pull out a few weeds before attempting to smooth it. The biggest issue was the cut on her scalp. It was less than an inch long and had already scabbed over, but it had bled pretty badly, and as she cleaned it up, she could already see the bruise forming around it. If it left a scar, she'd need to find a new way to do her hair.

Her hands were scraped, as were her calf and her knees. Going to bed was what she really needed to do right now, but that was out of the question. She didn't bother asking to borrow any of Caro's clothes, though the idea did cross her mind. Rex was wound pretty tightly, and it wasn't hard to imagine an explosion for any number of reasons.

She grabbed the green box from the apartment, a notebook from the cupboard beneath the phone, and the retractable razor blade Caro kept in the utility drawer in the kitchen. Even then she beat Rex to the truck. She was waiting next to the passenger door when he finally came into the garage. He hit the button that raised the garage door behind them, and strode purposefully to the driver's side while shoving his arms into the sleeves of his jacket.

It wasn't until she was climbing into the passenger seat that she remembered the earlier fear she'd had that the box wouldn't be in the apartment at all. The fact that it was still here meant the Cowboy and Horace didn't know where she'd been staying, or hadn't arrived yet.

"What's the box for?" Rex asked after starting the truck and backing out of the driveway.

Sadie touched the tape. "It might hold the key to everything."

"What's that supposed to mean?" he snapped, looking at her quickly before pulling into the street. He shifted into drive and took off so fast that Sadie was thrown against the seat. "I want to know what's going on here."

Sadie took a breath and laid it all out. Rex already knew about her BLM involvement, so she told him about Margo's history and disappearance, the conversation with Shel at the gallery Wednesday night, and her own kidnapping from the Fiesta. She explained the connections to the Standage family she suspected tied everything together, and then about her kidnappers' reference to something Sadie thought Margo had hidden in her room Monday night—the box.

"What does any of this have to do with Caro?" Rex asked when she finished. Whether he meant to or not, he sounded beyond angry.

"I'm not sure, but she made a comment about finding out what I was doing. She said she could figure it out if she wanted to." Sadie stared at the box, and a wave of regret and guilt washed over her. "The men who took me out to the desert were called back to the Fiesta. They'd been bothered by my talking to Ethan, maybe Caro talked to him too. If she'd done some poking around and discovered his tie to things, she might have put herself right in the middle of this, just like me." She wanted to believe something different had happened, but what other reason could there be?

"This is exactly why I wanted you to leave!" Rex bellowed, startling Sadie.

In her current state, responding in kind was not hard to do. She turned toward him and narrowed her eyes, almost glad to have a chance to let out some of her own aggression. "And that is *exactly* why Caro would have investigated on her own. Because she didn't know what was going on. Because *I* didn't tell her. Because *you* told me not to. I was just following *your* orders."

"Don't you dare put this on me!" Rex yelled, gripping the steering wheel so tight she felt sure she'd hear it crack any second. "I was trying to protect her."

"Well, it didn't work, did it?"

He glared at her and she glared back before they both looked out the windshield again. Sadie tried to keep her own guilt at bay, but she couldn't do it. They had no idea where Caro was or why. Making Rex feel worse about an already horrible situation was a waste of energy and not entirely fair. Sadie *had* brought this to their doorstep, and all the justification in the world couldn't hide that truth. It was also true, however, that if Rex hadn't forbidden Sadie from talking to Caro in the first place, Caro wouldn't have been investigating things on her own.

She was trying to find some way to say she was sorry for her part in things without making it sound as though Rex had won this argument, when Rex picked up his phone and touched a single button—speed dial. The ringing immediately sounded through the speakers of the truck thanks to a hands-free Bluetooth system that routed his calls through the sound system. Sadie had seen him use it over the last several weeks during the few times the three of them had gone somewhere in Rex's truck together. It rang four times before Caro's voice invited them to leave a message. Hearing her voice made Sadie sad all over again. Rex didn't leave a message and pushed a single button to hang up the call before putting the phone back in the middle console of the truck.

"I'm opening the box," Sadie said, shifting out of her melancholy and into the present. Regardless of fault, Caro was missing, and this box might hold the reason why. She turned on the interior light, then took the razor from her pocket and used the button to slide the blade out of the plastic holder. A shoe box and packing tape didn't seem to warrant the interest the Cowboy had in whatever it was Margo was hiding.

The blade cut through the layer of tape like butter, and she turned the box, severing the tape all the way around. After retracting the razor and putting it back in her pocket, she used both hands to lift the top off the box. Inside was cloth, just plain muslin. She hadn't thought about fingerprints until right now, and the reminder was just plain annoying—so annoying that she didn't heed it. There wasn't time.

She pulled back the first layer of cloth, and then the next; it was tightly packed, and after pulling back the third fold, she worried that the box was just full of cloth, but then she caught a flash of brown. She pulled back the additional folds, hanging the excess fabric over the edges of the box.

Inside the box was something that, at first glance, looked like a stick. Using a corner of the cloth, she picked up the item and turned it over to reveal the bowl of what she now realized was a ceremonial pipe. Intricate carvings covered every surface, and strips of rawhide attached skeletal remains of feathers to the end. She laid the pipe back on the cloth, suddenly realizing she'd seen it before—the only other time she'd seen an ancient ceremonial pipe up close. The acceptance of it was breathtaking. Scary.

"A pipe?" Rex asked regarding it in quick glances while continuing down I-25 toward Albuquerque.

"Not just any pipe," Sadie said, flickering her gaze toward him, though he was watching the road. "It's from one of Ethan Standage's photographs. In fact, I think it's on the cover of this year's anthology." She wished she'd taken the time to get Caro's copy of the book.

"I thought he left the stuff he photographed where he found it."

"That's what he says." She stared at the pipe lying innocently on the fabric. "At the gallery on Wednesday, Caro said that if Ethan were lying about leaving things be, it would destroy his art." Sadie remembered her earlier doubts about Ethan and whether he really left the artifacts behind, but then she thought back to the balloon ride conversation she'd had with him that afternoon. He feared someone was setting him up. What if he was being set up for more than murder?

"What if someone else is trying to destroy his art career for him?" Sadie let the question linger between them for a few seconds. "But who would want to do that? You know the family better than I do."

"I have no idea," Rex said, shaking his head. "He's pretty much a local hero."

"What about the ranch? Is there someone who's angry with the ranch?"

"There are always people angry at ranchers," Rex said. "Environmentalists mostly, but they cut down fences and burn down barns—this doesn't seem like something they would do. I don't know the Standages well enough to know if they have anyone else who might be out to get them."

"But you do know a little about the Standages. How supportive is Edward Standage of his son's work?" She envisioned a bowlegged, hardened cowboy who chewed tobacco and shot trespassers on sight. Basically, she pictured the Cowboy who'd abducted her that night. "He wasn't at the exhibit."

Rex shook his head. "Edward worships the ground his son walks on. He and Ethan's mother, Lacey, are the very picture of doting parents. When Ethan was young, I was sure he'd grow up to be a spoiled, worthless loser because of it, but as far as I know, he's an upstanding guy, and Edward is as proud as ever."

"What about Ethan's responsibilities to the ranch? I understand his art has taken most of his focus, and Edward has had to divide his time between the ranch and Lacey. Maybe that's created some discord between them." She felt like she was grasping at straws. Her knowledge of the Standage family dynamics was so limited that she had little basis for any of her assumptions.

"Last I heard, he *is* taking over the ranch," Rex said, casting a glance toward her. "There was an article in the paper about it a few days ago. I think Ed's been hoping his son would step up for a few years now. Guess he finally is."

Sadie leaned back against the seat and looked at the pipe again. "If we can figure out who wants to ruin Ethan, we'll be that much closer to solving this."

"Those men who took you to the desert seem to want that pipe pretty bad."

"Right," Sadie said with a nod. "And they were connected to Langley, who dealt in artifacts. Maybe he was going to help them sell this. But did they want profit or to destroy Ethan Standage?"

"Maybe both," Rex said.

Sadie nodded.

They passed a sign that read ALBUQUERQUE—21 MILES. Fiesta Park was located a few miles outside of Albuquerque, which meant they were about fifteen minutes away from the last place they knew Caro had been.

Sadie's thoughts cycled quickly, and then stopped at her next avenue of thought. "Why would *Margo* have this?" And how would she have gotten it? For that matter, how would anyone have gotten it? Ethan spent months finding the relics he photographed, and he claimed to keep his locations secret. If he didn't bring it out of the wilderness himself, how was this pipe here at all?

But that piece clicked into place almost as soon as she considered the question: the missing assistants. They were the only other people who knew where the artifacts came from. She mentally sorted through all the prints that she could remember from the exhibit Wednesday night. Of all the artifacts featured, only one seemed to be sturdy enough and small enough to be easily smuggled away from wherever Ethan had found it.

She imagined the pipe wrapped up and hidden within the supplies packed in and out of the wild. Ethan had said his assistants were good men, but they were also in need of money for their families. Maybe they were made an offer they couldn't refuse. But they were both dead, and Ethan had only hired one assistant at a time. Why kill them both?

"Ethan's assistants are the men buried out at the site," Sadie said out loud in hopes it would help her process her thoughts faster. "They disappeared a few months apart, one right before Ethan's expedition last fall and one right after the spring one." She wriggled in her seat and turned toward Rex. "What if the first one—Teodor—was asked to help bring Ethan down and was killed because he refused? Ethan said he hired Raphael quickly, so he wouldn't have known him as well. If Raphael smuggled this out, and then turned it over to whoever wanted it, the Cowboy and Horace could have killed him to ensure his silence. They obviously have no qualms about getting rid of complications. Except that Horace lied about my falling off a cliff and—"

Rex smacked the steering wheel. "Will you stop thinking about everyone else and think about Caro for just one full minute!"

Rage exploded within her, and she responded quickly enough to startle Rex with her knee-jerk reaction. "Will you open your mind to the fact that whatever is going on with Caro has to do with everyone else who is wrapped up in this mess? It's a puzzle, Rex, and Caro is the most important piece. But the way the other pieces fit together is the surest way for us to know how to proceed from here on out." Suddenly, Pete's face flashed into her mind. Pete! If anyone could help her put the pieces together, it would be him. He could help her explain all of this to Marcus too. She'd been un-kidnapped for over an hour and hadn't yet told the authorities.

"Can I use your phone?" Sadie asked Rex, who was still stewing over her last comment. Headlights from the other direction of traffic lit up his face intermittently. The phone was sitting in the middle console, and she reached for it, expecting he'd say yes. Before she got it, he grabbed it and put it in the pocket of his jacket.

"I need your phone," Sadie said, confused and wary.

"What for?"

"I need to talk to Pete about all of this and ask his advice."

"I don't think that's a good idea."

Sadie bristled. "Why not?"

"I don't want to tie up the line. Caro might call me back."

"I know how to answer a call if it comes through," Sadie said. It was all she could do not to roll her eyes. He was infuriating. "And I really need to call Pete."

Rex hesitated, then retrieved his phone from his pocket. Instead of giving it to Sadie, however, he pressed a button again—speed dial—and the speakers in the truck started ringing.

"Who are you calling now?" she asked, annoyed.

"Maybe she'll answer this time."

Sadie lifted her eyebrows and gave him an incredulous look. "Caro? She hasn't answered the other times. We need to take advantage of all our options, and Pete can—"

"Rex?" The shaky voice playing on the speakers of Rex's truck silenced Sadie in an instant.

"Caro!" Rex said, leaning forward in his seat, gripping the steering wheel with both hands. "Where are you? Are you all right?"

"I'm okay, but Sadie's in trouble, and I need your help."

CHAPTER 35

R ex cast a confused look at Sadie. "What are you talking about, Caro? What do you mean Sadie's in trouble?"

"I can't explain everything right now," Caro said, her voice shaking. "But Sadie has something that doesn't belong to her, and if you and I don't get it to these men, they're going to kill her, Rex."

It was the same story the Cowboy had told Sadie—that if she went with them, they wouldn't kill Margo. She grabbed a pen from the truck console and wrote on the notebook, *I'm not here.* Rex read it and nodded.

"Who's going to kill her?"

"These me—" The line went quiet. Rex and Sadie both froze. Of course the men were listening, but they were also orchestrating.

"Caro!" Rex yelled.

"I need you to find this thing Sadie took," Caro said, coming back on the line and talking fast. "It's got to be in one of the boxes she packed up on Thursday. The ones stacked in the apartment. We've looked everywhere else."

Sadie wrote *looked through my hotel and car* on the paper and showed it to Rex while Caro continued. The Cowboy had Sadie's purse, which had her hotel key. And Horace had found Sadie's car key when he'd searched her.

"I need you to go through the boxes and find this item. It's an artifact of some kind. Valuable," Caro said.

Sadie wrote *Don't say you have it* and showed it to Rex, who frowned. She held her breath until he spoke again.

"You're sure it's there?" Rex asked. His knuckles were white against the steering wheel.

"It has to be," Caro said, and the desperation in her tone convinced Sadie that she believed her life, and Sadie's too, might be forfeit if this artifact wasn't found. "We already checked her ho—" The line went mute again. Sadie circled the word *hotel* that she'd written earlier.

Rex pressed down on the gas pedal, and the truck sped up. He knew Caro was in Albuquerque and wanted to get there as quickly as possible. Sadie estimated they were still a good fifteen minutes from her hotel.

"I'll find it!" Rex shouted. A moment later the background fuzz from Caro's phone sounded through the speakers again. Rex relaxed the smallest bit. "I'll find it," he said again. "Then these people will let you go, right?"

"Yes," Caro said. "They'll let Sadie and me both go."

Rex was silent for a moment. "Where is Sadie?"

"I don't know where she is, Rex. But these same people took her. They're holding her somewhere, but she won't help them find this artifact. She said she'd rather die, and so . . . so they came for me," Caro said, almost in a whisper. "You have to find it fast, Rex. Where are you? You didn't answer at the house."

"I, uh, had to go to the store for some antacids," Rex said, looking at Sadie for help. She nodded that it was a good answer. "I'm almost back home. What do I do when I find this, uh, thing they're looking for?"

"Um . . ." Hushed voices on Caro's end of the call caused Sadie to lean forward, hoping she could make out a word or recognize a voice, but the sound was too distorted. "I'll call you back in half an hour," Caro said after a few seconds. "And—"

There were muffled voices in the background, and suddenly a man's voice filled the cab of the truck: the Cowboy. "You call the cops, I'll know about it, and she's dead. You got that?" He didn't give Rex a chance to answer as the connection broke.

They both sat in silence for several seconds, as if waiting for Caro's voice to come back on the line. Rex sped up even more. They were going to get pulled over. "What hotel were you staying at?"

"The Hampton," Sadie said as her fingers gripped the armrests. "By the airport. But she thinks you're in Santa Fe."

"I know. We're going to cut them off at the hotel."

"We're at least ten minutes away," Sadie said.

Rex wasn't listening. "We'll cut them off and get her back. The sooner the better. I'm not waiting half an hour while some mercenaries hold my wife for ransom. You've seen this van before. You know what we're looking for."

"They could be anywhere," Sadie said, trying to make him see reason while trying to think of a better idea. "Get off the freeway," she said a few seconds later.

Rex looked at her like she was nuts. "I'm going to the hotel."

She sat up straight, scanning the section of road in front of them and looking for the next freeway exit. "They won't be there waiting for you, but they think you're in Santa Fe so they're going to be heading your direction. If you get off the freeway and pull over on the on-ramp, we can watch for them. I know the van and when it passes, we'll be on their tail."

Rex considered that for a moment, still speeding down the freeway.

"And if you don't slow down, you're going to get pulled over. I saw on the news that nearly every cop in the city is working this weekend because of the Fiesta."

A sign for exit 233 came into view—the exit for Fiesta Park, in fact—and Sadie let out a breath when Rex started slowing down. "You better be right about this," he grumbled.

"I am," Sadie said with confidence. "They were driving the speed limit when they had me, and they were worried about the police so I bet they'll do that again. They weren't driving when we talked to them on the phone just now. It was too quiet in the background for them to have been in a car, so they likely called from the hotel. They're in a hurry to get this pipe back, so they'll come your direction." She paused, letting her thoughts catch up with her tongue. "Once we have a visual, we can call the police and set up a roadblock or something."

"They said no cops. I'm not risking it."

Oh, he was a stubborn man. "Well, we want to follow them anyway. Get off at the exit."

Rex nodded, slowed, then pulled off the freeway. He turned left, then left again, and pulled to the side of the on-ramp, positioning himself so that they both had a clear view of the traffic.

Sadie stared at every vehicle that passed by. Finding the van would be cake, and the success of her plan so far dispelled some of the rising tension. "They'll be driving in the slow lane," she said, thinking of the many cars she'd heard passing on the left when they'd been driving her out to the desert. She wondered if they were planning to go to the same location where they'd taken her. She hoped not. It would be difficult to follow them there. "I bet they'll be here within the next five or six minutes."

Rex nodded, but his expression was severe. This was his wife these men were holding. Every time her frustration with him rose, she had to remind herself of that.

"Please let me call Pete now."

"I'm not calling Pete," Rex said as resolute as ever. "He'll call the cops, and they said no cops."

"They also said to wait for them to call after half an hour, and we're not doing that."

"We are waiting."

He had a point.

She was working out a new argument as to why they had to call Pete when a white van sped past them.

"It's them," she said, hitting Rex in the arm. "Go, go, go!"

"You're sure?" Rex asked as he merged onto the freeway. The taillights for the van were a mile or so ahead of them by the time he'd reached freeway speed.

"It's a white van, I'm sure of that. See if you can get closer. If it's the one we want, there should be a crack in the back window."

"It better be the right van," Rex said between clamped teeth.

"Seriously, Rex, I'm this close to slapping you. I'm doing the best I can here, okay?"

He muttered something she chose to ignore, but he sped up slow and steady. When they were within twenty feet of the van, Sadie leaned forward and felt a rush of relief when she identified the crack. Thank goodness. Rex would likely have kicked her out on the side of the road if she'd been wrong. "That's it. Back off so they don't get suspicious."

Rex eased off on the gas and let another car get in front of him.

They passed a cop car with lights flashing on the side of the road. That, but for the grace of God, could have been Rex.

Each time they approached an exit, she worried the van was going to pull off into the desert, but they continued toward Santa Fe long enough for Sadie to know they weren't taking Caro to the same place they'd taken her. She was relieved, but then it opened up the new fear of an unknown location.

When the van did finally slow down, it took an exit Sadie had never taken before. They hadn't passed the airport yet, so they weren't quite to Santa Fe. There was a closed down gas station at the base of the off-ramp and a few boxy homes scattered here and there, but it didn't scream "residential area" and had a run-down look to it.

"Where are we?" Sadie asked. "Is this part of Santa Fe?"

"Not quite. It's gonna become obvious we're following them. I'll turn the other way. Circle back."

Sadie nodded, and Rex turned right as the van went left. He drove a hundred yards down the road before turning around on a ragged street. Another car got off the freeway and headed the same direction the van had taken—west. Rex fell in behind it.

There were scattered homes, most of them trailers placed with a lack of organization. Some of the lights were on inside the dwellings, but there wasn't a lot of traffic. The car between them and the van turned onto a narrow road, and Rex slowed down so as to give the van more space. Luckily, the van didn't pull onto a side street where it would have looked suspicious if Rex had followed them. Instead the van continued forward at least four or five miles before turning onto a dirt road. A mailbox was posted out front.

"It's a driveway," Sadie said.

"Watch them," Rex said as he drove slowly past the entrance while Sadie surveyed the property.

"There's a house back there," Sadie said. "No lights on inside, but the headlights of the van lit it up for a minute. Trailer, I think."

"Any other vehicles?"

"Not that I could see," Sadie said. The property was far enough behind them that she had turned around in her seat. "There's a shed and an old camper, I think. Lots of sagebrush and overgrown grass."

Rex drove another quarter mile, then turned around, shut off his lights, and drove back the way they had come. She looked hard at the area surrounding the house. A window was now lit up inside. Rex stopped in front of the driveway. They both remained silent, but the unasked question hung between them.

"Now what?" Rex finally asked.

"How long has it been since that call?" Sadie asked.

"Twenty-six minutes."

"Which means they'll be calling any minute. I think you should tell them you have the pipe when they call. They'll probably want you to meet them somewhere."

"What if it's a trap?"

"Which is why we should call Pete. Caro's his cousin, he isn't going to want anything to happen to her, which means he'll be careful. He understands how people like this think."

Rex shook his head; Sadie wasn't surprised. "Okay," she said, moving on. "Then I'm going to sneak up to the house and make sure Caro's in there and that she's safe. Do you have a flashlight?"

"I need to get out of the road," Rex said, pulling forward.

"Head over there," she said, pointing toward a dark, obviously abandoned trailer a hundred yards down the road. The windows were boarded up and a NO TRESPASSING sign had been nailed crookedly onto one of the plywood panels.

"I'm coming with you," Rex said as he pulled in behind the abandoned trailer.

"You can't," Sadie said with a shake of her head. She put the lid back on the box with the pipe and set it on the floor at her feet. "You have to stay here to take their call and arrange the trade-off."

"What if you don't get back before they call?"

"Then leave. I'll figure something out." She'd find a way to call the police is what she meant. She'd paid attention to the road signs, and the number on the mailbox was 89. She'd break into one of the other homes and use their phone if she had to. Her focus right now, though, was to make sure Caro was there and to get close enough to figure out who these men were and what part Caro played in their overall plan.

"I can't just leave you here," Rex said, but he sounded annoyed, making her wonder if he wanted to leave her but couldn't get past his own conscience.

"You will if you have to choose between Caro and me," Sadie said. "Now, do you have a flashlight in here somewhere? I can signal you from the house with it, let you know I'm there, and you can pump the brakes—I'll see the glow of the brake lights—to confirm you saw me."

"You've done this before?"

"I worked with Cub Scouts for too long. The flashlight?"

"In the roadside kit," he said, getting out of the truck and going around to the back door.

Sadie did the same, careful to be as quiet as he had been, and found a tire iron about the same time he handed her the small flashlight. She turned it on quickly to make sure it worked; it did. She had light and she was armed—it was a good start. If only her heart wasn't racing.

CHAPTER 36

"O kay," Sadie said after they rounded the edge of the trailer. "I'll flash the light once if she's there, twice if she isn't."

"She has to be there," Rex said.

Sadie nodded and kept to herself that the other part of her plan was to try to get Caro out of there. These men were killers, though she hadn't made a big deal about it to Rex.

"And then you'll come back to the truck?"

"Leave without me if you have to, I'll be okay." She was impressed by how calm she sounded despite how freaked out she was. She didn't want to be alone in the dark desert. But this was for Caro, and Sadie had to make sure she was safe.

"I should have brought my gun," Rex said.

Sadie almost made a joke about New Mexicans and their guns but decided now wasn't the time. Instead, she did one more scan of the truck for anything that might come in handy. She wished she had the walkie-talkies she and Caro had used when they were doing her informant work.

They found a place for Rex to stand that gave him a solid view of the house and determined where Sadie would need to be in order to give the light signal and see his response. By the time she hurried across the street, it had been thirty-four minutes since they'd talked to Caro. Why hadn't anyone called Rex back yet?

She kept to the thick brush and grass that lined the road, then darted across the driveway and went from a large bush to a small tree to a hiding place behind the shed, which was about thirty feet west of the house. From there she eased around the side and got a better view of the trailer. It was gray, old, and in disrepair. It sat on a concrete foundation, about half of which was covered in white lattice skirting. The windows were covered with either heavy drapes or old mini-blinds, which meant she had to get closer in order to make the visual confirmation of Caro. After crouching down as low as she could and still be able to walk with her incredibly sore muscles, she hurried across the open space toward the west end of the trailer.

Once there, she pressed her back against the metal siding, caught her breath, and then turned and went up on her tiptoes. She could just see over the windowsill—but even being this close, the blinds prevented her from seeing anything more than the movement of bodies. She could hear the murmur of voices and wondered if it were just Horace and the Cowboy in there or if the third man had joined them this time. She hated the idea of Caro being so horribly outnumbered, and that gave her more motivation to confirm whether or not Caro was even there. Rex was likely very antsy by now. She wondered if they'd called him yet.

She stayed close to the trailer and scooted around the back corner, hoping for another window that might afford her a better view. A large wooden porch—more like a deck, really—had steps coming down the side, parallel to the trailer rather than straight back from the back door. If she stood on one of the steps, she might be able to see through a gap where one of the blinds was bent.

Light caught her eye, and she moved back to the corner and peered around it to see a set of headlights coming down the driveway. It wasn't a car—the lights were too high. It must be a truck or another van. She heard a door slam from somewhere in front of the house a minute later. She glanced toward Rex's hiding place. He was probably completely freaking out over this additional member of the "party no one wanted to go to."

The front door opened, and she heard moving feet, then voices, the shutting of the front door, and more feet walking around the lit portion of the trailer. This new arrival must be the third man—the man the Cowboy and Horace had been waiting to arrive to talk to her in the desert. They must have been waiting for him as well.

She edged back toward the window by the porch steps but froze when hinges creaked above her and the back door swished open. She dove toward the space below the steps where the heavy shadows were her best cover and moved backward until she realized she was no longer under the stairs, but under the porch. She shivered and wrapped her arms around herself, envisioning all kinds of horrible bugs and rodents surrounding her. For the second time tonight she was in a totally creepy place she never imagined she'd go to on purpose.

"Describe it to me," a man's voice said—Horace, she thought. No one had come out with him. Was he on the phone?

Sadie looked up through the small spaces between the two-by-fours of the porch, but she could only see his form pacing above her.

"That's it," he said, sounding relieved. "Your wife will be very glad to hear that you found it. Here's what we're going to do: Get on I-25 and head south. I'll call you in ten minutes with more instructions. . . . I said I'll call you. And don't call the cops—we've got an in at the department and we'll know if you try to involve them. Your wife's life *is* on the line here. . . . Yeah, you can talk to her."

The footsteps above her turned, and Horace's voice moved back inside the trailer. "He wants to talk to you. You have ten seconds to convince him you're still alive, but he'd better—" The door slammed shut, and Sadie let out the breath she'd been holding. Caro was here.

Sadie crawled out of her hiding spot and went around the corner of the house to the spot where she knew Rex would be able to see her light. She turned it on and off one time, then waited several seconds before she saw the faint red glow of brake lights confirming he'd received the message. Horace had said he had an in at the police department, was that true? Could it be Marcus? Had Sadie been feeding him information all this time? She didn't think so, and the heavy thoughts were simply more fuel for what she had to do right now—get Caro out of there.

Moving as carefully as she could, she returned to the back porch, taking a deep breath for strength as she ducked back under it. After Sadie's sophomore year of college, she'd taken a teaching job in a small town in Southern Utah. The school district had let her and the other female teacher stay in a single-wide trailer not much different than this one. Because of that one summer, Sadie knew that trailers and mobile homes came with a trapdoor of sorts toward the center of the structure, usually accessed through a closet inside the house. The door led to the crawl space that accommodated the plumbing and—for the very bravest of homeowners—extra storage. Sadie's roommate had once bet her an entire package of Fig Newtons that she wouldn't go into that crawl space. Sadie had gladly lost that bet.

The crawl space of this trailer was perhaps three and a half feet high with a metal vent on each wall of the trailer's cement foundation. Sadie took a breath and scooted toward the vent underneath the porch. It was attached to the cement with hinges rather than screws, and they squeaked loudly when she lifted up the vent, even though she went slow. The voices above her didn't stop, however, and she was able to carefully hold the vent open while maneuvering her body through the hole.

The footsteps and voices were louder once she was underneath the trailer itself, increasing her anxiety as she shined the light around the horrible place. In addition to the concrete foundation, cinder-block supports made it look almost like a small city. Unfortunately the small city was tangled in spider webs, and as she moved her flashlight beam, something on the far side scurried away from the light.

Her every instinct told her to run, but instead she got onto her hands and knees—the tire iron in one hand and the flashlight in the other—as she made another, slower, scan of the crawl space. Her flashlight beam struck something bright green toward the center, and it took her a moment to realize it was a large plastic bin of some kind. Apparently these owners were the brave type willing to utilize the crawl space for storage.

She moved closer, having to hold the flashlight in her mouth to keep her balance as she crawled along the hard-packed dirt. Something squirmed beneath her hand when she put it down, and she squeaked but managed to keep from screaming outright. This might very well be her worst nightmare.

For Caro, for Caro, for Caro.

She attempted to block out everything but the green bin in front of her; it made a good destination goal within the maze. When she reached it, she realized that the trapdoor was directly above the bin. How fortuitous. Maybe the owners accessed whatever was in the bin through the trapdoor, though due to its size, the bin would have had to be brought in through the foundation vents; the same way she'd entered.

She tried to push the bin out of the way so she could access the door. It was heavy, and Sadie had to lie on her back and push against it with her feet. It scraped against the dirt, and Sadie froze, but the footsteps above and to the left of where she seemed to be didn't stop. The voices seemed to be rising too.

She pushed harder, though slowly, until the bin was out of the way. Carefully she pulled herself into a squat, put the tire iron on the ground and the flashlight in her mouth, and then reached her hands over her head, pressing them against the square piece of plywood. There was no hinge that she could see or feel, which she assumed meant the board was just a plug-type door that would remove completely from the hole. There would likely be carpet above it.

She held her breath and listened carefully to make sure she couldn't hear anything directly above her, then she pushed the board up. It lifted easily, and when she'd cleared an inch or two, she moved it to the side. Something was in the way of moving it perfectly, so she had to raise up on her knees a little more to get a visual. She took the flashlight out of her mouth, turned it off, and put it in the front pocket of her pants. She managed to fit one hand through the gap she'd created, and used it to pull back the carpet and a few shoes that were keeping her from being able to open the trapdoor completely.

Once she'd moved the trapdoor out of the way, she stood up; the floor of the trailer hit her hip-high. Whereas the crawl space had been cold and stale, the inside of the trailer was stuffy and musty smelling, like it had been closed up for too long.

She'd come up through a bedroom closet. The room was dark

and messy, and the door that led to the rest of the house was shut, allowing just a crack of light to seep in around the edges. She put the tire iron beside the opening before lifting herself up to sit on the floor. Sweat covered her scalp, but she kept a very clear picture of Caro in her mind and forced herself to continue.

She rose to her feet and picked up the tire iron before moving toward the bedroom door. It wasn't until she was next to the door that she tuned into the discussion taking place on the other side. She realized the volume of the voices had increased—and not simply because she was closer. The men were arguing.

" . . . is getting out of hand," a voice said. Horace?

"Getting?" said another voice. This one had an accent, but there was something familiar about it too. "This has been out of hand for a very long time. Everything is crazy."

Sadie blinked in surprise. It was Benny. Benny from the ranch. The foreman. Edward Standage's right-hand man. The man who bailed out Shel.

He burst out in Spanish, and the words rolled off his tongue much smoother than the English had. Horace quickly joined in.

The Cowboy's throaty voice interrupted them both. "You think I don't know what you're saying just 'cause you jabber away in Mexican?"

Another voice joined in, a woman's voice. Caro. "Where's Sadie?" she asked. "You said you'd take me to her."

Sadie was touched that Caro was so worried about her.

"Who is this Sadie?" Benny asked.

"Sarah," Horace said. "The woman we . . . took out to the desert earlier tonight. She has a couple of different names."

"Why are you doing this, Benny?" Caro said, a catch in her voice. "Ethan trusts you."

Benny didn't say anything, and the Cowboy spoke up. "What were you talking to Ethan Standage about?"

It was like someone was replaying a tape made of Sadie's capture.

Caro was silent, which Sadie was glad about until she heard a slap and Caro's soft gasp.

Sadie's hands balled into fists at her side, gripping the tire iron tightly. *You can't take on three men with a tire iron,* she told herself, but standing still was the hardest thing she'd ever done in her life.

"I ain't got time for games, lady. Why were you talkin' to Standage?"

"I—I wanted to ask him about the ranch."

"What about the ranch?" Benny asked.

"I'd been doing some research, and I found out that the ranch wasn't doing very well and that was why Ethan was taking a break from his art to help run it."

"Too late," Benny added. "He should have helped long ago. Why did you want to talk to Ethan about that?"

"Because it didn't make sense," Caro said. "He's making millions on his art. Why not use that to help the ranch? Why give up what he loved, ya know? I thought I could ask him about it, and it would help me understand what Sadie was working on."

"Blah blah blah and kumbaya," the Cowboy cut in. "Did Ethan tell you about the bodies found in the desert?"

"What?" Caro asked, sounding shocked. "What did he have to do with that?"

"She doesn't know anything," Horace said, sounding frustrated. "I can't believe you've taken this so far."

"I only done what you hired me to do."

"Hardly!" Horace said. "All my father wanted you to do was

turn Ethan's attention back to the ranch and you've turned this into a bloodbath. We should never have asked for your help. It's been a disaster."

Benny said something in Spanish, and since Sadie couldn't follow the conversation she pondered on what she'd learned. Horace was Benny's son. And Benny had hired the Cowboy to turn Ethan's focus to the ranch. But how, exactly? By ruining his art career through releasing the pipe publicly? Could a simple plan like that have turned into this? Horace had called it a bloodbath, and it seemed to be an apt description. Two assistants, Margo, Langley, and, as far as the men on the other side of the door knew, Sadie, too—all dead because Benny wanted Ethan to pay more attention to the ranching part of his life?

"Yer about to get yer pipe back," the Cowboy said, sounding bored. "Stop yer whining."

"We wouldn't have needed to get it back if you hadn't lost it," Horace said.

"I didn't lose it!" the Cowboy yelled. "Yer the one who said this Langley character would be a good contact. He's the one who lost it."

"Stop, stop," Benny said in his accented tones. "You forget that I talked to Ethan many times, Horace. I talked with Edward, too, but instead of Ethan increasing his role at the ranch, they talked of selling out, of leaving ranching all together. And then where would we be? It wasn't supposed to go like this, but we have to finish what's been started."

"Finish it how, Papa?" Horace said, frustrated. "How can you justify what's happened? Ethan's afraid, and he's turning back to the ranch like we wanted. There is no reason for anyone else to be hurt."

"Where's Sadie?" Caro cut in, fear tingeing her voice. Likely she, like Sadie, was beginning to understand how serious all of this was. How deadly it had been thus far. "When can I see her?"

"Sadie or Sarah or whatever the fool her name is, is dead."

The Cowboy's words were so final, so cutting, and so familiar. Sadie tightened her jaw, reliving the emotions she'd felt when the Cowboy had said the same words about Margo.

"What?" Caro cried out in horror.

Sadie put a hand to her own mouth and forced herself to take a full breath. *I'm not dead,* she said in her mind since she couldn't say it out loud. *I'm right here, and I'm going to get you out of this mess that I got you into in the first place.*

"What are you talking about?" Caro demanded. "You said you were taking me to her!"

"You really think we'd have taken you if we could have gotten the information from her? She fell off a cliff tonight, tryin' to make a run for it. You, however, became a delightful plan B."

"She's not dead," Caro said between sobs. "You're lying!"

"Horace saw it with his own eyes. Didn't you, Horace?"

Sadie strained toward the silence. Everyone waited for Horace to answer. "I did," he finally said. "She was trying to get away, and she fell. I . . . I'm sorry."

The Cowboy laughed. "Yeah, he's *real* sorry." The laugh turned into a cough. "Why's it so blasted hot in here?" Footsteps shook the trailer.

"Don't open the door," Benny said. "We need to be private."

"We're in the middle of nowhere," the Cowboy said. "Who's gonna see us? Ain't you supposed to be callin' that guy back, Horace? It's been ten minutes already."

"Yeah, I'm calling," Horace said. There was silence, and then Horace spoke again. "Take exit 271 and head east. There's a closed down auto body shop about a mile or so off the freeway. Park around back. We'll be there in ten minutes." There was another pause, and though Sadie strained for more information, all was silent until Horace spoke again in a different tone than the one he'd used on the phone. "I'm taking her with me."

"No way," the Cowboy said.

"The man wants his wife back, and I think we can trust them not to say anything—we know who they are and where they live."

"They know who we are too," said Benny. "We have no choice, *mi hijo.*"

Marcus had said Benny was a fabulous employee, loyal and protective of the Standages. Too loyal, perhaps. He was willing to do unthinkable things to keep the ranch going, perhaps preserving his job in the process. If Ethan had had any idea what Benny was willing to put into motion, Sadie had no doubt he'd have focused on the ranch long before now. It was hard to imagine that Benny didn't know what he was getting into when he hired the Cowboy; the man was a definite psychopath getting a kick out of the power he'd been given permission to wield.

"We won't say a thing," Caro said, her voice shaking. "I swear. We have children. Please, just take the pipe and let us go. We won't talk to anyone."

"It ain't up to you, darlin'," the Cowboy said. "It never was."

Caro started crying again.

"I'm not burying any more bodies," Horace said. "I told you that, Papa, I'm done with this. Her husband did what we wanted, and he didn't call the police. There's been nothing on the scanner. We can trust him. We don't need to kill anyone else."

Benny burst out in Spanish again, his words angry, harsh, and dominating. Horace didn't say another word and just took the lashing being dished out to him. Could Horace have been the one who buried the bodies of the assistants, and then given the tip to Ethan? He certainly had more regret than either of the other two.

Caro broke in with some Spanish of her own, and though Sadie didn't know what the words meant, the tone was pleading, begging. A slow trickle of sweat started down Sadie's back, and she shifted her shoulders while wiping at her damp forehead. It was stifling in here, but she felt bad complaining when Caro was hurt and scared for her life. If Horace left, that would leave two men she had to distract away from Caro.

"You ain't takin' her with you," the Cowboy said, cutting off Caro's pleas. "Simple as that. Get the artifact, come back here, and then we'll discuss what to do with her."

"Her husband will freak," Horace said, sounding genuinely scared. "He won't let me leave without returning his wife. He'll follow me back."

"Well, if he's stupid enough to do that, then you'll just have to take care of it. Won't be your fault at that point. Self-defense and all that."

"Please," Caro begged. "Please, you promised me you'd make it a trade. He'll trade the artifact for me. We won't—"

The sound of a hand hitting flesh and a startled scream from Caro made Sadie wince on the other side of the door. She put a hand over her mouth to keep herself quiet. A moment later, Caro was crying harder than ever.

Sadie put her palm on the door, holding back her own emotion as she felt Caro unleashing hers. Sadie had to get her out of here. She didn't move, but scanned the bedroom, glad her eyes had adjusted to the darkness. She thought she saw a cigarette lighter on the dresser. If she went back outside and started a fire, the men might leave Caro alone to try to put it out. But they might also suspect it was a distraction, and not leave Caro at all.

"Gag her," the Cowboy said, pulling Sadie's attention back to what was happening on the other side of the door. "Then get out of here and bring back that pipe."

"I don't want to do this anymore," Horace said. "Papa, please, this is too much. Killing women? Forcing Ethan's focus isn't worth all of this; it never was."

"We see things through," Benny said. "But it will end here, to-night. I promise."

"Tell me we'll send her back to her husband, Papa. Promise me."

"Maybe Benny should go to the meeting," the Cowboy said. "Horace can stay here and watch me hit her around some more. You choose."

Benny spoke again, this time in softer Spanish. Horace said something back, and then two sets of footsteps moved toward the front of the house.

"We'll be back soon," Benny said. "Do nothing until we return."

The front door closed, and a moment later the Cowboy chuckled. "You sure like thinking yer in charge, don't ya, Benny?"

CHAPTER 37

So, it's just you and me, huh, sweetheart?" the Cowboy said to Caro as the engine of a truck started up outside the trailer.

He laughed at whatever reaction Caro had given him. The laugh once again turned into a cough.

Sadie's fists were balled up so tight that her fingernails were cutting into the flesh of her palms. She recognized the rustle of cellophane and knew he was getting a cigarette out of the package.

"I'd offer you one, but I'm down to my last few. My night's become far more complicated than I expected. Good thing it's all about to pay off, right?" More laughing. More coughing. "Now, you best be a good girl so that I keep an open mind on what to do with you when them boys get back with our pipe. Good behavior can go a long ways with me. Man, it's too dang hot in here."

Sadie leaned closer to the door, listening to his footsteps. The sound of his footsteps changed when they hit linoleum, and then a door opened, but not the front door that Horace and Benny had just left through. He was on the back porch.

She could barely breathe as she realized this was her chance. Perhaps her only one. She'd followed her gut out in the desert and had gotten away; it gave her confidence to act quickly and capture the opportunity in front of her. She closed her eyes and prayed for enough presence of mind to use the next few minutes as wisely as she possibly could. When she opened her eyes, she put her hand on the doorknob and twisted it slowly before pulling open the door. It squeaked. She stopped. Listened. Pulled it open a little more, noting that the door opened into a hallway.

Poking her head out, she glanced to the right, where the light was coming from. There was a small kitchen with a cracked and faded linoleum floor. She could see the open back door. A wall separated the kitchen from a slightly larger living room set at the front of the trailer.

Sadie saw Caro in the living room portion, sitting on an old sixties-style chrome and vinyl kitchen chair. Her arms were pulled behind her back, likely tied together around the chair. Her ankles were tied to the legs of the chair. Her head hung forward, and her shoulders shook as she cried, her sobs nearly silent behind the gag—the same dirty bandana that had been shoved down Sadie's throat a few hours earlier.

She hadn't seen Sadie come in, and though startling her wasn't Sadie's first choice, she had no time to waste. The average cigarette took seven minutes to smoke; they were well into the second minute.

She moved as quietly and as carefully as she could into the living room, feeling able to breathe once the separating wall blocked her from the view of the open back door.

Caro looked up, then visibly startled as she stared at Sadie with wide, scared eyes that immediately began filling with tears again. The right side of her face was red and swollen. She tried to talk behind the gag, but Sadie shook her head, nodding toward the wall separating them from the kitchen. She could smell the cigarette smoke. She had approximately five minutes before he'd come back in—assuming he stayed outside to finish the whole cigarette.

She immediately bent down and started yanking at the knots tying Caro's ankles to the chair—feet were more important than arms right now. Thank goodness her son had shown such a propensity for knots when he was young. She never thought she'd be grateful for all the times she had to undo rope swings or shoelaces or ropes tied just for fun. In less than a minute, Caro's feet were free. Whoever had tied the knots hadn't seemed too worried about them being untied, which made sense, since even with her feet free, Caro was still tied to the chair.

The knots around Caro's wrists were not so kind, however. Sadie worked on them for thirty seconds before just grabbing Caro's arms instead and lifting her up, bending her arms painfully until they came over the top of the chair.

Caro whimpered, and Sadie sent her a mental apology; she didn't dare say anything out loud. She pointed toward the edge of the separating wall and moved forward. Caro nodded and followed after her. When they reached the edge of the wall, Sadie paused and peered around the corner. She couldn't see the Cowboy, but the back door was still open.

She put a finger to her lips, then tiptoed toward the bedroom, pushing Caro in front of her while keeping a close eye on the open door. If he came in right now, she didn't know what she'd do. She'd left the tire iron in the bedroom; maybe she could reach it in time.

Caro was a picture of obedience, and they crossed the exposed area without incident. Once inside the bedroom, Sadie waved her toward the closet and closed the door carefully before hurrying to join Caro, who stood in front of the open closet door watching Sadie with wide eyes. Sadie removed the gag.

"Sadie! I thought you were dead!" Caro whispered, but not quiet enough.

Sadie put a finger to her lips and pointed toward the hole in the floor of the closet. She pulled the flashlight from her pocket and picked up the tire iron from where she'd left it.

"We need to get you down there," she whispered, pointing the flashlight beam toward the hole. She put the flashlight in her mouth again—it tasted like dirt—and used both hands on Caro's ropes.

She felt the vibrations of the Cowboy's first few steps inside. She moved faster, frantically pulling at the stubborn knots. She heard the kitchen faucet turn on, buying them a few more seconds. The last knot finally loosened beneath her fingers, and she felt the rope slacken.

"Sit," she whispered to Caro, looking over her shoulder at the door. The faucet turned off. Any second now, the Cowboy would discover Caro was gone.

Caro sat and managed to finish wiggling her hands out of the ropes, which fell to the floor of the closet. She scooted forward and hopped into the hole before turning toward Sadie.

"Come on," Caro said.

Sadie was already scooting toward the hole, trying to take full breaths as the anxiety she'd kept tightly wrapped started seeping out of its bandages.

"I know yer still here," the Cowboy suddenly bellowed. "Did you forget what I said 'bout good behavior, 'cause I'm gonna remember that when I find you."

Sadie and Caro shared one horrified look.

"Go!" Sadie whispered.

Caro ducked into the crawl space, and Sadie scooted to the edge as heavy, angry footsteps shook the floor. She threw the flashlight into the hole at the same moment the bedroom door flew open. She jumped into the opening, but a hand clamped onto her shoulder. Sadie looked up into the raging eyes of a man she'd hoped to never see again. She attempted to twist out of his grasp, but she was trapped half-in and half-out of the hole in the floor.

"You!" he shouted, grabbing her with his other hand. Light shined up at her from the fallen flashlight.

"Sadie!" Caro screamed.

"Go!" Sadie yelled as the Cowboy pulled her upwards, surprising her with his strength. She threw her body to the side, trying to work her way out of the grip he had on her upper arms, but he was stronger than he looked. He wrapped an arm around her shoulders, pulling her into the room and causing her legs to scrape against the edge of the hole; they felt like they were on fire.

"Hurry!" she yelled toward Caro. "Get help!"

CHAPTER 38

As the Cowboy wrestled Sadie back into the trailer, she didn't wait for her head to catch up with her situation. She had to fight back before her enemy conquered. She twisted one arm out of his grip and grabbed the tire iron lying at the edge of the opening before jabbing it over and behind her head while the Cowboy attempted to pull her to her feet.

She was gratified to hear and feel the crack of iron against his skull, but the low-toned growl he let out in response sounded feral and angry; she hadn't hit him hard enough. She swung the tire iron a second time while she attempted to pull out of his grasp by twisting her trapped hand in the direction of his smallest, and weakest, finger. She managed to break his grip, but he grabbed the tire iron from her other hand and wrenched it away from her.

It was his turn to take a swing, but she used that moment to her advantage, doing a rather weak sweep kick that, though not good form, caused him to lose his balance and fall against the wall behind him.

Sadie ran for the closet again, but he lunged for her ankles and she pitched forward. She turned to her side as she fell, slamming into the sliding closet door and knocking it off the track. The paneling came down on the Cowboy, but it was cheap and flimsy, and she knew it wouldn't do much damage. It also blocked her access to the hole.

She got to her feet and ran for the bedroom door, hoping the closet door would slow him down. It didn't, and she heard him bellowing at her as he got to his feet, only a few yards behind her.

"You think we've done all this to be bested by the likes of you!"

He'd left the back door open, but she'd lost her sense of direction and ran toward the front door instead, pulling it open so hard it slammed against the cheap wall behind it.

Glancing over her shoulder as she crossed the threshold, she saw the Cowboy reach for something on top of the TV. She caught the outline of a gun in his hand, and adrenaline flooded through her as she pushed out the front door. She leaped off the front steps and landed hard on the packed dirt below. A twinge shot up her shin bone, but the pain didn't stop her as she ran for all she was worth toward the camper she'd seen upon her first survey of the property. She could take cover there. She hoped Caro was safe and far away.

A shot cut through the air, and a plume of dirt rose ahead and to the left of her. She cut hard to the right, which he'd likely been expecting because another bullet hit just a foot in front of her. She cut to the right again, instead of the instinctual left, and ran hard for the camper. She hadn't thought it was that far away. The Cowboy was screaming at her, but she couldn't sort out his words. Every ounce of energy she had was going toward creating distance between them.

The growl of an engine caught her attention, and she looked to the side as a set of headlights came barreling down the driveway. Were Horace and Benny back already? The thought of all three men coming after her sent a much-needed rush of adrenaline through her system.

She stared at the camper, certain Benny was about to plow her down if the Cowboy didn't shoot her first. She tripped and fell hard into the desert grass, the engine whined with increased speed behind her. As she scrambled to her feet, she risked a look over her shoulder in time to see that the truck wasn't coming toward her at all. Instead, it was heading toward the trailer, where the Cowboy stood on the steps with a gun in his hand.

He turned his head toward the headlights. But Sadie had a different angle than the Cowboy did, and she could see that the truck coming toward him was jet-black and gleaming in the moonlight as it plowed into the trailer at full throttle.

The sheet metal of the trailer wrapped around the cab of the truck, twisting off its foundation. The sound of breaking glass and crashing aluminum ripped through the night sky while one lone female voice cried out, "Rex!"

CHAPTER 39

"A nd then Rex drove his truck into the trailer," Sadie said, concluding her version of events. She was at the hospital, in a private waiting room, wrapped in a blanket and yet still shaking. She'd been checked out in the ER, then asked to return to the police station to give her statement, but she wanted to see Caro and make sure Rex was all right; they were still in the ER, or at least they had been when Sadie was escorted to this room with Marcus. "I thought Rex had gone to meet with Horace and Benny."

Marcus shook his head. "He saw that Caro hadn't come out of the trailer with the men, and when you didn't come back either, he snuck up on the trailer and was there when Caro crawled out from under the porch. He gave her his phone to call us and told her to get clear of the trailer. He thought he could create a distraction for you, but then when you ran outside, he had a quick change of plans."

Sadie was touched. No one had ever crashed into a house for her before, and she hoped it was the beginning of a new relationship between the two of them, though she'd never say so aloud.

She thought about Rex and Caro and wondered if anything would change between them now. Maybe this little "adventure" would be a new beginning. There was nothing like facing imminent death together to strengthen a relationship.

"He was able to give his statement? That's a good sign, right?"

"He'll be all right, but those air bags pack quite a punch."

Sadie nodded. She knew from experience how aggressive air bags could be. "He saved my life," she said, still visualizing those final moments.

Marcus was silent for a few beats. "Anything else you want to add?"

Sadie shook her head.

"Can I get you anything before I go?"

She shook her head again. There was nothing she needed or wanted right now that Marcus could help her find. She wanted to go home and go to bed. But where was home? Her hotel in Albuquerque which was being dusted for prints and fully inventoried since Horace and the Cowboy had searched it earlier? Or Rex and Caro's house she'd been asked to leave? Had Rex bulldozing the trailer changed things enough that she could expect to be welcomed back?

"There's someone else who'd like to talk to you," Marcus said as he got to his feet. He glanced at his watch. "I'll call Pete and see where he's at. I expect he'll be here within the hour. He should be in cell phone range by now."

Sadie nodded, and a new kind of longing washed over her. She would be fine once Pete got there. He'd hold her and let her cry and assure her that everything would be okay. She'd do her best to believe him, and he'd help her find somewhere to sleep. She was so tired.

She pulled the blanket tighter around her shoulders. It wasn't that she was cold, rather she just needed the comfort and this was the closest thing to a hug she could get right now.

Marcus left, and Sadie's eyes got heavier but she jolted awake when the door opened again. Blinking, she looked up, then jolted again when she recognized the person standing there, grinning at her with nice white teeth set in a round, brown, pockmarked face.

"Lily?" Sadie asked. But it couldn't be Lily. This woman was dressed in a black suit, cut to accentuate her curvaceous figure, and she had *hair*—a sleek black bob that curled beneath her ears. The woman approached the table and held out her hand for Sadie to shake.

Sadie stared at the faded tattoos on the backs of the woman's fingers, then up into the familiar and yet unfamiliar face of her former cellmate, Bald Lily, who wasn't bald anymore. She also had eyebrows, though upon closer inspection, Sadie could see they were penciled in.

"Agent Lillian Shannon of the Bureau of Land Management, artifact recovery division," she said, withdrawing her hand and sitting down across from Sadie. "I'm afraid we haven't been officially introduced."

She didn't *sound* like Lily either. Lily had a propensity for using improperly conjugated verbs and dropping her consonants.

"Agent Shannon?" This was Sadie's contact at the BLM? "What . . . ?" She couldn't even formulate a question, but her eyes were drawn back to the woman's hair. Lily had been bald. Could there be two of them? Perhaps identical twins with matching tattoos and very different ambitions in life?

Agent Shannon reached up with both hands and removed the wig from her head, revealing the completely hairless scalp Sadie remembered all too well. Sadie gasped but tried to cover it with a fake sneeze. It *was* Lily.

"Alopecia," Agent Shannon said, rubbing one hand over her

scalp. "It's an autoimmune disease that kills off hair follicles. It also makes me look like an instant criminal when I've got the mind to play that part. And thanks to being a stupid eighteen-year-old with lots of school spirit, I've got the art to fit the part too." She laced her fingers together and the tattooed letters spelled out "Go Lobos!"

Sadie looked from Agent Shannon's large hands to her face. Art? Autoimmune diseases? What did any of that have to do with her having been in Sadie's jail cell Monday night? "I don't understand."

Agent Shannon—Sadie couldn't think of her as Lily anymore—smiled a little wider. "Your reports impressed me from the start, and the fact that you not only verified your subjects but had conversations with them was beyond what most of our *trained* informants do. After those bodies were found, our interest in the site was officially halted, but I pored over your reports and took note of a few details regarding Kyle Langley. We knew someone had sold artifacts from D&E sites, and he'd worked on three of them. A little more research piqued our interest in him even more, and then we found out you'd been arrested, which got me worried. I wondered who exactly I was dealing with, and so I called in a favor with a friend at the police department."

"You were spying on me?" Sadie asked.

"I was making sure we could trust the information you'd given us, that's all. I didn't get to ask many of the questions I had, but the ones I tried you didn't even begin to answer. It validated our trust in you."

"Oh," Sadie said, not sure how to feel about that. "Did Marcus know you'd done that?" She thought of how angry he'd been when he found out Sadie and Pete had kept her BLM connection a secret.

"Not until he had to, but he took it pretty well. We've been working hand in hand since then, combining our knowledge, and, in the process, finding Kyle Langley's line."

"Line?"

"A chain of brokers and traders, pothunters and experts. He had a pretty extensive ring of people, which made him the ideal contact for Mr. Benito Ojeda, who was looking for a buyer for the pipe that would take down Ethan Standage's art career."

Sadie frowned, thinking hard. "So how did Margo get the pipe?"

"We're not sure just yet." It was obvious the agent did not like not having all the answers.

"You should ask Horace. He wasn't as committed to this plan like the others were, but he was still closely involved. Maybe he knows something that will help answer that question."

Agent Shannon pulled a pen and a small notebook from her pocket and made some quick notes. "We'll look into that. I understand he's been cooperating pretty well. We have a lot of questions to ask."

"He tipped off Ethan about the bodies, didn't he?"

Agent Shannon nodded. "I'd vote him most-likely-to-make-sense-of-this. He seems to have been in the middle of most of the action. I'm heading to the station after I finish up with you to make sure the BLM's interests are met during the questioning phase of this investigation, but I wanted to fill you in as soon as possible."

"Horace said something about things getting out of control," Sadie said. "That it was supposed to be simple. Do you know what he meant?"

"From what we've put together with the SFPD, Benny attempted to bribe Ethan's assistant to smuggle an artifact back from an expedition, then they would release the item into the black market through a string of contacts who would find a way to make it public. That would undermine Ethan's art career, but probably not to the extent that he'd serve prison time. Mr. Ojeda thought that would be enough to turn Ethan's attention back to the ranch. I guess there'd been some talk about selling out, but then the economy crashed and selling was out of the question. It looked as though the ranch would simply fold if it didn't get some more hands-on care."

"But the first assistant refused the bribe," Sadie said, thinking back to her own hypothesis.

Agent Shannon nodded. "They couldn't risk him exposing their plan, so Benny contracted Mr. Deveroux, a hired gun, to get rid of assistant number one. We think Mr. Deveroux killed the second assistant—who did go along with their plan—on his own to keep him from talking, and then at some point the artifact ended up in Margo's possession. She'd made contact with Tribal Preserve a few weeks before those two bodies were found, telling them she was on the trail of someone, but she had too many questions to ask before she felt she had enough information to get them involved. I'm assuming that, because of what happened to her daughter, she was uneasy about involving other people in whatever she herself was involved in, but we think she had the pipe at that time, though we don't know how she got it."

"So, when I went to her apartment asking questions, she decided to use that as a kind of cover for trying to find out who Crossbones was?"

"We think so," Agent Shannon said with a nod. "Though we don't know how she knew Langley's cover or what her ultimate plan was. She knew the item was important, though, because she hid it in your apartment. As soon as Langley realized what she knew, she was a liability."

"And then Langley became a liability for Benny and the Cowboy—Mr. Deveroux—too." Sadie filled in. It was all mush in her brain, and she wasn't sure she understood how everything had happened, but it was early in the investigation. More information would come to the surface in coming days to fit together what they had so far.

Agent Shannon nodded.

"Is Margo really . . . dead?"

"We don't know. We're trying to piece things together as best we can, and there's always hope that Margo will show up."

Sadie nodded, but she was thinking back to the mass grave she and Margo had uncovered a week and a half ago. Sadie had expressed how sad she was that the family had all died at the same time, while Margo had seemed to find comfort in the fact that they were together. Sadie believed in an existence after this one, and she believed a spiritual bond existed between families. Despite the horrible circumstances of what had happened, Sadie took comfort in believing that if in fact Margo were dead, she would at least be with her daughter again.

Agent Shannon stood up and straightened her jacket before putting her wig back on. "Is it straight?"

"Um, it's a little twisted to the left."

Agent Shannon adjusted it and raised her penciled-in eyebrows.

"That's good," Sadie said.

"Awesome. I only wear it so as not to freak people out. It's horribly uncomfortable, especially in the heat—ay, caramba! Well, I think we're done with you for tonight, or, well, this morning. How long will you be in town, in case we have some follow-up questions?"

"I have a court date on the fourteenth."

"Perfect. I'll make sure I'm there to explain things from my side."

"I'd appreciate that."

Agent Shannon headed toward the door, and Sadie followed her, not sure what to do now that the police didn't need to talk to her. Her phone hadn't been returned, and Marcus had been the one communicating with Pete on her behalf. She followed Agent Shannon to the main waiting area of the ER, then said good-bye as the woman swooshed through the automatic doors.

"Sadie?"

Sadie turned as Caro stepped out from behind one of the curtained areas. Her face was swollen, and she'd changed into a hospital gown that she totally rocked—the woman was in such excellent shape. They stared at one another for a few seconds, then Caro hurried toward her and threw her arms around Sadie's neck, crying into her shoulder.

Sadie hugged her back but tried not to cry; once she got started, she wasn't sure she'd be able to stop.

"I'm so sorry, Sadie," Caro said, stepping back and wiping at her eyes. "Rex told me."

"Told you what?" Sadie asked cautiously.

"He told me that he asked you not to talk to me about the investigation."

Asked seemed a little mild, but Sadie was in no mood to quibble.

"It was sweet of him to want to protect me, wasn't it?"

Uhhh. Once again, Sadie was unsure what to say.

Caro didn't wait for a response, however. "And then he ran over that trailer! I couldn't believe that was my Rex. I mean, who does that, right?"

"It was impressive," Sadie agreed.

"We had a good talk in the ambulance." Caro shook her head. "That is a sentence I have never said in my whole life, but we did. He apologized for telling you not to talk to me and said how he hated how much time you and I spent together. We're going to make some changes." Tears came to her eyes again, and she smiled. "Maybe he's not so different from that sexy linebacker I fell in love with."

"I'm very glad to hear that," Sadie said with complete sincerity.

"Mrs. Hoffmiller?"

Sadie looked over her shoulder to see an orderly coming toward her with a cordless phone.

Caro touched her shoulder. "I've got to get back to Rex. We'll talk later, okay? I want to know *everything* that happened."

Sadie nodded, then accepted the phone from the orderly.

"It's a detective," the woman said as Sadie lifted the phone to her ear.

"Hello?" Sadie said, wondering if Marcus had another question for her.

"Sadie?"

"Pete!" And then the tears came. She gripped the phone with both hands and sat down on one of the plastic chairs in the waiting area.

"Are you okay?" he asked, but the worry, the love, and the concern in his voice undid her even more.

"I'm okay," she said, trying to get control of herself.

"You're sure?"

"I'm sure," she said, forcing herself to take a deep breath. "I'm sorry you've had to come to New Mexico in the middle of the night twice now because of me."

"I don't mind. Honest. I'm just glad you're safe. Don't leave the hospital until I get there, okay?"

"Where would I go?" She leaned back in the chair, still wiping her eyes.

Pete was quiet for several seconds, and Sadie didn't try to fill the silence. Just knowing he was on the other end of the line was enough. He loved her; he was coming to her. What would happen then was anyone's guess. She had a court date next week, and she really needed to visit a chiropractor. Did Lois still need her help at the Fiesta? She didn't know where she'd go next or what her next move should be. So much had happened. Too much.

"Did you see the balloons, Sadie?"

In her mind's eye, she pictured the sight of all those balloons rising up over the crowds last night. And how they had filled the valley earlier that morning. She'd watched them float easily on the breeze, carried everywhere and nowhere all at once. Just thinking about them made her feel lighter. She nodded, despite the fact that Pete couldn't see her. "I saw the balloons. They were amazing."

"I've got half an hour before I get to you, and I don't want you to get off the phone until I can take you in my arms, so will you tell me about the balloons?"

Warmth enveloped her, and she leaned back against the chair and pushed away every ounce of worry and stress and concern. All she wanted to think about were the balloons. The amazing, beautiful, bright, and cheery balloons. "Well, the first time I saw them . . . "

Meringue Frosting for Tres Leches Cupcakes

1 cup granulated sugar
½ cup water
2 egg whites
Pinch of salt
½ teaspoon ground cinnamon

In a small saucepan, mix water and sugar. Heat on medium-high heat until boiling. Cook until soft-ball stage* (about 10 minutes), stirring frequently. Keep syrup on medium-high heat. (Use caution when handling hot syrup; it will burn you if not respected!)

In a separate bowl, beat egg whites about a minute, then add salt. Continue beating until soft peaks form. Add cinnamon and mix only until combined.

While still beating the egg whites, add hot syrup steadily and beat until the mixture reaches the consistency of marshmallow cream.

*To know whether or not you have reached soft-ball stage, drop a small amount of syrup into a bowl of cold water. If it gels together and forms a soft ball, you have reached the correct consistency.

For a filled tres leches cupcake, use an apple corer or small paring knife to remove a "plug" from the center of each cupcake. Add the three milks as directed in the recipe on page 4. Before frosting, fill hole with stabilized whipping cream, then frost cupcakes using a decorator's bag.

Stabilized Whipping Cream

1 teaspoon unflavored gelatin (one packet of Knox is a full tablespoon)
4 teaspoons cold water
1 cup heavy whipping cream
¼ cup powdered sugar

Mix together gelatin and water in a small microwave-safe bowl. Set aside and allow to thicken. In a mixing bowl, whip whipping cream with powdered sugar until slightly thick. Put gelatin mixture in the microwave and cook for 12 seconds. Remove, stir to even out any hot spots in the mixture, then, while mixing the cream on low speed, slowly add gelatin mixture. Once added, beat cream on high speed for about 5 minutes, or until very thick.

Using a decorator's bag, or zip-top plastic bag with a corner snipped off, fill the holes in the cupcakes. Store any leftovers in refrigerator.

Note: Leftover stabilized whipping cream can be used in place of frosting.

Acknowledgments

I love writing acknowledgments because it gives me the opportunity to marvel at the many blessings I have through the people in my life who help make this work.

My writing group: Nancy Campbell Allen (*Isabelle Webb: The Grecian Princess*, Covenant, 2013), Becki Clayson, Jody Durfee, and Ronda Hinrichsen (*Trapped*, Walnut Springs, 2010). These women are a priceless front line for me, and I so appreciate their patience and continual brainstorming and plot-hole-filling. I could never get these stories to work without their guidance.

Thank you to the beta readers I used this time around: Crystal White, Nancy Allen, Jenny Moore, and Lori Widdison. Without their final polish, my editor would know what an idiot I really am.

I should note here that I used my fictional license to alter some details concerning the Balloon Fiesta to better fit my story. The only balloon company authorized to give rides from Fiesta Park is Rainbow Ryders. If you've never attended the Balloon Fiesta, put it on your bucket list. It was an amazing experience, and I owe a big thanks to Jana Erickson for telling me about it—I had no idea.

The title of this book was determined via a recipe contest, and

I am so grateful to everyone who took the time to send their fabulous recipes my way. Lois Blackburn was the grand-prize winner—she developed the Tres Leches Cupcake recipe from scratch, and it was absolutely perfect. (She even made a delightful cameo in the story. You can visit Modern Cupcakes by Lois online at ModernCupcakesbyLois.com.) Big thanks to Shadow Mountain for sending complimentary copies of *Banana Split* to everyone who entered a recipe—I did not know at the outset that would be part of the contest but was so grateful for their generosity. And I will never forget the thrill of signing 150 books all at once. I felt like a rock star.

My production team at Shadow Mountain once again did a fabulous job: Jana Erickson, product director; Lisa Mangum (*After Hello*, Shadow Mountain, 2012), editor; Shauna Gibby, designer; Rachael Ward, typographer; and all the other people who bring the bits and pieces of brilliance together to make this happen. I have been so wonderfully supported and encouraged by everyone at Shadow Mountain that I cannot thank them enough for all they have done and continue to do for me.

Once again my test kitchen came to my rescue for this book: Sandra (Meringue frosting, Cinco de Mayo chicken salad), Whit (Dulce de Leche bars and Dulce de Leche frosting), Megan (Tostadas Compuestas, Posole, Green Chile Stew), Danyelle, Annie, Laree, Don, Lisa, and Katie. They are the reason I can be confident of how wonderful these recipes are, and I am so grateful for their priceless contribution to this book.

Someone recently asked me if any of my kids write. They are all very talented at it, but my oldest two have informed me that they *hate* writing. I think seeing my neurosis up close has completely banished the blush from the rose for them. How grateful I am, however, for their love and support of the crazy woman going on and on about the character she can't rein in and the plot hole that gobbled up every good word she managed to scratch out that morning. How grateful we *all* are for my husband, Lee, and his stable and calm presence. Without my family, there would be no words at all, and I credit them with making this career of mine possible.

How grateful I am for a Father in Heaven who has blessed me so very much, and for the journey I have taken as I've written these stories. I thank Him for everything, past, present, and future. It's been a wonderful ride.

Rainbow Ryders, Inc.
www.rainbowryders.com

Modern Cupcakes by Lois
www.moderncupcakesbylois.com

Enjoy this sneak peek of

BAKED ALASKA

Coming Spring 2013

CHAPTER 1

"Don't be a snob, Mom."

Sadie didn't look up from the gelatinous bread pudding she was poking with the serving spoon. "Bread pudding should not jiggle. If this is any indication of the food I can expect on this cruise, it's going to be a very long week."

"It's the first buffet," Breanna said as she spooned some berry cobbler onto her plate. "Don't judge it so harshly."

The cobbler looked okay, so Sadie took a small amount of it after Breanna finished, then followed her daughter down the line.

"You never get a second chance to make a first impression," Sadie said, narrowing her eyes at what was supposed to be cheesecake but looked like a stiff pudding. She settled for a cherry turnover that looked exactly like the ones she liked to get from Arby's. "On the cruise I took with Gayle in January, the food was just awful," Sadie said. The inexpensive, three-day Baja cruise had been a test to see if Sadie could handle the water issues of being in a floating hotel.

She'd always loved cruises, but she'd had some traumatic experiences associated with water that she worried would ruin future vacations. The cruise with Gayle had convinced her she was okay *on* the water, just not *in* it.

Now here she was on another cruise—a longer one—with a different cruise line and the first foray into the menus was less than confidence-inspiring. Good bread pudding was not hard to make. It should be dense, flavorful, and topped with creamy caramel sauce— like her cousin Kara's recipe Sadie had made for years and years. If they couldn't do right by bread pudding, what would their beef Wellington be like?

They finished the dessert segment of the buffet and headed for the salad bar—dessert first whenever possible.

"If you don't mind my saying so, you seem a little uptight," Breanna said once they finished dishing up and began walking around the dining room in hopes of finding an empty table. "Is everything okay? Have you already found a dead body you're afraid to tell me about?"

Sadie scowled at her daughter and gave her an exaggerated eye roll. "I'll have you know I haven't seen a dead body for eight months, if you don't count Brother Harper from church, but he was eighty-seven and properly laid out in his coffin when I saw him at the viewing. It was a lovely service."

"Eight months—that's got to be some kind of record, right?"

"Oh, stop it," Sadie said, wishing she had a free hand so she could playfully slap her daughter's arm. "I think that phase of my life is over." She scanned table after table filled with people already eating. "Is there not even one empty table in this entire dining room?"

"There's some back there," Breanna said, nodding forward. "Just calm down."

They made their way past their fellow passengers until they

finally slid into their seats, officially staking their claim on a table for four that looked out over the Seattle port.

"Seriously, though," Breanna said once they were seated. "Are you okay?"

Sadie took a breath and decided to spill—it often helped to talk about one's problems, or so she'd heard. "I'm worried about this trip."

Breanna unwrapped her silverware from her napkin, placed the cloth in her lap, then raised her brown eyes to meet Sadie's blue ones. Both of Sadie's children were adopted, and not for the first time Sadie though that Breanna's birth mother must have been as beautiful as her daughter.

"*You're* worried? This whole trip was your idea."

"I know, but I guess the worry didn't hit me until I realized Pete and Shawn would be on the transfer bus together. They'll be on that bus for half an hour, then in line for another hour. What if they decide they hate each other by the time they get here? Then we're stuck together for seven really lousy days."

"Shawn and Pete have been together before," Breanna said. "I'm the one who hardly knows your boyfriend."

"Oh, don't call him that," Sadie said, feeling her cheeks heat up. "It sounds so . . . young."

Breanna laughed and stabbed a bite of her salad with one hand while tucking her long, straight, brown hair behind her ear with the other. "I'd call him your fiancé, but he hasn't made it official yet, though I don't know what he's waiting for."

Sadie took a bite of her own salad to stall before she answered. The truth was that she and Pete had talked about marriage often during the last few months as Pete's retirement grew closer and the threat Sadie had been running from felt more and more distant. But

Sadie had always stopped the wedding discussions when they got to the point of timing and specifics.

Breanna had been engaged for more than a year now, and the happy couple had finally set a date for October. Sadie was loath to take any attention away from her daughter's special celebration of a joined life. Pete understood Sadie's reason to delay their own vows, but seeing as how they weren't getting any younger—Sadie was fifty-eight and Pete sixty-one—two and a half years was a really long courtship. This cruise, therefore, had multiple purposes—to celebrate Pete's retirement from the police department, to allow Sadie's children to get to know him better, and for Sadie to help with Breanna's wedding plans. Seeing as how Breanna lived in London and Sadie lived in Colorado, mother and daughter hadn't had a lot of time to talk things over.

"So?"

Sadie looked up, her fork halfway to her mouth. "What?"

"I asked if Pete was going to make an honest woman of you or not?"

"Breanna Lynn!" Sadie said, lowering her fork as her cheeks heated up again. "Are you implying that my relationship with Pete Cunningham is anything less than respectable?"

Breanna's grin widened, and she pointed her fork across the table. "Bazinga."

"Bazinga? What does that mean?"

Breanna laughed again and took another bite.

It must be European humor.

"Seriously, though, this whole cruise is about you making an announcement to Shawn and me, right?"

"No," Sadie said, shaking her head. *Is that what they thought?*

"It's a family vacation, and my chance to get caught up on your wedding plans."

"Oh," Breanna said with a shrug of one shoulder, showing how unconcerned she was about the information. "Shawn and I both like Pete, so I don't know why you're so worried."

Sadie considered how best to proceed as she and Breanna took a few more bites of their meal but decided she might as well lay all her concerns on the table. "I'm also a little worried about Shawn."

Bre kept her eyes on her food, a sure indication that she was hiding something, and Sadie's stomach fell, though she was relieved to know that Breanna was in the loop. As much as she hated being left out, if Shawn were in *serious* trouble, he wouldn't talk to Breanna about it, right? If Sadie hoped to get more information she couldn't push too hard. "Does he seem okay to you?" she asked innocently.

"Well, you know, he's finishing up school this summer, and it's not the best time to get a job and, well, it's a big transition."

It was obvious that school and the inevitable transition that followed wasn't *it*. "Why wouldn't he talk to me about that?"

She still wouldn't meet her mother's eyes. "Um, well, have you asked him what's wrong?"

"Of course I have," Sadie said, offended by the very suggestion that she wouldn't have called her son on his behavior. "He's assured me everything is fine, but he only calls me back about half the time these days. I just feel this . . . vagueness from him."

"Maybe don't worry about it, then," Breanna said, attempting a smile as she finally made eye contact. "When he's ready, he'll tell you."

"So he *is* having trouble that he doesn't want to talk to me about."

"Mo-om," Bre said just as the roar of a lion cut her off. Breanna rummaged in her bag and pulled out her phone. She'd majored in zoology and currently worked as a docent at the London Zoo, so of course her text message tone was a lion's roar.

"They're here," she said while typing a response.

"Shawn and Pete?" Sadie asked, sitting up straighter and instantly dropping her concerns in favor of an appropriate welcome for her two favorite men. "Where are they?"

"Shawn says they just had their 'Welcome Aboard' photo taken."

"Together?" Sadie said, a tender lump in her throat at the thought of Pete and Shawn superimposed in front of their boat, the *Celebration*.

Breanna smiled at her and sent a reply text message. "They're on their way up. Shawn said to save him some bacon."

"Does he know it's undercooked?"

When Pete found them, Sadie jumped up for a hello kiss and hug. It had only been a week since he'd dropped her off at the Denver airport so she could visit some friends in Portland before the cruise, but she'd missed him. Only when she pulled back from the embrace did she realize he was alone. "Where's Shawn?"

"He said he'd catch up. I think he saw someone he knew."

"Really?" Sadie asked with heavy skepticism in her voice as all her concerns came rushing back. What were the chances of him knowing someone on this cruise?

"He told me to go ahead and he'd be right behind me." They all looked behind Pete, but there was no 260-pound Polynesian man with an afro bringing up the rear.

"You go get yourself some food—avoid the bread pudding, though—and I'll find my boy," Sadie said to Pete. She hadn't seen Shawn since Christmas—far too long without one of his signature bear hugs. She knew she'd feel better once she saw him in person.

"Okay, he was one level down, in front of the elevators when I last saw him."

Sadie nodded and made her way out of the dining room and down the set of stairs just outside the entrance to deck eleven. Unlike level twelve, it was a cabin deck. She stopped at the bottom of the stairs to look around, and although there were several people waiting for an elevator, Shawn was not one of them. She headed to the port side and glanced down the long narrow hallway lined with turquoise doors that led to the passenger cabins. There was a couple coming out of a room but no Shawn. She crossed in front of the elevators to the starboard side, glanced left, and then right. She was relieved when a familiar set of shoulders and six inches of picked-out curls caught her eye. She smiled to herself and started heading toward Shawn's towering form when she realized he was talking to someone. And he didn't look happy about it.

Sadie slowed her steps and observed the scene with a little more interest. The woman Shawn was talking to had dark skin and long thin braids pulled back into a bulky ponytail. Some of the braids were dyed hot pink. She wore a black cotton dress and was very engaged in whatever it was she was explaining to Shawn, who had his arms crossed over his chest and a scowl on his face.

The woman was gesturing with her hands, but the expression on her face was somewhat pleading, as though she was trying to convince Shawn of something. As Sadie got closer, she realized the woman was older than Shawn, mid-forties, Sadie would guess, thickly built, and at least six feet tall. The two of them completely blocked the hallway.

Sadie stopped about twenty feet from them, not wanting to be rude and interrupt, but not inclined to back away either. Why was Shawn upset? Who was this woman?

The woman said something, then leaned forward slightly, awaiting his answer. Shawn shook his head and began to speak, then saw Sadie out of the corner of his eye. She smiled, but he didn't smile back and instead turned back to the woman with some urgency. Sadie couldn't hear what he said, but the woman looked at Sadie too. She didn't smile either, and Sadie found herself taking a step backward. Were they angry with *her*? What for?

Shawn said something else, and the woman nodded, turned away from Sadie, and proceeded down the hall. Shawn looked after the woman for a moment, then turned back to his mother. It took him ten feet before he managed to put a fake smile on his face.

"Who was that?" Sadie asked.

"Don't worry about it."

"But it seemed like the two of you—"

"Gosh, Mom," Shawn snapped, "can you please just not worry about it?"

Sadie lifted her eyebrows in surprise. Shawn never talked to her like that. At least not since he was twelve and she'd grounded him from his GameCube for sassing her.

His expression softened and he took a breath. "Sorry. I've got a lot on my mind right now. Where's the buffet?"

Sadie opened her mouth to ask what he had on his mind, but the way he was holding himself and shifting his weight from one foot to the other kept her quiet. Her son was twenty-three years old, and he'd been living on his own for a long time. He was a grown man.

Sadie forced a fake smile of her own and tucked her wanting-to-know-everything instinct away while putting out her arms, her signal that she wanted a hug from her favorite boy. "It's great to see you."

Shawn wrapped his strong arms around her back, but he didn't squeeze her quite as tight or hold on for quite as long as she'd expected. "Good to see you too, Mom." He pulled back and headed toward the elevators. "Is the food on deck twelve, then? I'm starving."

"Yeah," Sadie said, following him down the hall. "One deck up."

Just before they turned out of the hallway, Sadie looked over her shoulder. The woman Shawn had been talking to ducked out of sight.

A heavy feeling settled into Sadie's stomach as she and Shawn climbed the stairs leading to deck twelve. Over the last few years, Sadie had developed an extreme dislike for secrets. And now it seemed as though her son was keeping one of his own.

About the Author

Josi S. Kilpack began her first novel in 1998 and hasn't stopped writing since. Her seventh novel, *Sheep's Clothing*, won the 2007 Whitney Award for Mystery/Suspense, and *Lemon Tart*, her ninth novel, was a 2009 Whitney Award finalist. *Tres Leches Cupcakes* is Josi's seventeenth novel and the eighth book in the Sadie Hoffmiller Culinary Mystery Series.

Josi currently lives in Willard, Utah, with her husband, children, and dog.

For more information about Josi, you can visit her website at www.josiskilpack.com, read her blog at www.josikilpack.blogspot.com, or contact her via e-mail at Kilpack@gmail.com.

IT'D BE A CRIME
TO MISS THE REST OF THE SERIES . . .

ISBN 978-1-60641-050-9 $17.99

ISBN 978-1-60641-121-6 $17.99

ISBN 978-1-60641-232-9 $17.99

ISBN 978-1-60641-813-0 $17.99

ISBN 978-1-60641-941-0 $17.99

ISBN 978-1-60908-745-6 $18.99

ISBN 978-1-60908-903-0 $18.99

BY JOSI S. KILPACK

Available online and at a bookstore near you.

www.shadowmountain.com • www.josiskilpack.com

SHADOW
MOUNTAIN